DEAD WHITE

A Dakota Mystery

D1527652

M.K. COKER

Copyright © M.K. Coker. All Rights Reserved.
Cover Art by Glendon S. Haddix of Streetlight Graphics.
http://www.streetlightgraphics.com/
Edition: February 2012

ISBN: 1469922053
ISBN-13: 978-1469922058

This is a work of fiction. All characters, organizations, and events are the product of the
author's imagination or are used fictitiously.

DEDICATION

In Memory of Aunt Beige

Katharine Thayer
1941-2011

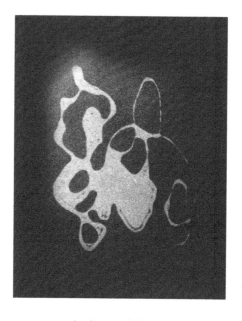

Artist and Muse
© Katharine Thayer

CHAPTER 1

DETECTIVE MAREK OKERLUND TRACKED THE faded center line of Interstate 29 through the pickup's cracked-open door. His booted feet, toes numb in the battered Blunnies, barely felt the gas pedal.

He glanced up into the rearview mirror to scan the backseat of the extended cab. Unblinking eyes stared out at him, adrift in the sea of blankets.

Not a word. Nor movement. Just the staring eyes.

But he knew she was cold. How could she not be? He was her voice now. Her interpreter. Unable to meet those frozen eyes, he looked back out at the blankness that had become his life.

Like the blizzard he drove through, he thought, death blocked everything in sight except the narrow path of necessity. Even then, it was so easy to slide off, into nothingness, rather than steer into a pain that seared.

A slash of red drew his eyes: a wound on the white.

He took his foot off the gas pedal. The red light was joined by blue. An exit sign jumped out of the canvas of night and white. Reunion, it said.

Marek turned the wheel and inched up the ramp.

He didn't want to stop; if he stopped, he might not get going again, but a squad car with its lights whirling blocked his way. The trickle of sweat froze to his back as he braked and put the pickup in park. He reached back and tugged the blanket over the frozen eyes. Then he went out to meet trouble before it came to him.

A uniformed figure—bundled, hatted, and booted in official browns—emerged from the squad car. From behind a scarf decorated with little white Christmas trees, a muffled voice asked, "Leif Okerlund?"

If the blizzard hadn't told him he was in southeastern South Dakota, the way the man easily pronounced the first name did. Layf. Not leaf. Not life.

No, not life.

Marek glanced back at his pickup and shaded his eyes against the headlights. As he thought, the license plate was snow-covered. He turned back. What he could see of the hatchet face beneath the brim of the hat didn't look familiar. But, more importantly, he himself shouldn't be familiar.

He'd always been called by his troublesome middle name. His father had been Leif. But he nodded.

The Eda County sheriff's deputy braced into the wind, then said, hand on the unsnapped holster, "You're under arrest."

Karen Mehaffey was about to pour herself some much-needed coffee in the sheriff's office on the first floor of the Eda County courthouse. Instead, she put down the dented thermos as a cold blast blew open the front doors and ushered in snow, deputy, and the man they'd been hunting.

Although she didn't recognize him, she recognized what he was: trouble.

He stood closer to seven feet than six, but his cheeks were sunken, his jeans hung on him, and his goatee...unkempt, was one word for it. As big as Paul Bunyan and haggard as a Byzantine saint, she thought.

He glanced down at the blanketed bundle he held. Then his eyes flickered up to her sheriff's badge. "What am I under arrest for?"

She glanced over at her deputy.

Kurt Bechtold took off his wide-brimmed hat. He placed it carefully on an antler of the stuffed jackalope—a whimsical pairing of jackrabbit and antelope—that sat on a file cabinet.

The oldest of her deputies, Kurt refused to exchange the old-fashioned hat for the baseball caps the rest of them wore. The yellow sun of the Eda County Sheriff's patch on the crown shone out against a diagonal slice of white and blue, snow and sky, symbolizing this county of extremes.

It could kill the unwary.

Kurt glanced at his watch then out at the dark night. "You said to find the man and bring him back in chains."

Not quite what she'd said but she waved it off. "Go on home, Kurt."

He snagged his hat and left.

Time to shut this down or none of them would make it home tonight. She'd lost enough sleep over the man now awaiting her judgment.

"The governor closed the interstate hours ago," she told him. "The whole county has been closed longer than that. Anyone found out on the roads is subject to immediate arrest."

The man shifted on the turf-green mat. The short leather boots—weird looking things with elastic gores instead of laces—dripped Sasquatch-sized prints. "And how was I supposed to know that?"

"Common sense?"

He blinked away snow-melt. "I kept thinking it'd get better." The snow sloughed off to show hair the color of the Karo's dark corn syrup her mother had kept in the pantry. "How'd you know it was me?"

"When they closed I-29 at the Iowa border, they saw a pickup going north with a New Mexico plate," she said. "They ran their sirens but he didn't stop."

"Used to having cops on my tail," he said with the faintest glint of white fang. "Didn't take any notice."

Now that she did believe. "You didn't have the radio on?"

"Had a tape on until it ran out a couple miles back."

Karen poured steaming coffee—Sisters' Blend—from the thermos into her mug. The hours of waiting, of worry, had taken their toll. Deliberately, she screwed the top back on the thermos.

"Well, given you got through just before they closed the gates, you're not arrested." She slammed the thermos down on her desk—metal against hardwood. "Except in development. I had to keep Kurt on the clock just to watch for you. What do you think you were doing?"

He didn't answer for a long moment. "I wanted it over."

"Are you suicidal? On a night like tonight, it could've been." Karen walked up to the man, refused to look up and make herself small. Something hard to do at six-foot-one. Instead, she reached straight out to what he held. "What've you got here?"

The man freed one hand from the bundle and tugged back the woolen blanket. Tendrils of black hair clung to it, as if in protest at

3

the loss of warmth or anonymity.

Oh, God. She'd never expected a child. School aged, likely, but not by much.

Karen lifted a hand, brushed back static-charged hair from the cold cheek, felt her own skin chill. The dusky face was studded with eyes the color of a Dakota winter sky: the palest of blues tinged with milky white. Wide, staring, they made her breath catch. When the dark lashes finally fell in a shuddering blink, she released her breath.

So, he had a daughter.

Karen looked back up at eyes the same familiar shade.

"Welcome back to Reunion, Detective," she said to the man four years her junior. "Or should I say, Uncle Marek."

CHAPTER 2

KAREN DIDN'T KNOW WHY IT should be so unexpected, that her half-uncle had a child, yet it was—a sucker punch. She tried not to resent what he had, tried not to remember what she'd given up so many years ago.

Shaking herself back into the present, she decided her new detective's face hadn't slackened just from the cold. "Didn't Harold Dahl tell you?"

"That Sheriff Mehaffey and Karen Okerlund are one and the same?" The deep voice scraped gravel. "No, he didn't."

So, Karen thought, they had something in common besides a name. They'd both like to kill the county commissioner.

When Harold had told her that he'd hired Marek Okerlund as the county's first detective, she'd laughed, thinking it was just his way of telling her that he still hadn't been able to fill the position.

But the joke had been on her.

"Where are you staying?" she asked the frozen man and child in front of her.

Marek blinked. "I thought I'd look up my Uncle Jim."

She knew Marek, while still in high school, had been apprenticed to his carpenter uncle. Until recently, she'd assumed he'd continued in the trade. "Jim Marek died several years ago."

A glimmer of grief there, she saw, but as if a pebble thrown on a whirlpool of frozen emotion. The ripple wouldn't come until the thaw.

"We lost touch," he said, shifting the girl onto his hip. "I always intended to...how?"

"A semi jackknifed on ice and slammed into his truck."

Marek Okerlund hadn't come to the funeral. Some said he hadn't cared. Instead, it appeared he hadn't known.

Karen hunched down to the silent girl. "What's your name?"

"Becca," Marek answered for her. "Short for Rebecca."

Must be shy, Karen thought. Like her father, then, and quite unlike herself. "Well, Becca, I'm your cousin, but that'll be awkward." She debated on Aunt Karen but that might stretch relations too far. "You can just call me Karen."

The child didn't say it, but after a long appraisal, nodded. The Okerlund eyes held true. They hadn't in her own case. Fjord eyes, her father called them, a much deeper, darker blue.

"You could stay here," Karen said, knowing she couldn't take Marek home with her. "We've got plenty of space in the jail right now."

Marek shifted his daughter closer. "What about the hotel?"

"We don't have one any longer, just some B&Bs during pheasant season. But there's always your house."

He looked puzzled. "My what?"

"I have a key," she said and he raised an eyebrow. "I've never used it. Never been inside. Not since..." She stopped, knowing he'd fill in the blanks. "Alice Winke at the realtor's office wanted us to have a key if something ever happened over there. It's been vacant for long stretches between tenants."

"Tenants?"

"You really don't know? Grandpa willed the house to your mother. When she died, her executor took control of it—for you, I assumed. It's been let out ever since."

Truth was, it was an eyesore, and her father talked about getting it condemned now that he had to stare at it much of the day.

Karen found the key and held it out. "Alice says it's not in the best shape. But it's shelter and, so far as I know, doesn't have any broken windows or the like."

His hand swallowed the key whole. "We'll make do."

She glanced out the windows to the snow piling up against the pickup. "Did Kurt get chains on you?"

That got a slight upturn of the mouth. "Already had them on."

"We're home: 21 Okerlund Road." Marek felt he had to say something, anything, to justify the old house to his daughter. "I grew up here."

He ran his flashlight over an exposed beam. Good bones. Isn't that what they said of the elderly who still had some claim to beauty? But in its present state, the bungalow—almost identical to the one across the street except for its condition—did little to warm flesh.

He should have called first, to find out if Jim Marek was still in town. But after so long, he hadn't wanted to make contact with a phone call. So he kept putting it off, just doing what had to be done, sorting through the life he'd led in Albuquerque. What was left of that life, other than what he'd brought with him in the pickup, was stuck in Denver.

He put Becca down. She didn't move, just stared.

Marek tried again to give her some connection to the place, so different from the adobe home she'd known. "My father was Leif Okerlund. You've seen his picture in his uniform, remember? He was the sheriff of Eda County."

An Okerlund had been sheriff for as long as the county existed, but Marek would never have returned if he'd known an Okerlund still held the job. All Dahl had said was, Karen Mehaffey had been a Sioux Falls dispatcher, not a cop, and needed a part-time detective on her roster. He'd never have guessed Karen Okerlund would end up back in Reunion. Obviously, she'd married. But it wasn't like her appearance was a giveaway.

Tall, blondish, and blue-eyed: an East River staple. The river being the mighty Missouri, which cut through the Dakotas. Scandinavians and Germans dominated the landscape, with a sprinkling of English, Irish, Slavs, and off-reservation and small-reservation Indians.

Still, if he'd been more awake, not snow-blinded, he'd have recognized the slightly broader build and assured stance of the young woman he'd been in awe of as a kid. No beauty, her face was too long and bony for that, but she had *presence*. Something he'd never had. His ex-partner Manny Trujillo used to say he was like the Sandia Mountains that loomed over Albuquerque.

Big and there. And ignored.

Marek swept the beam of the Maglite into the dark interior. Empty, shabby, and freezing. The Go Directly to Jail card began to look attractive. But he didn't think he could put either of them through another stretch on the road, no matter how brief.

He retrieved the car seat from by the door and set it by the empty hearth. Without so much as a wince, Becca sat down in it. He tucked the blanket back around her and kissed the top of her head, smelled the frozen sweat in the sleek, matted hair. And then felt the tremors.

Marek handed his daughter the smaller light he'd fished out of the glove compartment. "I'll see if there's any furniture in this place." At least someone had left wood in the bin. "Then I'll get a fire started."

He skirted the suitcase he'd brought in and headed toward the bedrooms. The worn plank floor creaked under his feet. He paused to run the light over it. Distressed, they called it these days, and it sold for big bucks in salvage yards. All it needed was some sanding and a new coat of varnish. Throw on some of his father-in-law's old rugs and...

Just look for something to sit on, he ordered himself, maybe to sleep on.

In the master bedroom, the William Morris wallpaper he'd helped his mother put up still clung, barely, to the walls, in faded swirls of sage and cream. The only piece of furniture in the room was his father's hickory rocker, which during the warm months had sat on the porch, in the neutral territory between the feuding Houses of Okerlund.

The rocker creaked and moved; his heart pounded.

A draft, he told himself, or his heavy tread on the loose planking. He reached out and stopped the motion. Then he picked the rocker up and took it back to the living room. He'd slept in worse over the years. Or, more often, not slept. Cop cars weren't bought with comfort in mind.

Deciding not to launch a Corps of Discovery into the rest of the house, he knelt by the hearth and began making a fire before his frozen fingers refused to work.

Karen inched the Suburban forward into the night-shrouded whiteout—a void, without shape or form. If she didn't get home soon, she thought, her body would be found hunched over the steering wheel, her eyeballs stuck to the windshield. More from instinct than anything, she turned onto Okerlund Road. She hoped. Otherwise, she might be driving into her death.

But the blizzard didn't top her list of threats. Leif Marek

Okerlund, her father's much younger and much disparaged half-brother, held that position.

If she'd thought of Marek at all since he'd disappeared after high school, Karen figured he'd gone the way of the maternal grandfather he'd been named for: a mishmash of a life, hammered together with nails and hard drink—and, if he was lucky, kept by a hardworking wife.

Instead, the boy who'd barely made it from grade to grade, who'd been taunted on the playgrounds of Reunion with the refrain *Dumb Polack*, had become a homicide detective, the elite of any city force.

If only he'd stayed in Albuquerque, she'd have cheered him from afar.

On paper, Marek Okerlund was her dream detective. In reality, he threatened everything she'd worked to build in her short stint as sheriff. Because she could only think of one reason why he'd return to rural Eda County, South Dakota.

It didn't matter she'd worked her butt off to learn her new job. Her main asset had been the Okerlund brand—that, and no one else wanted the job.

Mark my words, Mehaffey, her old boss at the Metro Council in Sioux Falls had warned her, when she'd handed in her resignation. *You'll be out of that backwater sheriff's office the second they've got a man on the ballot.*

A rainbow of color flickered across the windshield and she blinked—then braked. A few moments later, she shut the door of 22 Okerlund Road behind her. And reminded herself why, or rather for whom, she'd risked career suicide.

Karen let the warm air thaw her throat before she spoke. "Whew, if I'd realized it was going to be that bad out, I'd have slept in the jail." She started to peel off layers. "You just about need a rope to tie yourself to something out there. If you didn't still have the Christmas lights up on the roof, I might have gone right over the bluff. The shape the roads are in, I doubt I'd have been able to get back up."

Her father, used to her rambling monologues, didn't answer.

She hung her hat and coat on the pegs and stowed her gun in its case on the shelf above. "That would have been worth a line in the *Argus Leader*: Acting Sheriff Shoots Bluff." Only then did she realize she'd missed seeing another landmark. "Did you notice any lights from the other house?"

Arne Okerlund leaned forward in the recliner. "What, some

tramp's broken in?"

She closed her eyes.

Don't you ever think before you speak, her first commander had asked her, and she'd stared at him in bafflement. How do I know what I think until I *say* what I think, she'd returned. He'd suggested duct tape. In his day, he'd said, he'd have applied it himself, but now, he'd get hauled up on harassment charges.

"Whatever you think of him, Dad, he's not a tramp."

"Marek is here?"

Her father wasn't being personal by using the given name. It was a last name to him, one that hadn't had good press in Eda County. All of the good Marek's mother and uncle had done, all the bad they hadn't done, left no mark in her father's mind.

And that could not be blamed on her father's stroke.

The blame lay on Marek Okerlund's maternal grandfather, Lenny Marek, who'd done a spectacular job of making his mark on the memory of the populace.

"Yes, Marek drove up in this mess," she said. "God looks after fools and children, I guess." Karen hesitated, almost told her father about Becca, then decided not to give him that shock too.

"Everything secure?" her father asked.

She looked out the window. Even in the blizzard, she should see lights. With a big sigh, she yanked her coat on again. "Not quite yet. Back in a minute."

The wind that had whipped her into the house earlier now tried to keep her there, blowing snow through the gaps in her coat's zipper. Her footprints silted behind her. Once on the street, she smelled that primitive accompaniment of snowbound delight: wood smoke.

So they were there; they had heat. For all she knew, they'd gone to bed.

But her feet kept going. She ran right into the pickup, a Chevy Silverado, then followed the furrows of habitation until she hit the porch. Struggling her way up the growing drift, she made it to the front door. Her gloved hand made a dull thud on the wood. If they were asleep, they probably wouldn't hear it.

The door screeched away from the jamb.

She stared at the still-coated man then got a glimpse behind him: the hand of a child outlined in firelight. Waving to her.

Karen ducked in and Marek slammed the door shut on the blizzard.

"Hey, Becca, long time, no see."

A smile lit the flame-flicked face. Someone was happy to see her.

Only then did Karen realize she'd broken the family taboo. Unsure of what to do with herself, she looked around. The place didn't stir memories—she'd been younger than Becca when she'd last been inside.

Not since her father had famously said, when told of the engagement of Marek's parents, the widowed Leif Okerlund and the much younger Janina Marek, "No one from my family walks into this house again until you come to your senses."

But the marriage had gone through: and so had the threat.

Out of the wind, Karen felt warmer, so it took her a moment to realize why there were no lights on—and why her breath still came out in puffs.

She whirled on Marek. "You don't have electricity?"

His shrug turned into a shudder. "Must've been turned off after the last tenant. Not much left here but my dad's old rocker."

The rocking chair did stir memories, not only of its original owner, but also its maker: her mother's people, an old order of German Anabaptists who still lived in a small enclave in the county. Her mother had been shunned when she'd left to marry an outsider.

Well, Karen thought, never let it be said that shunning was a hereditary trait. Even if said family deserved it.

"You're coming home with me." When he hesitated, she clarified, "That's an order."

Minutes later, Karen stumbled back into the warmth of her father's bungalow. She set down the suitcase then stepped out of the way to let Marek in.

With a half-open mouth, probably a *Get Out* on his unguarded lips, her father saw the dark head pop out from the blankets in Marek's arms.

Into the dumbfounded silence, Karen said, "Becca, this is my dad. His name is Arne Okerlund." The girl pointed to herself. "That's right. He's an Okerlund just like you."

Karen was speaking, she knew, as much to her father as to the girl. "Same eyes as you, too. I didn't get those myself. I've got my grandmother's eyes. That's her over there on the wall. She was a Halvorsen. Norwegian instead of Swedish."

And if she hadn't died in a freak fall, Marek wouldn't exist.

"She's dumb?"

Karen couldn't believe her father said that. No, actually, she could. Although he'd recovered from the stroke that had almost killed him, it had loosened his iron control, over thought, over emotion, over judgment. But she knew he wasn't talking dumb stupid.

Karen reached out to Marek to keep him there. "My father means, she can't talk?"

"She'll talk when she's ready."

Talk about denial, Karen thought. Kids talked by about a year, didn't they? Two at most. Was Becca autistic or something? Even Marek, slow as he'd been, had never been that delayed.

Arne asked, "How old is she?"

A hand thrust out from the blanket. For a split second, Karen thought it was a plea to stop. But, no, all fingers and thumb splayed, it was an answer. "Five."

From the depths of the recliner came the comment, "Looks older."

Karen herself would have guessed six or seven.

Marek said, "Runs in the family."

The last word rang hollow in the room. Other words, anything but familial, remained unspoken—but heard nonetheless.

"Let's get you settled," Karen said to Becca. If she kept them focused on the child, they might all act like grownups. "You've had a long trip from New Mexico."

And not just in miles.

Marek shifted the girl to one arm and picked up the suitcase. His eyes were blank, all the way to the soul, Karen thought, as if he'd used up everything he had on this journey home.

Her father, eyes cold and temper hot, broadcast a wall of unwelcome that nothing could penetrate—except perhaps the girl. Though few knew it, given his brusque attitude toward them, Arne Okerlund loved children.

Which made it all the more mysterious to her why he'd determined to hate his half-brother. And it didn't look like he intended to keep his mouth shut much longer on the subject. Trust it to be the one thing Arne Okerlund couldn't shut up about.

Karen had won awards for thinking, or more aptly speaking, on her feet. Now she couldn't think of a thing to say. So she turned her back on her open-mouthed father, beckoned Marek, and headed up the stairs.

CHAPTER 3

MAREK BLINKED INTO THE HALF-light, his dreams lingering on a never-ending whiteness.

The knock sounded again. Then the door to the cramped half-story guest room opened a crack and he saw a slice of sheriff.

"Dale Hansen wandered out in the blizzard last night," Karen told him.

Marek freed one hand from the tangle of heavy wool blankets topped with a Prairie Star quilt. He rubbed his palm down his scratchy face. There'd been Hansens galore in the county, though they didn't quite rise to the level of that Anglicized equivalent: Johnson.

Dale Hansen. Oh, Dim Dale.

The older boy had been held back twice in school, landing him in Marek's class in the third grade. "You need rescuers?"

"Too late for that." Karen drew her ponytail through the gap in the back of her sheriff's cap. "The plow reported his body by the Reunion exit off I-29. Thought you might want to come."

The underplay: And get out of this house before Arne Okerlund kicked him out.

"I'm surprised I didn't wake you already," she went on. "Sound carries up here."

Another surprise. Turned out Karen still had her old room, with its second-story window looking out toward his own bungalow. He'd expected her to be living with a man, true enough, but her husband, not her father.

Marek flung off the cocoon of blankets, uncovering his sleeping daughter. He brushed a hand over her cheek, felt the warmth, the fluttering pulse, the silky strands of hair that had strayed there and stuck.

Not the only thing stuck. "I can't leave her."

"Dad can look after her. She doesn't need any special care, does she?" Karen must have seen the answer in his face, because she said, "You know, if you spoke more often, maybe she would. Where's her mother?"

"Gone."

Ten minutes later, Karen used a light touch and a prayer to keep the Suburban on the barely plowed road out to the interstate. The storm was over—but its aftermath lingered.

The morning sun strode down the white expanse and winked snow to diamonds. Nature's *femme fatale*: all glitter and tease.

Snatching a quick look at her silent passenger, Karen wondered if Marek had hooked up with the same kind of woman. And, if so, what had happened to her.

Gone.

He didn't wear a ring but a pale white scar still lingered on his finger. Divorced, she'd guess. Not uncommon for a cop, though uncommon for the husband to get custody. Unless...had the mother been illegal, perhaps? Deported?

Because Becca Okerlund, despite the blue eyes, looked Hispanic.

Karen turned down the ramp to the southbound stretch of I-29 and kicked up a ground blizzard. When it cleared, she saw the plow pulled off to the side. The driver had cleared the shoulder for them.

She used every last inch of it before she parked. The squad car that had been following—invisible in her wake—materialized to kiss her bumper.

When the odd couple of the dayshift got out, Karen nodded to the spare figure on the left. "Morning, Kurt." Then she turned to the other. Not spare. "Deputy Walter Russell, meet our new detective, Marek Okerlund."

The two men might have weighed in the same ballpark but they didn't play in it. Marek had half a head on him. And her deputy's head sported a shining bald pate that he covered with an orange hunter's hat.

"Call me Walrus." The ends of his long gray moustache streamed out like windsocks. "Everybody does."

Introductions done, they all moved toward the snowplow. A man jumped down from the cab, rubbed his bare hands together, then stuffed them back into his insulated coveralls.

"About time you guys got here. I need to get back to work." He glanced back at the path he'd cleared. The wind had already flung up finger drifts: thin snakes of white over the worn gray concrete.

"Sheriff Mehaffey," she introduced herself. "And you are?"

He ducked his head away from the wind. "Cal Bullard."

"Where's Dale?" Karen asked him.

The man jutted his chin toward the barbed wire fence across the ditch. Walrus and Kurt moved in tandem toward the furrowed footprints, but Marek remained behind her.

She tried not to let that bother her. "When did you find him?" she asked Bullard.

"And how?" her shadow asked.

Bullard blinked his eyes rapidly, as if to unfreeze them. "Okay, so I was going along, trying to keep up—they pulled us off the roads, you know, until early this morning when the wind died down."

The wind never died down on the plains but it had decreased.

"If they'd just let us stay out last night we'd be cleared by now," Bullard said, his mouth moving but his face frozen.

"Better to see by daylight," she said. "How did you see him at all? I mean, didn't you say he was in a snowdrift?"

The man shivered and not, she thought, with cold. "Weirdest thing. I look up from the road, making sure I wasn't going off the shoulder, and I see...I was up farther, you know, in the cab and...shit. You'll see it yourself. Saw his hand sticking out of that drift. Gave me a jolt, more than the coffee my wife made up for me, that's for sure. Always made a pisser of a pot of coffee, Mindy did, but I don't want to risk my balls by telling her so. Have to dump a ton of sweetness and light into it to drink the stuff."

Karen lifted her lips out of the lining of her coat collar, wishing she'd thought to bring along a thermos of hot coffee, no matter how it tasted. "What time was it?"

"You'd know better than me. I called you guys a few minutes after on my cell."

"How'd you know it was Dale Hansen?"

Her shadow again. This time, Bullard answered.

"He's a cousin of my wife's. Lost the family farm and she's never forgiven him for it. Some big hog operation bought it up on the cheap, I heard, to make one of those stinking feedlots that take up acres. But Dale did well enough by himself at the new meat packing plant there in Reunion. Started talking big, spending big, and I suppose he had his reasons."

The pursed lips said otherwise. No Dakotan allowed for bragging—unless it was on the kids or the sports team. "My wife, she said he should've bought the land back, but I keep telling her it isn't like it used to be. Hard to make a living in farming these days. Family farms, anyway. I should know. It's jobs like these that keep me from foreclosure myself."

Karen took the clues he'd given her. "You farm south of Fink, right? Married Mindy Hansen?"

The frozen face finally cracked. "You go to school with Mindy?"

"She was three grades ahead of me. Now, Marek here, he went to school with Dale."

That brought the eyes back over her shoulder. "Marek?"

There'd be plenty enough who'd remember the name even after all this time.

Her grandfather used to say that half of the hurt Lenny Marek inflicted while drunk wasn't meant but the half that was, could kill without meaning. And he'd killed twice. Thrice, if you included his own death.

"Detective Marek Okerlund," Karen said, seeing the inevitable question tremble on the bluish lips. "I think we've got all we need from you for now, Mr. Bullard." She picked up a handful of snow and dribbled it into the wind. "You can go tilt at snowdrifts."

He nodded, ran back to his plow, and went off in a cloud of glitter.

Karen followed Marek down into the ditch and then back up near the fence. She stopped beside her silent deputies, who had drifted together with backs to the wind, like cattle, to ward off the cold: heads down, puffs of white streaming from their nostrils, feet stamping.

All their eyes fastened on the same thing.

Snowdrifts on the plains baffled those not used to such capriciousness; there could be bare earth at the foot of a drift reaching up the side of a barn. Even in the open, drifts could make eddies and pools, a frozen sea, over a dead sea that once covered the plains.

For Dale Hansen, the whims of nature had made a satin white coffin.

The drift edges had risen higher than his face and while snow still held to his brows, giving him a sage look he hadn't possessed in life, his face remained clear. Unless one counted the snow settled deep into his nose, mouth, and ears.

Drugged with whiteness, she thought.

But the jarring thing was the left arm: it rose up out of the drift, clear from the forearm, with thumb raised high. Dale Hansen had hitched a ride with a lazy hand.

And death had found him a seat.

"That's odd," Karen said. "No gloves."

Walrus glanced over at Marek, who stood with his hands stuffed into the pockets of his leather coat. He had big hands, she'd noted, and his wrists stuck out, bare to the wind. Karen tromped over to the truck and retrieved a pair of mittens.

When she thrust them at Marek, he said, "Little small for me, I'd think."

"They're my father's."

He hesitated then wriggled his hands into the forgiving knit. "Thanks."

Walrus said, "Don't people who freeze to death start throwing off their clothes, thinking they're hot?"

"That could be it," she said. "Probably why Dale's got only a vest on and no coat."

She didn't know Dale Hansen well, only to nod to, but she knew his family, in a rumor mill sort of way. Wife and stepdaughter. "Didn't anyone call him in as missing last night?"

Kurt said, "I checked the dispatch log before we headed out. No calls after the storm hit. The only one out last night on this road was Marek." He turned and frowned. "What are you doing, Russell?"

Both she and Marek turned at the testiness in Kurt's voice.

"Looking for Dale's ride," the deputy said, digging at an odd-shaped drift, then pulling out an orange construction cone. He turned it upside down and scooped up a drift. "Snow cone, anyone?"

"Put that back," Kurt said. "It could be for a construction zone."

"If it is, they won't be back until the snow melts off." With a shrug, Walrus put the cone back. "So how'd Dale get here?"

She looked up and around. "His ride could be a ways off."

Marek spoke again. "Is this his place?"

"What place? The farm, you mean?" She glanced at Kurt. "Is it?"

The long-time deputy looked across the anonymous white landscape beyond the fence. A mile or two distant, a cluster of farm buildings sagged with the weight of neglect and snow. "Hansen place, all right."

"Dale lost the farm, remember?" Walrus rejoined them. "Lives on Bluff Road now. Had a new place built. But he could've been out at the farm, looking things over before the storm."

Marek stuffed his mittened hands into his jacket pockets. Knit might forgive, she knew, but it didn't fend off a stiff wind. "Why would he leave the farm to go out in a blizzard?"

"Just FYI," Karen said after a long pause. "Since you seem to have forgotten: in a whiteout, you can miss a building by inches." She still hadn't gotten over the risks he'd taken the night before, not only with his life, but his daughter's. "Or, for that matter, an exit, if there isn't a handy squad car waiting for you with all its lights going."

Marek just looked at her with that blank expression.

What was behind it? Anything?

With the seasoned eye of a Little League referee, Walrus shifted his bulk into the space between her and Marek. But he apparently decided distraction was the better part of valor. He asked, "If Dale didn't own the farm any longer, what would he be doing out there?"

Karen stamped her feet. Were those rocks in her boots...or her toes? "Maybe he was thinking of buying it back, like Bullard said. Time enough to find out when we're warm." She beckoned Kurt. "Let's get Dale out of the snow and turn him over to the coroner."

"Wait a minute," Marek said. "We can't just dig him out and tramp all over the scene. We've got a suspicious death here."

The wool watch cap she'd made him pull on before they'd left didn't seem to have done his brain cells any good.

"Geez, Okerlund," Walrus said, "you've lived in the sun too long."

"Sun doesn't have anything to do with it," Marek said. "Snow does. For all we know, Dale got hit by a car during the blizzard."

Kurt asked, "Yours?"

Marek's deep voice came out evenly. "I didn't hit anything but drifts." Then he hunched those big shoulders, glanced down at the exposed hand, and his last words barely rose above the wind. "I hope to hell he wasn't still alive, trying to flag me down, when I passed him."

Kurt shook his head. "If Dale'd been close enough to hear your engine, he'd have seen my lights at the exit."

Karen slapped her hands together to get them tingling again. "I know you want to show us your big city skills, Detective, but you're out of your frigging—frigid more like—mind if you want to treat this as a crime scene."

"Humor me."

She figured she'd have the last laugh. "All right, go ahead. Pardon me, gentlemen. I've got a call to make. In my nice warm Suburban."

The cold shoulder.

So, that's how it was going to be. But Marek didn't get to be a detective by being careless. Better a fool than a fuck-up.

He looked down. Which had Dale Hansen been?

Marek didn't recognize the ill-featured child in the man. The Coke-bottle glasses had disappeared. The teeth, once uneven and yellowed, shone unnaturally white in the bright sun.

A memory surfaced. On the first day of the third grade, the teacher had told Marek to share his brand-new pencils with the older boy. They'd come back with teeth marks in the wood and the erasers chewed off. That had soured their relationship from the start.

As a fellow school reject, he and Dale should have bonded, given how many times they'd been paired by exasperated teachers over the years, but they'd been far too different. Marek had desperately wanted to do well in school—Dale hadn't.

The older boy had often come to school late with the unwashed stench of animal on him—not from a lack of plumbing but as a badge of solidarity with those he considered his true friends. More often than not, those in smelling distance made pig faces, laying back their noses with a finger.

Marek couldn't flare his nostrils now if he wanted; they'd stuck together in defense against the cold. "Who's Karen calling?"

Walrus said, "That'd be Tisher. He's our coroner."

Tisher. Didn't ring any bells. Though they'd be distant enough bells these days, with names more like Arellano and Roybal in his mental geography map. "What happened to Dr. Ringold?"

Walrus smoothed down his moustache. "Who?"

Kurt pulled down his scarf to speak. "Ringold retired to Arizona years ago. Tisher came from North Dakota. People like him. Doubt he'll go south for the sun."

"Already came south," Walrus said, with the self-congratulation of a man who thought he'd gotten a good deal, being born in a warmer clime.

The three of them fell silent, shivered, and waited. Without being aware, backs to the wind, they drifted together.

A long twenty minutes later, a bright red Dodge Ram pickup with a long black shell on the extended bed hit the drift on the ramp. Then the pickup launched forward, looking like a mosquito aiming for a blood-letting on a winter white arm. Finally, it came to a sliding stop behind the squad car.

The chains, Marek thought, had saved him.

The door flung open and a figure uncurled from the interior. All bones and nerve, Marek thought, no wider than a toothpick. With one hand, the long-faced man held a battered hat on a salt-and-pepper head as he hurried toward them. "Where's the idiot who called me out?"

"That would be me," Marek said to the coroner.

"Big one, aren't you," Tisher commented. Then he turned to greet Karen, who had emerged from the Suburban to join them beside the highway.

"What was Dale doing out here?" Tisher asked her. "For all that he wasn't the brightest bulb in the socket, he did know the countryside. Comes from living off the land all those years, I suppose. How did he come to be out in it?"

"We don't know," Karen said. "But our new detective is suspicious."

"It's his job to be," Tisher conceded. "But he's got a thing or two to learn, I'd say, about what's considered a natural death out here." The lines around his eyes pulled into humor rather than irritation as he looked back at Marek. "All right then, Detective, lead me to the scene of the crime and I'll show you we're not the mean streets of—where did you come from?"

"Albuquerque."

Tisher took in the unlined leather jacket. "Frostbite and hypothermia aren't anything to brush off out here, Detective. Hope you've got something warmer than that—or I'll be carting you off as well."

Once again, *Dumb Polack* rang in his ears. How often had

Hansen heard the echo of *Dim Dale*? "The moving van's stuck in Denver with the rest of my stuff."

The man nodded then, seeing where the body lay, made his own way over the drifts, puppet-jointed, legs sinking in and then jerking out of pristine snow. When he reached Dale Hansen, he squatted down, knobby knees near his ears.

When he remained there for long moments, Karen asked, "Well?"

The coroner pulled a small notebook out, looked at his watch, then jotted down the time. "He's dead."

"Thank you, Dr. Tisher, I wasn't sure."

The coroner glanced up over the body to the sheriff. "Smart aleck."

Tisher slid on gloves and brushed snow away from the pale neck and around the head. Then he pulled back, sighed, and got to his feet. "I don't suppose his family knows yet?"

"I want to tell them in person."

Marek glanced over at Karen. *Want* wasn't the word any cop he'd known would have used. Obligated, more like. No one *wanted* to notify next of kin. Being sheriff, she could have ordered him or one of the deputies to do it. Looks like she knew how to stand up to the job, even if she didn't know much about securing a scene.

"You'll want to take your new detective with you—what was your name again?" Tisher put one hand back on his hat. "Wind snatched it before my ears did."

"Marek Okerlund."

Tisher looked between sheriff and detective. "Long lost cousins?"

Karen didn't look at Marek. "Something like that."

"I guess there are still things about this county and its people that I haven't learned." He stuffed his gloves back in his pocket and puffed on his free hand. "But I know one thing. You're one sharp cookie, Marek Okerlund."

That had all of them staring.

"Dale Hansen has a dent in his skull."

Walrus snorted then coughed up cold air. "So Dale took a slip on the ice and fell. That's probably why he froze to death. Knocked himself out. Maybe he got lost in the blizzard. Maybe he'd been drinking. Wouldn't be the first time."

"Maybes don't cut paychecks, Deputy Russell," Tisher said. "Regardless, I'm on the clock as of now. Let me get my camera and then we can clear him off."

Marek forced himself not to protest. He wasn't, as the others had reminded him, in Albuquerque any longer. He didn't have the same resources to call on, even on what might turn out to be a hit-and-run, and he'd have to rely on the coroner to do his job.

After the clicks of an old SLR camera and a few hurried notes before the ink froze in his Bic, Tisher let them clear the snow away from the body.

CHAPTER 4

ARNE OKERLUND EYED THE SHADOW at the top of the stairs. "Don't just stand there, come on down. Your dad's gone out on a call with Karen. I expect you're hungry."

He rose unsteadily from the recliner, cursed his stroke-weakened limbs, and made his way to the kitchen. When he got out the milk for the raisin bran, he turned and found Becca already sitting at the table.

She poured the cereal in the bowl and started eating.

"Here now, you need to pour the milk on that." But when he tried to pour, she covered the bowl with her hands. "It's good for you. Makes you grow." One hand fell to her tummy. "Makes you sick?"

She nodded.

What was it they called it, lactose intolerant? He put the carton back in the fridge.

She didn't look or act like a retard, or whatever they called them these days. Developmentally disabled. No matter what words they used, it'd still end up an insult, then they'd move on to some other word until they ran out. Maybe retard would come back in style, like the ridiculous bell-bottomed jeans the girl was wearing.

Funny. His own daughter had worn them at that age.

Thinking of Karen, he frowned. He'd seen her horrified look when he'd asked if Becca were dumb. Substituted her own words for his. She'd been doing that. Treating him like a burden.

Like her good-for-nothing husband.

Patrick Mehaffey hadn't even managed to give Karen a child. That girl there, she should be his granddaughter, not his...whatever she was. Nice. He screwed up the fist on his bad hand. The words didn't come like they used to. Niece.

Finished with her cereal, Becca slid off the chair and went to the window. Blanket-shawled like an Indian, she stood there, dark hair gleaming and dusky skin touched with sun.

Striking girl.

Marek didn't deserve her.

Or anything in Eda County. Arne wished he'd locked his half-brother up when he'd had the chance. Then there'd be no danger that Marek could take Karen's badge. Oh, Arne knew, he himself was done for as sheriff. Able-bodied was the unspoken requirement, even before able-brained, but he'd do whatever he could to make sure his daughter kept the job she'd chosen.

He still had some pull here in Eda County, after all.

Arne turned on the TV but it filled with snow then went blue. No connection. He heard the old plank floor creak and looked up. The girl had her hands clasped below her waist. He pointed to the bathroom door. "In there."

She ran.

It was a change to have a silent child in the house. Karen had talked to fill the silences as if they'd devour her if she didn't push them away. Always on the go, too, ever since a baby. She'd climbed out of her crib so many times he'd finally put chicken wire over the top for her own safety.

When Becca returned, leisurely, Arne watched her go back to the window.

"You get any snow down there?" he asked her.

Her head tilted as if she wasn't sure how to answer that. By which he decided that they did get snow, which surprised him, but not as much. "You want to go out?"

She nodded.

"You can't go out like that."

He pondered. The rafters of the attic bulged with boxes of things Hannah thought might be passed down. His wife had organized them during those slow months of dying, as if a gift to the world, or to grandchildren not yet born.

Arne made his way up the stairs; it hadn't been that long ago that it would have been beyond him. Functional recovery, they called it. Muscles, memories, skills. But in his world, the world of action and decision, it wasn't enough.

Once he'd gotten Becca bundled in Karen's winter castoffs, she stood uncertainly by the front door, looking out at the snow. Maybe she didn't know what to do with it.

"You can make angels." That caught her attention. "You know," he said, miming as best he could, a flawed angel with a wobbly wing. "You lay down in the snow and move your arms and feet. Then when you get up, there'll be an angel there, come down from heaven."

She shot out the door. He had to shut it for her.

Kids.

Despite himself, he felt one side of his face lift. Then as he thought about how it was only the one side, it fell.

So much lost at a stroke.

Marek shifted his gaze from Dale Hansen's body to the coroner. "Got any idea of the time of death, Dr. Tisher?"

To Marek's surprise, everyone huddled over the body laughed. Even Kurt huffed out a couple puffs.

"Goodness, Detective," Tisher said, dabbing at an eye before the tears could freeze on his eyelashes. "I'm not a doctor."

His brain must be numb. "You're the coroner, right?"

"Longest serving coroner in Eda County as of this last election. Took over from Dr. Ringold after he went to Arizona. The new doc, Hudson, wasn't interested. But I never said I was a doctor. Don't have to be. Not in South Dakota."

Even in his father's time, the coroner had been a doctor. "Then what are you?"

"To your mortification, I'm sure," the man said with a tug on his hat, "I'm a mortician."

Marek thought he'd be able to work with the more relaxed rules of rural policing. But not *that* relaxed. He found that he could still care. Even for Dim Dale. "And that makes you qualified to do the autopsy?"

The figures before him froze.

"Of course not," Tisher said. "I send the body up to Sioux Falls. They've got the setup there for forensic work. You want to be there, you let them know."

The only whistles of laughter now came from the wind. "Sorry, I just didn't know how things worked here."

Tisher gazed at him for a long moment then nodded. "I'll admit

I'm a bit testy about the matter. I don't have to do this job and I wouldn't, not if I wasn't also the only mortician in Eda County." At Marek's puzzled look, Tisher said, "Unfair competition, if you see what I mean, my being first on the scene."

Marek had had too much knowledge, too young, of local morticians. "What happened to Jorgens in Reunion and Brodski in Valeska?"

"I married Jorgens' daughter and took over the business," Tisher said. "As for Brodski, he only did cremations—until he became a client of mine."

Tisher winked, pulling laugh lines on his long face. "Al Brodski didn't want to go to the Good Lord in sackcloth and ashes, per his last will and testament, so he went to the earth whole for the judgment day."

What did it matter if there were ashes...or desiccated bones. No body stayed whole and any God worth his salt could make matter out of nothing.

But He couldn't make anything matter to Marek.

"All right, let's lift him," Tisher said. "With your permission, Detective?"

What Marek wanted was a full crime scene investigation team. Specialists. The works. Even on what might be an accidental death.

The sheriff must have read his hesitation. "We can't call in the state boys for help. No way DCI can get down here from Sioux Falls with the interstate closed."

Division of Criminal Investigation, Marek translated. "Where are we moving the body to?"

Walrus nodded back at Tisher's ride.

Marek took a closer look at the black shell on the extended cab. The windows weren't tinted as he'd thought but curtained with black crepe. He shuddered. "Let's do it, then."

But when they lifted Dale Hansen, the right arm tugged down to earth, exposing a length of white arm, bare from the shoulder, where the flannel shirt had been torn away.

"What the hell..." Walrus breathed.

Block capital letters ran down the arm in a ragged and blood-encrusted line.

Walrus poked at the letters. "W-H—what's that next letter?"

"Needs to take a class in penmanship, whoever he is," Kurt said. "An A or an I?"

Marek let them try to decipher it. He began brushing the snow away to get to the buried hand.

He uncovered the chained wrist just as Karen said, with the triumph of a spelling bee champion, "It says WHITEOUT."

Her yard was full of angels.

Karen pulled the Suburban up to the curb of 22 Okerlund Road and said to Marek, "After the scene we just left, I wish I were a kid again, with nothing to worry about but making snow angels."

Marek had insisted they stop home. Karen hadn't argued because she felt the need to take a breather herself before she informed the family.

Six months on the job, half of it away at law enforcement training, and she had a homicide. Not unheard of in Eda County but nothing like this.

The letters cut into the arm had been bizarre; the chain had been an abomination.

When they got out, Becca launched herself into Marek's arms. And held on. Marek knelt down to disentangle himself. "What is it, Becca? Are you cold?"

The girl shook her head.

And, indeed, the heavy woolen coat, which looked vaguely familiar, had come unbuttoned at the top. Karen saw one of her German mother's handknit sweaters—in one of the Scandinavian designs she'd tried to emulate—poke out.

"I told you I'd be back," Marek said. "I have to go out again but I'll be back."

Becca pointed at the angels.

Karen said, "Very pretty."

For a moment, the girl seemed distracted, her eyes going to the coat, then back to Karen.

"It's all right, Becca. I always have ambitions to get into a smaller size but I think that's a losing battle." She'd put on some weight recently, something that shouldn't be happening, given her more active lifestyle as sheriff. "You can have the coat." With a pang, she forced herself to finish. "And the sweater, too."

But her gift didn't bring a smile. Instead, tears fell, silent, sparkling. Before either of them could react, Becca pointed to the sky then at the snow angels.

The door of the house creaked open. "What's she telling you? I haven't done anything to her but let her have some fun in the snow."

The girl glared at Arne then pointed at the angels then back up to the sky.

"What, you want more angels?" he asked her. "I don't think there's enough snow, or enough angels in the heavens to—"

"Is that what you thought, Becca?" Marek interrupted. "That you could bring down an angel from heaven?"

An angel. One. Not many.

Now Karen understood what she'd seen in Marek, the blankness, the soul-deep whitewash of grief. She knelt into an angel's wing to level with the heartbroken face. "I'm sure your mother can see your angels from heaven, Becca."

Becca, however, held up two fingers.

"Peace? What?"

Marek crumpled the two fingers into one of his big hands. Then he picked his daughter up. Over the top of her head, his words dislodged wisps of static-charged hair. "Two angels."

Oh, God, Karen thought. Two dead.

CHAPTER 5

THROUGHOUT SOUTHEASTERN SOUTH DAKOTA, THE river bluffs—the one constant landmark in the undulating prairie—rose up from wide floodplains filled with rich, dark soil. The new Hansen home sat on one such bluff several miles outside of Reunion.

Marek trudged up the uncleared driveway. Only a few years old, the house was showy, but he noted a window casing wasn't straight and soffits flapped in the wind.

"You do much of this?"

Marek looked back. Those were the sheriff's first words since they'd left Becca in the care of Arne Okerlund. He didn't remember Karen being so close-mouthed.

"Much of what?" he asked. "Homicides? Every day. It was my job."

Still is, he reminded himself. Just not every day. Only his first day.

He'd bet his boots Karen had never worked a homicide before. Whatever training she'd had in investigative techniques must be recent.

"Notifications," she said as they slogged up the steps.

"My share." He'd dealt with a number of reactions: anger, tears, laughter, even a punch to the mouth. Sometimes he'd wondered how he'd take the news. Now he knew. He'd frozen, as if by not moving, not saying anything, not even breathing, reality would pass him by. "It never gets easier."

If anything, it accumulated, so that the scab never healed.

"As a dispatcher, I dealt with grief plenty of times," Karen said.

"But I've never caused it before." She pushed the doorbell. "Never shattered a world with a few words."

Maybe that's why, he thought, she hadn't probed.

Karen pressed the doorbell again.

He glanced around. The snow lay pristine for as far as he could see. "Maybe Dale's family's gone for the holidays. Who'd he marry?"

Karen peered through the side windows. "Krissy Martin."

Marek blinked his disbelief. They'd called her Kissy. Kiss and tell. Three years older than himself. "I thought she married Troy Ringold, the doctor's son, when—"

"When she got pregnant and Troy's father made him play the gentleman?" Karen turned to face him. "Stuck for a dozen years or so. But when his daughter turned up with some genetic disorder, Troy got DNA tests done."

"She wasn't his."

"Legally, she was, and he's still paying for it, but I'm not sure even Krissy knows who the real father was. She got around. Even you..." The sheriff bit her lip, obviously wishing she'd kept her mouth shut.

Marek just shook his head. "Krissy didn't go for younger, not then, and I moved to Valeska before I got to high school."

After Leif Okerlund died, his mother had moved back to her hometown, a haven for Slavs to the west of Reunion. The small towns of southeastern South Dakota often had a predominant heritage, like to like, whether Dutch or Indian.

Karen knocked this time. "Where the hell is she?"

Marek started down the steps. "I'll go look in the garage."

When he reported two vehicles in residence, they decided to wait.

Shifting away from the endless horizon beyond the bluff, Marek asked, "Why did Krissy marry Dale Hansen after someone like Troy Ringold?"

"She likes her toys even better than her boys."

On that damning statement, the door flew open. Krissy Martin Ringold Hansen stood before them in a royal blue velour bathrobe; one hand pushed back artfully mussed blonde hair from a cosmetic-drenched face.

"What a surprise. Come to check on reports of orgies, Sheriff?" But her gaze fastened on Marek not Karen. "Or are you wanting to start one?"

For the first time since he'd crossed the state line, Marek felt heat.

In his face.

Karen's voice came with an edge. "Can we come in?"

Did the sheriff really think he was going to hit on the woman? From what Marek knew of Krissy's family, she didn't deserve this blow. Her mother had run off when Krissy was still in grade school. Her father—who'd owned The Shaft, a dingy just-outside-city-limits bar his own grandfather had often frequented—hadn't stood in anyone's book as a model parent.

"Hurry in, then," Krissy said. "It's beastly cold out. I've got the fire going inside."

Karen went first and Marek followed. He blinked at the expanse of glass panes opaqued by a creeping frost that separated the sunlight into cold splinters of color.

Their hostess went over to the ostentatious marble fireplace that didn't match the rustic plank flooring in the great room. He'd guess that the Jekyll and Hyde look of the place meshed with the two personalities who inhabited it.

Stairs snaked up to a loft and as his eyes climbed, he saw a teenager in tartan-red flannel pjs leaning against the railing.

"Who're they and what're they here for?"

Krissy put hands to hips. "Show a little respect, Darcie. It's the law come to call. If you can't be civil, why don't you go back to your beauty sleep?"

"Beauty never sleeps," the girl said with a dryness that told Marek she was older than she looked.

Krissy's heavily lashed eyes fell again to Marek. "Truer words were never spoken. Now, what can we do for you?"

Marek wasn't stupid. He remained silent. Usually he'd let his partner say the shattering words, while he stood ready as a shoulder to cry on—or pound on.

Karen said, "Mrs. Hansen, I am sor—"

The laugh stemmed the flow of regret. "Please, just Krissy. It's not like we don't know each other, Karen. You'll have me thinking I'm Dale's mother instead of his wife."

But she wasn't. She was his widow.

"It's Dale, isn't it." The girl's words fell on their heads first. "What happened? Where is he?"

Marek couldn't read the face for the fall of dark hair. "Where do you think he is?"

"At the plant, of course," Krissy's shrug pulled velour. "He said he wasn't coming home last night because of the storm. That's Dale. All plant, all the time. He wanted to make sure there wasn't any damage to the roof with all the snow." Now a flicker of concern shone through the artful face. "Has there been an accident? Did the roof fall in?"

The sky was falling, the sky was falling, said Chicken Little.

"Can you come down, Miss...?" Karen asked. "There's something we need to tell you and your mother."

As the girl came down the stairs, she pushed her hair away from her face. "That's Ms. and it's Ringold."

Marek upped the age again. Not a teenager. Maybe even into her twenties. Darcie Ringold must feel gypped in the gene lottery. She was short, five-foot tops, and had a face like a Picasso: mismatched angles in a swarthy face with thick dark eyebrows that slanted downward.

Krissy asked, "Is Dale all right?"

Karen said, "I'm afraid not."

Half an hour later, Krissy Hansen showed them to the door, her makeup still intact. She held up a hand to stop Marek then placed it on his arm. "You never did introduce yourself."

Feeling Karen's eyes on him, he said, "I'm the county's new detective."

"Oh, goody, new blood. It's about time." The tears on her lashes sparkled in the fractured light. "If you didn't know, the Okerlunds have a dynasty going here."

He let out a breath. "I *am* an Okerlund."

When she registered just who he was, the hand fell from his arm.

To his surprise, it was Darcie Ringold who said, "Cool. The prodigal son."

The silence in the Suburban became intolerable.

In her various incarnations, from basketball player to communications specialist to dispatcher, Karen hadn't needed to keep her mouth shut, and she saw no reason to now.

She drove over a clump of rust-red autumnal bluestem, a native prairie grass scraped free by the plow. "I think it's obvious Krissy hadn't a clue about Dale's death."

"Is it? The wheels on that Hummer in the garage still had snow caught in the chains."

Point to her new detective. Both mother and daughter had said they'd been home from well before the storm. It had been dry and brown before the blizzard hit.

"I don't know, Marek. I can't see Krissy doing anything to ruin her manicure. Which, if you noticed, was not. Ruined, I mean. Likely she or Darcie went out for a bit, maybe turned back, and just didn't remember, what with the shock and all."

He simply tilted his head, staying neutral—and silent.

Before she could stop herself, she blurted out, not the question she wanted to ask, but maybe one that would lead to it: "How did your wife die?"

He stared out into the white road before them. "Does it matter? She's gone."

Insert frozen foot into unfrozen mouth, she thought.

"I'm sorry for your loss." And, unlike with Krissy, she actually felt the futility of that standard statement to the bereaved. But what else could she say? So she returned to the investigation. "What did you think of Darcie Ringold?"

The big shoulders relaxed. "Think she didn't much like her stepfather."

Karen slid through a small drift, skidded a bit to the side, then corrected. "You don't think..."

"He molested her? You never know." But he didn't sound like he believed it. "The silver Lexus in the garage is probably Krissy's. I didn't see a clunker for Darcie. Maybe she doesn't drive. Do you know who owns the Hummer?"

"Actually, I don't," she said. "Maybe Krissy's got a visitor from out of town."

"Plate is local."

She mulled that. "Krissy could be two-timing Dale. That would be a motive for murder."

"Could be."

"Well, I can pretty much guarantee there's not another Hummer in the entire county. It shouldn't be too hard to find out from vehicle registration." Thinking of the paperwork, she asked, "Aren't you going to take notes on the interview?"

"If you want them."

He fished into his pocket and pulled out, not a pen and notepad, but a tiny digital recorder. He gave time, date, and repeated, as far as she could tell, word for word what Krissy Hansen and Darcie Ringold had told them.

Which hadn't been much. They'd learned that Dale Hansen had had a cell phone with him. And his pickup had been at Gotsch's for repair. So how, she wondered, had Dale gotten from the plant to the interstate, miles away?

Marek clicked off the recorder. "Good enough?"

For a moment, Karen couldn't think of a word to say. "The lawyers will want it on paper."

"In Albuquerque, they had someone transcribe the recordings."

Did he really think she had the money for that in her tiny budget? "I don't know if you noticed, but we don't have any sagebrush rolling around out here."

The seat creaked as he shifted. "What do you want? A full transcription?"

"Incident reports. Written notes." She throttled the steering wheel in lieu of his neck. "We don't have a secretary anymore; we have you."

His hand fisted over the recorder. "That'll take a lot of my time."

"It wouldn't if you took the notes during the interview." How many times, in how many ways, would she have to remind him—he wasn't in Albuquerque anymore. "You might have left that kind of thing to the uniformed officers when you were a homicide detective, Marek, but no one will do your work for you here."

He turned his head to face her fully. "Are you trying to be difficult?"

All in all, she'd been as welcoming to the prodigal son as anyone could expect. But she had limits. "Me?"

"You do know I'm dyslexic."

Karen fishtailed into the sheriff's parking spot and bumped into the barrier.

His hand on the dash, Marek stared at her. "Don't you? I told Dahl."

CHAPTER 6

K AREN LINGERED IN FRONT OF the Suburban. "Go on in," she told Marek. "I just want to make sure I haven't done any lasting damage."

He looked down at the bumper and opened his mouth, probably to tell her it looked fine. Then he went. Because he'd likely guessed that it wasn't the damage she wanted to ponder.

Her father used to say, See what happens when you have kids late. End up with a halfwit. Don't wait to have kids. Karen hadn't, not that it had done her any good.

But if Arne Okerlund got the blame for calling Marek a halfwit, Marek's mother had unwittingly supported it, unable to disguise her disappointment at her son's continual problems in school. Not behavioral problems. So far as Karen knew, Marek had never shown any signs of the violent temper of the maternal grandfather he resembled.

But he hadn't won any points for brains either.

Dyslexic. That put a different spin on things. No matter how much she ached for the child Marek had been, Karen *really* wanted to talk to Harold Dahl about the man.

That game plan in mind, she went in, aiming for the stairs, but found her swing-shift deputy, Travis Bjorkland, and night-shift reserve deputy, Rick Gullick, in the hallway. Rick held up a sealed evidence bag. "Tisher just dropped off the stuff he found in Dale's pockets."

She took the bag. "You two aren't on the clock."

"Mmm. Just curious," Bork said. "Tisher caught us coming out from getting an update from Walrus. We were just going to drop that off then scram."

"So scram. I need you two fresh and rested, since you won't have backup on your shifts." Karen decided that her confrontation with Dahl could wait.

She went into the office, put the bag on her desk, and slid on gloves. Marek, Kurt, and Walrus circled her. She took out the wallet and found license, social security card, credit cards, self-inscribed business cards, even $287 in cash.

"Robbery's out," Kurt said, staring down at the small pile on her desk.

No surprise there, she thought. She rummaged in the bag and pulled out a keyring.

"Geez, that thing looks like it weighs more than I do," Walrus said.

She clunked the keys down onto the desk; sunflares of brass and steel shot off from the ring. One key glowed a mellow copper.

Marek asked, "Is there anything else in that bag?"

She flattened it. "That was it. Why?"

"It's what's missing," Kurt said, his narrow face turning toward Marek. "And that would be a cell phone, right?"

After Marek nodded, Kurt beckoned them to his own desk. "We've got some other evidence for you."

Karen walked over to find a mishmash of chains—like something out of a torture chamber—snaked across the desktop. Just thinking of what Dale Hansen must have felt, endured, being tethered to Nature's rack, had her shivering.

But she forced herself to concentrate on the evidence: two cut-up chains of unequal length and origin, held together by a single padlock. The long one, from a tow chain by the looks of it, had been used to tether Dale Hansen to the fence. But the smaller chain, what and where had it come from?

Kurt rubbed at the reddened webbing of his hand. "Had to use the heavy-duty cutters to get that short chain off Dale's wrist."

Walrus leaned down, nose almost to metal, and Karen wondered when he'd last had his eyes checked. "I'll bet it was cut off a longer chain," he said. "No, wait, not cut."

Kurt's lips pursed. "It's a weak link. Pried away. Takes a lot of force to do that. Or was made cheap. Foreign, likely."

"No markings on it," Marek said. "Unless we can match it to what it came from, we won't be able to trace it."

With a gloved hand, Walrus nudged the padlock that had kept

the short chain taut around Dale Hansen's wrist. "Nice solid lock. Brass. Takes a key." He flipped it over. "Master Lock, it says." He dropped it in disgust. "They're all over the place."

"And the tow chain's no different than the ones we've got in our own squads," Kurt said. "Made in China. No distinguishing marks."

"Great." Karen blew out a breath. "Take it up to the crime lab, Kurt, once the roads are open and let them take a look." Then, thinking of the turnaround times Marek must be used to, she told him, "It'll be a while. Things don't move real fast here."

"Probably faster," Marek countered. "Less crime, less backlog."

"Good luck on getting any fingerprints," Walrus said, as Kurt wrapped the chain back up in the plastic bag. "In this kind of weather, our guy is bound to wear gloves—if not for the cold, the crime."

Karen glanced at Marek's once-again bare hands. He stared down at them, as if just now realizing their wind-chafed condition, blew on them, then winced.

"The pain means they're going to be okay," she said, wondering what he'd done with the mittens.

His hands fisted and fell. "Does it?"

Karen deflected her deputies' questioning looks; it wasn't her place to tell them of Marek's loss. Keep him busy, she told herself. That's how she'd gotten through her own loss—loss in limbo, more like. Or denial. But she pushed that thought aside.

"So what's next?" she asked Marek, knowing she needed to learn the investigative ropes. That's why she'd asked for a detective on her roster.

"Next? Uh...talk to people at the plant." He pulled the watch cap back on. "If you let me know where it is, I can walk back and get my pickup then start interviewing..."

Apparently dyslexics could read faces fairly well, because he trailed off and gestured for her to lead the way.

He wasn't the only one who needed to stay busy.

It didn't take a detective, Marek thought, to figure out why the sheriff didn't want him working alone. She had some serious questions about his abilities. But at least he didn't have to deal with small talk—or worse, personal questions—on the way over to the meat packing plant.

Piles of loosened snow and ice ringed the company sign: PBI, it read, in large black letters painted on whitewashed plywood. In smaller letters underneath: Plains Beef, Inc. The corrugated-metal building behind the sign gleamed dully out of the snowdrifts. In the neighboring field, dead cornstalks poked up like sentries, guarding a small army of shabby trailers.

Marek got out of the Suburban, reached for his badge, then remembered. "Don't I need an ID or duty shirt or something?"

Karen joined him on the short walk to the plant from the parking lot. "Your badge is a custom job. There aren't many county detectives around. So it'll be a while yet. As for what you wear, you don't work for me but for Harold Dahl. I don't know what he wants."

That meant that he could probably get out of stepping back into uniform. "If he's anything like his father, Harold won't care as long as it doesn't cost him anything."

She surveyed him. "You'll need something."

"Because otherwise no one will believe I'm really a detective?"

Her eyebrows closed ranks as he opened the door for her.

Workers huddled in groups, drinking coffee from a big cafeteria roaster and cupping their hands around their mugs for warmth. The concrete floor under their feet was wet with mud and snow tracks.

Marek heard snatches of Spanish and the accents, if not the content, of something Slavic and an Asian flavor he'd guess was Laotian or Cambodian. The two tall blacks by the counter might be Sudanese or Somali. Wherever war was, immigrants soon flowed out. But he'd never expected to find them washed up in the white-bread county of his childhood.

Cautious eyes passed over him to Karen, who wore her official brown jacket with its starred badge and the cap with SHERIFF embroidered above the county patch.

"Who's in charge here?" she asked.

The man didn't step forward so much as the others edged back. The workers trickled then flowed out of the side door.

"I'm Jack Thompson, the manager of this outfit." The man hitched up his sagging pants. "Not that we've got work with the highway still closed. We're waiting for a couple truckloads of cattle from the feedlot in Iowa but they're stuck in Sioux City."

Bleary eyes turned on Marek in a face that could have come from anywhere in the country: the doughy spread of inactivity had blurred the bones beneath. "Who're you?"

"I'm Detective Okerlund." He had to bite back the APD. The smell of overripe coffee reminded Marek of long nights at work. Too long. "I work for the county."

The manager took in the rumpled jeans and battered leather jacket. "Got an ID?"

Karen said, "I'm his ID. We have a few questions about Dale Hansen."

Thompson tightened his hold on the clipboard at his side. "Dale? Listen, if he's in trouble, it's nothing to do with me. I'm administration. He's operations."

Then the manager batted at his thinning hair and sighed. "But if he's with you people, that explains a few things. I tried to call him early this morning to see how the roof held up but I didn't get an answer. Left a couple messages but he didn't call back. So as soon as I could get out of my drive, I got over here. About eight, I guess, by then."

Karen asked, "Did you call Mrs. Hansen?"

"Why should I do that? Dale's got his own cell, and as appealing as the wife might be, she's got no eyes for me—nor interest in PBI except what comes out in greenbacks."

Marek traced the scrapes in the concrete. "So you opened about eight?"

"Opened isn't the word. Damn door was already open." Thompson gestured at the main door. "Snow all over. Took an hour just to shovel it out."

Marek rubbed at his temples. "And no Dale."

"Not a sign of him. Where was he, down at The Shaft last night getting drunk?"

He didn't answer Thompson's question. "Has anyone been in the operations area today?"

"Told you, we can't run the chains without the cattle."

Before Marek could, Karen asked, "The chains?"

Thompson beckoned them toward the swinging double doors. "If this was GM, it'd be called the assembly line. Here it's the chains. They hold the carcasses."

Once in the cavernous room beyond the doors, Marek veered toward the area where hooks descended from chains.

"Stop!" Karen yelled. Marek stopped midstep.

"There's blood there," she told him. "On the floor."

But Thompson laughed. "It isn't called the kill floor for nothing."

Marek backed away from the smears on the concrete floor. "You don't clean up every night?"

"Of course we do. Steam hoses hot enough to burn *E. coli* in its tracks. We don't want another huge recall like we had a couple years ago. Nearly bankrupted us. But you don't always get every little bit...that's odd." Thompson was looking up, not down. "There should be a chain there. One that attaches to the hide, to pull it off the carcass."

"How does it work?" Karen asked. "The whole process, I mean."

Marek wasn't sure he wanted to know. He'd given up pork after his mother had read *Charlotte's Web* to him as a child. Now he might have to give up beef.

Thompson pointed to one side of the large room. "The cattle come down that chute over there and are stunned with a bolt gun. Then they get bled and the hides pulled off with this machine here. The carcasses get swung up on the chains and moved around to get gutted and cleaned." He pointed to the pulley system that went to the far side of the room. "End up in the chill room to dry and cool."

Marek stared down at the floor, the iron-smelling smears filling his nostrils. Animal or human blood? Once again, he realized how much he'd taken the APD team, the process, for granted. He'd have closed off the whole plant at this point and called in the crime scene investigators. Now it fell to him. Should he question Thompson or secure the scene? God, he needed sleep—and a working brain.

"Marek, you want me to get the evidence kit from the truck?" the sheriff asked.

He loosed a breath. "That'd be a good idea. Camera?"

"In the kit," she said and walked out.

"Evidence of what?" Thompson straightened and his belly drooped out like a feedbag over the tailgate of a pickup. "Is this about last night? Listen, if one of the workers gave you some sob story about an injury, they're making too much of a scratch. Knives are sharp. Sometimes people get nicked. Besides, they shouldn't be going to the law about that kind of thing anyway. We send them to the clinic."

"I imagine it was closed last night," Marek said.

"Well, yeah, I suppose so, but that young kid filling in for Doc Hudson over the holidays, he's got to still be around." Thompson rocked back on his well-worn heels. "Is Dale answering questions down at the station about this? I tell you, if you think you can make a federal case out of a scrape, our lawyers will—"

"I never said anything about lawsuits." Marek spread his hands. "Just trying to find out what happened here."

"I'll tell you what happened," Thompson said, his voice low but biting. "Some lazy spic got careless and blamed the company for his own incompetence."

Marek's placating hands fisted.

"Would you like to say that again?" Karen stood with the kit cradled in one arm, voice clipped, with a military edge Marek hadn't expected from her.

Thompson sputtered. "I didn't mean...I just get tired of all the claims, you know? My poor back, my poor hands, if it's not one thing it's another." He stuck up his thumb in a strange parody of Dale Hansen's. "One son of a bitch actually took a hammer to his own thumb—did it in front of me, no less. Said he was filing for worker's comp. And I couldn't say a word because he was legal and a minority."

Marek took the kit from Karen. "And one man makes all his race?"

"No, no....of course not." Thompson stepped back. "Sorry. I just...we've got production quotas to meet. I can't afford workers crying wolf." He appealed to Karen. "Our injury rate is no higher than any other in the industry."

"Somehow that doesn't reassure me," Karen said, as if she knew what he was talking about.

The ability to bluff was a necessary job requirement in law enforcement. His new boss—or colleague or whatever she was—had the raw material for her job. But that didn't make her any less raw. He needed to focus. Remember Dim Dale, he told himself, and got down to business.

Karen drew the manager's attention. "Tell me what you know about the injury."

Not only a bluffer but quick, Marek thought, as he pulled open the lid of the kit.

"Not much," Thompson said. "Dale called me last night in a real steam because he had to finish the cleanup himself. Some kind of trumped up injury."

Marek snapped a few shots with what he was surprised to find was a digital camera. The flash glanced off stainless steel all around the room. Then he hunkered down to take swabs of the blood.

"Trumped up?" Karen asked in a neutral voice.

"I tell you, that blood's got to be from the meat," Thompson said, "but even if it isn't, it's not that much. What'd this guy tell you anyway?"

Marek bagged the swabs and caught Karen's look of *What now?* So he asked, "Did Dale tell you who the worker was?"

"It's got to be one of the foreigners. Nobody likes working cleanup and they're the only ones willing to do it. Anyway, all Dale told me was that he'd taken care of the guy."

Marek had few illusions about the corporate definition of *care.* "Fired him, you mean?"

"Look, the guy took off and left Dale to do the dirty work. I'd think anybody would fire a worker like that."

Glancing around, Karen said, "You're telling me there was only one other worker besides Dale to clean up this whole place?"

"No, there's a crew. Subcontracted. Dale deals with them, not me. I figured it must have happened at the end of the shift, since it looks pretty clean in here, except for that bit there."

Karen puffed on her hands. "How many locals do you hire at PBI?"

"Well, there's not many people in this town to hire, are there," Thompson grumbled. "Dale, of course. Maybe a dozen more."

And not a one, Marek would bet, on the kill floor, much less the cleaning crew.

Karen pulled on her gloves. "Not exactly the salvation of the town as billed five years ago."

"Listen, this is tough work. Hard work. We thought you people knew what that meant. If you took these jobs instead of the foreigners, we wouldn't be—"

"Hiring illegals?" Karen asked.

"Oh, no, you're not going to pin that on me," Thompson said. "If that guy who got hurt was on our payroll and an illegal, he did it by stealing somebody's identity. I told you I've got papers on all of them." He hitched up his pants again. "But if it was a member of the cleaning crew, they're independent contractors. We don't keep tabs on them."

Thompson twitched as the camera flashed again. "Injuries aren't even under your jurisdiction."

Marek put away the camera and rolled out the yellow tape. "Assaults are."

"What assault? Hey, what do you think you're doing? This is an assembly line not a crime scene."

Marek kept pulling the tape while Karen distracted the irate manager again. "You just told us you don't have work to do today," she said.

"I'm trying to persuade the trucks to drive up as soon as they re-open I-29," he told her. "They could still be here this afternoon."

Marek tied off the tape. "You have any knives here?"

Karen gave him a look. Oh, yeah, he reminded himself. Meat packing. "Where are they kept?"

"That'd be the fab floor."

He rubbed at his ears. "The Fab Four?"

Thompson snorted and walked toward another part of the building. "The fabrication floor. The bloodless stage, if you like, after the blood's drained and it's all been refrigerated. It's where the skilled work goes on. The knives are kept locked up after the last shift. After they're cleaned with a steam hose. Only two keys, mine and Dale's."

The manager stalked over to a wall cabinet and took out a distinctive copper-colored key—mirror to the one on Dale Hansen's keyring—from his pocket.

Before Marek could do so, Karen took the key from Thompson. "Permit me."

Good instincts, he thought again, and watched her open the cabinet. All the slots were taken. All the blades gleamed clean. She shut the cabinet and glanced at Marek. He shrugged. Unless it had been well cleaned and Dale's key used, the knife hadn't been from the shop. Besides, these knives were too thin, too sharp, to have made the letters on Dale's arm.

They started back down a hallway when Marek stopped by a bin attached to the wall. "What are the padlocks for?"

"Basic safety." Thompson pulled out one of the brass padlocks with its key inserted. From another bin, he picked out a hole-punched card stamped with hazard warnings and labeled LOCKOUT/TAGOUT. He opened the lock and slipped the tag onto it. "Workers put them on the machines after the last shift."

Karen stared down at the padlock. "After cleaning, you mean?"

Thompson shot the sheriff a look that made Marek feel better. He wasn't the only village idiot.

"Before, Sheriff. That's the whole point. Keeps the equipment from getting accidentally triggered. You know, like when people are cleaning."

Karen's expression remained as cool as the air. "And are all the machines locked out?"

Thompson threw the lock and tag back into their proper bins. "It's the law and we follow it. Stupid not to, with liability." At Karen's glance down to the half-full bin, he sighed. "Look, we've got extras. Better too many than too few."

"Humor me," the sheriff said. "Let's check the machines."

Marek lingered behind and snapped a photo of the padlocks. When he caught up, he found the manager and the sheriff in front of a gleaming piece of machinery.

Thompson scratched at one reddened ear. "Must've missed it, that's all. Grinder. Look, it's clean. The hose is right there. Dale must've been in a hurry to get things done last night and just forgot to tag this one."

Marek took another photo, which got a scowl from the manager. "You done here?"

"For now," the sheriff said, after a nod from Marek. "Don't remove the yellow tape without our permission. And don't start up production again until I say so."

Thompson grumbled but said he needed to repair the hider anyway. As they returned to the kill floor, he said, "Listen, if you'll just tell me where Dale is—"

A small man in a ratty red goose-down jacket slapped the doors open in front of them. "I want to talk to Dale."

Thompson glared at him. "Take a number."

"Then I want to talk to you."

"I'm not talking to you, Sanchez." Thompson brushed off the smaller man as they all went out to the lobby. "Get off the property or I'll have the sheriff take you in for trespassing."

Sanchez had the unfortunate look of a rooster, arms flapping, sharp nose poking out like a beak under the thatch of cowlicked black hair.

"It's you the sheriff should be after, Thompson." Little white feathers flew from a tear in Sanchez's jacket. "After what happened last night."

"I don't know what you're talking about." Thompson looked meaningfully at Marek and Karen. "Now get off my property."

"I'm not going anywhere until you—"

"Mr. Sanchez," the sheriff cut in. "You *are* going. Outside. Now."

Marek prepared to step in, but after a short silence, the beak of a nose dipped as if taking a delicate peck at the air, then Sanchez walked out.

Thompson grinned. "Well, look at that. You bowled him over, Sheriff. Doubt he's ever met a six-foot female sheriff before."

"Six-one." Karen turned back to Thompson. "Is that the worker who left Dale in the lurch last night?"

"Sanchez? Are you crazy? Lazy son of a bitch. He didn't work here more than a few days. Fired his ass the minute he started complaining about the cold in here. Would have run him out of his trailer too except he signed a year lease. No, he's a union agitator."

"Unions have a right to org—" Marek began.

"Go on out to the truck, Detective." Karen's tone dismissed him but her eyes said: take a hint. "I'll finish up here and meet you out there."

He closed his mouth and went.

CHAPTER 7

"WISH I COULD DISMISS SANCHEZ that easily," Thompson told Karen. "Little man thinks he rules the roost and all he does is sit in his own chickenshit."

She was glad to be out of the cavernous slaughter room. "I take it you don't have any love for unions."

"Hell, no." Thompson put his clipboard on the coffee counter. "They just drag down production and morale, making demands that can't be met. We're operating on a very slim profit margin here, Sheriff." He pulled at his limp tie, an avocado paisley that made Karen seasick. "Of course," he said, "we could ship all these jobs to Mexico."

Instead, a chunk of Mexico had been shipped here—legally or illegally.

The manager's hands rose to encompass the plant. "Look, it ain't pretty, but it feeds the multitudes for peanuts. As for me, I do what I have to, to keep from having to take a white hat."

That gave her pause. "You have something against the good guys?"

The man rolled his blurred eyes. "White hard hats. The ones on the chains. On the lines."

Ah, she thought, the ones who did the actual work.

When the cell phone in his pocket burbled, he jerked it out, stared at the readout, then stuffed it back. "My ex. She'll be wanting more money that I don't have. I was hoping it was the trucks in Sioux City."

So that's where his money went, she thought, instead of into fashionable ties or another starter castle like Dale Hansen's.

Thompson retrieved his clipboard. "Now, if you've got Dale cooling his heels—"

"I'm afraid, Mr. Thompson, that Dale Hansen's heels aren't all that's cool." She watched him carefully. "He's dead."

The face before her went white then red. "Dead? Are you saying—did that Mexican kill him, is that what's going on here with all the crime scene tape?"

"Why do you say Mexican?" she countered.

"Because odds are, it is," Thompson reminded her. "We've got lots of nationalities here but that's the main one. Cleaning crew especially."

"It should be easy enough to find out. You've got time cards, don't you?"

"Not if it's the contractors." Thompson pulled at his tie again. "But I'll bet Sanchez knows. He was just on about something last night. Maybe you should take a good look at him. I'd like to see that little cockamamie in chains."

No love lost there, she thought, and hoped Marek got her hint to question Sanchez.

"We're still in the preliminary stages, Mr. Thompson. The cause of death has not yet been determined. We'd appreciate it if you kept this to yourself for now." When he opened his mouth to protest, she cut him off. "You won't be working today and tomorrow is Sunday, so I suggest you use the time to start looking for a new operations manager."

Now he did look grieved. "We can't afford this kind of disruption."

Karen kept her tone even, polite, professional. Basic dispatcher training. But she hadn't had as much practice keeping her expression in line. "Dale couldn't either."

"Sorry. I just can't get my head around it. I mean, Dale was no great brain, but he had the best production figures in the business, even with the high turnover." He tapped his fingers on the clipboard. "It's been more stable the last couple years and I was hoping...well, it doesn't matter now."

No doubt he'd hoped to use Dale as a stepping stone out of the Siberian steppes. "Mr. Thompson, can you tell me where you were last night?"

"Where do you think? I was at home praying I wouldn't freeze to death."

She stared at him but he didn't blink.

"If you don't believe me, just ask the neighbor kid I called up and bribed to clear my drive. Tommy Jensen. He'll tell you the snow was pristine over my car. And I live a couple miles from the plant."

Marek locked the evidence kit in the Suburban then walked over to the bouncing red ball that was Sanchez.

"You can't run me off." With the hood of the goosedown jacket pulled tight, only the eyes and nose poked out. "Your boss told me to wait outside and that's what I'm doing."

Marek took Karen's hint, if that was what it was, and got to work. "Thompson said you got fired for complaining about the cold."

"Is that the reason he gave you?" The man's snort puffed out frozen. "All I said was, it's cold in there. A fact. Nothing more. The real reason I got fired was that they found out I was a union organizer. Their hiring policy says they can fire anyone without notice or appeal within the first 90 days. Can I prove it? No, so there I am, out."

But still here and still agitating. "What happened last night?"

"Nothing you'd care about." Sanchez kicked at a stone in the graded gravel. "People like you don't care about lives like ours."

Marek rolled his tongue over teeth that ached with the cold. "*La vida es difícil.*"

The head snapped back up. "Life's difficult, that's for sure, but what does an Anglo like you know about it?"

Marek didn't blame the man for his fixation on race. It had been fixated for him. *La vida es difícil.* Life is difficult. It was the first thing his partner, Manny Trujillo, had taught him, over the dead body of an old woman who'd gotten killed for the twenty dollars in her purse.

And it was the first thing that had come out of Manny's mouth after he'd pulled Marek over that awful morning six months ago.

"I can't claim to have worked in a meat packing plant, Mr. Sanchez, but I've worked in the fields, hung dry wall and molded adobe, spent several years as a carpenter and more than a decade as a cop. I've seen a lot of work and a lot of life."

Too much work, he knew now, and not enough life.

"Looks like you've seen something of death too," Sanchez said after a moment, reaching out. "Something personal."

Marek felt the hand on his arm. He cleared his throat. "My wife."

"I lost mine to breast cancer seven years ago."

"Car accident," Marek said, hedging his guilt so he could speak over it, around it, without going through it.

"That's worse," the little man said, stuffing his hand back into his pocket. "No goodbyes."

Marek took a deep breath, seared his lungs, and coughed up the cold. But Karen wouldn't be any more impressed, he thought, with the too-cold-to-work excuse than Thompson. "Are you going to tell me what happened last night if I tell you I don't care about legal status?"

That stilled the dark eyes. "I'm a citizen. I was born in Oregon. In the middle of a strawberry patch, as my mother told it."

"I meant the man who was injured last night."

That rocked Sanchez back. "You know about that? Is that why you're here?"

"In a roundabout way."

Sanchez stared up at him then the beak of a nose dipped. "Follow me."

When Karen went back outside, she found the parking lot deserted except for her locked Suburban. Looked like her ploy had worked. But where had Marek and Sanchez gone?

She turned toward what the locals called trailer city. Dozens of the old beaters tottered on their blocks, the rust demurely covered with gleaming white drifts. She glanced back across the road at the small row of tiny tract houses there. No one stirred. Not even a child out to play in the winter wonderland.

Then Karen picked out a sled abandoned on a makeshift hill and the beginnings of a snow fort at the end of the first row of trailers.

A curtain twitched as she stared.

It finally dawned on her. They were afraid. Of her.

She hadn't gotten into law enforcement to terrorize people. Quite the opposite. She'd been in a land, the former Yugoslavia, where what went for the law terrorized anything in its path; she'd wanted to make sure that kind of terror never reached these shores.

Somehow, without fanfare, it had.

Karen kicked at a snowdrift then saw a pair of tracks: Bigfoot and Chicken Little. She followed them into trailer city.

"Aiyee!"

Hearing the agonized scream from inside a nearby trailer, Karen dodged under the rickety steps of the trailer opposite and jerked out her gun. "Police! Open that door!"

The door flung open and crashed against the siding.

She slowly released her trigger finger. "Don't ever, *ever*, do that again."

So far as she could tell, Marek didn't appear to either understand or care that she'd nearly put a hole through his heart.

"You said to open the door."

"I didn't mean for you to slam it open like a—" Another scream cut her off. "What's going on in there?"

When Marek disappeared back into the trailer, she followed. What she found in the dank little trailer made her stomach roil.

Marek watched the color pass out of Karen's face. He stepped between her and the man lying on the ratty old couch.

She swallowed then asked, "You've sent for an ambulance?"

Behind him, Marek could hear Sanchez pleading with Julio Chacón's wife but, so far, the union rep wasn't getting anywhere. The three Chacón children huddled in the corner, the eldest cradling the two younger against him.

"He's refusing treatment," Marek said.

"You can't be serious." Seeing he was, Karen beckoned him back outside. Whether to speak privately, or to get fresh air, he wasn't sure. "What happened to his hand?" she asked.

Marek had gotten the story from Sanchez on the way to the trailer. "Julio Chacón triggered the grinder last night when he was cleaning."

She slid hands down her sickly pale face. "Dale Hansen must have cleaned it up afterwards."

"But forgot to lock and tag it. Chacón stuffed his hand in the snow to numb it then holed up in his trailer. By morning, the pain got so bad, his wife went to Sanchez."

"Why not us? Or the doctor?"

Marek could have told her but decided to stick to surface truth. "She went to the only person she felt she could trust."

That didn't satisfy her. "Why didn't Sanchez take him to—"

A squishy thud sounded from inside the trailer. They rushed

back in to find Julio Chacón collapsed on the floor, the soaked linens around his mangled hand dislodged, blood and pus running out on the floor.

"That's it. He's not in his right mind." Karen yanked her radio out and turned away. "You get him ready to transport. I'll get the Suburban."

Nodding, Marek slipped off his belt, knelt down, and wrapped it around the man's wrist. Then he kept his fingers on the man's pulse—and his eyes on the terrified children.

An hour later, Karen paced the small waiting room of the dime-store-sized Reunion Medical Clinic. Her stomach had finally settled but her feet hadn't. She'd seen worse than a mangled hand on her tour of duty, but it wasn't the same.

Work shouldn't be a war.

In one of the cheap plastic chairs, Sanchez tapped fingers against his thighs and stared at the clock. Marek stood nearby with Maria Chacón and the children. He spoke to them in low tones in Spanish, something that surprised Karen. She'd thought he'd had a hard enough time in school just with English.

The slap of swinging doors had them all turning to see Dr. David Echols.

The young resident's fallen face told them the verdict. "If you'd gotten your husband to me right away, Mrs. Chacón, I might have been able to do something."

"Don't you lay that on her." Sanchez sprang up from his chair. "PBI's the one at fault. Dale Hansen didn't bother to call you, didn't even get out a first-aid kit, just turned Chacón out in a blizzard." He turned and kicked at the chair. It didn't move. "Nailed down. Figures."

"I'm afraid what's left of the hand will have to be amputated." Echols pushed his own hand through his lanky blonde hair, leaving streaks of blood, highlights of violence. "I've stopped the bleeding, given him antibiotics, and sedated him. According to the radio, the highway just re-opened, so I've called for the ambulance. He'll have to be transported to Sioux Falls. I'm sorry."

The faces of the Chacón family didn't change. Karen imagined they had the same unfocused look of cattle shocked before slaughter. The woman murmured something to Marek about *dollares.*

How much was a hand worth? Or, in this case, the severing of one?

One thing was for sure: no way had Julio Chacón carved those words into the arm of Dale Hansen. Or, for that matter, chained him to a fence out on I-29.

Even if Dale Hansen deserved it.

As the EMTs loaded Chacón into the ambulance, Karen turned to the union organizer. "Where were you last night, Mr. Sanchez?"

Hand on the door of a battered white pickup, he frowned. "I was in my trailer. Why?"

"Wife? Kids?"

"Wife is dead." His gaze flicked to Marek, who stood talking to the Chacón family, then returned to challenge her. "Kids are in college."

"Best place for them, these days." She pulled on her gloves. "You were alone?"

"That's right, until Chacón's wife came knocking this morning." He watched the EMTs close the doors of the ambulance. "I couldn't get Julio to go to the clinic, he was that afraid he'd be depor—" He stopped and shifted. "Then I went to confront Dale and ran straight into you and *El Gigante.*"

So, Chacón was illegal. That explained much. Except…"El who?"

"The giant," Sanchez said. "Your detective. Biggest man I've ever met in a uniform."

Metaphorically, apparently, since Marek wasn't wearing one. "Then you haven't met Deputy Russell."

"The one they call Walrus? I don't trust him farther than I could throw him—which isn't an inch. He covered for Dale Hansen."

Now he'd lost her. "What do you mean?"

"They said you were still in Pierre for training, but you must've given the okay, right? To bust up our strike back in August?" When she shook her head, he said, "The night before we were going to strike, your deputies came in with guns and handcuffs."

Karen wanted to defend her men, but why would Sanchez bother to lie?

She forced her face to blankness. Don't *ever* show the opponent your disgust with the mistakes of your own team, her college coach had told her, after her first loss. "I didn't authorize any such action. What happened?"

"Your deputies busted in my trailer and hauled a bunch of us down to the station. Dale Hansen claimed we were going to keep workers from crossing the picket line. That's a lie. They didn't have a leg to stand on, not legally. They finally let us go with a warning not to cause any more trouble. After that, no one wanted to talk about unions any more. If you want something to go after, Sheriff, I tell you, there's some pretty il—"

"Mr. Sanchez," she interrupted. "When was the last time you saw Dale Hansen?"

"Hansen?" The head tilted. "Why? What's happened?"

"You tell me."

"I'd be happy to tell you he was six foot under but... *Madre de Dios*. Is he?"

Marek, who'd come up behind, said, "Why don't we take this back to the station?"

CHAPTER 8

NOTHING EVER CHANGES IN SMALL TOWNS.

That, Marek thought, was as big a lie as the one that said you couldn't go home again. Bigger, really, given he was home, except it wasn't.

He and the sheriff walked down the middle of the barely cleared Main Street.

The Ben Franklin general store, the Piggly Wiggly grocery store, even local staple Lindstrom's Drugstore: all gone. Another block and the dime store was another hit. He'd spent a lot of time perusing the backroom racks there. Comic books. He'd gotten a paper route to pay for them, as his mother refused to support superheroes on her dime.

What the hell happened to this town?

Marek glanced sideways at Karen, about to ask her, but she was looking straight ahead, probably thinking of the interview they'd just conducted.

Sanchez told them he'd been in his trailer. Asleep. If you want to know who'd want Dale Hansen dead, he'd said, get in line. When they'd pressed, he'd said, "There used to be another meat packer here in Reunion, you know. Small outfit. Got run out of business by PBI."

A plow approached, its operator giving a friendly wave. Marek wasn't used to the common rural courtesy. In the city, he'd gotten more of the one-finger variety.

Marek raised a belated hand and waited for the plow to pass. Then he crossed the street to where Milstead's Bakery—a favorite haunt for a sugar high—had been. Wait, still was. Then he saw the little sign. It took a moment for the words to sink in: closed until further notice.

"Don't worry, it's just for the holidays," Karen said. "Helen Milstead still makes the best butterhorns in the state."

Three boarded up storefronts later, they found Sig Halvorsen knocking snow from the overhanging sign that showed a butcher knife dangling over slices of succulent meat. Medium rare, Marek judged, about what an independent butcher shop must be these days.

Marek had grown up going down to Halvorsen's on his bike for a cut of this or that, mostly beef, occasionally something more exotic like chicken or turkey. His mother hadn't been an adventurous cook and working full-time as she did, they'd had a lot of pot roasts in the slow cooker. Over the summers, the roasts yielded to hamburgers grilled out back, dripping with juice, ketchup, lettuce, red-ripe tomatoes, and pickles.

The slam of the shovel onto concrete covered the grumble of his stomach.

The man caught sight of them and leaned on the shovel with a grin of delight. "Hello there, Karen. You checking how we've fared the storm?"

Sig Halvorsen must be in his early sixties now but his hair was still thick, blonde, and his shoulders outsized to the rest of his lanky body. Marek wasn't quite sure how the two were related, but Karen looked more like Sig than she did her own father.

"Last blizzard I saw like this it was, I don't know, '75?" Sig went on without waiting for an answer. "Just don't get them like we used to."

Did the elder generation always say that kind of thing to the younger? But Karen was saying, "It's been since I was a kid anyway. School was off for days, sleds went out on the bluff, and Mom made barrels of hot cocoa. Dad, of course, hated it."

"Well, then, he had to go rescue the idiots caught out in it, didn't he." Sig missed the glance that Karen sent Marek. "But it wasn't the people, so much, but the animals. Lost an awful lot of cattle. So far as I've heard, we've fared better this time."

Sig Halvorsen took a leisurely look at Marek. "You'd be Leif Okerlund's youngest. The one who couldn't watch the grinder going without turning green."

After seeing what was left of Chacón's hand that morning, he was pretty sure that hadn't changed. "I'm Marek."

He waited for the inevitable comment, one that had yet to be voiced. It would be a relief, he thought, to finally hear it. A Marek doesn't make anything but trouble.

But all he heard was the grumble of his own stomach.

"Hmm. Yes. Well, come on in, Marek Okerlund." Sig swung the shovel over one shoulder and pulled open the shop door. "I can see you've got more on your mind than your stomach can handle."

Karen knew when she took the job that she'd have to question, arrest, and jail people she'd known since childhood. But Sig wasn't just a man she admired. Although technically he was her father's cousin, she'd always called him uncle.

But Sanchez had one thing right: Sig Halvorsen had more than enough reason to want Dale Hansen dead. Or, more particularly, PBI, Inc.

She watched Marek try to pay for some beef jerky and get stonewalled.

"You gnaw on that long enough and I'll interest you in a prime rib," Sig said. "Of course, city boy that you are now, you may not know what to do with it."

Marek stopped mid-gnaw but it was Karen who asked, "How'd you know he came from the city?"

"His uncle, of course. Jim Marek said the boy'd come back in his own time."

The beef jerky went down with a bob of the adam's apple. "How'd he know?"

"Hired some PI in Sioux Falls," Sig said to Marek. "You weren't exactly hiding. Jim was a bit disappointed you left carpentry, said you had a knack for it, but I think he got a kick out of you turning cop like your dad. I kept after him to contact you but he said that was your move."

Her detective no longer looked hungry. "Too late."

"The name of Marek is a better one because of him," Sig said. "He was a good man, if a bit...closed off. But he did good work. At the house, here, at my plant."

Which was why they were here, Karen reminded herself. "We've got some questions for you, Uncle Sig."

Marek straightened, stuffed the remaining jerky into his pocket, and wiped a careless hand over his jeans. He wasn't wearing gloves again and the knuckles were chafed and red.

Dammit, she wasn't going to say a word if he lost his fingers.

"Ask away," Sig said. "If it's about another raid, I'm all for it."

Seeing the puzzled expression on Marek's face, she said, "Last year my dad worked with Sig to bring the Feds in to raid PBI for illegals."

The hand still absently wiping against the wrinkled jeans stopped.

Sig's affable face tightened. "I think we'd better sit down while I explain to the detective here why I shouldn't be flayed for wanting better for people—*all* people—than what goes on there."

Marek settled uneasily in the straight-back chair in the tiny office at the back of the shop. Karen, in a move that spoke of long familiarity, hooked the stool in the corner with her foot.

On the wall, nearly obscured by a montage of grinning blondes, hung a framed diploma: Sigurd Halvorsen, B.S., South Dakota State University. That would be in Brookings, to the north, but still well within East River.

As always, such credentials made Marek sink into himself, into his failures, into the dashing of his mother's hopes. He'd gotten his high school diploma, as had his father at a time when few did, but his mother had had a master's degree.

She'd have gone to college around the same time as Sig Halvorsen. But she'd gone to the rival University of South Dakota in Vermillion, just to the south on the border with Nebraska. As, Marek knew, had Karen. Only true affection could have made Sig tack Karen's picture up there in the red and white of the Coyotes instead of the blue and yellow of the Jackrabbits.

Sig sat down in a rickety swayback chair behind his desk and looked across at Marek. "I'm not down on people for trying to better themselves and their lives, Detective. But if people come here illegally, they're vulnerable to the lawless, because they can't call on the law for help."

That was a different take on it than he'd expected to hear.

"You know about Chacón?" Karen asked.

Sig glanced at her. "Who?"

"Never mind."

"I know Sanchez, the union guy," Sig said, as if the jump from one to the other was obvious. Maybe it was. "Can't say I like the lean of his politics but he's a good man. Cares. That's what it all comes down to in the end. You care or you don't. Too many in this business don't."

"How did you meet Sanchez?" Marek asked.

"On that failed raid. He was so furious on all sides of the coin that he could hardly say a word. He didn't want the Feds snagging Mexicans, but he also wanted people to know what was going on there. Plus, illegals undermined his efforts to unionize. None of us were happy with the result. Made everybody but PBI look like a fool. Somebody tipped them off."

Marek shifted in the hard chair. "Them?"

"Bunch of workers, maybe twenty or thirty, disappeared that day. A week later, once the Feds had left, they came back and things only got worse. Most of my people who went to work for PBI when I closed, they left after a week or two."

Marek blinked. "In this economy?"

Karen frowned over at him. He could read the question in her face, even if she didn't voice it. *Who would work for PBI after what we just saw?*

He had to remind himself, she wasn't Manny, his old partner. She hadn't picked up on what he was doing—but, on the other hand, did she know what she was doing?

Marek sharpened his tone. "One of my great-uncles, Bill Kubicek, he worked for a big meat packer in Sioux Falls." He didn't know if it still existed or not. "Got good money. Hard work, true, but no harder than the farming he grew up with—less, he said. Tried to get me to work there, but I didn't think I could handle the blood and guts."

Sig just smiled. "Interesting you ended up in homicide, then."

People didn't care to see the slaughter—but they ate up the results, whether in Big Macs or *Forensic Files*. He needed to push Sig, to get some kind of reaction. "I just don't get why your ex-workers left PBI, Mr. Halvorsen. Are they lazy?"

Finally, red stung the butcher's cheekbones. "My people aren't—weren't—lazy. Good people, willing to work hard, but not be taken advantage of. PBI may look sleek and high tech to you, but they've pushed the chain speeds to insane levels, endangering workers and the quality of the product. Your great-uncle got out of the business just in time, with a pension and his health. Things have changed. He'd have told you that, if you ever bothered to contact him."

Marek didn't let himself react to that. It was true enough.

Then the butcher let out a long breath. "Maybe you've forgotten, Detective, but people here, we like working for ourselves or, barring that, our neighbors." His hands touched on his chest. "If I mistreat my workers, it comes back on me and business falls off. But if Dale Hansen mistreats his workers, pushing them beyond what's human, he gets a bonus."

Karen upped a foot on the rungs of the stool. "You're saying the managers at PBI don't care what Reunion thinks of its business practices?"

"They don't have to, more's the pity, because no one connects the dots. People who buy the overstressed, overdrugged beef PBI sells to the chain stores, they don't see what happens at the plant. Just like farmers here, it's all about crop yield, but the fertilizer that makes bumper crops, it flows downriver and makes huge dead zones in the gulf. Puts the fishermen out of business."

Marek steered the man back. "Just like PBI put you out of business?"

Sig bobbled on his chair then righted. "My little plant did maybe a hundred head a week at full production; PBI does more than that in an hour. That's economy of scale, sure enough, but it isn't humane. My people can—could—produce hour for hour better than anyone. With more quality. But the customer never has a chance to see what I've got to offer, because the big guys keep me off the market."

His knife-nicked hands came together in his front of his face and the fingertips almost met. Almost. "Buyer and seller never meet."

His hands fell. He dug into his shirt pockets, drew out two more sticks of jerky, and handed them over. "Me and my customers, we've got a relationship; they've got a transaction. Everything's so impersonal these days—and so messed up."

Marek wondered if, technically, the jerky could be considered a bribe but slipped it into his pocket. "But it's more jobs for Reunion, isn't it," he pressed, ignoring Karen's baffled glare. "More than your operation employed. Isn't it good for the town?"

Sig intertwined his hands and let them fall to his midsection. "You notice anything different, Detective, walking down Main Street?"

Marek felt himself lose traction again. He wasn't supposed to be answering the questions. "Most of the shops are gone."

"We used to have a thriving downtown with more than enough

people and produce to go around. Now look at it. We live in the breadbasket of the world and can't even get fresh vegetables."

Not exactly a problem for him. "I don't do much cooking."

"Your wife will find out soon enough." At the awkward silence, Sig looked uncertainly at Marek. "I'm sorry. I seem to have put my foot in it."

"I'm a widower." That was the first time he'd ever said it. A strange word. What made a woman a widow and a man a widower? Sounded like someone who made widows. When that thought hit, he could barely snatch breath to say, "She died six months ago."

Whatever questions arose behind those inquisitive eyes, Sig must have decided it wasn't the time or place to voice them.

Instead, the butcher went on, briskly, "To get back to your question, yes, I got run out of business. Frankly, if I can't run my plant so it's decent to human and animal, I'd rather not run it at all."

When silence fell again, Marek realized Karen wasn't going to ask, so he was going to have to do it himself. "Mr. Halvorsen, where were you last night?"

Karen came off her stool, one foot still on the rung, like a one-legged crane. "Marek."

He kept his eyes on Sig Halvorsen.

"Where? Right here in the shop, that's where, listening to the weather reports and praying we weren't going to be losing animals." Sig slid a hand through his hair, rippling it like winter wheat under a Dakota wind. "From your tone, Detective, I'm guessing something else was lost last night—and not animal."

CHAPTER 9

KAREN CONTAINED HERSELF UNTIL THE butcher shop door closed behind them. "You had no right to question Sig like that."

Marek turned on her so fast that her nose dipped into the hollow of his throat. So he wasn't always slow. About some things.

He said, "You weren't asking."

Because he was right, it burned the more, and she shoved at him. "Get out of my way."

For a moment, he didn't move, and she could smell the heat, a pungent threat, then he stepped back and the icy wind blew it away. "I'm trying to solve a case," he said. "It was an interrogation, not a family reunion."

That's for sure. She stuffed her hands into her pockets, walked around him, and took off.

He caught up with her in a few unhurried steps. No one else could do that to her. Walrus would huff and tell her to slow down, Kurt would simply walk behind her in measured steps until she fell back, and her father would ask what fire did she think she was going after.

Karen shaded her eyes from the sun's glare off the snow. Okay, he might be right, about the asking, but not about the rest. "Uncle Sig's no killer."

"He's a butcher."

"So? It's like a hunter's code for him, honoring the sacrifice of life to sustain life. You know, like the Indians worshipped the buffalo, but they still killed it. That's how Sig feels about cattle. A quick killing, a merciful one, not the kind of death somebody put

61

Dale Hansen through." She upped her pace but it didn't faze Marek. "I can't believe you'd defend Dale and PBI after what happened to Chacón," she told him.

A frozen mist appeared as he exhaled. "Is that really what you think I was doing?"

He sounded tired and, to her chagrin, hurt. She replayed the scene back in the butcher shop. Finally, she got it. Bad cop. Classic interview technique. And she'd missed it because, dammit, she knew Sig Halvorsen.

Torn between loyalties, sworn and familial, she fixed on their destination. The courthouse rose majestically out of the snow in roughhewn rose-colored Sioux quartzite. Built in the late nineteenth century, the Richardsonian Romanesque building—festooned with fanciful turrets—housed all the functions of local government, from highest to lowest, court to jail, third floor to basement.

Marek pulled open one of the heavy double doors for her. She hesitated.

"Hey, close that door," a yell came from inside. "This building is drafty enough as it is."

She went into the office, intending to apologize to Marek, then caught sight of Walrus. Blood spattered his pant legs. "Where have you been, to a massacre?"

"It's sure not Wounded Knee." He twitched the spattered fabric between two fingers. "Think it'll come out? The wife's going to kill me."

"More like Harold Dahl," she commented. "You're going to need new uniform pants. What happened?"

He released his pant leg. "Those cattle trucks you said Thompson wanted up here at the plant—well, they made it to slaughter after all."

Had everyone decided to ignore her authority today? "I told Thompson to shut down over the weekend. I don't care if the interstate opened again."

"Well, don't have a cow." When Karen didn't smile, Walrus put his feet up on his desk and grimaced at the spatters. "The trucks didn't make it to the plant. The first truck skidded off I-29 and rammed into the embankment off the Alford exit overpass. The truck behind rammed into the first. Hell of a mess. If they'd had any sense, they'd have waited until the roads were clear. There's ice under that snow."

Marek asked, "Anybody killed?"

"Other than cattle?" His moustache drooped. "The driver who hit the embankment got life-lifted out to Sioux Falls."

Karen wondered if Thompson knew. "Why wasn't the highway patrol doing that one?"

"They figured the cattle were our business. Good thing I had enough bullets."

As if all the talk of meat had gone to his stomach, Marek pulled out the jerky from his pocket and began to gnaw. "So what's going to happen to the meat?"

"We left the carcasses stacked in the ditch, nicely packed in snow. I figured you could tell Thompson, Sheriff. That's why they pay you the big bucks."

"You know, I took a big pay cut from my job in Sioux Falls to become sheriff of this county." Karen pushed his booted feet off the desk and sat down on it. She could play bad cop too. "Walter, what were you and Rick doing at PBI back in August, right before the planned strike?"

"I hate it when you call me Walter. What'd I do?"

"That's what I'm trying to find out."

Walrus shot Marek a put-upon look and shrugged. "Don't know why you're interested. Nothing came of it." He shifted under her continued stare. "Look, this is a right-to-work state, isn't it? Dale Hansen said he'd heard the union people were going to bust some balls, stage a strike, keep people from crossing the line. So we went to look things over."

"And?"

"And nothing. That union ringleader, Sanchez, we found him with some other agitators; he mouthed off, so we brought them down here to talk. That's all it was, just talk. We got no evidence of anything illegal, so that was the night. Dale was pissed, yeah, but we had to let them all go." His eyes widened. "Hey, you figure Sanchez did for Dale Hansen?"

She leaned over. "The only thing I'm trying to figure out right now, Deputy Russell, is where the report is on that incident."

He chewed on his moustache. "Uh, I'm not sure there's much of a report to speak of."

She liked Walrus. But, as had her father before her, she found he could be a little careless when it came to paperwork. "You claiming to be dyslexic too?"

Walrus blinked over at Marek then looked back to her. "Come

on, Karen, you know we were short-staffed with our secretary retired and you gone for training and—"

"Walter, where was Kurt?"

He let air stream down through his moustache. "Guess."

Now she sighed. "Eva."

Kurt Bechtold's unmarried sister, who lived with him, had as many phobias as years, the most prominent being fear of the dark. After sundown, you could see the Bechtold place lit up until sunrise the next morning. Anything that threatened the electricity, threatened Eva. "There was a storm that night?"

"Knocked power off for two hours," Walrus confirmed. "Made it hell trying to find anything or anyone in that camp of trailers out there. Muddier than a cowpatch."

Remembering what Sanchez had claimed, Karen asked, "No damage to person or property?"

Walrus tugged at his spattered pants. "Okay, so Rick got a little excited, knocked a door off its hinges when we didn't get an answer. But we took care of that."

So Sanchez hadn't been lying; it had been his door. The repair job, he'd claimed, had been half-assed and let the cold in. If he made a stink, her office could be in a shitload of trouble. And she hadn't even known about it. Not an excuse, she knew, that would go over well with her constituents.

From his desk, Marek said warily, "I need Dale Hansen's phone records. Cell, landline, whatever."

Karen wondered if she'd have been better off as an office, or officer, of one. "I'll get the warrant from Judge Rudibaugh."

She pulled open the side door that led out to the main hallway of the building, slammed it behind her, and made her way to the third floor.

The crack in the plaster around the side door let out a burst of white particles that swirled in the light then slowly dissipated. Marek itched for spackle. If that plaster wasn't taken care of, it might release who knew what—asbestos, even, in a place this old.

"Ouch. She's not usually so uptight," Walrus said. "Sorry you got the backwash."

"No, you got mine," Marek said. "I asked Sig Halvorsen where he was last night."

Walrus whistled. "Can't blame that one on dyslexia, Detective."

No one had even heard of dyslexia when he'd been in school. Now it tripped off the deputy's tongue as easily as dermatitis and with about as much concern. How much different his life might have been, if it had been discovered earlier.

His gaze fell on the line of pictures on the far wall—all the past sheriffs plus their respective wives who'd taken the title if not the office when the law had once stipulated term limits.

Marek walked over, contemplated the black and white—more gray—of his father's picture. Light eyes pulled sad, a gentle hand held out palm up rather than riding his gun, Leif Okerlund embodied the term Keeper of the Peace. He'd seen too much death, dying, and dead as a young man in the last world war. He'd kept the little wars of rural Eda—of turf, of politics, of religion, of water and rights—from turning bloody.

A just war was harder to find, he used to say, than just war.

What would he have thought, Marek wondered, to know his youngest son had come home, to take up the badge in this same office?

He honestly had no idea. His mother, on the other hand, had made him promise to leave Reunion. And he had, right after her funeral, though not by choice. His gaze slid sidelong to the last picture.

Walrus tapped the frame of the full color photograph. "A good man, good sheriff, but not exactly all sunshine and light, if you know what I mean."

Marek kept his thoughts to himself on Arne Okerlund. Enforcer, his photograph might be titled. And not necessarily of the law.

He turned away from the collected gaze of Okerlunds past; one not past enough.

"I'm surprised none of you took over the job of sheriff," Marek said to Walrus. "How many deputies are there, besides you and Kurt?"

"Three." But Walrus held up two fingers, making Marek wonder if his dyslexia was bleeding over into nontextual areas. "Deputy Two Fingers keeps getting shipped off to the Middle East."

An Indian, Marek mused. Not just the storefronts had changed in Reunion.

"Then there's Bjorkland; he's mad for climbing rocks. And we've got a reserve deputy on call during the night shift, Rick Gullick."

That made three deputies Marek had yet to meet—all likely

younger men. Marek didn't remember Kurt, but he was old enough to have been a night shift deputy during the last years of his father's reign as sheriff. "Why didn't you or Kurt go for sheriff?"

"Kurt's got his sister to look after." Walrus circled the air around his ear with a finger. "Batty as a fruitcake—but makes up for it by baking for us. As for me, you couldn't pay me to put up with the potshots people take at you once you put your hat in the ring. I figure being a deputy is the safest way to keep my friends and still be a hero."

Walrus linked sausage fingers over his paunch. "And, of course, I'm not an Okerlund. Karen's got a bit of a pass that way. It's like the family business. Besides, people feel sorry for her, what with her husband and all."

Marek almost asked about Karen's husband then decided if he wanted her to respect his privacy, he'd better return the favor. Instead, he asked, "You have kids?"

Walrus beamed. "Sure, I've got three boys and plan on living to see them give me a passel of grandkids one day. Just hope there's still some halfway decent girls here for my boys to marry when the time comes." He considered Marek. "Heard you got a daughter. She hunt?"

"She'd be out there protecting Bambi."

"Time to convert her. You a hunter?"

Marek had hunted once when he was twelve. He'd liked the actual excitement of the hunt and the triumph of hitting his target—but then he'd picked up the squirrel, felt the heat still in the supple body, felt the life drain out of it.

He'd buried it where he'd brought it down; he'd have done better to leave it, fresh, for others to feed on, but humanity always buried its shame. His father hadn't said a word, simply accepted his decision; later, they'd shot at targets.

Marek turned, stared at the crack above the door, and took his life in his hands. "Not of animals, no."

Walrus shook his head. "You've been gone too long, Marek Okerlund. Gone soft."

He kept staring at the crack. "It's been said."

Karen stalked down the hallway of the third floor.

The two men she'd left behind were probably plotting a coup.

Takes a man to do the job, they'd be saying.

Well, too bad. A man hadn't stepped up to the plate. She had. Besides, she'd overheard it all already.

Can she shoot somebody, that's what I want to know—she's got ball, I'll give her that, but balls is different—couldn't put the final shot down, could she—don't hold with a woman sheriff—not like she can talk a gun to death—now, that husband of hers, that's a shame—look, she's here, so I say, let her be and we'll see—

Yes, they'd all see.

Karen halted in front of the double doors to the judge's outer chambers, forced herself to stay there, instead of slapping her way in, as Sanchez had onto the kill floor.

As a dispatcher, she'd missed being in the action physically; now that she'd stretched her legs—and her mind—she liked where she'd found herself. For now, anyway. So she'd shaken sun-spotted hands, eaten lutefisk and downed brats with beer, and waited for an opportunity to prove herself.

Now it might all unravel because of one man: the man she'd fought to hire.

Eventually, Karen thought, she could handle detective work herself, but she had no practical experience and a whole county to patrol. A scary proposition. None of the towns, not even the county seat of Reunion, had its own police force, not since her father had folded his two-man force to take the position of sheriff from his own father.

She'd wanted a part-time detective on her roster, maybe one easing out of the life, to help her make the transition. She'd even had one lined up in Sioux Falls, until he'd had a heart blip and his wife stuffed him into a Winnebago.

So instead of a mentor, she'd gotten a competitor.

Taking a deep breath, she pushed open the doors with decorum—something the office and the man who presided there demanded—and wasn't surprised to find the door to the inner chamber open.

"Afternoon, Judge."

The Honorable John Franklin Rudibaugh looked up from his legal tome. He swept reading glasses off of the ruddy and bulbous nose that sat oddly on his patrician face—and had given him his nickname. Judge Rudy.

"I did not expect to see you today, Sheriff." The sonorous voice cut its consonants close. "I would have thought you would be out checking up on the old and infirm for quite some time yet, there being so many of them in your constituency."

She shifted awkwardly. "Kurt's out doing that now. Most people had the sense to stock up and stay home. The electricity held for the most part."

"Well, then, what can I do for you?"

"I need a warrant for Dale Hansen's phone records. His cell phone and his landline."

She wasn't prepared yet to ask for the records of Krissy Hansen and her daughter, but she might get lucky and find they used the landline.

"On what basis do you wish to interfere with the man's right to privacy?"

"That the dead have none."

The judge stared at her over his clasped hands then slowly let them fall to the open book in front of him. "While I admire your uncharacteristic brevity, Sheriff Mehaffey, I must say that death is not a condition whose mere existence dictates that privacy be violated. Try again."

The last time she'd been in his office, he'd accused her of circumlocution. She couldn't win. "Probable homicide."

"Expand on probable."

Karen told him what she knew. When she finished, he pulled open a drawer and brought out a form.

With a fountain pen, he filled in the blanks with a looping longhand that in most places had yielded to the standard font sizes. Judge Rudy believed that justice required impartiality but not impersonality.

When he finished filling in the required spaces, he capped the pen and set it aside. But the warrant remained on his desk.

"Whiteout? Or white out? Two words or one?" he asked, leaning toward her. "An atmospheric condition, an erasure of a mistake, an expulsion of a people, which is it? The case, I imagine, may hinge on the words."

He looked like he relished the challenge of presiding over such a case; he had few challenges here, so far as she could tell.

Before she could censor herself, she asked, "Isn't this job a waste of your talents, judge?"

"Is this a personal question?" he threw back at her. "Because if you think you are wasted here—"

"No, I just..." Well, maybe she did, in the long term, but that wasn't what worried her. "I don't know if I'm fooling myself, that I'm cut out to be sheriff. I just blew up at two of my people."

He leaned back, into dispassion, and she regretted her words. "Why?" he asked finally.

She had to think about that for a moment in terms that the judge would understand. "One asked a question that I didn't want asked. The other didn't ask enough questions and didn't put down the answers."

"The former is the one that troubles you."

She rubbed at her forehead. "That's why I wonder."

He picked up the warrant and handed it to her. "That you wonder is the reason you will learn." The faintest of smiles touched his lips. "Learn fast or you won't have to wonder: the good people of Eda County will do it for you at the ballot box come November."

When she returned to the office, she nearly ran into a ladder that blocked the side door entrance. Walrus leaned negligently against the inside wall, one of his hunting boots on the bottom rung of the ladder. Higher up, her eyes rested on Marek's short leather boots. She could read the word Blundstone molded into the sole. She looked higher and found her new detective sanding down a recent spackling job.

So much for visions of catching them counting coup.

Her eyes dipped back to Walrus. "I think there's a leftover can of paint in the basement."

"I'm holding down the ladder," he protested.

She put her size-eleven boot on the bottom rung. With a sigh, Walrus trundled off. After the door to the basement slammed shut, a product not of anger but of a spring-loaded door, she said, "Sig Halvorsen is like...well, like an uncle to me."

The pale blue eyes brooded down at her. "Unlike this uncle."

"I didn't mean..." Better, she thought, to change the subject, to something less loaded than the gun she carried. "What made you turn from carpenter to cop?"

For a moment, she thought she'd trod too heavily on his privacy, the way his face closed up, but then he said, "Actually, carpentry led me there. Maybe I'll tell you the story one day."

"Why not now?" The door to the basement creaked open again and that was her why. Under her breath, she said, "I shouldn't have told Walter about the dyslexia."

He glanced over her head then came down the ladder. "Deputy Russell's already figured out I'm an idiot for questioning

Sig Halvorsen."

"That's right," Walrus said, holding out the open paint can. "Here you go, Sheriff."

Now that she'd made overtures to Marek, she'd extend the same to Walrus. "Why don't you paint it over?"

"Me? I hate heights," Walrus said, but with a smile. "Get Bjorkland in here if you want any climbing done. Besides, I stirred it up for you."

So she took the can and the brush he handed her. Deputy and detective each held a foot on the ladder while she painted over the last evidence of the crack.

CHAPTER 10

HALF AN HOUR LATER, KAREN turned the Suburban off Main Street onto Okerlund Road. With one ear captive to her cell phone, she stopped beside the drift-ensnared Silverado.

"Yes, Mayor, I'll be there in a few minutes." She swiveled the cell phone down to speak to Marek, who sat in the passenger seat. "The roof of the senior activity center collapsed. No one got hurt but the mayor wants us out in force. You go ahead and interview the workers in trailer city. I'll catch up, if I can, otherwise I'll trust you know what you're doing."

That hadn't come out quite right after their little détente in the office. She just didn't want to be shut out of the investigation.

"What was that?" she said into the phone after Marek got out. The bright sound of Greta Dahl tinkled through her earpiece. "No, it's Marek. I had to drop him off. Yes, he's here. No, he's not coming with me. You'll have heard about Dale Hansen."

It wasn't easy to turn the gas hog around in the snow—and one hand on the wheel. But she got it headed back to Main Street. She tuned back in to catch the mayor's question.

"Cause? Most likely, Dale died of exposure, but we can't be sure until the autopsy."

All true as it went. If Greta Dahl hadn't heard the whole of it, then no one else had. Karen would give it another day or two before the story broke, what with the blizzard being the banner news.

Marek slogged his way through thigh-high drifts to the last of the tract houses across from the plant, home to the line supervisors. Might as well start at the top and work down, he'd decided. So far, no joy.

He raised his hand to knock. He rapped dead air.

"Are you goddamn crazy, soliciting out here after a blizzard?"

Facing the business end of a shotgun, Marek held up his hands. "I'm not soliciting, Mr. Yarnik. I'm Detective Marek Okerlund. I work for the sheriff's office." Sort of, he thought. "I've got a few questions for you about Dale Hansen."

The name Okerlund apparently rang no bells with the man whose gnarled finger fit into the trigger as if made there. "Where's your badge?"

"I don't have one yet. I just got to town. If you want to call the sheriff's office and ask, they'll vouch for me."

"You carrying?"

"Carrying what? Oh." Marek edged open his jacket to show he had no gun. "Not yet." If anything, that seemed to disturb the man more. "Got handed a case straight out of bed this morning. I haven't even gotten coffee."

And it was now past the half-day routine he'd been promised. With leeway, he conceded, for major cases, but why did one have to hit his door just now? He had things to do. For Becca. First on the list, rescue her from Arne Okerlund.

"Why should I talk to you about Dale, I'd like to know." Yarnik didn't lower the gun. "What's he been up to?"

"He's dead."

The man considered him for a long moment then put his gun back on a rack inside and pulled on a coat. "Let's take this over to the plant. I want to talk to Thompson."

They found the manager by the coffee counter, his hands ruffling his thinning hair up into tufts. "Yarnik, I was about to call you. We've got a mess on our hands."

The bony shoulder jerked in Marek's direction. "So he just told me. Thought I'd come talk to you about that."

"Well, we can't run the chains." Thompson glared at Marek. "Sheriff taped off the kill floor. I just called her and she said it's a no-go, even though we've got bodies stacked up like cordwood."

Yarnik blinked for the first time. "All I heard was Dale. Who else?"

"Not people. The *shipment.* Two trucks. Idiot driver rammed into an embankment and our beef got stacked in a ditch off the highway. The only good thing is that they're on ice, so to speak. Tell me, how are we going to deal with that if we can't run the chains?"

The older man scratched at his grizzled face. "You'll need somebody to take over operations."

"Get me those carcasses here without spoiling them and you've got the job." Thompson tamped down the tufts of his hair with steadier hands. "Otherwise, they're a dead loss. One we can't afford."

"Excuse me, gentlemen," Marek said, "but I'm here looking into another dead loss, human life, not animal."

"Human, animal, same difference," Yarnik said.

Marek found he still believed in one thing: it *was* different. It had to be. That's why Marek wore a badge. Figuratively speaking, at the moment. "I need to ask you some questions, Mr. Yarnik. Where can we go?"

Ignoring him, Yarnik told Thompson, "Start calling in the workers. I'll find out who can skin and dice the old-fashioned way, without all the fancy equipment. Send the rest to retrieve the carcasses." The bony shoulder jerked up again in what might have been a come-hither gesture to Marek. "I need to suit up."

Marek followed him into a locker room where the man stripped to his skivvies. Faded blue-ink tattoos—anchors, mermaids, sea dragons—covered much of his torso. Gnarled, body and hands, with bowed legs, he might weight 120 pounds wet, but Marek wouldn't like to take him on.

That kind often fought fast, hard, and dirty.

So he'd hit first. "Where were you last night?"

"Where any man with a brain in his noggin was, at home. What's it to you?" Then the beady eyes steadied on Marek's face. "It wasn't an accident? No, course not, your type don't show up to ask people about accidents. What did for Dale, then?"

Stupidity or cruelty, he almost said. "Exposure."

"You telling me you're wasting my time, and yours—which *is* mine given I'm paying your salary—on some idiot getting caught out in a blizzard?" He stomped into a rubber boot. "What happened, did that fancy pickup of Dale's go belly up on the way back to that love palace of his last night?"

"Love palace?"

The sly smile showed yellowed teeth. "You must've seen the wife."

Marek wasn't going to play that game. "I'm afraid it's looking like it wasn't an accident."

The man donned what looked like fine-chained armor over his head. "No? Well, he wasn't popular, if that's what you're asking, except with Thompson. But that's what you take on when you move up, getting the work done, not mollycoddling whiners."

"Whiners?"

That earned Marek a single birds-eyed stare. "In my day, we worked hard and we worked hurt. Patch 'em up and put 'em back in. I could pull my count with the best of them."

"Pull your count?"

Yarnik spat into the drain; the brown liquid ran into the rusting metal. "Keep up with the chains. You know, the chains that move the meat from station to station."

From what Sig Halvorsen had said, the chain speeds had reached insane levels. "Tell me, Mr. Yarnik, did you start out on the chains here? Or did you go straight to a supervisor spot?"

"I've put in my time over the years—all over the country. Not like some others."

"Like Dale Hansen?"

"If I'd got here first, I'd have been his boss. Seniority, see?" He showed the scars on his gnarled hands. "Surgery three times. Can't afford it no more but I ain't complaining. I'll work 'til they put me in the ground. Man was meant to work."

"What's your take on unions?"

He spat again; this time it pooled and left a stain on the concrete. "Had their place once but don't see much use now." He tweaked the body armor. "They've got all these newfangled getups we never had."

Thinking of Chacón, Marek said, "We've had reports of inhumane working conditions."

"Is that a fancy word for saying it ain't a walk in the park? Not everybody can take it. You go outta this job by quitting, by getting hurt, or by dying. I'm planning on the last." He smashed the sunny yellow hat onto his head. "I don't know about you but I got work to do."

Marek addressed the man's back. "What do you think happened to Dale?"

"Think he got himself froze to death. The chains'll keep moving without him." He paused at the doorway. "But at least he went out dead, not a quitter, and that means he was a good man, in my book."

And now, Marek thought, he had Dale Hansen's job.

Karen picked her way up the partially cleared courthouse steps to the sheriff's office. She'd wanted to talk to Harold Dahl about Marek, but the commissioner had been arm and arm with the mayor, aka his mother, surveying the damage to the senior activity center.

So Karen had tasked Kurt and Walrus with getting the few seniors who'd ventured to the center that day—for bingo, for pete's sake—back to their homes. But when she'd started toward the plant to join Marek, she'd been diverted by the highway patrol to a five-car pileup on the newly opened interstate.

Fortunately, no serious injuries, just seriously pissed people.

She was one of them, given she now had to fill out the paperwork. Evil, but necessary. So she'd better get to it. First rule of effective management: do as I do, not just as I say.

But when she stepped into the office, Walrus hailed her. "You've got a call from DCI."

She took the phone, thankful for the reprieve. "Sheriff Mehaffey here."

"Dirk Larson. Sioux Falls." The words came out like impact-exploding bullets. "I know you're wet behind the ears, Sheriff, but why the hell weren't we called in on this?"

If this Larson thought berating her would win friends and influence investigations, he was mistaken. "Strangely enough, Mr.—"

"Agent."

"—Larson, we didn't need you."

"It's a homicide. Of course you need us." His breath whooshed into her ear. "God knows you've never handled one before—"

"God may, you don't," she said, though she did wonder how Larson had heard of it. Most likely through Tisher, who'd have contacted the forensic pathologist in Sioux Falls about an autopsy. "We've already got someone on the case."

"Hell you do. You didn't call Pierre, did you? They'll only shoot it back to us. Didn't they teach you anything at the academy? You don't have the resources for a case like—"

"I have a detective." She cut across him because if she didn't, she sensed the rant would go on for some time. "And the road was closed when we needed you on the crime scene. We handled it. Now, you might have time to—"

"Don't tell me you hired your dad."

"No, I did not hire my father." She spaced out every word. "I hired my uncle."

She hung up on a roar of protest.

Walrus grinned at her. "You'll be happy to know that you're not the first sheriff of Eda County to hang up on the man."

That got her attention. "I've never heard my dad talk about Agent Larson."

"Only came here a couple years ago. From Chicago."

"With a name like Larson?"

"Word is, he's got relatives around here somewhere, though no one can pin him down to where." Great, she thought, another prodigal son, as Walrus went on, "We all wish he'd change his name to Larski and go back to the windy city. He's more their kind than ours."

East River Dakotans partook of the spillover from Minnesota Nice. Or, as they liked to think, Dakota Decent spilled the other way.

"Are Larson's skills better than his manners?"

The moustache blew out in twin streams. "Sorry to tell you, boss, but they are."

Marek eyed the falling sun; he had maybe an hour, two at most, before full dark.

He knocked at the second to the last trailer on the lot. He hadn't identified even one worker on the cleaning crew. Chacón would know, even if he wouldn't tell, but he was in a Sioux Falls hospital.

At the moment, Marek didn't hope for a break in the case but a break for himself. Or, more aptly, his daughter.

Instead, here he was, standing in the cold, trying to take notes that looked like chicken scratches—he was pretty sure he couldn't read them much less anyone else—and talking to people who had no wish to talk to him. Some likely were illegal but most were, as Thompson claimed, legal; they simply had little reason to trust those in authority.

The door flung open into his thoughts, into his face, and Marek stumbled back. His boot heel caught in the porch slats and he was only saved from a long fall backwards by the man who grabbed his arm. The strength in the long-fingered hand didn't appear to fit its owner—a thin man with old clunky glasses sitting askew on a sliver of nose.

"Please, you should have care. Much ice."

Marek pushed himself off of the porch rails. With care. He'd have bruises, but they were better than a cracked skull. "Thank you." Concentrate, he told himself. Only one more trailer and, no matter what Sheriff Karen Okerlund Mehaffey said, he was done for the day. "My name is Marek Okerlund. I work for the police. I have some questions for you."

He'd given up telling people he was a detective after the first three blank faces. He'd given up the word sheriff after a few more. This long face blanked too but not, Marek thought, from incomprehension but the see-nothing, hear-nothing, stay-alive kind.

The long-fingered hand curved around the doorjamb and held. To keep him out?

From what Marek could see into the interior, no TV flickered. Instead, a book lay on the table alongside a notebook and pencil. "Your name?"

The rigidity drained from the man. "Name? I am Dr. Ahmed Sabanovic."

Marek blinked. What was a doctor doing here? "Sab—what?"

The lips curved and turned the thin face into a gentleness, with a glimpse of...soul, for want of a better word. "People, they call me Dr. Ahmed. You come in?"

Marek accepted the invitation, not only for the warmth of the tidy trailer, but to get a better look at the notebook on the table. For all the good it did. He rubbed his eyes and still didn't have a clue.

"It is equations," the man apologized. "It is for fun."

Equations were a language as foreign to Marek as any he'd heard that day. He could do basic practical math—the kind required for carpentry—in his head. But this? No way. "Why are you working for a meat packing plant if you can do this kind of thing, Dr. Ahmed?"

The man pushed his glasses up higher. "I get permission to come to America because I am civil engineer. I think, I will work as engineer. But when have bad English, no one want. I keep learning. Maybe, one day, I am engineer again." But his voice held little hope of it. Given he was, what, early fifties perhaps, it didn't seem likely.

The man glanced at a framed photo on the wall: Dr. Ahmed, a woman, and three children. Where were the rest now? Deciding he didn't want to know, Marek forced his eyes away. "You speak better English than many I've spoken to tonight."

The head, with its close-cropped graying hair, bowed slightly in acknowledgement. Marek waited a beat then asked the engineer-turned-meat-packer where he'd been the night before.

"At home."

He'd gotten the same reply from everyone he'd talked to: at home, with or without family. "Do you know who might have wanted to hurt Dale Hansen? Or why?"

"I do not have good words."

Did that mean that Dr. Ahmed didn't have any good words to say about Hansen or that this man didn't have the words to say what he meant?

Maybe Marek could take something back to the sheriff after all. "Try."

"Dale Hansen, he is cold, you understand?" If Marek hadn't seen the earnestness in the man's face, he'd have taken that as sarcasm. "To the people. To the animal."

Marek had not been surprised by the first, as few had been kind to Dim Dale in his day, but had been by the second. Dale had loved his animals; they'd been his saving grace through a miserable childhood.

He nodded. "So I've heard."

"I do not like Hansen. He is not good man. But I do not kill. Do not know who kills."

Marek held the dignity of that statement, savored the simplicity of it, before he asked, "Do you work the cleaning crew?"

"I do not."

What story, Marek wondered, did this man hold behind those sad eyes; so many stories in this backyard lot in a town that wished it gone.

Or at least out of sight.

He wasn't sure where this man came from, with his Slavic accent and weak-tea skin, but likely a place where the civil authority had been corrupted by the power of fear or shredded by terror.

"Do you know Julio Chacón?" Marek asked.

The head tilted and the glasses stayed in place—the nose piece had broken. "I do not think."

"Think so."

"Pardon?"

"That's how we say it," Marek explained. "'I do not think so.'"

"Oh. Thank you." Dr. Ahmed tried it out, slowly, then he shook his head. "English is strange language, I think so."

Marek decided not to tell him to drop the *so* in that last statement. His mother might have been an English teacher, but he himself had no business correcting anyone's wording.

"Julio Chacón was hurt. His hand." Marek cupped his own hand. He'd been doing a lot of miming that afternoon. "In the grinder." But he saw no recognition of the name or the injury. The Chacón trailer was on the other side of the lot. So it wasn't surprising that Dr. Ahmed didn't know of him, especially since he worked the day shift and Chacón the night.

Marek asked his final question. "Do you know who lives in the last trailer?"

He'd noted it was dark.

"It is Mr. Sanchez."

"The union representative?"

The man nodded.

Well then, he was done. Something tried to tug at him, a memory or a connection, but he cut the thread of it, too tired to think. "Thank you, Dr. Ahmed. That's all the questions I have for you."

The man looked bemused. "You do not want papers?"

Marek looked down at the notebook on the table. What and where had Dr. Ahmed come from, that his equations were taken? Then he got it. Immigration papers.

"No, I don't need to see your papers." Marek walked back to the door, turned, and said what he'd wanted to say to all the others but hadn't, because he didn't think it would make any difference. "You can trust me, Dr. Ahmed."

The doctor's eyeglasses remained tilted even as his head straightened, showing the naked beauty of one eye, a wild gold-green.

The nod didn't come.

Marek left, watching his feet, while the one-time engineer watched his back.

CHAPTER 11

ARNE OKERLUND WOKE TO A ringing in his ears. Tinnitus.
Then he blinked open his eyes. Not tinnitus after all. He
maneuvered himself out of the recliner, reached out with
the wrong hand for the phone, and knocked it right off the cradle.
With his good hand, he reached the receiver. "Sheriff Okerlund."

"You back in the saddle, Arne?" his long-time friend asked.

"No, Vern. Just habit." He stared down at the offending hand. It
took a moment to make a fist, a weak one at that. "If you're looking
for Karen, she's out riding herd on Marwit."

"What was that?"

Arne still had occasional difficulty pulling up a word. "I mean,
Marek."

"Oh, I see." Vern Gullick cleared his throat. That awkward pause
had never been there before. It hurt more than his hand did.
"Listen, I wouldn't bother you, or Karen, but I wanted to let you
know that someone emptied my BLF tank. Not sure when. I only
noticed it this morning when I went to check the outbuildings after
the storm."

Liquid fertilizer wasn't anything to play around with. "The cap
wasn't off, was it?"

"No, no, they had that much sense, at least. I just need to get
the insurance people down here and they'll want a police report.
Wasn't much, only what was left from last season, but I can't afford
to lose it."

Although crop prices had risen in recent years, the farm crisis
that had started back in the 1980s had never really ended, at least
not for small family farmers like Vern Gullick.

In a place where memories were long, debts were longer.

Vern continued, "Can you tell Karen to send one of her deputies out when it's convenient? Wouldn't look right for Rick to do it, him being my son and all. I don't suppose you—"

"Can't. Don't have the authority." At a noise in the street, Arne turned and looked out the window. "But I don't see why I can't send Marek. He just pulled up across the way. Looks like he thinks he's done for the day."

The bellow of an outraged taxpayer came over the line. "He's *what?*"

Grudgingly, Arne admitted, "He's got a little girl to look after." He sent a hurried glance around the living room. With relief, he saw the small body curled up at the end of the sofa, blinking off the easy sleep of youth. "Lost her mother not long ago."

Arne knew what that was like, to lose mother, to lose wife.

"Well then," Vern said, "I can't ask him to come—"

"I'll get him. You just sit tight."

Arne hung up then glanced down at a tug on his arm. The girl already had her coat on. Karen's coat, that is. "Come on then, let's go talk to your dad."

That Marek Okerlund was anybody's dad didn't register; the last time Arne had seen him, the scarecrow of a boy had been eighteen years old and scared shitless—and right where a Marek should be.

Behind bars.

When Arne opened the door, the girl ran out. Marek caught her up with one arm, making a grunt that must have been for effect. Arne'd had an arm like that once. Oh, not so big, but that taut. Even now it held some lingering memory of that form, rippling as it tried to grasp it, then failing, falling into slack flesh.

Arne came to the street curb. Marek saw him, the mouth tightened, then relaxed. As one relaxed, Arne thought, by sheer will, before getting stuck with a needle.

"Thanks for looking after Becca."

Not a heartbeat of heartfelt, Arne thought, but he shrugged. Politeness had been drilled into both of them. "She's no burden."

Marek proved that easily enough, transferring the girl to the other arm without even thinking about it, something Arne would never do again. He heard his own voice snap out with an enunciation that would have done his speech therapist proud. "You'll want to get back in the pickup."

That iced the winter blue eyes—a mirror of his own. "You're not going to run me out of town this time, Mr. Okerlund."

The *mister* had been stressed and it burned. "Someone stole Vern Gullick's fertilizer."

"So call it in to one of the deputies. I'm supposed to be part-time. I've already put in more hours than full-time since daybreak." He gazed at the falling sun. "We've got an hour of daylight left, if that."

"The taxpayers here don't take to slackers, especially on a homicide." Why was he bothering to warn him? He wanted Marek Okerlund gone, where the past wouldn't haunt him in those familiar eyes. "But I'll go with you since you don't know what to— how to get there."

Don't know what to do, he'd been about to say, but his wife Hannah's angel eyes had him pinned. "Vern's had a hard couple winters."

The ice eyes melted. Just like Leif Okerlund. Tell him a sob story and he was out the door. Always out to save someone else's day, someone else's life, someone else's child.

Poor little boy, Arne Okerlund snarled to himself. Grow up. "We going, or what?"

Shading his eyes from the sun, Marek drove in silence. His passengers, Becca and Arne, weren't any more inclined to talk than he was. He gazed fixedly out the windshield, thinking it wasn't all that different from driving in the blizzard.

The snow hid even the pretense of scenery, if by that, one meant the land, but in the Dakotas, the land only framed the real show: the sky. But here and there, just to relieve the eye, something jutted out between white and sky.

A few old gravestones poked up their gray heads above the drifts near an abandoned Lutheran church. What made people bury their dead, he wondered. Was it for the sake of the dead, or for the survivors, somewhere to go, to remember?

Marek didn't want to remember his dead. He wanted them back.

He went past the church and turned down the section line road. Like most of the West, the Dakota Territory had been surveyed and struck off in 640-acre sections, dissecting the landscape in orderly squares.

The wandering wheels of the Silverado caught on the gravel. The plow had done a good job here. He passed another old building, peeled of paint, sagged with weight. A leaning cupola sheltered a rusted bell. Furrows in the snow led to the door, so someone must be looking after it.

"One room schoolhouse," Arne said into the silence, nearly causing Marek to jerk the wheel. "Didn't go to one myself but I know Vern swears by them. Says we lost our way when we started to console everything."

A strange word to use, Marek thought, but Karen had told him about her father's stroke. "Console?"

Arne touched his forehead then after a moment said, "Consolidate."

Which had started to happen when Marek had been at school. "I remember when Dutch Corners and Fink closed and the kids got shipped to Reunion." Rumors had also circulated his senior year at Valeska High that it too would be closed. He just about asked if it had, then decided it didn't matter.

Instead, he asked, "Do you know when school starts again in Reunion?"

Arne glanced back at Becca in the extended cab. "What grade you in? First or second?"

"She's five," Marek reminded him. They passed the shelterbelt then the rural sprawl of a family farm, from house to barns to silos and assorted outbuildings. "Kindergarten. They still do half days here?"

"Don't know."

And didn't care. But Marek needed to care. He thought he'd have time to get all this sorted out. Right now, though, he had work to do.

As that thought seeped in, that automatic deferral, he nearly stopped and turned around. Would have, if the man in the passenger seat had been anyone else—a man who expected him to fail.

Marek pulled into the Gullick farm, unbuckled his seatbelt, then turned. "I'll leave the heat on for you, Becca."

But she shook her head. Not unexpected. But at least he didn't have to tell her to keep quiet. "All right, you can come, but keep close."

Arne frowned at this exchange. "She not like her car seat?"

Marek worked at the buckle. "Do you know any kid that does?"

"Didn't have car seats when I had to worry about Karen," Arne said, unbuckling his own belt with some difficulty. "You can turn off the indig—I mean, the ignition. I'll come with you."

Ignoring Arne, Marek pulled Becca into his arms. He smelled the scent of her, of baby shampoo and fear, and whispered into her half-covered ear, "It's okay, Becca. I love you. I'm here."

It wasn't okay, of course, but he did love her and he was working on the *here*.

When they got out, the side door of the farmhouse opened then clattered shut behind its owner. Vern Gullick had a barrel chest stuck on short, lean legs. In his worn sheepskin coat, he looked, Marek thought, like a wary old coyote who'd managed to outwit death. And, when it came, he'd rather go down fighting then go belly up in submission.

In other words, an old-fashioned Dakotan.

"Arne, I didn't know you were coming too." The man stutter-stepped then gave a crinkle-cornered smile. "Good to see you out and about again."

The face of the ex-sheriff didn't move, only the neck, with a stiff nod.

Vern Gullick looked sideways then up. "You'd be Marek, then. Don't know that we've ever met. You'd have been quite a bit older than my Rick. He works nights for you people when Karen needs him. Seems like that's more and more these days."

"Haven't met him yet."

"Well, maybe you won't, if you only work half days. Not everyone's so lucky as you, getting a plush job like that on the tax roll." The man hiked up his jeans from off of a nearly nonexistent butt. "Almost lost the farm a couple years back. Without Rick's help, I would have. Agri-business is busting my chops and my crops. County pays well, though."

Compared to a struggling farm, perhaps, but hardly well, Marek thought. His part-time wage was a pittance of his APD salary—and worth it only for the health insurance. And the chance to start over. Eventually, he'd have to find other work to supplement his salary, but he had some breathing room.

"This won't take much of your time," Gullick said as he started toward the outbuildings. "Just need a report filed."

Becca wriggled in his arms and Marek let her down.

"What is she, Mexican?" Gullick asked.

Marek didn't bother telling the man about Becca's tangled heritage. "She's my daughter."

"Farms aren't safe places for kids from the city."

Knowing that for the blunt truth, Marek reached down to snag one of Becca's mittened hands. But she pulled away and went to Arne.

The ex-sheriff took her proffered hand, saying, "We'll let your dad do his work, then, with both hands free."

Translation: the new detective of Eda County needed all the help he could get.

Marek didn't let that bother him; but it did bother him that Becca had taken to the old man. She must associate him, in age at least, with her maternal grandfather. Another loss.

Gullick directed Marek to where a bulk liquid fertilizer tank—covered with a smattering of warning labels—sat on the small cradle of a trailer.

Marek frowned down at footprints. "Yours?"

"That's right," he said.

"So there weren't any other prints in the snow?"

"Expect they got to it well before it snowed."

The tank's gauge hovered a few ticks from empty. "When was the last time you checked it?"

"Oh, I don't know, weeks ago. Not needed, really."

Marek heard only truth in the exasperated voice. "How much did you lose?"

"Almost 500 gallons."

"You have documentation?"

The man stared at him, then at Arne, and said, "You can call the inspectors. They logged it in the fall. That's their *job*."

Implying Marek wasn't doing his? He was here, wasn't he, on his own time, something he shouldn't have let happen. If he didn't hold the line, it would be crossed, over and over again. But now he was here, he'd better finish the job.

"You didn't notice anybody hanging around the farm in the last month or two?"

"Not that I can remember right off. Strangers, I mean." Gullick scratched his head. "We've had family and friends over, some suppliers too, but none of them would—"

"Make me a list." Marek glanced over at the round face in the picture window of the ranch-style house. "Ask your wife too."

"Aren't you gonna take fingerprints?"

Marek turned at the challenge in the man's voice. "No, I'm not. First of all, any thief knows to wear gloves or brush off their prints.

Most people wear gloves this time of year anyway." Gullick glanced down and Marek stuck his bare hands into his pockets. "And I'm not taking the cap to check for evidence. I'm sure you know why, Mr. Gullick."

"I do, but I didn't think you would."

The toxic plume from the remaining fertilizer could poison them.

"Believe it or not, Mr. Gullick, I've heard of BLF tanks before." Though not, Marek acknowledged, in this particular context. Fertilizer had many and varied uses, as the nation had found out in the Oklahoma City bombing. He headed back toward the pickup, with the farmer at his side and Becca skipping ahead, tugging at Arne. "I'll get your report written up as soon as I have time."

"When's that?"

Marek opened the Silverado's door and placed Becca back in her car seat. She resisted for a moment then went limp. "When we've got Dale Hansen's killer."

"Killer?" The man stared at him. "Thought the blizzard killed him."

Before he could answer, Arne said to Gullick, "It's looking like homicide. That's confidential, but Rick'll probably tell you—it won't stay quiet for long."

Nor did Marek, once back on the road. He'd had enough of Arne acting like he were still sheriff. Had enough of being branded a halfwit—or worse. As if time contracted, to their last encounter two decades before, Marek said, "I wasn't drunk."

Arne just snorted, proving the stroke hadn't damaged his long-term memory. "Puking drunk."

"Puking, yes. Drunk, no. I had half a bottle of lowpoint beer." Which had been legal back then in South Dakota for 18 year olds. He'd thrown it up outside the bar. After, that is, Krissy Martin's father had said to him, About time the Marek came out from hiding behind the holier-than-thou Okerlund.

"Weaving all over the road," Arne continued, glaring out the windshield.

"I was crying too hard to see."

Because he'd lost his mother that night. His grief, his anger at the way she'd died, had led to rebellion. But Arne Okerlund hadn't listened, hadn't checked at the bar, hadn't believed the breathalyzer results, hadn't done anything but say, Knew you'd turn out a Marek.

Arne slouched down in the bucket seat. "Let you go, didn't I."

Because the night jailer had called Arne's wife. Hannah Okerlund had marched into the jail, taken the keys, and set Marek free. But the sheriff hadn't let him go without a last threat—implied, if not stated.

"You told me to never come back." The exact words: *After the funeral, you get the hell out of my county and don't ever come back.* The silent words in the iced eyes: *Or else.*

"Opinion hasn't changed."

No, Marek thought, but Arne's position had. Marek now held the authority. He could make waves for Arne Okerlund.

Tempting, yes, but if Marek smeared the Okerlund name in Eda County, he wouldn't have an honest name to hang his hat on. He could take some small revenge, though, in letting Arne know he knew what the sheriff had done back then—fudged the breathalyzer results.

Marek opened his mouth. But all that came out was silence as the sun plunged into the whiteness behind them, turning all to dark before them.

Karen kicked the right rear tire of the Suburban. Flat. Which is what she was after a long and exhausting day.

She'd deal with it tomorrow, God willing and the dispatcher didn't call. If she had a callout, she'd use her own vehicle, though she'd have to dig it out of the garage first.

Using her frustration as fuel for warmth, she walked gingerly out of the ice-covered parking lot and down the moon-drenched street toward home. If it had been subzero, she'd have called Walrus, but she could make the walk without risking frostbite.

Karen kept her head down, eyes on her boots, until she turned off onto her own street. She skirted a pile of silvery snow and puffed out a breath. Light spilled out from 21 Okerlund Road. It looked like somebody'd had some spare time to take care of the utilities.

She hadn't been pleased to find Marek had clocked out for the day without leaving her any updates on his interviews at trailer city. And she had no way to reach him. She'd even tried calling her father to see if Marek had returned home, but there'd been no response.

Maybe they'd killed each other.

But when she snuck into her own dimly lit house, she found her father alive, if somewhat less than alert. He snorted awake, pushed himself up in the recliner, and said, "Taught you to work, didn't I."

That stung more than the cold. He'd never, not since she returned to Reunion, not since she'd taken the job, said a negative word about her work. It was nine o'clock and she hadn't had dinner yet. What did he expect?

Before she could find her voice, he made a satisfied nod. "You bet I did. But Marek, now, he tried to knock off well before sundown."

Thank God, she thought. Marek, not her. She stowed her gun. "What do you mean, tried?"

He told her about Vern Gullick's stolen fertilizer. Half way through his recital, she realized her father had actually gone out with Marek. What she wouldn't have given to have been a fly on the wall of the Silverado. She bet neither had said a word.

But the theft meant more paperwork for Marek. They really needed a secretary. "You think Mrs. Lindstrom might rethink the whole retirement thing?"

"Why should she? Josephine earned it."

Karen bit her lip to keep from telling him. But it came out in a whoosh. "Marek is dyslexic."

Well, it was out anyway, she consoled herself, since Walrus knew. He'd tell his wife Laura. And Laura...well, it would get around. Maybe, Karen thought, it would mellow her father's view of his half-brother.

But Arne Okerlund's expression didn't change. "Always told you, didn't I, he was a halfwit." Then a glimmer of hope glittered. "Did he forget to mention it to Dahl?"

So much for softening. "No, Harold's the one who has something to answer for, not Marek."

Her father slumped back into the recliner. "That's a Dahl, always looking for a cheap bargain."

Karen ducked into the refrigerator, pushed around some salad going brown, then settled on raisin bran. Had she even had breakfast? No, she hadn't. She poured out the last of the crumbs into a bowl. "Thought I had a couple days worth yet. You get hungry?"

He didn't like raisin bran, so her cache was usually safe. He did their shopping now, but they generally made their own meals, if it could be called that. Home cooking had long been a thing of the past, for both of them, but he'd had to eat more healthy after the stroke, which meant she did as well. At home, at least.

"Not me," her father said. "That girl of his. What's her name again? Bertha?"

Short-term memory still had glitches. "Becca."

"She had to eat something." As Karen peered into the milk carton, he said, "Should be plenty. She won't use it. Makes her sick."

"Dry cereal? Yuck."

"Better than starving. Marek didn't so much as call. I could've been doing anything to that girl, for all he cared."

Despite her own bitching, fair was fair. "For pete's sake, Dad, he just pulled into town. His moving van isn't here yet, his place is a dump and unsafe without heat, and I got him up at the crack of dawn and kept him at it. I don't think he ate anything at all." She looked out across the road. "At least he got the electricity on."

"Didn't. Alice Winke had it turned on. Her husband came over and moved the suitcases too. It's all taken care of."

So the status quo could go on: never the twain shall meet. She sagged down into a kitchen chair and stared at the soggy mess of cereal. "That shouldn't be possible."

"It's done."

"No, I mean, I just put the milk on. The cereal is soggy."

Her father just grunted then asked, "You know when school starts up again?"

That surprised her from taking her first bite. "School? What school? You planning on taking up a new career?"

"I did," he snapped. "I took yours—taking calls—and you took mine."

That made her put her spoon down.

Her father shifted in the recliner. "Sorry. I know I'm done as sheriff. And you've had to put up with me, taking all that time off, seeing me get back on my feet."

Still, it had come out. "You know I wished it were different, Dad."

"What will be, will be," her father said.

But he didn't like it, the tone said. Who would?

"That girl of Marek's, she needs somebody to look after her," her father said after Karen started on the cereal. "I'll do it when he can't." He appeared to force out the words. "You tell him that."

It wasn't exactly an apology, to either of them, but she took it. "School should be starting soon. I'm scheduled to give the DARE spiel sometime the end of next week."

"You could call Laura."

Laura O'Connor Russell. Walter's wife. "I could."

"You two were like pits in a pot."

Peas in a pod, she translated, though it made her smile. "Odd colored ones."

Tow blonde and flame red. The years had darkened both—and their friendship.

"You and Russell work together," her father said testily. "You're gonna have to deal with her. Can't figure why you two haven't talked out this fight of yours a long time ago."

"We never fought."

Call it disconnect of ambition, Karen thought. Then of geography. Not to mention she'd hid the biggest secret of her life from her best friend, duping Laura as well as her own parents. Becca, not a stroke, had stoked those memories, ones she'd locked down hard at the age of 22. She didn't let herself think about that period of her life. There lay madness.

Karen finished as much of the cereal as she could stomach then threw the rest out. Her father narrowed his eyes but didn't call her on it. He didn't like waste. Neither did she, but there wasn't much use for mush in their home. Not since Hannah Okerlund had died, much too early, of ovarian cancer.

She felt her father's glare between her shoulder blades. "All right, all right, I'll call her."

Karen stomped upstairs to her room. That she had to look up the phone number only underlined the disconnect in their relationship. When Laura picked up, Karen tensed. "Laura? It's Karen."

A pause then, "Oh, Karen. Of course." A laugh. Forced, Karen thought. "You'll be wanting my husband. Did he turn off his cell?"

Don't be a coward, she told herself. "I was calling for you."

Liar, liar, pants on fire. What she wanted was to get beyond the call—to some sort of resolution of what they meant to each other now. If it was nothing, so be it.

Laura said, "Oh. I know you've been busy. I've heard your father's done quite a bit better and..." Something crashed in the background. The phone was muffled against an outraged maternal breast. "Junior, you put that baseball away or I'm putting it in the trash." Laura came back on. "I'm looking forward to school starting again. It's calmer."

Given Laura was an elementary school teacher, that was saying something, and it was as good an opening as any. "When does school start?"

"You want to turn in your badge for a ruler?" Before Karen could answer, Laura went on, "I heard you got yourself a homicide and a new detective today. That must be... Hang on. I told you, Walter, it's in the laundry basket. Men. Where was I?"

Karen settled herself against the slatted headboard of her bed.

"Oh, yeah, Marek Okerlund," Laura said. "Whew. What a blast from the past. I'm all agog." Another aside. "No, Josh, not a dog. Agog. Go look it up."

Josh would be the middle son, if Karen remembered right. The last son, what was his name? "Once a teacher..."

This time there was a pause. "You've never forgiven me for that, have you."

Avoidance, her father had said. He didn't know the half of it. "For what?"

"Come on, this is your longlost childhood buddy. You didn't think much of my coming back to Reunion to teach snot-nosed kids. Not to mention marrying a hometown boy."

"So I was an idiot," Karen mumbled. "They seem to be cropping up in my family."

Now she heard the schoolmarm. "Dyslexia is not the same as—"

"I didn't mean Marek." She pulled on her lower lip. "Did your talkative husband tell you everything that happened today?"

"The highlights, in between doing the Heimlich on Davy and rescuing the goldfish from the toilet bowl."

Davy, that was the last son. No wonder Walrus tended not to stress on the job; he got all the excitement at home. "Did you get the biggest newsflash about Marek? He has a daughter. School age."

"No, Walter didn't tell me that." Now a coolness entered Laura's voice. "Is that why you called me, to find out when school starts? Why isn't Marek calling?"

"I haven't given him time." Karen wanted to slink down into her bed. Sleep. Not try to find the right way to say what should have been easy. "Laura, listen, I...we...I just want to know if—"

"If we're still friends?"

Karen let out a breath. "Yes."

"Let's find out. We need to get together somewhere, somewhen, that we won't be interrupted." Over the line came a bellow, another crash, and Walrus's yell for help. "Listen, Karen, I really do need to put down the insurrection here."

"School, Laura. Becca is in kindergarten."

"Oh, yes, we start school again on Monday. Tell your—what is Marek? Your nephew?—no, no, it's the other way around, isn't it. Your uncle. Tell him to be there with Becca at eight sharp at the principal's office with records in hand."

"I'll tell him. Thanks. Good luck with the mutiny, Captain Bligh."

Karen put the phone down on a laugh she hadn't heard in years. With a smile, she slumped down on the bed and fell off to sleep before she found the energy to get undressed.

Which was good, because when the early call came, she not only had to roust her detective but commandeer his ride.

CHAPTER 12

A S KAREN SLID INTO THE Silverado's passenger seat, Marek punched out a cassette tape from the console and snapped off the radio. Considerate of him. Few people had the same taste in music—and the case that lay between them read *Animal Tales*.

Given the sticker said GREAT FOR KIDS, he must have had it on for Becca

But as the miles dragged out, Karen decided anything had to be better than the silence. She pushed the tape back into its slot.

Endless...beginningless. A grey waste...an empty silence...a boundless cold. Snow fell; snow flew; a universe of nothing but dead whiteness.

Marek stabbed the eject button and the tape screeched out.

Not *Animal Tales*. Nor was Becca the recipient, she'd bet. Though Karen wasn't much of a reader, she did remember this, from perhaps the most famous book to have been written in this little slice of South Dakota.

Ole Rölvaag's *Giants in the Earth*.

Written in Norwegian, published in Norway, it had only later been translated into English with the help of its immigrant author. The book had been required reading in the high school English curriculum designed and taught by Marek's mother. And hadn't that been awkward, but it was college prep, so Karen had gritted her teeth and done the work—and gotten reprimanded for *not* talking in class.

But she hated not talking. And she and Marek had already broken the family taboos.

"If you don't like the tape," she asked Marek, "why are you listening to it?"

"Didn't say I didn't like it."

With a sigh, she checked her watch then turned on the radio and input the local station. After a mile of Norwegian fiddling, a canned voice said, "This is YRUN. Your low-power FM out of Reunion, South Dakota. YRUN when you can't walk? From your legless connection, Rusty 'Nails' Nelson."

She got a glance from Marek. "He's a Vietnam vet. One of the Bandit Ridge Nelsons."

Now the voice came on live. "Morning, folks, we've got some hot news this morning to warm up that frozen tundra out there. By now, you all should've heard about Dale Hansen. Froze to death off I-29. Here's what Sheriff Mehaffey had to say at the crack of dawn this morning."

Actually, it had been before dawn, right before Marek had brought the blanket-draped Becca over to the spare room in the attic. Daybreak didn't come until about 8 AM this time of year, the same time as Nails' first broadcast. The earlier call had been Kurt, telling her that the Hansen motor vehicle and phone records had been waiting in the fax machine.

Karen heard her own voice saying, "All I can tell you at this point, Mr. Nelson, is that the circumstances of Mr. Hansen's death appear suspicious."

Okay, she thought, so that sounded evasive. But it was the truth. So far as it went. She wasn't going to jeopardize their investigation by giving out too many details.

Nails chimed back in. "If you didn't know that our new sheriff was an Okerlund by birth, you'd know it now. A talent for understatement runs in that family, though it's the first time Karen Mehaffey's shown any sign of it. But here's the hot news. The unofficial line says that Dale Hansen was found chained to a fence, his head bashed in, and a message carved into his arm. W-H-I-T-E-O-U-T. White out."

She dropped her head back against the headrest and groaned. Their job this morning had just gotten more complicated. Who the hell had tattled?

"The killer, and yes, I said killer," Nails went on, "was either keeping a weather journal or he wanted us whites out. Now tell me, who wants whites out of this town?"

Static crept into the broadcast and she knew they'd be out of

94

range soon.

"And, no, I'm not making a dig at our natives, so you can take both fingers off that trigger, Two Fingers. At least until you get back to the Middle East. But, tell me, what else could it mean? Sounds like something coming out of trailer city. You got a better idea, you call me."

Marek had to be touchy about race, given his daughter's mixed heritage, but if that's what the message was, well...it was what it was.

"Karen Mehaffey's done a decent job in the last six months, filling in for her dad, but now we'll find out if she's got more than the Okerlund understatement down pat."

Before she could decide if that was a pat on the back or on the head, Nails changed targets. "And we'll also see if our brand new detective, never the brightest bulb in the land according to our retired sheriff, has the watts to figure it out if she doesn't."

She sunk down into the seat and hoped they'd drive out of range.

"If you hadn't heard, that'd be Marek Okerlund, the grandson of the man who baptized the courthouse steps with his brains. Not that Lenny Marek had much to lose. If you'll recall, he went down for murder in an unusual way; he jumped from the clock tower after his conviction. We'll see which family our detective takes after, now that he's come back home from Mexico."

As the signal cut out, Karen saw only a faint tightening of Marek's mouth. She'd learned to read these little signs, having grown up watching for them in her own father.

"Doesn't check his facts," Marek said. "Why do you listen to him?"

"He'd have called you if he had a number. Do you have a cell, by the way?"

Marek pulled one out of his jacket pocket.

She input the number into her own cell. "Pretty much everyone who's in range listens to Nails. He takes call-ins, if you want to correct him on Mexico."

That earned her an eye roll.

"He just lost us our leverage," Marek said.

Probably, she thought, but wasn't ready to give up yet. "We might get a line or two in the *Argus Leader* but it won't be picked up for a while yet in Sioux Falls." She handed Marek back his cell. "As for why I listen to Nails, other than to find out what he knows,

I'm sheriff. I have to know what people are saying if I want to be elected."

He didn't react to that for a long moment. "You aren't elected?"

She'd become sheriff at the stroke, not of a pen, but of the body of Arne Okerlund.

"Harold called me into his office after I came home to take care of my dad last spring. He said he'd like to appoint me acting sheriff. I didn't take him seriously at first. I still intended to go back to my job in Sioux Falls, but...well, here I was, twiddling my thumbs, and Dad didn't need me hovering every minute of the day."

Maybe she was being too frank. Was Marek looking for an opening to take her job—or perhaps more to his view, his father's, or even her father's?

Just as she worked up the courage to ask him, he jammed the tape back into the player.

Blizzards from out of the northwest raged, swooped down and stirred up a grayish-white fury, impenetrable to human eyes.

Now she ejected the tape. "You'd think snow's the only thing memorable about the Dakotas."

She got no response. Like the vast prairie sky before them, the man beside her embodied the presence of an absence so huge that it depressed the spirits of some, lifted that of others.

Maybe she could get him to talk about the case. "If Kurt hadn't snagged that fax so early this morning and called me, we still might not be anywhere. You think it's going to break open the case, now we know who owned that Hummer?"

He shrugged and she gave up.

Minutes later, Krissy Hansen opened her front door before they'd even rung the bell. She wore a black form-fitting sweater over designer jeans. Behind her, an artificial fire raged in the split personality of a fireplace. Krissy didn't, so far as Karen could tell, have makeup on, but no one could call her natural state a burden.

"We'd like to speak to your daughter, Mrs. Hansen."

Unlike the last time, Krissy didn't insist on informality. "I don't think so. Not without a lawyer."

From behind her, Darcie said, "I'm not afraid to talk to them, Mom. I'm 22, not 12."

She'd been way off on the age, Karen thought. Not a minor. That was good.

Krissy turned to her daughter. "Believe me, honey, lawyers know the games these people play. I don't care if you're about to graduate summa cum laude. You haven't a clue."

Darcie had dressed in black as well, but it only emphasized her Picassoid face, dark and slanted.

Karen said to her, "You're listed as the owner of that Hummer in the garage."

"Dale gave it to me." The college girl grimaced. "I'm not saying it doesn't come in handy in the odd blizzard, but most of the time it's overkill."

Somehow Karen hadn't imagined that, even as the operations manager, Dale had done so well, but what did she know. "Did he use the Hummer on Friday night?"

"Don't be ridiculous," Krissy said. "No one used it. We told you—"

Now Marek spoke up. "I saw the Hummer in the garage yesterday morning. The chains still had snow caught in them."

When Krissy looked at the detective, the only heat was of anger. "You didn't have a warrant."

"Mom," cut in her daughter. "Yes, I took the Hummer out that night." Darcie Ringold swept back her fall of black hair. "And I killed Dale."

CHAPTER 13

THE WALLS OF THE CRAMPED interview room bulged with filing cabinets. Karen wanted to pace, but there wasn't enough room. So she stood instead. And kept quiet. You couldn't lead until you learned, she told herself.

"All right, Darcie," Marek said in a gentle rumble from his seat at the scarred table. "Tell us what happened Friday night. Take your time and give us details."

Though Darcie Ringold's feet dangled off the floor like a child's, she didn't come across as one. Not now, not full face. Force of personality, people called it, a different kind of punch than her mother's blatant sexuality.

"Dale called me that night," Darcie said.

"Yes, we know." Marek tapped the phone records he'd laid out. "What did he want?"

"A ride home." Darcie cradled the cup of coffee they'd given her from the communal pot—no sister blend this time. "He decided not to stay at the plant, not if the roof was going to come down on his head."

Marek asked, "Do you know what happened to Dale's head?"

Why had her detective made that leap, Karen wondered. Word association?

"Yeah," Darcie said, "the Mexican who—"

"Wait," Karen interrupted. "What Mexican?"

Impatience stirred in that slanted face. "Whatever Mexican coldcocked him at the plant."

So there'd been an assault prior to the murder. Interesting. If tangential.

"Just to be clear," Marek said. "You didn't hit Dale?"

"Of course not. He showed me where he got hit when I picked him up. It could have been a subdural hematoma, I told him, but he wouldn't listen."

At their stares, Darcie said, "I'm pre-med. I want—wanted—to be a doctor." After a sip, she scowled down at the dark liquid. "Guess that's down the drain too."

Karen had made the coffee strong. You could, after all, dilute the strong, she thought, but you couldn't pump up the weak. She wanted to get to the meat of the girl's confession, but since she'd told Marek to control the interview, she'd better let him.

"Go on, Darcie," Marek said.

"Dale said that Dr. Hudson wouldn't be at the clinic, just a resident, and no way was he going to let some spanking new MD get anywhere near his head."

"What about his arm?"

"What about it?"

Karen let out an exasperated blast of air. That detail had already left the station. "Are you telling me you didn't get the scoop from YRUN this morning, Darcie?"

"We can't pick it up out there. Why? What's Nails saying? Is he dissing my mom?"

Marek looked thoughtful. "You haven't spoken to anyone this morning?"

"Mom pulled the plug on the phone. I swear, if they're pointing the finger at her—"

"You pointed the finger," Marek said mildly. "At yourself. What happened?"

Darcie shrugged—or hunched. "We argued, I told him to get out, and that was it."

The tape recorder whirred into the silence.

Karen expected Marek to ask about the argument but, instead, he asked, "Where were you then? When Dale got out?"

"By the road. Where you found him, I guess." Her mouth trembled. "It wasn't that bad out yet and other people were still out. I know I should have tried to call him later, make sure he was all right, but I figured he'd stay the night at the plant. Before he got out, he said he had forgotten to do something back there anyway."

Karen couldn't keep herself from saying, "That doesn't cover the chai—"

"Tell us again, Darcie," Marek cut in. "With more details.

Physical details. Where you were, what you did, what he did."

The girl glanced between the two of them. "I don't understand. I was on the way toward home and—"

"Which way?" Marek asked.

"Main to Bluff Road, of course. How else? We hadn't gone that far from the plant. No more than a mile, I swear."

Karen waited for Marek to call the girl on it, but he just nodded.

Was he taking this seriously? If true, how had Dale gotten from Bluff Road to the interstate?

"So you argued," Marek prompted.

The girl looked down at her coffee, cooled now, and pushed it away. "Yeah, it's not like we never have before. I didn't like the way he ran the plant." Darcie stopped, glanced over at the recorder, then said, more firmly, "But he didn't want me butting into his business, so I said, fine, he could go back to his precious plant. I pulled off the road. He got out. I went home."

Now he'd nail her, Karen thought.

"Not quite," Marek said. "Your mother must have known that you—"

"You leave my mother out of this," the girl said, rising out of the chair. "She's had enough grief, people always talking about her behind her back. Besides, she was in bed when I got home. She didn't know, not until I told her, after you guys went, that I'd left him out there." Darcie sank back down. "That's some kind of negligence, isn't it? Involuntary manslaughter? How long...if I plead guilty, how long do you think I'll be in prison?"

Marek draped his hand over his mouth, but what it hid, Karen didn't know. His silence, however, apparently provoked Darcie as much as it did her.

"I know I should've told you right away, but I was scared, okay? I was getting ready to come to you when you drove up. That's why my mom was up so early. Usually Sunday mornings she's zonked out until noon."

Marek leaned back and the chair creaked. "What time did you pick up Dale from the plant?"

"A few minutes after he called." Then she glanced down at the phone records. "Okay, not a few. More like fifteen or twenty."

"Takes that long just to make the drive," Marek said. "Much less to get the chains on."

"I'd put them on earlier," she said, almost clinically calm now. "It wasn't the first time Dale asked for a ride in bad weather, and I knew his truck was in the shop."

What was Marek doing, Karen wondered. He should be confronting Darcie Ringold about the chain, about the message on Dale's arm, about the dropoff point on the interstate. Not to mention getting the Hummer impounded so they could check the chains—maybe they'd match the short link around Dale's wrist.

Marek leaned over the table. "Who did you see, Darcie?"

The girl stiffened on the edge of the seat. "What do you mean?"

Marek didn't answer for a moment. Maybe he hadn't expected that reaction. "You said people were still out. At the plant? On the road?"

Darcie looked puzzled. "Well, yeah, at the plant and...I guess I passed a car or two."

Was her detective trying to trip Darcie up, Karen wondered, to prove she'd been on the interstate instead of Bluff Road?

But he didn't ask about the cars. He asked, "Who did you see at the plant?"

Karen was thoroughly baffled now—and afraid her detective had dropped the ball. Keep the heat on, her academy instructor had said, but Marek hadn't even turned it on yet. Why was he being soft on the girl?

"I—well, I don't know who the guy was," Darcie said. "I'd never seen him before. I only saw his face in my headlights when I pulled up."

"What did he look like?"

"Hispanic," she said. "But that's about all I can tell you."

What did it matter who was at the plant, Karen mused, unless Darcie had gone back into the plant and confronted Dale there. Was the girl trying to backtrack on her confession? Had she made up the Hispanic to cover herself? She could have easily gotten a padlock from one of the bins before taking Dale out to the interstate. Possible, Karen supposed, if it had been Dale's blood on the kill floor instead of Julio Chacón's.

Marek said, "I think you can do better, Ms. Ringold. Was this Hispanic man you saw outside or inside? With Dale? How were they together? Was he taller or shorter than Dale? What was he wearing?"

The girl blinked at the barrage of questions. "He was outside with Dale. Waiting, I guess, to make sure I got there. They waved at each other, the other guy ducked into his car, and Dale got in the Hummer." Her face screwed up in a ferocious look of concentration.

"He was shorter than Dale. Couple inches maybe."

Now Karen felt her curiosity prick. Dale hadn't been above 5'10 himself. Sanchez? That didn't make any sense. Those two wouldn't have been friendly.

"He wore one of those mountaineering jackets with all the bells and whistles. Like he was going to scale Mt. Everest or something." Darcie's voice chided the man for overkill. Though as it turned out for Dale Hansen, maybe not. "It was dark. Blue or black. Pants, boots, everything."

Not Sanchez, then, in his red goosedown. Nor did it sound like any immigrant worker Karen had ever seen or heard of. If that was prejudiced, well, it was a matter of money, not class. Which of them could afford that kind of getup? And what native wouldn't be laughed out of Eda County for it?

Marek asked, "What kind of vehicle did this mystery man drive?"

"An SUV, I think, dark like his clothes, but I wasn't really paying attention. I was ma—um, it was snowing harder and I wanted to get home."

Mad? That fit the scenario of Darcie and Dale having a confrontation at the plant and not in the truck. As for Sanchez, he drove a battered old Dodge Dakota. What wasn't rust or primer was white.

Marek creaked again into the silence. "Did you see where this Hispanic man went?"

"Sure, he went out on Main headed toward the interstate. I headed the other way to get to Bluff Road."

Karen tapped fingers on her crossed arms.

"All right," Marek said, apparently sensing Karen's impatience. "You said you passed a car or two?"

"Yeah, on my way to the plant," Darcie said, with a twist of her lips. "I saw one of your people."

"That would have been Kurt Bechtold," Karen explained for the record. "I sent him out to look for Detective Okerlund at the Reunion exit."

Marek's next question came with suspicious rapidity. "You passed a second car?"

For the first time, Darcie Ringold smiled, her mismatched face realigning in a flash of charm. "That one I can tell you for sure. It was Sig Halvorsen's."

CHAPTER 14

MAREK KNEW HE'D BEEN SKATING on thin ice.

Now he'd fallen right through. His new boss planted both hands on the table. In front of their suspect. "You're lying."

"About what?" Darcie asked. "Sig? Why should I? I saw his truck—you know, the refrigerated one for deliveries, coming in the direction of the plant."

Marek decided he'd better get to his next question or Karen might break out a rubber hose. One attached to the exhaust of her anger.

Time to hit harder. "Darcie, what does the word whiteout mean to you?"

Darcie looked at them in confusion. "Is this some weird kind of good cop, bad cop, because I don't get it." She settled on Marek. "And anyone who grew up here should know what a whiteout is. You can't see a thing."

One thing he did see. "Tell me how Dale Hansen died, Darcie."

Her hands clasped together tight enough to show the whites of her knuckles. "He froze to death because I kicked him out of the Hummer."

Marek tried again. "What did you use to keep him there, Darcie?"

"Keep him where? He must've gotten disoriented in the blizzard. I didn't think his head wound was all that bad, he seemed coherent and his pupils looked okay, but it could've been worse than I thought. Why all these questions? Can't you just get it over with? I've already told you that it's my fault."

"Did you run him over? Knock him down?"

"Did I—*what*? I told you. He got hit on the head at the plant. Some deal about Mexicans." Her mouth tightened. "He was a bigot, okay? Nobody'll be surprised to hear it, and I know they say you shouldn't speak ill of the dead but, you know what, I'm not sorry he's dead. But I'm sorry he died. If that makes any sense."

Marek didn't want to make sense of death; it was nonsense. He tried a different tack. "Do you mind if we check the tires on the Hummer?"

Darcie looked at him for a long moment then said to Karen, "Mom told me he wasn't too bright. If he wants to play with my tires, let him. It's probably more up his alley than detective work. Put me in a cell or whatever you have to do, but I'm done talking to him."

Karen gave Marek a hooded look.

"Not crazy enough to let you go," he said to their suspect, "before you tell me where you really were when Dale called you for a ride."

Only a quick intake of breath recorded the hit. "What do you mean? I wasn't—"

"I may have been gone a long time but Reunion hasn't changed *that* much."

When he got no response, he placed his right index finger on the table's peeling varnish. "Here's you at your place on Bluff Road." Then he stabbed down with the left. "Here's Kurt Bechtold at the courthouse on Main." He started moving them—in the same direction. "You head to the plant and Kurt to the interstate." Then he stopped with the fingers still equidistant. "The cars would never have met, Darcie." He tapped the phone records. "And the timing just doesn't work. Try again."

Darcie sank back down, her eyes fastened on the invisible trail of evidence. "Okay, I just...I didn't think that part mattered. If you really want to know, I was at the clinic when Dale called me. You can ask David Echols. He's the resident." Her hair fell over her face. "I've always said I'd never do something stupid and get pregnant like my mom did, but...um, I thought I might be." Her head came back up. "But I wasn't."

Better, Marek thought, to let the sheriff take that one. But when he looked up at her, she appeared frozen, until she leaned back against a filing cabinet.

"You went to the clinic in a snowstorm to see a doctor you didn't even know, at night, just to see if you were pregnant, when you could've picked up a kit at the drugstore?" she asked Darcie.

"What drugstore? Lindstrom's closed years ago, if you've forgotten. Not that I'd have wanted to buy it there. Might as well call up YRUN." Her chin jutted out. "I figured there wouldn't be anybody else around and I would've been too embarrassed if it were Dr. Hudson. I wanted to know what to do. I'm like that. I need to know things, like what's going to happen to me now."

Marek asked, "Did you tear off his shirt?"

She stared at him. "Echols?"

"No, Dale."

Darcie startled them both as she laughed. "You think that I was sleeping with *Dale*? Cheating on my own mother? Are you kidding? No way."

"What was Dale wearing when you picked him up?"

She considered. "He had a heavy coat, jeans, work boots. No hat because he showed me where he got hit. I don't know about gloves. He may have had them in his pockets."

"Where did you go after you kicked Dale out of the Hummer?"

"Straight home." The white knuckles showed up again. "When are you going to tell me what you're charging me with and what I can expect to get? I hate not knowing."

That was too bad, Marek thought, because until he knew what happened, she wouldn't get an answer. "What did you do with Dale's cell phone?"

"Nothing. He still had it. I don't know why he didn't just call me back or call somebody." Her gaze fell on the phone records. "Or did he try? Was the cell tower down?"

Instead of answering, he opened a folder and pulled out the stack of crime scene photos he'd selected. Tisher had dropped them off the previous night. Turned out the mortician was also an amateur photographer and had developed them himself in his basement. Marek handed Darcie the first one. "Take a look at that and tell me what you see."

Her lips parted. "I thought it would be worse. But he looks...almost peaceful. I don't think I ever saw him like that. Usually he looked hard, suspicious, like he thought somebody was pulling his leg all the time."

Marek handed her the next one of the bloodless bare arm.

"What's this?" She turned it sideways then squinted. "It looks like...are those letters? It looks like a tattoo, all blue like that, but I never saw a tattoo on him before. W-H-A-T. It says what." Now

Darcie looked at him as if *her* leg was being pulled. When he kept his eyes steady on hers, she glanced back down. "I can't read the rest. Except the last letter is a T. Is this a joke or something?"

"Or something," he said and gave her the final picture, showing what wasn't visible in the previous: the chain.

She gasped then dropped the photo as if it burned.

"You think *I*—I swear, I never. That's...that's sick. You never said anything like this, you just said he froze to death, that someone might be involved in his death, you didn't say he was—this, this is *murder.*"

She'd turned the color of the dingy white interview room. "Please, you have to believe me. No matter what he'd done, do you really think I could do *this*?"

Now she looked up at Marek. "Is that why you wanted to know if I passed anybody on the road? Was it Mr. Halvorsen? But I saw his truck much earlier, not after I dropped Dale off, but when I was on my way to the clinic. It looked like he was turning off into the plant, though I can't be sure, but there isn't anything else out there but the plant and trailer city. I know he and Dale had some run-ins but—"

Marek didn't look at Karen. "What run-ins?"

"Oh, more on Dale's side. Mr. Halvorsen came over to the house once to try to work out some kind of deal with PBI."

"What did Dale say?"

"He said Mr. Halvorsen would have to compete or die. I felt sorry for him. Mr. Halvorsen, I mean. I think he really cared, not just about his own workers, but what happened to those people out there."

"You mind if we check the chains on your tires?" Marek asked again. "And your tow chain, if you've got one?"

"Mind?" Darcie let out a breath. "I insist."

Downstairs, Karen handed Darcie Ringold over to the day jailer and dispatcher.

"Don't tell me," said Tammy Nylander, who rivaled Walrus in weight and nearly in moustache as well. "Don't process this one, just keep an eye on her?"

Karen wondered what Tammy had seen in her face. "That's right."

"If she gives me any trouble, I'll sit on her."

Darcie didn't smile. Neither did Tammy.

Although Marek had gone to check out the Hummer, Karen expected that Darcie's story would hold up.

So much for a closed case.

Going back up to the office, Karen retrieved the tape recorder, took it to her desk, and ejected the tape. She stared at the little plastic tines, the shiny brown surfaces, the flat plastic casing with its blank label.

Yestermillenia's technology. But fairly new to Eda County. Welcome to rural policing on a shoestring budget, she thought, so different than her years in Sioux Falls, where she'd had the latest in technology at her fingertips. It must be even harder for Marek, who'd likely had covert audio and video feed in interviews. Getting a videorecorder had been on her upgrade list.

First had been a detective.

Karen labeled the tape, started to take it to the evidence room, then hesitated. Even if Marek had managed to get somewhere in the end—though not the end she'd been counting on—the interview had been off kilter from the start.

She wondered who she could ask for a professional opinion of the tape's contents. She couldn't ask her father. Talk about bias. She couldn't ask any of her deputies. Evaluations were her job, not theirs, and she still didn't know if Marek was officially hers to review.

Besides, Harold Dahl wouldn't fire Marek over what was on the tape. He hadn't been abusive, he'd followed the basic procedure, but...it didn't seem like he'd had a clue what to ask. For pete's sake, his big guns, he'd left for last. He'd dragged it out for far too long.

Then she had it.

At the academy in Pierre, DCI Agent Gary Longwell had lectured on interview techniques. Or at least, what not to do, like lead the witness. That much she could exonerate Marek of, but the rest?

Karen made a copy of the tape and slipped it into a mailer. She'd just finished a quick note to Longwell when the door opened. Guiltily, she sealed the mailer and pushed it into the out box. "Well?"

"All chains present and accounted for," Marek said. "I took pictures."

She nodded toward the computer and printer she'd managed to

scrounge for him and bullied IT—a department of one—into setting up. "Make printouts."

Though he raised his eyebrows, Marek sat down at the antiquated computer and, at least in this area, didn't seem to have any trouble.

When he was done, she handed him the original tape of Darcie Ringold's interview. "Secure this tape with the printouts and the flash card."

"Where's the evidence room?"

"Downstairs," she said. "Ask Tammy."

He paused. "Tammy Nylander?"

"You know her?"

"Met her once." He looked down at the evidence in his hand. "Didn't know she was still here."

When he'd left Eda County, Tammy would have been the night jailer, which made Karen wonder. But her father would have crowed that news from the silo tops: to have Marek in jail. "She's been the day jailer for, oh, ten years at least. She also dispatches. We couldn't run the place without her. Tell her to send Darcie back up."

He hesitated. "You are letting her go, aren't you?"

"She kicked her stepfather out into a blizzard."

"But she didn't kill him."

"Maybe. Maybe not. But there's acting blood in that family." She read the faint twitch. "You didn't know?"

"Only actor I ever knew who came out of Eda County was one of your class."

"Adam Van Eck," she said with a wry smile. "A stunning Romeo to my pathetic Juliet and the only one tall enough to do it. He's still on Broadway, putting Reunion on the map."

Marek scratched at his overgrown goatee. "Is he Darcie's father?"

"Are you kidding? Two blue-eyed and fair-haired people don't make a black-haired and brown-eyed child." She stared at his pale blue eyes. "It's unusual, isn't it, that Becca has your eyes, or did her mother have—"

"Brown," he said. "But Val's mother had blue."

That stopped her line of thought. "Val? Your wife's name was Valerie?"

"Valencia."

"Oh, well, I guess Hispanics do sometimes have lighter—"

"Val's mother wasn't Hispanic. She was Anglo. And no mother at all." He picked up the printouts from the printer. "Val was raised by her father."

And now Becca was being raised by Marek.

"Getting back to Darcie," Karen said. "Her grandmother, also no mother of the year, was one of those itinerant actors who put on kiddie shows in the schools. At least by day. At night she had other talents."

Krissy Martin had done far better in life than had her mother.

Marek slowly nodded. "Think I remember Dad talking about her disappearance. People said she ran off, but he wasn't so sure. Martin was alibied up at the bar. Is the case still open?"

"As open as it is cold." She looked at the evidence in his hands. "Kind of like this one."

Marek stepped down into the jail. Cold, dank, with weak light filtering through small, barred windows mounted just above ground level, the room hadn't changed since he'd last seen it.

"Well, well, well, look who's back in my parlor," Tammy said.

"Am I the spider or the fly?" Marek asked.

The woman boomed out a laugh that shook yards of khaki fabric. She'd put on at least a hundred pounds, he noted.

"Hon, you are talking to the biggest flytrap this side of the river," Tammy said. "Heard you was back and a big bad detective now."

"Big anyway," he said and looked over at Darcie, who sat in the chair by the dispatch desk as if she'd been strapped to it. Awaiting execution, by her expression. "You can go on upstairs."

She latched onto his face with hope. "I'm free?"

"The sheriff didn't tell me what she planned. You'll have to ask her."

The shoulders slumped a bit but Darcie got to her feet and glanced over at her jailer. "You really should think about that surgery."

"No hotshot doctor is going to get any blubber off me," Tammy said. "I need every bit of it this time of year. It's you runts of the litter who want to cut us all down to size."

With a sad shake of the head, the doctor-wannabe went back up the stairs.

"Still chatting up the prisoners, Ms. Nylander?"

"Passes the time," she said. "We get along fine unless they try to pull one over on me. Then they find I'm no lightweight." She hefted her bulk out of the chair with ease, proving there was still muscle beneath the extra layers. "And you're no longer a kid. You can call me Tammy now. What you got there? Stuff for the evidence room?"

He nodded.

She took out a key and went to a door on the other side of the hallway. Her eyes skimmed over him but with none of the overt sensuality of Krissy's appraisal. "Grew into that beanpole body of yours, didn't you, but looks like you're off your feed. I was real sorry to hear about your wife."

If he'd thought he wouldn't be reminded of Val here, where no one knew her, he should have known better. He was new. Better, he was new and he was old.

Lots to gossip about.

"What you need is time."

How he hated that platitude. Time was eternal when grief knocked at the door.

But Tammy went on, "Doesn't do much good to hear that now, though. Me? I lost my mother two years ago. She went in for some routine tests after she had some eye trouble and came out with a death sentence. Brain tumor. Finished her off in seven weeks."

Marek envied her those weeks. "I'm sorry."

"I still catch myself calling her number to tell her something and, each and every time, it stabs me all over again. Just doesn't go in as far. They say, remember the happy times, but that's not it; it's that you can't share them anymore." She shoved the evidence log at him. "Here, you'll need to sign those in."

He forced himself to relax, take his time to decipher the headings of each column, and then write down the few words needed.

Tammy put away the cassette tape, then the printouts, and shook her head over the flash card. "Tell me what happens, I'd like to know, if one of these goes bad? Photos like the ones Tish makes, they'll last a good long while, but these things?" Her booming voice died to a whisper. "Corrupted, just a *little* corrupted, and you can't read it."

Marek raised his eyes from the log.

Her lips crumpled into her rounded face. "Arne doesn't know that I saw him tinker with the breath test. Or that I told you. Once Hannah let you out, I...I just let it go. I was new at my job and didn't know if anyone would believe me. And I never saw Arne do anything like that again, not in all the years we worked together. But that doesn't make it right. I should've done more."

Marek handed her the log. "You did enough."

He walked away from her relief and heard the door of the jail close shut behind him. Memory echoed the sound a thousand-fold.

CHAPTER 15

THOUGH THE BUTCHER SHOP HAD the CLOSED sign hanging, what he'd expect on a Sunday, Marek could see Sig Halvorsen hard at work inside. The man he'd known hadn't believed in working on the Lord's Day. Unless, of course, one worked on a farm: animals and plants didn't observe the rituals of deity.

Marek didn't want to be working himself, whatever day it was, especially since Karen had informed him that school started tomorrow.

"This time," Karen said at the door of the butcher shop, "I'm doing all the talking."

"What am I here for, then?" he asked.

"You can take down Sig's statement."

As they entered, Sig held up one bloodied hand in greeting. "You've caught me red-handed, working on Sunday, but I don't want the meat to go to waste. Looks like you're working as well, so you can't turn me in. How's the investigation going?"

Karen hooked her thumbs into her belt. "We have more questions, Mr. Halvorsen."

The butcher put down the knife he'd held and wiped his plastic-gloved hands on his apron. "Ask away, Sheriff. I've nothing to hide."

The tone sounded, Marek thought, more considering than offended.

"You said you were here at the shop on Friday night," Karen said.

"I was."

"You don't let anybody else drive your delivery truck except your

boys, and I know they're in Omaha with your wife for the holidays."
Karen's hands dropped to her sides. "The truck was seen out on the
road that night. You *lied* to me."

"I did not. You are my—" Sig took a deep breath. "My
goddaughter, my kin, and, I thought, my friend."

Karen just stood there, limned in misery, and Marek decided
that the two had probably never had so little to say to each other.

So he was the one to break the silence. "Who was driving your
truck, then, Mr. Halvorsen?"

Sig looked over at him. "Bryan McNulty. Used to work for me
before he went to PBI. Stuck it out longer than most. When he quit
at PBI, I hired him to help over the holidays."

The *rigor mortis* drained out of Karen's body.

Marek asked, "What would McNulty be delivering in a bliz—"

"If you don't have something to write with," Karen told Marek,
"turn on that recorder you call a brain and keep your mouth shut."

Now Sig looked amused. "I don't mind."

She shifted on her feet and said, "It's a matter of following
orders."

"It's not the Army, Karen, and he's the detective. Keeps his
mouth shut too much, I'd guess, if he's anything like his father and
yours. As for the truck, that wasn't a delivery but a pick-up. The
Bolvins wanted us to get one of their cows before the blizzard hit.
That's what I'm carving up right now."

Bolvin. That name, Marek did know, and it didn't make sense.
Wrong direction again. This time the sheriff caught it.

"The delivery truck wasn't on the county road out to Bolvins,"
she told Sig. "It was seen going toward the plant."

That brought trouble into the butcher's face. "The plant? Why?"

"If we knew, Uncle Sig, I wouldn't be asking," Karen said, then
bit her lip. "You had a confrontation with Dale Hansen."

Marek frowned down at the pitted but gleaming floor. Karen was
making statements and letting Sig Halvorsen confirm them. If
people didn't know what you knew, sometimes they lied.

Sig fingered the knife. "Dale wasn't interested in anything I had
to say."

"Which was?"

That was better, Marek thought.

"I told Dale we could work together and both keep in business—
that's how we do things out here. We help our neighbors. Or did."
Sig hefted the knife and the sun shot bright smears of red onto the

walls. "He told me to put up or shut up, that my kind was over and done with."

Marek heard the hurt beneath the words.

Then Sig laid down the knife in a slow, controlled movement. "God knows, Dale Hansen learned the hard way that life's unfair, losing his farm the way he did, and make no mistake, he did care for the animals. Back then." He let out a breath. "But I wasn't looking for a handout but a partnership. We could take the European trade at a slower chain speed or do special testing for mad cow disease. Whatever clients are willing to pay more for."

Karen relaxed against the counter. "Sounds reasonable."

"Dale said I didn't get it. It wasn't about the meat; it was about the money. People don't care about the quality, barring contamination by *E. coli*, only the lowest price."

"How much did you lose when your plant closed?" Marek asked, earning him an exasperated look from the sheriff.

"Just about my shirt. But you have to go on." Sig looked again at his bloody knife. "Or you're dead."

Marek looked around the shop, at the bright displays, the new equipment. "Doesn't look like you're hurting too much."

"I was headed for bankruptcy court when an old classmate called me up. He owns a fancy restaurant in Sioux Falls, wanted to know if I could supply him with grass-fed organic meat. Healthier. Tastes better. Business picked up. Word of mouth mostly." Sig smiled faintly. "So we kept the butcher shop open; I think of it as the smallest processing plant still in existence. We work with locals, family farms and small-scale ranches, some with just a few head."

Karen pulled out a beef stick from a canister then stuck it back. "Maybe you're on the cutting edge."

"Ha-ha." The butcher didn't look optimistic. "Me, I *know* the connection, know what goes into what I eat, know how it's been treated. But most people? They just want the pretty packages then end up chucking most of it because they're too busy to cook. One thing about plenty: it makes for plenty of waste."

Thinking of the many times he'd let food go bad, Marek looked away. He found Karen doing the same. Maybe food *should* cost more, he thought.

Sig picked up his knife again. "You look like you're biting your tongue, Detective. You have more questions for me?"

Ignoring Karen's annoyance, Marek took the offer. "You have a car?"

"My wife and boys took it down to Omaha last week. I'm pretty much stranded, since Bryan's still got the delivery truck."

"You were working here that night?"

"Sure, I was on the phone with my suppliers. In between listening to radio reports."

"Cell?"

Sig placed his hand on the old beige phone near the register. "Land line. Lots of places farther west don't have towers anyway. If you want, I can make a list."

"That's not necessary," Karen said.

Before Marek could find the breath to disagree, Sig said, "If it's more convenient, you can get my phone records. I've no problem with that."

"Thank you, Mr. Halvorsen." He just couldn't call the man Sig, not when his memories of the man came from twenty years ago. "Did you see anybody out that night?"

"Through the windows here? Sure, I saw headlights every so often, mostly four-wheel drives, but I didn't pay much attention. Those I did take notice of, they had their lights whirling: gravel trucks, plows, cops, people you'd expect." He rubbed the back of his wrist against his nose. "Wait. I did see that Hummer that belongs to the Ringold girl. Saw it twice. Coming and going. Does that help?"

Karen butted back in. "Which way?"

Sig's answer confirmed Darcie Ringold's story that she'd driven to the clinic and then back to the plant.

After a moment of silence, Sig said, "If that's all, Detective, I'd like a word with Karen, if you don't mind."

Not at all, Marek thought, and went outside without a word.

"Karen, I don't want to tell you how to do your job—"

"Then don't." She bit her lip in distress. She had to remember that her new badge made her an uncomfortable person to be around, even with family.

When she was a child, her exasperated parents had sometimes shooed her out of the house with her questions. She'd run down to the butcher shop. Sig had been a bachelor back then with plenty of time for her.

Since returning to Reunion, her relationship with Sig was one of the few she'd renewed, even though he was married now with twin sons in their senior year at Reunion High.

She sighed. "Sorry, Uncle Sig. Go on."

He tipped his knife toward her detective outside. "He's just trying to do his job."

So it wasn't her apparent distrust of him that Sig was calling her on. "He should *know* you wouldn't kill Dale."

"Why should he know any such thing? Why should you, for that matter? Don't you believe anyone is capable of murder, given the right circumstances?"

"No, I don't. I think very few people are. If murder were natural, we'd be awash in blood, day in, day out, and there'd be no law: just survival."

"Karen, you were in Bosnia."

"That's war."

"How do we get into war but something akin to bloodlust?" As she opened her mouth, he waved away the question. "Marek Okerlund's got enough on his plate without butting heads with you over me. You know what it is to lose someone. Walk in his shoes."

She glanced out at Marek, standing on the sidewalk talking into that digital recorder, then down at her size eleven boots. What size did he wear, that made her feet look dainty? "That would trip me up, Uncle Sig."

Under his steady gaze, she caved. "I do care about him. I always did. But it was just easier not to talk about Marek in our house. He's got a daughter now...she's beautiful and sad and silent. I'd like to see her grow up. But that's separate from work. I need Marek on top of his game." She let her fear show. "And I don't know what game that is—down the road, I mean."

Understanding lit his fjord eyes. "You can play any game he throws at you, Karen. Just let the detective do what you hired him to do, okay?"

When she got into Marek's truck a few minutes later, she said, "You can take the resident. Dr. Echols."

When Marek didn't respond, she guessed what he was thinking. He should've been the one to question Sig Halvorsen.

But, dammit, Uncle Sig was...Sig.

As Marek pulled into the clinic parking lot, her phone rang. She glanced at the readout. "It's the pathologist in Sioux Falls. Go ahead. I'll catch up after I take this."

He hesitated, glanced at her phone, then got out. Did he think she'd hold back information if she didn't happen to like what she heard?

Her father had said it often enough: you can't play favorites with the facts.

The resident doctor—or doctor resident?—at the clinic had clearly been expecting a patient, not a detective, when Marek buzzed him.

"I can't tell you anything," David Echols said, his young face resolute. "Doctor-patient confidentiality."

"But Darcie Ringold was here that night?" Marek asked.

"Oh, yeah, she stayed until she got a call." Echols hadn't taken off the hastily donned labcoat. Maybe it gave him confidence, as a uniform did a rookie cop. "She said it was her stepfather. He's the one that got killed, right?"

For a doctor in the making, Echols sounded pretty happy about that. But, then, the young man had seen the result of Dale Hansen's callousness with Julio Chacón's hand.

Marek nodded. "You have anybody else come in that night?"

"Give me a warrant, Detective, and I'll tell you—not before."

He wasn't ready to give up. "Do you know Darcie Ringold? I mean, other than giving her a pregnancy test that night?"

Echols blinked then bumped up his round-rim glasses. "I've talked to her some, that's all. We've got a mentoring thing going at the U and she's pre-med."

Yet she'd claimed that Echols was a stranger to her.

"Were you the potential father?"

Echols started. "Me? As if."

"Her stepfather?"

Echols gripped the lapels of his labcoat. "Detective, if you want medical information on Darcie Ringold, ask her or get a warrant. That's the last time I say it—maybe you didn't hear."

Repetition sometimes got different results. Three times then out, his old sergeant used to say. He changed tactics. "Do you get many illegals here at the clinic?"

Now the hands fisted into the fabric. "I don't check papers. I just heal people. When I can. I'm only here over the holiday break. Dr. Hudson will be back next week. I can't wait."

"You don't like working in Reunion?"

"Do you?" the doctor countered.

Like wasn't a word that made much sense to Marek anymore. He did what he had to do, one step at a time, to keep from falling into nothingness and taking his daughter down with him.

After he returned to the Silverado and reported on the interview to the sheriff, she said, "Okay, looks like Darcie Ringold is off the hook. We need to find out what happened to Dale Hansen after she kicked him out of the Hummer. Do you think he could've wandered all the way out to the interstate?"

Marek wondered what exactly Sig had said to Karen. She'd used the *we* word.

"Depends on his direction and the severity of his head wound." Marek pulled to the road from the parking lot. "What's *our* direction?"

"Bryan McNulty," she said. "He rents an apartment on Norbeck. We've got some new juice."

He didn't think apple or grape. "Care to share?"

"It's preliminary, the pathologist said. He won't get the final report out to us until tomorrow. But he wanted to give us a heads-up. Dale had some kind of burn on his back. Sort of in a zigzag or Z pattern. Before his death by several hours. Mean anything to you?"

"Zorro?"

Now she turned her head. "Are you being serious?"

He didn't smile. "I don't know."

"Well, the pathologist said the burns would have healed in a couple days." They pulled up in front of the fourplex. "Otherwise, I didn't get much. He wasn't willing to commit to anything else until he's finished the autopsy."

"Who's *he*?"

"Oh, sorry. Dr. White." Her lips curved up then leveled. "You'll have to form your own opinion when you meet him."

Arne Okerlund had figured the colored pencils might keep the girl busy fifteen minutes, tops, yet the clock on the mantel told him it'd been three hours now.

The fall of hair hid the paper—the last of many—the girl worked on.

Why, he wondered, had he gotten a girl like Karen, who couldn't sit still for more than fifteen minutes, much less keep her mouth shut that long? And Marek had gotten...well, what had he gotten? Watching the girl, he felt sad that such a life, a life on the cusp, had been damaged. If she couldn't speak now, she wouldn't, no matter what Marek hoped.

No, Arne wouldn't want to switch Karen for Becca, but it sure was a change to have such silent intensity in the house.

Finally, he put down the remote, pushed himself up from the recliner, then fiddled with the dishes from their lunch of canned chicken noodle soup. With the last bowl dried, Arne turned and looked down at the papers that littered his kitchen table.

And found no words for what he saw.

CHAPTER 16

KAREN KNOCKED ON THE DOOR of the second-floor rental.
A stocky, dark-haired man jerked it open with a scowl.
"I'm not buying anything you're selling so...Ah. It's the law come to call."

"We're hoping you might tell us about working at PBI."

Bryan McNulty opened the door wide. The TV blared behind him; the Minnesota Vikings were once again about to snatch defeat from the jaws of victory.

For a bachelor, McNulty kept a tidy pad, more so than her own room in her dad's house. Sometimes, Karen wished she had her own place again, could take her things from Sioux Falls out of storage, but for now, she didn't really have much choice. Her dad needed her—and she needed him.

The Packers went wild with a game-ending field goal. McNulty picked up the remote and turned it off.

"I'll tell you honest," he said into the defeated silence. "I didn't shed tears when I heard about Dale Hansen."

She heard the faintest lilt. "Where are you from, Mr. McNulty?"

"Little dot of a place in Derry. Came over when I was a little kid after my uncle got blown to kingdom come for wanting better than he was allowed."

When Marek remained silent, Karen decided he didn't have a problem with her taking the lead this time. Contrarily, she wished otherwise. She could only think to ask, "How was Dale as a boss?"

McNulty blew out his disgust. "He got those chains moving way too fast. I challenged him once to keep up, you know, and he couldn't. Nowhere close. You know what he said? Those who can't do, teach." He laughed, short and bitter. "Teach? Give me a break. He wasn't called Dim Dale for nothing."

When Marek twitched beside her, she wondered what he'd picked up then remembered that he'd been called similar names in his time. "Did you keep up?"

"Barely," McNulty admitted.

Karen shifted on her feet, starting to feel the long hours since they'd discovered Dale Hansen's body. "How long did you know Dale?"

McNulty waved her to the sectional couch. "Seven months too long."

Karen sank down on leather and McNulty did likewise. Marek disappeared into the shadows of the room. Was he going to look around or was he lost again to the world?

Keeping her attention on McNulty, Karen asked, "Why did you go to work at PBI after being with Sig Halvorsen?"

"Figured one place was as good as another and PBI was a big outfit. Steady work, I thought. I'm a hard worker. But that place was brutal, even for a line supervisor. I went back to Halvorsen and begged for work. He gave me this short-term gig."

She didn't know Bryan McNulty, even by rumor, but his plate was clean according to the quick check she done on him. "You do the deliveries?"

"That's right. I like being on the road. My mother, she lives in Alford, married a trucker based there about...ah, a dozen years ago. He used to take me on long hauls over the summers while she worked as a waitress at the truck stop. I've been saving up for a rig of my own."

"Tell us what it was like at PBI."

He leaned forward. "Violations out the wazoo."

"What kind?"

"Every possible kind." He ticked off fingers. "Health and safety of the workers, humane treatment of the cattle, contamination of the meat, all the stuff the government is supposed to watch out for."

"Aren't there inspectors to catch that kind of thing?"

"There aren't enough of them and they can't see what it's really like, day to day. Besides, when they did show up, the chain speed was always slower, everything shipshape. When Hansen and Thompson ignored my complaints, I went direct to USDA and OSHA. Next thing I know, I'm being pulled off the line and told if I don't take a white hat, they're firing me."

She'd prefer not to get the take of a disgruntled employee. "So you were fired."

"No, I quit, then and there, which looking back is what they wanted. I don't like that I fell in line. I never did hear back about the violations. Swept under the rug, most like, or they handed out some piddly little fines. Easier for PBI to pay them than fix the problems."

McNulty picked up the remote, twirled it in his hand as a gunslinger might a revolver. "That's how they treated a line supervisor, Sheriff, so what do you think they did to the white hats? Especially the illegals."

Karen thought of Chacón. "You knew for sure there were illegals?"

"Dale liked to give them the shittiest jobs—the kill floor or cleaning crew—because he knew they couldn't go to the inspectors or the police. Most of them were off the books. Cash only. And if they got hurt, he'd fire them. He also dished out some—"

"Were you there when the Feds raided the plant?" the shadows asked.

So Marek hadn't zoned out. McNulty blinked but nodded. "People with guns, stomping all over the place. They held, what, more than two dozen workers overnight, maybe another half dozen for longer, but it turned out they were all legal. Some even natives." He traced a finger down his pale cheek. "They didn't even look at me."

The shadows spoke again. "Who tipped off the illegal workers?"

"Had to be Thompson or Hansen. Or both. Don't know how they knew, though. Someone higher up in the food chain must've told them."

Someone always knew. But she wasn't here to investigate the failed raid. "You mind telling us where you were Friday night?"

"I was stuck out at Bolvin Farm," he said, finger on the power button. "All right and tight—and well fed, too."

Before she could refute his statement, Marek sauntered back into the light and said, with bored cop in his voice, "So you haven't been to the plant at all since you quit?"

The man seemed puzzled. "I was there on Friday."

Karen let a breath out. "You just said you were at the Bolvins'."

"That was after I left the plant." McNulty flung an arm over the back of the couch. "Don't be looking at me for your killer, Sheriff. Dale Hansen was alive and kicking when I left him."

While Karen mulled that, Marek said, "Dale had a burn across his back. Sort of a Z shape. Know anything about that?"

"Like Zorro? What do you know. How poetic of me."

Just to be sure, Karen asked, "You did that?"

"Hell, yes, I did that. Grabbed a steam hose from one of the workers and—"

"Wait a minute," Marek said. "What workers?"

"Cleaning crew. Mexican, at least the one I grabbed the hose from, but I just don't remember. I had a red haze in front of my eyes, I did, and a beef to pick." That shot up one side of the mobile mouth. "Yeah, I had one hell of a beef with Hansen. I'm not afraid to say so."

A straight shooter, Karen thought. "What was your beef?"

"I'd been waiting months for my backpay. Called several times and left messages. Nothing. So I thought, before I go out to the Bolvins' place, I'd stop at the plant and get what I was owed. I found Dale there with the cleaning crew. I told him he'd better get my money then and there or I'd file in court for it."

Karen said, "I take it he wasn't cooperative."

"He said I owed PBI for an equipment fee. That's bullshit. I worked there for seven months and the only thing I didn't already have was the yellow hard hat. No way I owed him."

"So what happened?"

"He told me to get lost. If I didn't like it, I could sue. Like I had the money to hire a lawyer. But someone takes what I've earned, I've a right to be angry, and if you want to charge me for the burns, go ahead." He lifted a Coors can off the coffee table. "I'll be lifting a glass to whoever killed him."

When she wondered how many "glasses" McNulty usually consumed, he smiled wryly.

"No, Sheriff, I'm no drunken Irishman. My temper is no hotter than most, colder than many, and I'm no murderer. Nor was my uncle: just a peaceful protestor, he was, when he got blown. Near to killed my mother too, as he was her only brother, and me, his namesake."

Marek spoke up again. "You have any ideas about who might have killed Dale Hansen?"

"All I can say is, there's people in that plant who've seen lots of violence and not been able to go to the law to get satisfaction. When you can't see to survive another day with the likes of Dale Hansen in your face, it's not so surprising someone took the only path available."

Karen rose slowly to her feet. "No one tried the law, Mr. McNulty, not when it came to Dale Hansen, or I'd have heard of it."

Then she remembered the union-bashing raid and winced. But McNulty wasn't looking at her. He'd gazed over at the picture of a man on his wall. Bearded, gray eyes, holding a toddler, who'd be Bryan himself, she'd guess.

The now-grown man turned back to her. "He was a lovely man, Bryan O'Dell. No one ever paid for his death, Sheriff. Law or no law, if I ever find out, he'd be a dead man."

Because she knew outrage could bud into revenge, she said, "Looks to me like he was a man who'd have wanted better for you than to turn into what killed him."

She and Marek left the man in silence, hands fisted, damp gray eyes on gray.

When she got back in the Silverado, she asked Marek, "Do you think he knows who did it?"

Marek paused in the middle of holding that dinky little recorder up to his mouth. Which reminded her, she needed to bring up his dyslexia with Dahl. In the morning, she promised herself, when Marek was getting Becca registered at school.

"Hard to say. I'll check his story out with the Bolvins. But no one is admitting to being on that cleaning crew. It would've helped to get some names." He summarized the interview and dropped the recorder back into his pocket. "We should talk to Thompson again."

She glanced at her watch and weighed the emptiness of her gut. "Let's swing by the café first and get something to eat. My treat."

Now he looked at his own watch, his focused face going blank. "Becca—"

"I called Dad after I talked to Dr. White. Becca is fine. She's busy drawing."

His brows funneled down. "Drawing?"

"Yeah, on paper, not on the walls." When he didn't put the Silverado in gear, she asked, "Don't you remember where the café is?"

Moments later, they parked in front of the Reunion fixture. The weathered sign above the corner restaurant was barely discernable: The Café. What some might take as a lack of imagination, Dakotans took as a lack of pretense. Besides, café was itself exotic—French, even.

"What'll you have, Sheriff?" Ella Rasmussen asked as they took stools at the counter. Then she nodded at Marek and said, as if she'd done so for years, "Detective?"

"We'll take two specials," Karen said, to save her detective thought.

When Ella glanced at Marek, he just shrugged and said, "Coffee, black, would be nice, Mrs. Rasmussen."

When the woman hurried off to the kitchen, Karen tapped fingers on the counter. Ella had waitressed at the café for, what, twelve or thirteen years now, ever since her husband had been disabled in a farming accident. Not long enough for Marek to have met her here.

Karen traced an old watermark on the counter. "You know Ella?"

"She used to clean our house in Valeska," he said.

Ella returned and placed a mug on the counter in front of him. He wrapped his hands around the mug and said to the waitress, "I should apologize for taking off like I did all those years ago, Mrs. Rasmussen, without even seeing if you'd been paid."

"Oh, never you mind that, I was paid by the estate," Ella said with a wave of a workworn hand. "Your mama said, once she was gone, you'd be gone too. I just wish I could've given you a proper send off. I baked a bunch of stuff for you. Thought you could've used it after the funeral and all."

Karen watched Marek's face slack into that blank look she hated.

"I'm sorry," he said.

"It didn't go to waste." Then, to Karen's surprise, the woman reached out and ruffled the dark hair. "I'm glad you're back."

The waitress had said that just loud enough to have Karen realize there'd been grumbling in the peanut gallery. Well, why wouldn't there be, with Nails Nelson stirring up the populace, putting her and her detective on notice?

In the awkward silence, a voice came clear from a table behind them.

"If the sheriff's office would get off their duffs instead of stuffing their faces, maybe we wouldn't have any trouble catching killers. Seems to me, it's good money thrown after bad, when they can't even solve a murder every dick in town knows who done."

Another voice said, "Maybe that's the problem...our sheriff don't got one."

A dick, he meant. When Ella opened her mouth, Karen held up a hand. Better not get the house involved.

She swiveled on her stool.

Her years as a dispatcher had taught her: be calm, be patient, be firm. Oh, and be polite. You were being recorded.

Karen identified the first speaker. "Well, Mr. Gotsch, you're entitled to your opinion."

"Not an opinion," he said, dunking his French fry with a bloody dollop of ketchup and shaking it at her. Splatters fell on his bistro white plate. "Fact."

"Well, sure, we could sit in our vehicles giving out more speeding tickets to finance our sitting out in them," she said and got a few huffs of laughter. Myron Gotsch had picked up more than a few tickets over the years. "Just might pay the increase in gas prices." A few groans echoed. "But, see, there's a thing called community policing."

The second voice piped up. "Is that, like, policing the community?" queried Myron's son Wayne with a finger gun going off at his head. "Duh."

Her father hadn't often talked of his work. But Wayne Gotsch had been an exception. Trouble, he'd said. That put Wayne on par with the worst there was: a Marek.

"It isn't only the waitresses who get tips here." She kept her smile. Barely. "See, if I was out in my truck patrolling the back lanes of the county, I might've missed hearing that your dad's already solved this homicide. Care to share?"

"I'm not gonna do your job for you," Myron said. "All I'm saying is, it's gotta be one of them foreigners at trailer city."

"What about you, Detective Halfwit," Wayne said. "You got an opinion?"

Karen cast a wary eye at Marek but he didn't even move, his eyes drowned in the coffee he cradled in his chafed hands. Maybe he hadn't even heard.

"He's not paid to give one," Karen said. "He's off the clock."

Myron glared at her detective's back. "What do you mean, he's off the clock? Policing is a full-time job."

The stool creaked as Marek swiveled. "You pay me half-time and work me full, you get a halfwit."

Another man at a booth called out, "Heard you didn't want to be a wit."

"You'd be right."

At the disapproving looks, Karen said, "He's got a little girl to take care of. On his own."

That cleared most, if not all, of the expressions, excepting the Gotsches Grim.

Her radio crackled to life.

"Sorry, duty calls," she said, digging out a ten dollar bill and putting it on the counter.

What would barely cover a meal in Sioux Falls, here encompassed hers, his, and a generous tip. She rose to her feet as Mrs. Rasmussen came out of the kitchen with two steaming plates of tuna noodle casserole. "Thanks, Ella, but we just got called out."

"You just hold on a minute and I'll box it up for you." She transferred the contents into Styrofoam containers. "Can't go without dinner, no matter what's got you called out."

Karen took the containers then walked over to Myron's table. "Every time we take a call, Mr. Gotsch, it could be our last meal. That's what we take on with the badge. Now, if you'll excuse us, we'll have to finish this chat another time."

Wayne leered up at her. "How about tonight at my place, you come do a bit of community policing, since you're not getting any from your hus—"

The hand that hit the table rocked the plates. To her surprise, that hand belonged to the elder Gotsch. Apparently some things were still taboo. Karen looked down at Wayne with a shake of her head. "I doubt I'd wring much out of your...tip."

As she pushed out the door to a chorus of hoots, she heard one of the tow-headed kids in the red-vinyl booth by the window ask his parents, "What's so funny?"

Not much. The sweet thing was, though, Wayne's father had laughed too.

But Marek hadn't even smiled. She might have expected Kurt Bechtold to disapprove of that little rebuttal but not Marek.

He stalked over to the Silverado and opened the passenger door. For her. "Little shithead."

So, he'd been upset on her behalf. "No pleasing a Gotsch and no appeasing them." She slid into the passenger seat, a warm fuzzy feeling pervading her. She told herself it came from the containers she balanced on her lap.

An hour after leaving the café, Karen parked her Suburban at 22 Okerlund Road. She'd gotten her ride back in fair trade. The callout had been from a plow operator, who'd discovered a stranded tourist in an RV on a remote county road. She and Marek had transported the half-frozen man—with his no-bars cell phone stuck to his hand—to the clinic. She'd filled out the paperwork and Marek had fixed her tire.

Behind her, the Silverado slipped into its own messy slot across the street.

She picked up her container of now-cold casserole and got out. Marek stood out in the middle of the street, holding his own container, and she frowned at him. Surely he wasn't proposing to come over for dinner. Was he? "What?"

"You want to send Becca home?"

"Oh, sure. I'd forgotten. She's such a quiet thing that I..." Too quiet, she remembered. "Uh, not at all like me, now that I think of it. I was a terror."

"I'm sure your opponents on the court thought so."

He wasn't talking a court of law. Basketball. "Yeah, well, past glories. Long gone and forgotten."

His shadow, thrown from the street lamp behind him, reached all the way to her boots. "Becca's going to be tall."

"If she stays, she'll play, even if she's got two left feet." That first *if* played in the street between them. "I'll send her out."

When she pulled open the door, she collided with Becca and bobbled supper. "Whoa, what's your hurry?"

Although she expected the girl to keep right on going, as she herself would have done at that age, Becca instead backed up and held out a drawing.

She took it. "For me?"

Prepared to make lemonade out of an artistic lemon, Karen could only stare. Then she looked up, over the girl, and into Arne Okerlund's eyes. "My God, Dad, you said she was drawing but...my God."

"She did a whole batch of them. Gave them all to me except that one." He cleared his throat and glanced down at the girl. "Never saw the like."

Karen hunched down into the anxious gaze of the artist. "You have a gift, Becca."

The girl's nose wrinkled. She pushed the drawing closer to Karen.

"Yes, I know, it's my gift. What I mean is, it's good, Becca. Really good." She heard Marek call the girl for dinner. "Don't you want to take one to your dad?"

Her head shook. Decisively. Well, Marek likely had drawings coming out of his ears. "Okay, but I'm going to put it over my desk. My first Becca Okerlund."

Becca gave Karen a lunging hug, nearly overbalancing her, then ran over to Marek.

As the two disappeared into the broken-down house, Karen got up and went inside with her father. She didn't quite know what to say, so she asked, "You eat yet?"

"Not if that's from the café."

"Guess you haven't eaten, then."

She put the casserole in the microwave, pulled down plates, found the silverware, and set the table. Her mother's stricture: it takes a minute to sit down to a meal and a lifetime to talk over one.

"You've been pretty quit about the case, Karen."

"Quit? Oh, quiet." Freudian slip or stroke, she wondered. "Well, it's not that I'm holding out on you. I just haven't had time. I'd like to get your take, actually. It's kind of hard to talk freely to Marek."

"Why? He keeping you out of the loop?"

"No more than any other close-mouthed man in my life." Her father grunted, not looking a bit abashed at being among their number. She pulled out the casserole and placed it on the table. "But Marek's the one with the bigshot homicide credentials. I wasn't sure...well, I'm still not sure, how much of it's merited. But when the election comes up..."

"Nobody's going to elect a Marek in Eda County."

He always spoke as if there were a marauding horde of Mareks out there, though she supposed Lenny Marek had been big enough to encompass one. And her father ignored both Jim and Janina Marek, neither of whom had been in trouble with the law. Which was beside the point.

Karen sank into her seat and picked up her fork. "Dad, he's an Okerlund."

"You're a better one." Her father stabbed his fork into the casserole and out came a pyroclastic flow of peas and shredded tuna. "You've got something Marek doesn't, something he never had, never will."

"What's that? Brains? Dad, Marek is dyslexic, and that's a problem I need to bring up with Dahl, but he isn't an idiot. He's got over a decade on me when it comes to experience."

"You're a natural leader. So, lead." He dug into the casserole.

"Tell me about the case."

Her need to discuss the case warred with her hunger. So she alternated—a few words, a few bites—until she'd finished. She pushed away her plate. "Now we've eliminated our best suspect. I may think it was pretty callous, or at least careless, of Darcie Ringold to boot her stepdad out into a blizzard. But she stood up for what she did, I'll give her that. Dale Hansen was last seen headed back to the plant on Bluff Road. We don't know if he made it or not, or how he got out to the interstate. Basically, we're nowhere."

"Look harder at the plant," her father said, picking up his plate with his good hand. "The cleaning crew."

Frustration filled her. "No one other than Chacón will admit to being on it."

With more patience than she'd have given herself, her father said, "That's why you need to look harder."

Marek gave Becca the plastic spoon and kept the fork for himself, mentally thanking Ella Rasmussen for including utensils. The cold casserole wasn't half bad. But he'd be glad to have his microwave again. On Tuesday, if the weather held, they'd have their things back.

If not their life.

He watched Becca nudge doubtfully at the casserole with her spoon. "Tuna noodle. It's a Dakota specialty, especially at potlucks." In Albuquerque, the potlucks had run more to *posole* and *chile rellenos*. He took a bite himself, didn't have to mime his pleasure, and she spooned up a bite.

And sniffed.

Well, if he couldn't get her to eat, maybe he could get her to talk. "You have a good day?" Becca peered at him over the casserole, as if judging his sincerity, and he had to remind himself he had the interviewing skills, not her. "Well?"

She nodded. Not a dad-you're-full-of-it kind but a real one.

"That's good." He felt so tired but knew he had to make the effort. "What did you give Karen? A drawing?"

Becca shoveled the casserole in her mouth.

"Okay, be that way. Once we're fueled, it's bedtime. You've got school tomorrow." When he saw the fear, he put down his fork.

"Don't worry. I'll take you to school in the morning and I'll come get you at lunchtime. It's only half-day here, Karen told me. That's a big break, kid."

His daughter stabbed her spoon into the middle of her casserole. Good thing it was cold, he thought, or they'd have cream of mushroom all over.

When the remains had been trashed, he scoured the bungalow until he found a lumpy mattress upstairs. He dragged it down in front of the fireplace, got his daughter settled, then got a fire going. The heating system wasn't doing its job.

Was he?

Sitting back in the rocker, he wondered what he'd let them in for. Had he really done this for Becca? Or for himself? His partner had tried to tell him, battering away at him, that there were other ways, less disruptive, to get what he wanted for his daughter.

And himself.

He hadn't listened. Val would have said: you have to melt a glacier, not chip away at it.

But he couldn't melt. There wouldn't be anything left of him. He watched the sparks leap, catch wood, smolder, then burst into flame. His daughter fell asleep and he knew he'd follow soon.

When his cell rang, he groaned, flicked it open, and scanned the readout. And took the call.

"You bored yet up there in the Great White North?" the voice on the other end asked.

Marek could picture Manny Trujillo, fingers pulling restlessly at a pitiful excuse of a moustache, sitting on the edge of his chair, elbows on his desk.

"Bored? Not exactly. I've got a homicide. What about you, *El Jefe*? Get any paper cuts lately?" Expletives exploded in his ear. "Hey, it's a dangerous job, paper pusher."

"I'm the man here now," his former partner said. "Just one M now."

Manny and Marek. M&M.

At first it had been a gag, pinned on a mismatched pair, then a brand. For all of the fifteen years they'd been partners, they'd argued who was plain and who was nuts.

But M&M had been killed that early morning six months ago when Manny had pulled him over. Marek had been put on leave and Manny Trujillo had been propelled, not entirely against his will, into management.

"We've got a nice little gang killing here, right up your alley," Manny said into the present. "You want in?"

"Mine's more challenging," Marek said. He filled Manny in on the details. "The cause of death could still be accidental, I suppose, depending on the extent of the head wound, how he got it, and when he died. He could've been dead before he was chained out there. Though according to what he told his stepdaughter, the head wound was an assault, so it'd still be manslaughter." Then he remembered the hand, jutting up from the snow. "But it's more likely he died of exposure in the blizzard—and that makes it murder. We're waiting on the autopsy report."

"Weird stuff," the new sergeant said. "Can I come and help?"

"It's 10 below here."

"Scratch that. No wonder they grow them tall up there. Keeps your brains from figuring out your toes are freezing. So how're the *gringos* treating you? They impressed with your credentials?"

Hardly, he thought. "Sheriff here's a *gringa.*"

"That's right. How's that going?"

"She's also my niece."

The line whistled with stunned silence. "Thought she had some Irish name."

"Sheriff Karen Okerlund Mehaffey."

"You're telling me that your new boss is the daughter of the man who kicked you out of the county?"

Marek had gotten chatty one night after 36 hours of sleep deprivation and told his partner why he'd left Eda County. "She's not really my boss, since the county commissioners thought it looked funny and decided that they were my boss instead."

"Boss by committee? That's gotta suck. How many are there?"

"Three. But really only one."

"What, like the Trinity?"

God, Marek thought, when had he last laughed? "Not unlike."

CHAPTER 17

STANDING IN FRONT OF THE principal the next morning, head bowed, Marek tried to remember he wasn't the child here. "I didn't know I'd have to go through the third degree just to get my daughter enrolled."

He discounted the faint memory of Karen telling him something about papers.

"Does she speak English?" the principal asked with a honk into a handkerchief.

Marek barely got it out from between clenched teeth. "She doesn't *speak*."

That muted the principal. Marek took the time to read the nameplate almost run off the desk by papers. Blanche Hagaman. Hadn't there been Hagamans in Fink?

Recovering her voice, Principal Hagaman said with nasal emphasis, "You really should have contacted us before bringing a special needs child. We have a special ed teacher come in once a week but—"

Marek brought his daughter closer to him, fought not to cover her ears, and instead said what she needed to hear. "Nothing is wrong with her. She just doesn't talk."

"In English?"

Becca knew some Spanish, courtesy of himself and her maternal grandfather. Val had shrugged off her own lack of fluency: she was American, wasn't she. "In any language."

"Is she autistic, then?"

"She's fine. She just doesn't talk."

"Got it. She's mute."

Marek shook his head. "She *can* talk. She'll talk when she wants to talk."

The woman stared at him then sighed. "Her birth certificate?"

"She's legal," he said, trying to keep from leaning over and strangling the woman with her handkerchief. Now he had an inkling of how Sanchez must have felt. "Her birth certificate is coming with our stuff. Tomorrow, I hope."

The red-rimmed eyes said: Right. "I'm sorry, but until you do have it, I can't let her enroll. We have rules."

Their work was education. His was murder. "Can't she just go to class and then we'll sort it out later?"

"Marek, is that you?" A woman with a carefully touched up face under coiffed white hair stepped into the room. "I'm right, aren't I, you're Marek Okerlund?"

She didn't look like a teacher, Marek decided, not in her powder-blue suit and flashy diamond accents. Besides, he remembered the faces of every teacher who'd given up on him.

"Okerlund?" the principal queried.

The woman beamed at him and he had it. Mrs. Winke. Mother-in-law of Alice Winke of the real estate business. If anyone could be said to have money in Reunion, it was the Winkes, though for all that, they weren't snooty with it. Just refined.

"Haven't you turned on YRUN lately, Blanche? Our new detective blew into town with our first homicide in years. Hands on favorite, he did it, to give himself work. And this must be Becca." Mrs. Winke reached out and patted his daughter's dark head. "I'm so sorry."

So much for salvation from that quarter. What was he going to do with Becca, take her back to Arne again?

"About your wife's death, I mean."

Marek couldn't so much as open his throat to answer that.

But Blanche Hagaman got hers open. "You can vouch for this child, then, Meredith?"

"Absolutely, I'd recognize those Okerlund eyes anywhere," Mrs. Winke said. "I'm delighted to see the Okerlund name won't die out."

The principal didn't share her delight. "He says she doesn't talk."

"Trauma affects us all differently, doesn't it?" Mrs. Winke said. "Why, when my husband died, I just threw myself into every and anything I could, just so I didn't have time to think. That's when I started volunteering here at the school."

In a much subdued voice, Blanche Hagaman said to Marek,

"Why didn't you just tell me that her mother had...passed away?"

Marek shifted Becca around so her back instead of her front was plastered against his legs. "Why should I have to tell you about our personal life just to get her enrolled?"

She balled up her handkerchief. "Detective, you're the seventh parent trying to get their child enrolled this morning without the proper paperwork."

Marek didn't see anyone hovering behind him. "What happened to the other six?"

The principal sighed. "I simply can't turn away people who want so much for their children to learn. But purely as a practical matter, it's hard to meet the needs of all the children in a class when there's such a disparity in basic skills. I've had half a dozen of our English-speaking students transfer to smaller schools like Alford or Valeska so they could get more personal attention."

Hell, that was the one thing he'd thought Reunion had going for it. He didn't want Becca to get lost, a silent ghost, falling behind, with no one to catch her.

As if sensing his thoughts, the principal leaned over the desk and put a staying hand on Becca's shoulder. "Let's start over, shall we?"

Twenty minutes later, Marek was back at work, with Karen looking annoyed, though it didn't appear to be with him. Not directly, anyway.

"I've scheduled an incident meeting at eleven," she told him. "You okay with that?"

Incident meeting. Fancy word for a sit-down in the sheriff's office. Shouldn't take more than an hour, he decided, given what little they had, so he nodded.

"I've got some foreclosure papers to deliver then a court appearance." Karen glanced at her watch. "What're you going to do now?"

"Check out stories."

"Which stories?"

"You want to hold this meeting now?" he asked, then held up his own hand. "Sorry, school always has this effect on me." He pulled up his mental checklist. "I'm going to check out Bryan McNulty's story."

"I'll await your report, then."

"Written?" he asked her back.

"You're so far behind on those," she said, pushing open the door, "that it would be kind of counterproductive."

And out she went.

Stroking his moustache, Walrus said, "She didn't *sound* mad."

"No, she sounded resigned," Marek said. "I think that's worse. I can write a report. I just haven't had time."

The radio crackled and dished up details on another stranded motorist.

"That's mine." Walrus got to his feet then hesitated. "Just a heads-up, Okerlund. You'd better rustle up something new to tell the boss. She looked all business this morning when she came in—disappeared for a little while upstairs and came back pissed."

"Where'd she go?"

Walrus shrugged into his jacket. "Maybe she talked to Judge Rudy, I don't know, but she's in a ship-shape mood. Almost saluted her, but I didn't think she'd appreciate it, not today. My guess is, if something doesn't break soon, Nails is going to start crucifying her—or you."

Minutes later, from the large office windows, Marek watched Walrus lumber down Main in a squad car that looked like a lowrider, the frame sunk down to the wheels. Difference was, in Albuquerque, they did that on purpose.

He went to his desk and pulled the phone to him. Five calls later he found the right OSHA inspector.

"McNulty?" He heard the clickety clack of nails on a computer keyboard. "Yes, I logged that complaint." The prim voice gave him the time, date, and particulars.

He waited for the followup. "And?"

"And what? I've logged it. That's all I can do. We don't have the authority, or scientific data, to cite a company for excessive line speed. We don't even know what excessive is."

He rubbed at his ear. "What?"

"Deputy—" she began on a longsuffering sigh.

"Detective," he said. "If you don't cover injuries, then who—"

"We cover injuries," she said coolly. "But we have no data that line speeds or repetitive stress cause disabilities that require our intervention."

"Do you really believe what you're telling me?" he asked her. Then gave it up. "Never mind. I assume you would be interested in an injury resulting in amputation."

He heard a long pause broken by the clacking of keys. "I have no report from PBI on such an injury." Now she did sound interested.

"His name is Julio Chacón. He triggered the grinder while cleaning. "

She stopped typing. "Cleaning? That's an entirely different category. I'll transfer you."

Before he could protest, he found himself talking to a young man who took down the particulars on the lockout/tagout violation. His drawling questions were punctuated by yawns.

Maybe the government would be more interested in violations in the food supply, Marek thought. He tried USDA next.

"Violations?" The sound of a coffee mug being placed down on a metal surface rang in the earpiece. "Oh, sure, PBI's got them. They all do. They don't care. Just pay their fines—or appeal them and never pay them."

The cynicism had hardened to acceptance.

"Did you get a report from a man named Bryan McNulty?"

"Yeah, I did. Called me up personal. Took guts. I filled out the report, filed it, and my boss calls me into his office the next day. He says McNulty's just a troublemaker who got himself fired, so I'm to ignore it."

"McNulty says he got demoted *after* he reported the violations," Marek said. "He walked instead."

A thoughtful grunt came on the other side. "Sounds more like it."

"So...are you going to do anything?"

"Detective, what comes down from the top is: be business friendly. I've got three more years to retirement. If they'd let me do my job, I'd gladly do it, but I've got to put food on my family's table. And I'll be honest; it's not meat."

After he hung up, Marek stared out the window. Why bother with laws, with agencies, to oversee and regulate, if politics kept them from doing their job? It was like someone reporting a murder to him, Marek thought, and he just said, sorry, we'll log it, but that's all we can do. It's against the law, sure, but it isn't good for business.

Rising to his feet, Marek looked around for somebody to tell where he was going. Then he realized he was alone, something he'd never encountered at APD, with its constant traffic of accusers and accused.

Finally, he found a yellowed legal pad in the bottom drawer of his desk, wrote his destination in capital letters, and propped the message against the lamp on Karen's desk.

Bolvin Farm lay nestled in the slowly rolling hills to the east of Reunion, not far from the state park that preserved the highest point in the county.

Marek turned off the county road onto gravel and rumbled over the barely exposed cattle guard.

He'd been friends with one of the Bolvin sons; there'd been, what, five of them. All began with *N*. Ned, Nate, Noel—he'd taken a lot of flack for that—Nick, and...what was the last? Oh, Norman. The Conquest, his older brothers had dubbed him, always on the bottom of the pile. Or, given the family obsession, pinned to the floor.

Marek drove past a churned up mess of dirt, ice, and snow. Had the cows gotten out and had an orgy?

Two round plastic sleds, one red and one blue, sat discarded at the base of the nearby hill. Kids must live here, then. Another generation of Bolvins.

Marek pulled up in front of the nearly invisible two-story farmhouse, white paint against white hills. He stopped behind a Ford F250. Gravel-spattered snow still sat on its rear bumper except where it'd been cleared around the tow ball.

He contemplated that, got out, then headed toward habitation. He knew better than to go to the house; instead, he followed the path to the barn. Standing on the threshold, he waited for his eyes to adjust but his ears had already pegged one Bolvin. He followed the sound. The family had another talent besides racking up wrestling championships; perhaps the wrestling had even been necessary because of it. All the Bolvins sang.

I spied a young cowboy all wrapped in white linen
All wrapped in white linen as cold as the clay

Recognizing *The Streets of Laredo*, Marek slid in with an ad-lib counterpoint, but the singer didn't react. Fallen bangs the color of the russet cows outside hid the downcast face. Finally, the head jerked up and the voice broke off. "You're not Ned."

That eliminated one of the five. The russet hair narrowed it down further but not conclusively. "Neither are you."

"Ned's gone to the feed store," the man said with an absent

wave. "Whoever you are, you've got a true bass voice. I mean, *true*. All of us Bolvins...well, we're baritones, even if we try to cover all the parts. Just because I'm the skinniest, I get bumped to tenor. Who *are* you?"

Marek decided to hide behind his new title. "Eda County Detective."

"Detective?" The unfocused eyes met Marek's. Sharpened. "Well, I'll be. Marek Okerlund, all grown up."

Since he doubted YRUN reached all the way out here, Marek assumed word of mouth had betrayed him. The grin came then, a sort of shy half-slash, and that clinched it. "Back at you, Nick Bolvin."

His childhood friend rose from where he'd been fixing some kind of tractor attachment. Whatever it was, it looked capable of doing major damage. "You really *did* grow up. Even Noel would have a hard time taking you down."

"Noel? Thought he was going to change his name on his eighteenth birthday."

"He made people shut up about it instead. Took all-state in wrestling four years and did serious damage in college. Went to the Olympics and missed a bronze by a hair, then got it after the other guy was found to be doping. Coach at Iowa now."

Not a small feat. "Impressive."

"The last time I saw you must've been, what, all-state chorus? Your voice grew up along with the rest of you. You still sing?"

"Only in the shower."

Nick looked affronted. "With that kind of voice, you could have gone professional. Took a while for it to hit but, whew, that's almost subsonic. Stealth bass."

Marek wasn't used to being praised for his voice, not after high school. Manny used to elbow him when he'd start humming.

A long plaintive bawl from one of the stalls startled Marek enough to have him reaching for his nonexistent gun.

Nick laughed. "City boy."

"Very funny," he muttered.

Nick poked into a bucket full of metallic odds and ends. "You aren't here for just old time's sake, I take it." He fished out a washer, pursed his lips. "What have we got to do with Dale Hansen?"

Marek considered that tone. "I take it you didn't want anything to do with him."

"We sell our cattle to Halvorsen. Or, I should say, he butchers it for us. Had to cut back on the supply once his plant went belly up." He slid the washer on and screwed down the nut by hand. "Business is picking up again, though."

"So you're doing well?"

That earned him a wry look. "Well enough to keep off the auction block. Of course, I couldn't do it without my wife teaching at the high school. Ned works at the feed store for benefits. You won't find many full-time farmers these days. Can't make a living at it."

How had farming become the odd job? "Bryan McNulty."

Nick picked up a wrench that looked half rust. "What about him? He works for Halvorsen."

"How well do you know him?"

"Not very."

Marek wasn't used to dealing with Dakota slow-talkers but rapid-fire Hispanics: hands waving, mouth working, passion in every line.

The first time he'd met Manny Trujillo, introduced himself, the other man had said, how do you manage to talk without your mouth moving, eh, *Gigante*? Since he'd given the man his name, he thought his new partner hadn't heard him, so he'd repeated, with more volume, I'm Marek Okerlund.

That had earned him the expression that had graced the faces of so many of his teachers over the years: idiot.

Partly to prove he wasn't, he'd asked his new partner to teach him Spanish. Somewhere along the line, they'd gelled into the candy store of M&M. Marek's advantage over his coworkers was that urbanites tended to run off at the mouth when confronted with silence.

It wasn't working on a Dakotan. "When did you last see McNulty?"

"That would be the night Dale died. And, yes, Bryan was as hot as the night was cold—and blowing just as strong. But that's all it was. The delivery truck got stuck here until yesterday morning. Royal mess we made getting him out. You must have seen it coming in."

Marek sneezed as one of the cows kicked up hay dust in its stall. "How'd you get him out? Towed him?"

"Took two pickups and two chains."

He'd take a look at those chains before he left. "Why wait that long?"

"Took that long before we could get a plow out here on the county road." Nick threw the wrench into the bucket and stood up. "And, I'd guess, Detective, that takes him out of your little story."

Not so little. "I'll have to check it out."

"Check what out?" a grim voice asked from behind them. "Nick, have you gone and talked to those flaxseed people behind my back? I told you to wait. I'm not sold on it."

"Nagging Ned, never changes," Nick said. "Take a closer look, big brother. See if you can put a name to our visitor here."

The man was taller than Nick, with bigger shoulders, hair the color of bark, and none of the *aw shucks* amiability. Dark and close, his eyes roved from Marek's unkempt hair to boots and back again. "Well, if it isn't our Little Honey."

Marek would prefer Dumb Polack any day.

On a sleepover at the farm courtesy of his parents' tenth anniversary, Marek had been bullied into singing with the brothers Bolvin. When he'd finally let loose, their mother had swung around on that little piano stool that pretty much disappeared under her broad expanse and exclaimed, why, Marek Okerlund, you've got a honey of a voice.

From then on, he'd been known to all the Bolvins as Little Honey, even though he'd been bigger than all but Ned, even at that age.

"I'm nobody's honey."

Hand to chin and then a slow nod. "Yep, same reply, same pink cheeks behind that stubble, but the voice...Nick said it went south later on. Still sing?"

Marek sighed at the hopeful tone. "Not really."

"What a waste."

Marek turned at the female voice. Patty Bolvin stood at the threshold, hands on ample hips, shaking her head. Our bulwark never failing, Nick had called her.

"If you boys are going to gab the day away," she said, "it's warmer in the house and I've just pulled a pie out of the oven. Come on in, now."

She turned and headed out. The men looked at each other then followed out in her tracks like cows after the farmer—or the farmer's feed.

CHAPTER 18

WHEN MAREK RETURNED FOR THE incident meeting Karen had called for 11 AM, he found an unfamiliar Eda County deputy in the office. Perhaps thirty, under six foot, medium build, receding sandy hair cut close against his head.

Walrus made a grand gesture from his seat. "Detective Okerlund, meet Travis Bjorkland."

Marek held out his hand. "Nice to finally meet you, Deputy."

The calloused hand shook his own with a faint twitch that told Marek he'd thought about playing the crush-and-see-if-he-flinches game.

"Mmm." The musical sound seemed assessing. "Bork."

Picking up two pens from his desk, Walrus struck them together then threw them over his shoulders onto the floor where Kurt, with a shake of the head, stooped to retrieve them.

"You're not that young, Okerlund," Walrus said at Marek's blank look. "Didn't you ever see the Muppets when you were a kid? Mmm. Bork, bork, bork."

The deputy stuffed his hands into his pockets. "I don't cook."

Finally it sunk in. "I doubt the Swedish Chef did any real cooking either."

"Mostly he just throws things," Walrus agreed. "But Bork here just likes to climb things."

Marek thought of the majestic Sandias, the Sangres, the Jemez of New Mexico. "You're in the wrong place, Deputy."

"Not all climbing's about elevation. The Palisades are good for bouldering."

Marek vaguely remembered them: cliffs of rose-colored

Sioux quartzite.

His fingers waving like sea anemones, Walrus said, "I'm feeling outnumbered here: three Scandinavians to one English, that'd be me, one German, and one Native. Kurt thinks we need more Germans, but sheriff's half that, so there's got to be bonus points there."

The steady hazel eyes took in Marek's Slavic-slanted features. "Mmm."

Walrus let out a gusty sigh. "We figure he's still learning to say the name of his home state."

Marek let out a hiss of air. "A Minnesotan?"

With that, Bork strode out of the office into the break room. Had Marek managed to offend the man? But when Bork came back, he handed Marek a mug of coffee and one of hot water to Walrus. "Farm straddles the border. My trailer's on the South Dakota side."

Probably for the tax break, Marek thought, then took a sip: hot and strong. Flavorful to boot. "Thanks. Better than the fare I got in Albuquerque."

"Sheriff brings it in," Bork commented. "Some fair trade deal from her church, she says, but I think she just wants the good stuff, no matter how she gets it."

Walrus pulled out a tea bag from his desk drawer and dunked it. It took Marek a moment to read the little tag on the tea. Native American Tea Company. Green Tea. That wasn't something he'd have pegged for Walter Russell.

Kurt didn't seem to have a need for liquid. The twitch of fingers against his mouth, however, told Marek that the man smoked—or had at one time.

From the side door, Karen walked into their coffee break. He'd forgotten she was in the building. In court. She dropped papers on her desk and picked up the scrap he'd left for her. "What's this? Don't tell me we've had another cow massacre."

Marek stared at the big letters: BOVINE. "Uh, I was out chasing leads at the Bolvins."

As Walrus wheezed, her lips twitched. "Well, you weren't far off."

Karen sat down on the edge of her desk, took the cup of coffee that Bork handed to her, and addressed Marek. "What did you find out at the Bolvins?"

That Patty Bolvin made the best apple pie he'd ever tasted, spiced with cinnamon and topped with homemade vanilla ice cream. He had a tin of the leftover pie in his Silverado and refused to feel guilty about it.

Marek sat on his desk. "Bryan McNulty's off the suspect list. He's alibied."

"I'd like the details," the sheriff said. "Now that we're all here, let's get started. Marek, bring us up-to-date."

Whatever else his faults, Karen had to admit that Marek Okerlund knew how to lay out a case.

He didn't ramble, didn't hesitate, at least not after the first few seconds. He hadn't expected her to yield the floor, she thought. And it was true, she had an agenda today: her father had told her to lead. But leading often meant delegating.

Once Marek finished, she asked, "You checked the tow chains at the Bolvins?"

"Nick's was in the back of his pickup. Ned's was still wrapped around the tow ball."

Bork asked, "What about Halvorsen's delivery truck, does it have one?"

Karen stiffened but Marek glanced over at Bork with what looked like approval. "I checked that out on the way back. Halvorsen said, so far as he knew, it didn't have one."

"Mmm."

Karen didn't like the questioning sound of that. "I thought Sig had been eliminated."

"No, I said he wasn't high on the list," Marek responded. "When the phone records come in, we'll need to contact the people he talked to."

A waste of time, she thought, but managed to keep that to herself. "Okay, that's where we've been. Next question is, where do we go from here?"

Walrus opened his mouth but she held up a hand. "That was rhetorical. I made up a list while I was waiting to give testimony in court this morning. Marek, I want you to go to Sioux Falls this afternoon. See if you can shake loose the report from Dr. White and interview Chacón. He must know who was on that cleaning crew. You get me names and I'll go with you to trailer city after you get back."

Protest gathered on the scraggily face. "But I—"

"Kurt, you get to work on Sig's phone records," she interrupted.

Marek had had the floor for long enough. "Walrus, you get in touch with the crime lab. We need any forensic evidence they can give us. If they give you grief, let me know and I'll goose them myself."

"For all the good it will do," Walrus muttered.

"We need information."

She handed out the rest of the assignments. And watched Marek's eyes jump up over her head. What was he doing, checking out his spackling job?

Her own gaze wandered down to the clock; they'd just have to go over lunch.

She hadn't been able to snag Dahl that morning; he'd gone to Sioux Falls to talk with people about grant proposals. But she still wanted to find out why she hadn't been informed of her detective's dyslexia.

When Marek interrupted Bork to say, "I need to—" Karen had had enough.

"You need to shut up when someone else is talking," she told him, wondering if he was trying to assert his position over hers. So much for the warm fuzzies.

A few minutes later, as Kurt turned the discussion to Darcie Ringold's mystery man, Marek got to his feet. She thought he might be headed for the bathroom or the break room to get more coffee. But as Kurt trailed off, the draft of cold air hit her, and she whirled in time to see the front door slam closed.

Karen couldn't believe he'd just done that. Got up and left.

Grabbing her coat, she took off in pursuit, hearing Walrus say before the door closed behind her, "He's so cooked."

That wasn't the half of it, Karen thought, as she nearly clipped a car on her way out after the quickly disappearing pickup. She thought about running the sirens but, as he'd proven already, Marek was used to having cops on his tail—and ignoring them.

Moments later, Karen pulled up behind the parked Silverado. She'd had to stop for a red light or she'd have been right on his bumper. She got out of the Suburban and stalked out onto the playground. She found a tear-streaked Becca sitting on the steps of the school with a young and harried-looking teacher. One of the year-and-out variety, she thought.

Marek wasn't in sight.

"What happened?"

To her surprise, Becca stuck her tongue out at her. Karen saw red. The rough, raised, ugly wound of a playground prank.

"One of the older boys taunted Becca into licking the flagpole," the teacher babbled. "Before I could get to them, she pulled her tongue off, it started bleeding, and her father came up and he took Jimmy into the school and said he'd take care of it but I'm afraid— he looked pretty mad and he's so—so *big* but I didn't want to leave Becca alone—and I should tell the principal or something but I—"

The woman, Karen thought, had picked the right age group to teach; she had all the narrative instincts of a kindergartner.

"I'll take care of it," Karen said, trying to remember if Marek had had a belt on. Yes, she thought he had, to keep his baggy jeans on.

She raced down the lunch-vacated halls to hear Marek's voice rumble out of a classroom, "I'll show you."

Marek let go of the boy's arm. The kid looked up at him, fear in his eyes, a piggish look to his fair, round face beneath the fine blonde hair.

The boy blurted, "My dad says you were a cop in Mexico and that's why you're siding with Mexicans."

Marek lifted one hand off his belt. "Do you know what this is, Jimmy?"

The boy followed Marek's finger and said, "A map of the United States."

Of course. You big dummy. "You learn the capitols yet?"

The blonde head shook. Jimmy was only seven or eight at most, Marek reminded himself. "Do you know how many states there are?"

"Lots."

"Fifty."

"I can count to fifty," the boy declared. "I can count to a million."

"Please don't. Do you know where Mexico is on that map?"

After a moment, Jimmy stabbed it with one stubby fingernail etched with dirt.

"Looks like you know your stuff. Show me *New* Mexico."

Hands slid into the back pockets of the miniature Levi's. "It's not on the map."

Marek pointed to the yellow-colored state between Arizona and Texas. "What's that say?"

The boy's lips moved then shut tight.

"New Mexico is one of the fifty states," Marek told him. "Became a territory in 1850 but was settled long before then by the Spanish. Do you know when South Dakota became a territory?"

"Like a hundred years before then?"

Stupid, Marek thought, to forget the lawyer's mantra: don't ask a question you don't already know the answer to.

"The Dakota Territory was established in 1861," the voice of his salvation intoned. "It was divided into north and south and entered the union in 1889."

Karen stood in the doorway of the classroom, her cheekbones red-tinged and not, he thought, with cold. Not salvation after all. Her voice, however, had been calm and factual, no doubt in deference to the child.

Marek turned back to Jimmy, his shield from that temper. "Becca's granddad's family came over to the New World in 1600. I don't know when your people came over—"

"He's a Forsgren," Karen supplied. "It was in the 1870s."

Marek didn't take his eyes off the boy. "Point is, you're the newcomer, not Becca."

The sheriff reached down and put a hand on the boy's shoulder. "Becca's family to you, Jimmy. You're cousins. So protect her, don't pick on her, okay?"

He looked baffled. "She can't be my cousin."

"You know I'm your cousin, right?" When she got a slow nod, Karen went on. "Well, Detective Okerlund here is my uncle; we both have Forsgren blood. Since Becca's his daughter, she's your cousin too." When that didn't appear to make a dent, she said, "I don't care if someone did that tongue-on-the-flagpole thing to you once, Jimmy. It isn't funny to hurt people, family or not. Got that?"

The lower lip, full and red, pooched out in the fair face. "My dad says you're not gonna last as sheriff."

Marek coughed and Karen ignored him. "Jimmy, if you don't get out there and apologize to Becca and her teacher for what you did, I'll talk to your dad."

Jimmy Forsgren's lip trembled and he stalked out.

Marek asked, "Would that be Jerry Forsgren's kid?"

"Recognized the pug-nosed stubbornness in that face, did you? Yes, he's Jerry's, but I won't tattle on him." Her gaze dipped to his belt. "Jerry probably would belt him, not for what he did, but for getting caught doing it. Jerry always was a bit of a bigot—and chauvinist."

Marek waited to get walloped.

"Marek, you have to know, I came after you to fire you."

That jerked his hands into fists. "It's Becca's first day. I promised her I'd be here after school to get her. At noon sharp."

"You know, I kind of figured that out myself, no thanks to you, but leaving the incident meeting like that was inexcusable."

"You wouldn't *let* me tell you."

She blew out the red from her cheeks. "I thought you were objecting to my orders."

That too, Marek thought. He needed to talk to Dahl; somehow Karen didn't seem to understand what he'd signed up for. "Becca needs me."

"You don't clock out on a homicide. Time's critical. If you solve it this week, I'll see if Dahl will let you take next week off." Now she got in his face—or as close as she could come. "You should've let me know when I set up the meeting this morning that Becca needed to be picked up. I could have called Dad to get her. He's safe to drive now."

"I promised I'd be here for her."

"Talk about pug-nosed stubborn." She pointed out the door, just as she had with Jimmy. "Go calm your daughter down then take her to my dad. I'll call him to expect her. Then I want you in Sioux Falls."

Her voice cooled when he didn't move. "Take it or leave it, Marek."

CHAPTER 19

AREK PASSED A POPULATION SIGN. If he'd read it right, Sioux Falls—always the biggest city in a state well short of a million—had gained tens of thousands of residents in his absence. Where there'd once been miles of corn and soybeans, cookie-cutter homes and condos now sprang up out of the upturned earth.

But he still found his way easily enough to the hospital complex where his mother had died, shunted into a dark corner room, denied her last wish to die in the summer light. After all these years, it still burned that the staff had ignored his pleas to move her.

In the forensic pathology unit, he discovered Dr. Oscar M. White writing up a report using the two-finger method but with great rapidity. Now he understood Karen's amusement. Dr. White was black. That wasn't something you saw every day in the Great White North.

Marek knocked on the doorjamb of the cramped office. His chafed knuckles protested.

"Go away, Detmeyer, and bother someone else for your monthly stats," the pathologist said. "I have to get this report out before those country yahoos come lynch me."

Rubbing at his knuckles, Marek contemplated the bowtie. No scrubs for this man, though a labcoat hung on an old-fashioned coatrack. "Lynching's not usually a Scandinavian MO."

Dr. White swung around and rose to his feet. "What did they do, feed you on raw meat and tubers?" Below the neatly trimmed beard, the pathologist gripped his throat with one hand. The other he held out. "You must be Detective Marek Okerlund."

Marek shook the hand, gently, feeling the bones. "Must I?"

"If you're Sheriff Mehaffey, I'll eat my labcoat." The throat-throttling hand fell to tug at the bowtie. "Mehaffey being an Irish yahoo, I wasn't sure my neck was safe."

Given the accent or lack thereof, Dr. White had never been south of the Mason-Dixon line.

"That would be Sheriff Karen Okerlund Mehaffey." Not for the first time, Marek wondered about Karen's husband. He couldn't see her keeping the name if she was divorced. Nor would she keep the ring on her finger. So was he dead or, like the missing Deputy Two Fingers, in the service? "My half-brother Arne's daughter."

Somehow that sounded better, more professional, than niece.

"Shocking amount of inbreeding," the pathologist said. "Now that you mention it, I do believe I met her once, but I didn't catch her married name or realize she'd taken over her father's job. She came to thank me for keeping Arne Okerlund out of my clutches—the morgue, I mean."

At the quizzical look on Marek's face, he continued, "You don't know? Sheriff Okerlund had his stroke right here, in this office. Fortunately, I managed to remember that this is, after all, a hospital, with people who actually know how to treat not-yet-dead people."

He tsked at Marek's silence. "You're more like your half-brother than you look. No chitchat. You know, I would have had that report done in another minute and faxed it to you. You wasted a trip."

Marek shook his head. "I'm here to see a witness of interest."

"Are there witnesses of disinterest?" the man asked as he settled back in his chair.

"Far too many." Marek sunk his weight against the door. There were no chairs for visitors. "What did you find?"

"Forensically speaking, it's an interesting case, what with the different injuries occurring at different times. First the burn to the back. A spray, perhaps hot water, with some chemical residue...ah, I see I am right. Good, good. Then the head trauma. Probably knocked him out but wasn't in itself the cause of death. Not even close."

"Someone hit him from behind?" Marek asked.

"Looks to me more like a fall against a flat surface—floor or table perhaps—but I can't rule out a blow, though the weapon would have to be flat like a pancake griddle. However, given the bruising pattern, I vote for the floor."

According to Darcie, her stepfather claimed to have been hit over the head. But Marek needed the punch line. "Dale Hansen froze to death?"

"In layman's terms, yes." The pathologist pulled again on his bowtie. "None of his injuries were life-threatening."

Marek nodded and turned to go. Homicide. No big surprise there.

"Whoa, there." Dr. White swiveled back to his computer and attacked the keys. The printer revved up, vibrated on top of a desk-height metal file cabinet, then spat out a report. "There you go, Detective. I think you might want to look at that last page."

Marek hadn't the energy to focus on words. "Spell it out for me."

"You didn't let me get to the hypergraphic."

"The what?"

"The obsessive-compulsive writer. Your killer must not have had anything else handy to write on." White flashed unexpectedly in the dark face. "I saw that twitch, Detective. So nice to know you have a sense of humor. Your brother's a different kettle of fish."

The pathologist's smile vanished. "I don't know if the message was racially motivated, that's your job, but I'll say that it's no less chilling—and no, that's not a pun—for being aimed at whites. Hate's hate." He paused. "But to get to the forensics, I'd say someone carved those words in Dale Hansen's arm when he was out, not after he was chained to the fence."

He'd already figured that one out. "No defensive wounds."

Not a big leap, yet people always seemed surprised he could make such connections. It wasn't the halfwit thing, he thought, but the inverse body-mass thing: the larger the body, the smaller the brain.

Marek had one last question. "Can you give me an estimated time of death?"

"Regretfully, I cannot. Too many variables."

Marek tucked the report under his arm and started to turn.

"Oh, and I'll fax a copy to Agent Larson, as requested."

That turned Marek all the way around again. "What agent? FBI?"

Dr. White laughed. "Hardly. State. DCI." Then he blinked up at Marek. "I assumed that you were working with him on this case."

Had Karen called in DCI to assist with the investigation—or was she preparing them to take his place? "Who made the request?"

The pathologist speared a piece of paper on the desktop and slid it nearer to the lamp. "The message just says to copy Larson and gives his fax number. He's on the up and up, if you're wondering. I've dealt with him before."

And he didn't look too pleased about it. That made two of them. "Then I suppose you'd better send Agent Larson a copy."

He headed down the hall.

Dr. White yelled after him, "Next time send the Irish. At least they know how to talk!"

Minutes later, Marek walked into another cramped room, where he found Chacón soused on morphine. The right hand lay, or rather didn't, on the coverlet, the stump covered with white bandages, the edges frayed with red.

"Mr. Chacón?"

Dark, doped eyes stared up at him.

"I want to talk to you about what happened Friday night." When that didn't get a response, he repeated it in Spanish.

Now pain showed, its echo more than its reality. "Grinder."

"Has an OSHA inspector been to see you?" Marek asked. "Workers comp? Anybody?"

"Mr. Sanchez, he come. Say he will talk to inspector."

But the dark eyes didn't hold hope.

"Where are you from, Mr. Chacón?"

"Ciudad Juárez."

A genuine Mexican, then, from one of the most crime-ridden places on the continent. Drug cartels, feuding for the lucrative US drug market, had spiked the murder rate high, brutal, and endless, with the innocent often killed in the crossfire.

A nurse came in, checked Chacón's vitals, then went to the other side of a curtain, where a voice complained, "You can't stick me with an illegal. My boy had to go to Denver to get a job because *his* like is taking all the jobs here. Stealing, that's what it is—they cut people's hands off, don't they, in some parts of the world, for taking what's not theirs."

Ignoring the nurse's murmured assurances that she'd look into the matter, Marek asked Chacón whether he'd seen anyone confront Dale Hansen.

"A white. Not know him."

When Marek tried to pull out more details in Spanish, he got more vagueness: maybe as tall as Dale, maybe dark hair, maybe light eyes.

That fit Bryan McNulty.

"He took hose out of my hand," Chacón said, returning to English. "Hansen, he turn his back. This man, he use hose on him. I think it is this, what this man do, it give me..." The one brown hand fisted. "*Coraje.*"

Courage. "For what?"

"After the man leave, I take Hansen to chain."

For a moment, Marek's brain froze. Was this his killer after all? Then his brain sputtered back to life. It didn't make any sense. "You chained him out on the interstate and *then* got messed up in the grinder?"

"No, no." The blood-tinged stump swung up in tandem with its dark and whole brother. "Take to chain on hider. Metal, it not strong. Danger."

Marek rubbed at his tired eyes. "The links of the chain were weak?"

"Yes, links. Hansen laugh at me. Swing on chain." His fisted hand rose then snapped down.

So the chain had broken. That would fit with Dr. White's opinion, that the head wound had come from a fall to the floor. "What happened then?"

"We think, Hansen, he dead, and we run."

And they'd left him on the floor. "Who is we?"

"*No sé.*"

Oh, he knew, but Marek could see it'd be a waste of time to press him. "Mr. Chacón, if you left the plant after Hansen fell to the floor, how was your hand hurt in the grinder?"

"I go back," he said with a regretful dignity. "Not right to leave if not dead. I do not want on my heart, that he die."

Dale Hansen had had no such squeamishness about Julio Chacón. "How long?"

"Half hour. More." Chacón shrugged. "He is mad everyone gone. When I start to clean grinder...Hansen stop but too late. He say no one care I hurt. I am...what is word? Disposable."

How anyone could see that mangled hand and not do something...but this was, Marek reminded himself, a plant that sold mangled meat as a product. "What happened to the chain?"

"Think he take. No proof, see?" His lips trembled. "When I run, I see he turn hose on grinder."

So Dale Hansen had tried to remove any evidence of the injury. But why hadn't he locked and tagged the grinder? Maybe that's what he'd forgotten to do back at the plant. But what of the chain on the hider, where had it gone? If it was the one around Dale's wrist, it was only a small link of it, so where was the rest?

None of those questions, he knew, could be answered by the man who'd sunk back into drug-induced indifference. "Dale Hansen was alone and alive when you left him?"

The dark eyes rose and held. "Yes."

A snort came from the patient behind the curtain.

"Thank you, Mr. Chacón. I may want to talk to you again." Then in Spanish, Marek said, "You gave a hand to a man who had no heart. Your loss is less than his."

He left the man staring at his stump, turning it to what would have been palm up, as if looking for a life line on his missing hand.

Karen skidded into the sheriff's office. Walrus and Kurt looked up at her.

"Why hasn't maintenance put down salt on the steps?" she asked. "I shouldn't need an ice pick to get in and out of here."

Kurt got up and went to a small closet.

"I didn't mean for you to do it," she told him, belatedly remembering the county's meager resources.

But Kurt went out with his bucket and shovel like a kid going off to the beach. A moment later, she heard an oath, a thud, and a crash. "Great, we've got a lawsuit on our hands." When Marek limped into the building with Kurt in his wake, she said, "Oh, it's just you."

He glanced up from his foot. "Disposable?"

Maybe he was thinking of his grandfather, Lenny Marek, who'd been killed on those steps. A jump from the clock tower would do that. "You all right?"

Marek tested his foot then nodded. "Tried to avoid Kurt and tripped over my own feet. Not the first time. Won't be the last."

Clumsy had been another tag on the young Marek Okerlund. For all his size, he hadn't been any kind of standout in the sports arena, at least not when he'd lived in Reunion. "Get your weight off that foot and let's get an update."

Marek limped over to his desk and sat on top of it. Kurt put away the bucket and shovel then sat down behind his desk. Walrus slumped back in his own chair and put his feet up.

Karen turned to her senior deputy. "Kurt?"

He folded his hands over a neat stack of jury summonses. "The phone records show Sig Halvorsen was on the land line pretty much nonstop that night. The longest break was twenty-two minutes."

Karen let out the breath she hadn't known she'd been holding. "That should let him out."

"Assuming that he was the caller," Marek said, perhaps the only one who dared. "Still, it wouldn't take him long to go out to the interstate."

Was he serious—or just yanking her chain? "Not if he had to go track down Dale first."

"Maybe Dale came to see Sig. Or Sig saw him wandering in the street." Marek shrugged. "We don't know what happened to him after Darcie kicked him out of the Hummer."

Kurt said, "Timing would be awful tight."

When Marek stared down at his feet, Karen wondered if he'd really done damage to himself.

But, no, he appeared to be thinking, not wincing. "Real question is, why kill him? Or, why now?"

Not one to be left out, Walrus piped up. "Crime of opportunity?"

"I don't like it," Marek said before Karen could, surprising her. "Something else happened—something with the chain from the hider from PBI."

As he filled them in on Julio Chacón, she paced back and forth on the marble floor. Her brain calmed when her body moved: a legacy from her basketball days, perhaps, or just the way she was made. In Sioux Falls, they'd rigged her dispatch station so she could stand instead of sit.

Karen halted in front of Walrus's camouflage boots. "Did you call the crime lab about any fingerprints on the chain?"

"Yep. Seems it got tagged priority. You got pull with DCI, boss?"

"I'd be about dead last in the pecking order," she said, thinking of Agent Larson. "Must have been a slow period for them."

"Whatever it was, they sure worked fast." Walrus stroked down the droops of his moustache. When his hand fell, it revealed a huge grin. "We got ourselves a match."

CHAPTER 20

"**W**E'VE GOT A SUSPECT?" MAREK asked, forgetting his aching foot. He hadn't thought Walter Russell would be the type to keep quiet if he held the winning hand.

"Uh, no," Walrus acceded. "They found Dale's fingerprints on the padlock and the chain around his wrist."

Marek felt the pain return.

"Gee, Walter," the sheriff said, returning to her pacing. "Do you think Dale might've tugged on them, trying to get free?"

"No, what I mean is, Dale got his prints from the *chained* hand on it." Walrus encircled his own wrist with one hand then flopped the captured hand in a vain effort to touch the restraining fingers. "Can't be done."

So, Marek thought, Dale had touched that chain before.

Running with it, Karen said, "If it was from the hider chain and the padlock from the plant, Dale would've handled both, likely the last to hold them, other than the killer." Then she waved it away. "We need something *new*."

"The tow chain also had Dale's prints on it." Walrus plopped his feet down and leaned forward. "But they also found a possible partial match."

Marek watched Karen stop in a holding pattern. "To?"

"Guy named Bruce Wilson. He's got a sheet, mostly burglary with some petty drug possession charges, including marijuana and meth. Bounced around in various seasonal jobs between bouts in lockup—walked beans, detasseled corn, did some road construction and snow removal, that kind of thing. He just couldn't stay clean."

Given no one was chiming in, Marek figured the name wasn't

familiar to any of them. "What's his connection to Hansen?"

"Uh, none, that I know of, and well..." Walrus cleared his throat. "Problem is, he's been locked up in the medium-security prison at Springfield for the past three months. I talked to him myself. He says he never met Dale Hansen. He doesn't have a car either—it was impounded seven months ago—but it did have a tow chain in the trunk."

Marek rotated his ankle. Slowly. Just sore, he thought. "Who was the car sold to?"

Walrus slumped. "Seems it never got sold. A real clunker. It's still sitting on the lot. They asked if we wanted it for evidence."

"Tow chain?" Kurt asked.

"Tow chain included."

Karen picked up her pace again. "I hope you said no."

"Far as I'm concerned," Walrus said with a grin, "you can never have too many lawn ornaments."

"Walter."

"Just kidding, Sheriff. Just kidding." He shrugged off her glare. "Okay, so it wasn't such a big break, but it's more than any of you came up with."

The heels of the sheriff's leather boots slapped on marble. When they stopped, Marek found himself staring at them.

"Who was Chacón working with that night?" Karen asked him.

Marek decided to keep watching the boots: to avoid getting kicked. "Chacón wouldn't cough up names."

"How hard did you try?"

Marek was tired. His foot hurt. He wanted to ask the sheriff if she'd called in DCI. He wanted to go rescue his daughter from Arne Okerlund. He wanted to contact the moving van to see if their life was ever going to catch up with them. Maybe he should tell the driver to head back to Albuquerque. "The only rubber hoses handy were breathing tubes."

"Marek..."

Now he did look up. "Chacón wouldn't give them up and I didn't have any leverage. It's not like I could offer him a green card."

Her boots moved. Away. "So now what?"

Whatever was going on with DCI, the sheriff still seemed to want his input. "So we talk to Thompson again to see if he's found any records on the cleaning crew. Even if he hasn't, we can still check trailer city for those who weren't home before."

"Then let's go."

Karen didn't like the way Marek limped out to his vehicle.

"Maybe you should have that foot looked at," she told him as she moved toward the Suburban.

"It'll walk off," he said, pulling open the door of his Silverado.

She decided not to press him. But if it continued, she would insist. His foot wasn't the only thing wrong, though; she felt something from him that she hadn't before. Distrust? Anger? Affront?

Whatever it was, it had destroyed any bonding they'd done at the café. She supposed he might still be upset about what happened at the school. Or maybe it was sending him off to Sioux Falls to interview Chacón. But he had signed up for a job, not the dole, and if he couldn't take orders from her, where did that leave them?

Maybe, she thought, she'd been too abrupt, too pushy? Her Army career hadn't stressed the touchy feely.

Karen pulled out into the street and waved at someone too bundled up to recognize. Minutes later, she got out in the plant's parking lot, strode down the sidewalk, then skidded on the refrozen ice. Marek caught her arm before she went down.

"Always in a hurry, that's me." She got her feet back under her, decided to get the apology over with before they got to work. "I'm sorry if I'm pushing you too hard on this case, Marek. I get things done, get them off my plate, but this murder just won't go anywhere."

Marek blinked then released her arm. "Murder never goes anywhere. It has no statute of limitations."

But it did have the limitations of its investigators, Karen thought, herself included.

When they walked into the lobby of the plant, they were almost overrun by white-hatted workers. Shift change, she wondered, or end of business? She elbowed her way against the flow and saw Thompson. A man in a yellow hard hat shook a gnarled finger in his face. Unfortunately, she wasn't close enough to hear their conversation.

She'd given PBI the green light to begin work that morning, somewhat reluctantly. But if the plant started up again, it might pull Dale Hansen's killer back in as well.

Once across the room, she tapped Thompson's shoulder. "We

need to talk to you."

He whirled, his face almost as ugly a color as his tie, some shade between brown and purple. "Wait a frigging min—Oh, Sheriff. You aren't going to shut us down again, are you?"

After she shook her head, Thompson spread his hands toward the counter behind him. "You want some coffee? We've got sugar, creamer, and—" He nudged a small white packet. "What's this?"

A white hat said something as he passed by and took it off the counter with him.

Thompson squinted after him then said, "Oh, lite. I figure if you can't have the real thing, what does it matter. I like it black, myself."

Karen doubted she could stand the coffee here black. Nor did she want *faux* cream. "I'll take sugar."

She slurped sweetness as the last of the stragglers moved out, except for the man in the yellow hat, who Marek now greeted with a nod, saying, "Yarnik."

So this was Dale Hansen's replacement. He looked brighter in brain but dimmer in disposition underneath that cheery yellow hat.

"We're looking for the cleaning crew," Karen told them.

"So am I," Yarnik said.

Marek lifted his lips from his coffee cup long enough to say, "All we need are the names."

"I tell you, we don't have them." Thompson put down his own coffee. "We used to employ a nationwide cleaning service, the same we use at our other plants, but Dale found some folks here willing to do it for lower wages. I let him worry about it."

"Off the books?" Karen asked.

"We just report it as an expense to the IRS. It's up to the worker to report the income." Thompson yanked at his tie. "Look, Dale's wife said he didn't keep any records at home. As far as I can tell, these guys and their families just broke their leases and vamoosed. But it seems all of them were Mexicans."

"Yep," Yarnik agreed. "From Guatemala mostly."

"Then they weren't Mexicans," Marek said and got a blank stare from Yarnik.

Whatever they were, Karen thought, if they'd fled, then the most obvious reason was to save themselves from prosecution—or deportation. Or both. Had they discovered what had happened to Chacón, despite the latter's disavowals? Had it been a group effort?

Marek ditched his empty coffee cup. He'd taken it black. She wondered if the caffeine would affect him—not much else seemed to, but grief could mask reactions.

He asked the manager, "Has anybody from OSHA been in contact with you today about Julio Chacón?"

Thompson smoothed down his tie. "And he would be?"

While Marek explained about the grinder and the mangled hand, Karen watched concern rise but not, she thought, much for the man. The machine, more like.

"You were there," she reminded Thompson. "When we discovered that the grinder wasn't locked and tagged."

"That doesn't mean it caused an injury." The manager fiddled with his tie again. "Could be, Dale was working on the grinder."

Yarnik spat on the concrete. "Needs regular maintenance."

Thompson glanced away from the stain. "All I'm saying is, I've seen it before. Get an injury hotdogging around on your own and try to blame the company."

Though Marek didn't move, Karen grabbed his arm with her free hand. He vibrated. And not, she decided, from excess caffeine. "That's why we have inspectors, Mr. Thompson. Detective Okerlund has already called OSHA and sent them photos of the lockout/tagout violation."

Though Thompson blanched, Yarnik didn't even blink. "We gotta get more men for cleanup," he told Thompson. "If we don't, we'll have the USDA after us and headquarters too, if it turns up *E. coli*."

Karen put down her half-drunk coffee on the counter.

Thompson's voice rose to match the whir of a machine somewhere in the bowels of the plant. "Dale recruited the cleaners, he paid them, he knew them, not me. You wanted this job, Yarnik. *You* find men."

The new operations manager swore, spat, then stalked off.

"Sorry, things got a bit dicey today," Thompson said. "It wasn't just the cleaning crew who went missing. We were short-staffed on the kill floor too."

Karen dropped her hand from Marek's arm. "And you didn't think to tell us?"

"Figured you already knew. Besides, I've got other things to worry about than Dale Hansen's killer. I'd like to kill him myself after today."

Marek walked gingerly up the ice-covered steps of the rickety porch. Karen had insisted on going through trailer city again, looking for the cleaning crew.

He knocked on the door and felt it bow under his fist. Flimsy. They must freeze in these things in subzero weather. He turned to Karen when no one answered. "Must be another that took off."

They'd noted down the empty ones so she could get a warrant to search them. But she didn't move from where she stood on the ground below. "He's here."

Marek looked around, caught the twitch of a curtain, if it could be called that, a sheet hung over the window.

Before he could knock again, the door opened and a man stepped out. He wore a faded tan workshirt and jeans that looked like they'd become skin over bone. This man would keep up his count, Marek thought, through sheer grit.

"Can we come in, sir?" Karen asked from below. "We'd like to talk to you."

The man didn't budge from the doorway, his face shadowed in the dimming light. "I do nothing."

The words were slow, the accent marked.

Karen advanced up the rickety steps. "Then it shouldn't be a problem for us to sit and talk."

Marek repeated that in Spanish. The man hesitated then opened the door for them. He gave his name as Emilio Jaramillo. Once they'd gone in, he shut the door and stood there in front of it, his eyes falling to the shag carpet at his feet.

The wail of wind through the old trailer sounded human in the small space. Although Marek had seen some pretty poor places in trailer city, he thought this one outdid the others. The shabby interior sported only one ornament: a pewter crucifix.

It seemed sucked empty of what...hope? Something lost. Something vital. Then as he turned back, he saw it. The only color, so much of it, concentrated, it drew the eye like a mirage on the dingy sand-colored room.

He moved toward the framed photo of a young girl wearing a dress woven of bright-colored chevrons; she cupped a shucked ear of yellow corn in her small hands.

Maize, they'd call it.

Behind her squatted a man in an elaborately embroidered red jacket. The man he recognized as Jaramillo. The girl with the harvest in her hands...had he lost her? Who had taken the photo, his wife? What had brought the man from that lush and vibrant world to this one, a bleak place in a barren field still stubbled with the lifeless stalks of corn?

Marek thought of the photos on Dr. Ahmed's and Bryan McNulty's walls. So many losses. He saw them now wherever he went.

Karen didn't appear to be in a hurry to talk for once. So Marek turned from the photo to the man. "You work at the plant, Mr. Jaramillo?"

After a moment, perhaps to translate that in his head, the man simply nodded.

"The night of the storm," Marek prompted. "Were you one of the cleaning crew? No? Do you know who was?"

Jaramillo shook his head.

Marek asked, "Where were you that night?"

The muffled wail took Marek by surprise. How could Jaramillo make a sound like that—filled with rage, despair, and plea—without so much as twitching?

Even as his brain registered that the source came from behind him, he whirled, reached for his gun...which he'd given up with his badge.

But Karen had drawn her weapon and moved to the side of the trailer from where the chilling wail emanated. She opened the door.

Tied hand and foot to a narrow bed, a woman screamed at them behind a white cloth gag.

CHAPTER 21

A SMALL MERCY, KAREN THOUGHT, that the woman wore a thick flannel nightgown reaching down to her bony ankles. If she'd been raped, it wasn't readily apparent. Her face, pocked and scarred, indicated either bad diet or ill health. Or both. Brittle hair the color of a field mouse streaked across the sweat-wrinkled pillow.

And in those red-rimmed eyes a fear so deep, or a need so deep, it obliterated all else.

Karen placed a hand on one thin, trembling arm. "We're from the sheriff's office. The police. I'll get you untied in just a minute. You're safe now, do you understand? Marek? Reassure her."

Spanish flowed in gentle swells of sound that Karen couldn't find the beginning or ending of, until it stopped.

Slowly, the eyelids came down and tears leaked out. Without looking back, Karen told Marek, "Restrain Jaramillo then go get the evidence kit."

When he returned, she took pictures of the bound woman. Marek kept tabs on Jaramillo, sitting dejected on a kitchen chair.

Karen removed the gag. "What's your name?"

The woman's tongue circumscribed her mouth, showing yellowed teeth, before she answered, her voice husky. "Blanca Jaramillo."

The man's wife, Karen decided, and got to work on the cloth bonds. The skin underneath had rubbed red but wasn't yet raw. "How long have you been like this, Blanca?"

"Way too long," she said, in far better English than her husband. "I have to go."

Karen didn't think she meant elsewhere, though that too, after the first pressing need. She unknotted the last of the bonds, helped the woman up, and then steered her into the small closet of a bathroom, where she gave her privacy.

What kind of man tied down his wife—and why? To keep her from fleeing him? Karen kept her eyes on the small door.

The rush of the toilet saturated the silence.

The bathroom door opened. The woman had washed her face, tried to brush the brittle hair back into contact with her head, with indifferent success, and asked with a kind of desperation, "You let me go?"

Karen wasn't quite sure what she meant. "Yes, I let you go."

"Let me go *now*?"

Not a native speaker after all. "Oh, yes, of course, you're free. But we'll need you to come to the sheriff's office to give a statement and document any injuries."

The white-knuckled hand still gripped the bathroom door. "No, no, I am not hurt."

Karen knew, in her head, that women did this, but she couldn't comprehend it. She stepped between Blanca and her husband. "Do you want him to go to jail, Blanca? Do you want us to lock him up, away from you, so he can never hurt you again?"

From behind them, Jaramillo said, "Blanca."

The small jaw hardened under reddened skin at the plea—or demand. The petite woman might have once been pretty, Karen thought. No more.

The woman stepped up—and burrowed into Karen's shoulder.

"He's crazy," she said in a muffled voice. "*Loco.* Lock him up."

Minutes later, Karen strode out to the parking lot, hit a patch of ice with all the acceleration of her anger, and this time went down hard.

A big hand scooped down to help her up. "You all right?"

"Yeah, just peachy." She brushed off her pants, gave herself a moment to cool, then blinked. "What are you doing?"

Marek paused in the midst of undoing Jaramillo's handcuffs. "You didn't see his face."

Karen shook her head, sure she'd misheard, that he was only adjusting the handcuffs, but no, he'd taken them off. "*His* face?

What about *hers*?"

"That too."

Jaramillo was now free, though he didn't move.

Karen turned on Marek. "You think you can cool him off then send him back to abuse that poor woman?" Blanca had told them she'd come to the office later to give her statement but hadn't sounded convincing. "Are you out of your frigging mind, Marek?"

"You didn't see—" he began again.

"What's not to see?" The pain of scraped knuckles and burgeoning bruises dissolved in incredulity. "That woman was bound, hand and foot, and you think it's what, just a bit of playful S&M? You think the fear I saw in her eyes was a con job?" Before he could speak, she went on, "Have you forgotten what it is, to be abused?"

That rocked him back. Did he think she didn't know? Hadn't she heard him scream, over the endless thwacks of leather on flesh that had carried across the street: *I'll try harder.* He'd screamed it, over and over. He'd been what, about ten, on report card day.

Horrified, Karen had called her grandfather, who'd rushed home and charged into 21 Okerlund Road. All she'd heard after that had been sobs, then quiet. Until then, Karen been neutral on Janina Marek Okerlund; afterwards, she'd respected the woman for her mind, but not her heart, if she had one. Did her son also lack one?

"My mother only lost it once; she never forgave herself for it." He didn't look pleased that Karen knew, though the widening of his eyes told her that he'd figured out how she'd known—and who she'd called to stop it. "Karen, you have to lis—" His cell phone rang to the tune of the *William Tell Overture.* Lone ranger, indeed. He snatched it out, turned, and after a pause, said, "I'll be there."

"You're not taking off on me," she began, then saw his face as he turned back. "What is it?"

"That was your dad."

Her dad had called Marek? Had the world gone mad?

"Becca's sick. I have to go."

Jaramillo, who stood forgotten, asked, "Go?"

Karen grabbed the man's arm. "You're not going anywhere, Mr. Jaramillo." She quickly got her own cuffs on him. "Marek..."

But he'd already gone to the Silverado. She stuffed Jaramillo in the back of the Suburban, got in the driver's seat, then pulled out her cell phone. "Dad? What's going on with Becca?"

"Growing up," he said, his voice shaky. "All over the place."

"Growing up? Oh, throwing up. Does she have a fever?"

"Don't know. Don't know what to do. Hannah took care of you."

Karen eased into dispatcher mode. "Dad, kids get sick. I tossed my cookies in the squad car once, remember? Fine and dandy afterwards. You sprayed me down along with the car."

A pause, then, "Smelled for weeks. Got a new vehicle. Passed off the old one to Kurt. Took a spin with him later and the Pinesol was so strong it nearly gagged me."

She told her father that Marek was on his way. Then she gunned the Suburban out of the parking lot and headed for the office.

What with Marek AWOL, she'd take this case herself. She couldn't believe she'd misjudged her new detective so badly. Had she thought him soft? Anything but. The small tendril of kinship died.

Once Karen got Jaramillo in the interview room, he wouldn't talk to her, wouldn't even look at her. Fine. She'd get his papers from Thompson and see if they checked out. If he was illegal, she'd get him deported, away from his wife. That way it wouldn't matter if Blanca Jaramillo gave a statement or showed the extent of her injuries.

If he was legal but not naturalized, a conviction should still get him deported. If Blanca was herself illegal...well, that might explain her reluctance to come to the sheriff's office.

After Karen booked Jaramillo into the jail, she conferred with Bork on a drunk and disorderly then went out and sat in the Suburban. She needed to talk to someone about Marek. Someone outside the small circle of law in Eda County.

Perhaps Laura...no, too awkward, too soon. Nor would it be right, given Laura's husband was in the mix.

After a moment's hesitation, she made a call then headed for Sioux Falls.

She'd get a hearing, at least, and maybe that's all she needed.

Back in the trailer, still stunned at her own temerity, Blanca Jaramillo slipped on her coat. It had been her first gift in this strange land: a gray wool herringbone. She'd wondered at the generosity of these people, before she'd learned of discarded fashions.

Before she'd learned what cold was, how deep it went, how long it stayed, in the barren white lands. So different from Guatemala. Her hands shook against the zigzags of the fabric, trying to thread the buttons, to warm herself, as she stepped outside.

The dull pain that pulsed in her head kept rhythm with the crunch of her moon boots on the dirt-worn track between the trailers. Eyes on the ground, she didn't see the man, until he grabbed her arm.

"What have you done?" he demanded.

"Leave me alone." When the hand didn't let go, she took what little courage she had left. "Or the sheriff comes to get you too."

Those clunky, skewed glasses slid down the thin nose. He released her. But he didn't move out of her way. "Dale Hansen, he is dead."

"No!" She sank to her knees in the snow, hands digging into the dirty white of it, then spreading out to plea. "You lie to me."

The pitiless answer: "The white is dead."

She scrambled to her feet and ran to the plant. He lied. He had to lie.

But Dr. Ahmed was right: there was no white.

After Marek carried Becca back home, he checked her out. No fever, no flushed face, no lethargy, nothing. Though her tongue still looked like a battleground. Given the way she'd strangled him when he'd arrived home, he suspected nerves.

Or too much Arne Okerlund.

Satisfied she was okay, he started a fire. When he rose, his daughter tugged at him, her Nintendo clutched in one hand. "Bored already? The moving van should be here tomorrow afternoon. You'll have all your stuff." He poked her midriff. "Be able to wear something else besides that old sweater."

Funny, she'd managed to throw up without getting anything on it. Its bright colors reminded him again of the picture on Jaramillo's wall. Such beauty, such vitality, such peace and contentedness, could all be taken at any time.

When he heard a growl from the little tummy, he asked, "You hungry now?"

When she nodded, he looked around the still-empty place and wondered if he had the energy to get them bundled into the Silverado to hunt something up. Then he remembered the tin he'd left in the Silverado. "You want pie?" Her pale eyes rose to meet his with a quirk over them that he recognized: in the mirror.

"Apple," he answered. "Think your tongue can handle it?"

She stuffed the Nintendo back in her pocket. He took that as a yes. They ate off the tin with their plastic utensils, in silence, watching the fire he'd stoked.

What was going on her head, he wondered, after this first momentous day of school? She'd had to do it twice: start kindergarten in Albuquerque and now here. At least the first time, she wasn't the new kid. Today she had been. Did that damage a kid?

Becca banged her plastic spoon against the tin. "What?" She pointed at his barely touched slice. "You want it?"

She shook her head, pointed at the slice again, pointed at his mouth. "Looking after your old man? Okay, okay, I'll finish my supper. See? I'm eating."

After he finished up and got her to bed, he let himself think of going back to Albuquerque. Not only for her but himself. He couldn't work with someone who wouldn't listen to him. He didn't talk that much. When he did, people usually listened, if only for the novelty of hearing him speak.

Truth was, as soon as he learned who the sheriff was, he should've called it off.

Why had he come back here anyway? To this little dying dot of a town in one of the least appreciated states in the union.

Except for perhaps North Dakota.

Somewhere he'd picked up that North Dakota had thought about dropping the north from its name, to warm its public image, but he doubted it could be done. Hell, it was probably best now that *Fargo* had been engrained on the public mind. True, South Dakota had *Deadwood* and *Dances with Wolves* but that was West River and the past. Who did a movie about corn and soybeans and the towns that grew between them or the tiny Indian reservations that weren't Pine Ridge or Rosebud?

What was there, really, to stick around for?

Everything here was the past. He hadn't expected open arms. No, that had never been a possibility. But what he hadn't known to be wary of, and he should have been, was being found wanting. He'd forgotten how that felt. How Dale Hansen must have felt, after losing his farm, being one of the dispossessed.

Ever since Marek and Manny had made their first homicide, a

cold case no one had expected them to solve, he'd taken in, basked in, the startled gleams of respect from the older detectives. In time, M&M had gone from a rag to a tag and, more often than not, a collar. They'd had the best conviction rate in the department.

When Manny had started feeling him out a year ago about breaking up the candy store, about riding a desk, he'd resisted. Why did people want to ruin a good thing? Then Marek's father-in-law, Joseph De Baca, had been given six weeks to live. That had been the beginning of a letting go that had ended in a brutal taking.

Why was he here?

If he had to get away, he could have gone to a dozen other cities, could have stayed in the southwest, or if he wanted something completely different, one of the coasts. Instead, a snatch of sneering laughter over a job ad in the bullpen had caught his ear, an ear desperate for distraction, and heard: Reunion.

Fate? If it was, fate was a killer. How did you hunt it; how did you make it pay?

Sometimes he didn't want to take another breath. But he'd been cast as Sisyphus and had to keep heaving the stone up the hill for a bit of breathing space before it came tumbling down on him again. His mother used to say teaching knuckleheads was the same way—he'd never asked if she meant him specifically.

Sisyphus. If he ever said such a thing in front of anybody, the men in the little white coats would be sent for him. White. Coats. Hats. He frowned. Something...white hats. What was it? He needed Manny. He needed his partner's mouth to give voice to what his brain wasn't saying.

Maybe he just wasn't the man for the job.

But as he watched the flames, another thought took spark. He'd never flown solo before. Maybe, he finally admitted to himself, he wasn't even up to the job *period*.

Karen's footsteps echoed off the long institutional corridors. The building was old and, from the outside, imposing. At one time, the staff had known her and let her pass without the usual rigmarole. It had been easier as the years went on, to find excuses not to go; there'd been plenty of turnover in staff since she'd last been here.

"Visiting hours end in forty-five minutes." The man at the final door to her destination noted her official togs. "No exceptions.

Doesn't matter if you've got a badge."

Karen just nodded. He opened the door to the wing for her.

She took a breath, walked through, heard the door shut behind her.

She stood on the safe side of the bars: safe from the man who didn't turn to look at her. He wouldn't, no matter what she said. She'd accepted that, finally. She ignored the clanks and wheezes, an argument down one hall, someone crying down another.

"You know you always said nothing ever happened in Reunion?" she asked him.

Not a flicker of response, but she couldn't help herself from looking for one. "Well, guess what, a lot's happened."

By the time she finished, he hadn't even twitched, his pasty, sun-deprived face stubbornly turned up toward the ceiling.

Well, what did she expect?

Patrick Mehaffey was serving a life sentence, a living death in this small cell, and she'd put him here.

Marek told himself to stop staring at the cell phone cupped in his hand as if it were the oracle that held his fate. Flicking it open, he dialed.

When he heard it pick up, he said, "Manny, have you been shouldering me all these years?"

"Hell of a load, too," his ex-partner said without hesitation.

"I mean it."

A pause. "You've got one whacked out brain."

Marek rubbed at the head that contained that brain. "I know that."

So too did all of Eda County, apparently, and its sheriff in particular.

"Makes weird connections, you know?"

Marek's hand fisted around the arm of the rocker. "I know I've got dyslexia, what I want to know is if—"

"I'd be jamming away on some lead, thinking I'm the man, and you'd just shake your head at me. Drove me nuts. Because nine times out of ten, you were right."

Marek stared into the dying fire. "Was I?"

"You think I pulled you into homicide with me just for brawn?" A muffled ting sounded against tin. Likely Marek had interrupted the man's one avocation. Painting. "The desk was my pension plan, not yours. You were supposed to stay in the field and make me look good. I've still got a reserve badge with your name on it. I'll make it official anytime you want."

Marek's hand relaxed on the phone. "Yeah?"

And with the ease of a veteran interrogator, Manny got it all out of him, the doubts, the case, the dicy familial relationships. Before he signed off, Manny told him, "If those *gringos* up there don't know what they've got, they don't deserve to keep you. Come home."

What was home, Marek wondered, when the people who'd made it one were gone? He stuffed the cell phone back in his pocket and stared at his sleeping daughter. He wished she would say the word. Stay. Go. But he was going to have to be her interpreter.

Unless, of course, he got himself fired.

Karen made her decision on the way back to Reunion. Venting to Patrick had cleared the air—and her head. It was simple, really. Marek hadn't seen spousal abuse as a crime. That made him something she couldn't afford: trouble.

A Marek after all, just like her father had warned her.

It wouldn't be the first time she'd fired somebody. But that didn't make it any easier.

She turned down Okerlund Road and saw the lights still on at Marek's. Maybe she should just go now and tell him. Get it over with. But when she parked, she didn't move from her seat, thinking of the little girl with the Okerlund eyes.

Karen couldn't stop herself from wondering—had the daughter she'd given up had those same eyes? She forced herself to accept once again that she'd never know, had lost the right to know, and put it away, far away, in a time-frozen locket of her heart. She had to deal with the now, with Marek. Her job demanded justice, not kinship.

Then she remembered she didn't have the authority to fire Marek; she'd need Harold Dahl's approval first.

Happy to delegate that task until tomorrow, she entered her own darkened house just as the phone rang. She snatched it up before her father could awaken. And she was given her most compelling reason yet to get her new detective—and his daughter—out of the county.

When she knocked on Marek's door moments later, he pulled it open immediately. He looked relieved to see her, which didn't make sense, given the way they'd left things at trailer city. Had it been so inconsequential to him?

"Come in."

She went in, noted that his things still hadn't arrived. Just as well. "I got a call."

He blinked at her like he'd expected her to say something quite different. "Can't it wait until tomorrow?"

Karen glanced over at the sleeping child, bundled into a blanket on the old mattress in front of the fire. "No, it can't. Marek...someone just called me to threaten your daughter." Her hands fisted in her coat pockets. "A man. It came from a public phone. I can't trace it. But I think you should take it seriously."

He seemed unable to process the news, sinking down into the rocker, shaking his shaggy head. "Because she's Hispanic?"

"Not exactly." She looked again at the child, fire dancing in the gleaming hair, and explained. Then she asked, "Does Becca have family back in New Mexico?"

"You want me to send her away?"

No, Karen wanted to send both of them away, but Marek had gone on.

"Her grandfather lived with us and took care of Becca while Val and I were at work. He died eleven months ago. Pancreatic cancer."

Becca's second angel. "I'm so sorry, Marek. Aren't there any aunts or uncles down there? Cousins? Anything?"

His chin fell to his chest. "Break in ties."

Trying to connect the few dots he'd given her, she asked, "Was Val's family involved in her death?"

His head snapped up again as if someone had yanked it back for a killing slice. "Yes," he breathed out. "I killed her."

That brought her hands, still fisted, out of her pockets. "*You* were the drunk driver?"

Just how closely had Harold checked into Marek's record, his recent record? An involuntary manslaughter charge should have ended his career, if not his freedom.

His gaze fell to his daughter. "I was drugged."

Drugs? No, that's not what he'd said. Drugged. Had someone slipped him something before he got behind the wheel, unknowing? Why? For revenge?

"Drugged on work, on one more followup, one more break in

a case."

She flexed her fingers, hooked her thumbs into her belt. "It's been a long day, Marek. I don't have time for riddles."

"Val called me at work. Asked me to bring a carton of milk on my way home. I forgot all about it," he said over the spit and crackle of the fire. "When she couldn't reach me later that night, she went to the grocery store herself around midnight. So Becca would have it for her cereal the next morning."

Oh, God, the milk. Her father had said something about Becca being lactose intolerant. But that wasn't it at all. "Who was the drunk driver?"

"Does it matter?" At her silence, he looked into the fire. "My wife was run off the road by a state legislator, coming back after a campaign fundraiser."

Turning from the flames, his pale eyes met hers, without warmth, without color. "Daniel Elwell didn't stop or call for an ambulance. He kept going, hit another vehicle, killed himself and two more people. No one knew about the first crash until daylight. I'd been on that road over and over again that night, but I never saw anything. They'd hit an embankment and gone down into the arroyo."

Even in her short stint as sheriff, she'd seen crash victims—or what was left of them. "Were you the one to find her?"

"No, one of the patrols found the minivan. They had my partner pull me over. I knew, as soon as I saw Manny's face." Marek reached down, stroked his daughter's cheek, ran his finger up over her forehead, lingered, then retreated. "When they found Val, she was still warm."

Minutes, she thought, ticks of time, between life and death.

"Becca was strapped into the child seat in the back," he said, his deep voice so low she could barely hear him. "Trapped there as Val bled to death in the front seat."

Horror kept her silent.

"We don't know what, if anything, happened during those hours, except Becca's vocal cords were strained. From shouting for help, we guess. She hasn't spoken a word since that night. It's not physical, not any more, but they told me not to push it, that she won't talk again until she's ready."

After a long silence, Marek shook his head, cleared his throat, and looked up at her. "About the investigation, Karen, will you listen to my..."

She had no choice but to listen. But not to him.

The sound the sleeping child made didn't have a name, because it had no shape, no form, only a keening pitch. Marek snatched her up and held her against him. His tears doused the fire in Becca's hair as he rocked her.

Karen mumbled that she had to go and left. Somehow she couldn't choke out the words, you're fired, even if it might be best for all of them if she did.

CHAPTER 22

I N THE OFFICE THE NEXT morning, Karen turned on the FM radio just before 8AM.

"Where's Marek?" Walrus asked over a local barbershop quartet's rendition of *Mr. Sandman.*

"Listen," she told him.

After the last refrain, Nails Nelson came on. "We've got a big news flash this morning, folks. I want every single one of you to pick up and run with this one since I can't. The sheriff called me up earlier this morning."

Kurt and Walrus shared an *uh-oh* look while Bork just said, "Mmm."

Nails said, "Seems that our new county detective—that'd be Marek Okerlund if you haven't been paying attention—is getting too close to whoever killed Dale Hansen."

That raised eyebrows all around. She hadn't said so, or thought so, but she supposed Nails might have reason to jump to that conclusion.

"Didn't seem that way to me," Nails went on, "but somebody called up the sheriff last night and threatened the detective's little girl if he didn't lay off."

Walrus's feet came down to the floor with a thud, Kurt shot to his feet, and Bork laid his hand on the butt of his gun.

"Now, before you go off half-cocked, or full for that matter, gunning down what more than a few of you've called fricking foreigners, and I'm being polite here, you gotta know a few things. This man, and that's what it sounded like to the sheriff, spoke without any kind of accent. Phoned from the Casey's gas station at

11:18 PM last night. If anyone saw anything, let the sheriff know."

Now all eyes had gone to her but she let Nails do the talking for her.

"Whoever you are, you are a yellow-bellied coward to threaten an innocent child. If anyone lays so much as a hand on that girl's head, I can assure you, the whole county will get themselves deputized to come after you. I can't run after you—heck, I can't even walk—but I can shoot. And let me tell you, they won't be blanks."

Karen snapped the radio off.

Now it was Kurt who asked, "Where's Marek?"

"At the school with Becca," she told him.

Which meant that Karen would have time to see Harold Dahl before Marek got back.

Once again, Marek stood in front of the principal, head bowed.

"Do you like causing trouble, Detective?" the principal asked him, her nose peeling and her voice still nasal. "How serious do you believe this threat to be?"

He raised his head. "I don't know. It could be nothing."

Still, he'd had a hard time letting go of Becca, handing her off to Mrs. Winke at the classroom door.

"We aren't a prison, a fort, or a security detail, Mr. Okerlund. I simply cannot guarantee Becca's safety. However, if you wish her to stay in school, I will alert the staff to watch out for her."

Doubtfully, the principal eyed the kindergarten teacher standing in fig-leaf position by the door. The young woman hadn't said a word since she'd been called in over the PA system. But she bobble-headed her agreement.

Principal Hagaman tapped fingers on her desk and looked back at Marek. "No one but you will be allowed to pick her up after class."

He modified that, reluctantly. "Or the sheriff or Arne Okerlund."

"Very well." Then she looked back at the young teacher. "Don't forget to tell Mr. Okerlund about your concerns about Becca's behavior, Deborah."

If she'd looked nervous before, the teacher now looked terrified.

"What kind of problem?" Marek asked her. "Is Becca disrupting class?"

"Um, not exactly, but she's...well, she's not doing the lessons like the other kids. Even the, um, immigrant kids."

His greatest fear held him immobile for several long seconds. "So what is she doing?"

"I have to show you."

The teacher led him back to the classroom, where Mrs. Winke was reading the kids a story. Something about a magic stone. He could use one of those himself.

The teacher asked him to wait, went to retrieve something from her desk, then returned. She handed him sheaves of cheap paper, the kind that came from tablets with a big Indian chief on the cover. He looked down. Then he put his hand over his eyes.

"I'll talk to her."

As Karen watched, Harold Dahl reached out across his desk, signed this, that, and another, before his secretary, Avis Dixon, bore the papers efficiently away in the feeding chain of bureaucracy.

God help them if he ever quit.

A ball of a man who reminded Karen of an octopus, the county commissioner had his tentacles in everything. Technically, Eda County had three county commissioners. One showed up only every four months, the required minimum to stay in office, to make sure no one had slipped in anything banning guns or restricting fishing. The other had Alzheimer's but had clung stubbornly to the ballot.

If a county could ever be said to have a mayor, Harold Dahl was it.

"Morning, Sheriff." He gave her an absent salute before pulling more papers into signing range. "Avis said you've been trying to see me since yesterday. Something come up in the investigation?"

"The investigator," she said, deciding to start with her first beef against Marek. "He's dyslexic."

Harold looked up at her over his reading glasses. "Yes, he is."

"You knew? And you didn't tell me?"

"Figured you knew. He's *your* family." The commissioner put hands to paunch. "The fact is, Marek Okerlund's an experienced detective who has a local tie that might keep him here. What more did you want? Or do you think he's a halfwit, like your dad always said?"

Even with his shortcomings, Marek had never been that.

"It's not just the dyslexia," she said, letting some of the heat leak. "Yesterday he got up and left an incident meeting, without a word, just to go get his daughter from school."

"Yes, I see," Harold said with a somber nod. "The man should be shot, especially since his daughter was threatened with bodily harm."

"This was before the threat." She'd been in charge of her own department long enough that having to explain herself, to rationalize her choices, didn't come easily. "I know we hired Marek part-time but we need him full-time on this investigation. Unless we want to bring in the state guys to take it over."

Although the thought of Dirk the Jerk from DCI taking over the case gave her pause.

"Karen, the man's only just hit town." Harold leaned back in the ergonomic chair—by far the most expensive thing in the office—and the buttons of his shirt strained. "Make allowances. I'll bet some were made for you at one time."

She couldn't meet his eyes on that.

"As for the dyslexia, there's a thing called the ADA," he told her in the kind of reasoned tone used on the unreasonable. "You have to accommodate his disability."

"We don't have a handy dandy transcriber to take down every honeyed word."

"Given he's an Okerlund, it shouldn't cost much." His stubby hands went through what was left of his hair. "Look, I've got real problems here."

She stiffened to attention. "I've got a dead body."

"And I've got a dead business; the dead are dead but the living have to find another living." He flicked at the paperwork on his desk. "You think I want to tell the Sorensens that their loan extension got turned down?"

She had to think a minute: the little card shop on Norbeck. Every once in a while, someone tried to get a new business off the ground, people got excited, it survived a couple months then...slow and agonizing death.

Not so slow any more.

But she wasn't going to be distracted. "Marek isn't doing his job, Harold."

"What, because he hasn't solved this homicide soon enough to keep Nails Nelson from lighting a fire under your feet? Get used to the heat, Sheriff."

Avis Dixon snuck in and got a signature from Harold without his ever looking away from Karen. "I didn't hire Marek Okerlund because he was the only thing I could get," he said. "I had a long talk with his ex-partner, Sergeant Trujillo, before I decided to hire Marek. Albuquerque didn't want to lose him any more than Sioux Falls did you. Besides, I had my cousin check him out."

Bigwig FBI in DC. "Is that precisely legal?"

"He's a public servant, isn't he? Turns out the FBI did a workup on Marek."

That perked her up. Maybe she wouldn't have to lay down her trump card. "For what?"

"Get a clue here, Karen. For themselves. Marek worked with the FBI on a couple cases down there and impressed them. But you know how those people like paperwork."

"It's part of the job," she insisted.

"So give him the time to do it. You got a brand name at a bargain price, Sheriff." When she remained silent, his jaw unhinged. "Good grief, you want me to *fire* him?"

The guilt ate at her gut—but she had a job to do. "Take a good look at this, Harold." Karen pulled the picture from her pocket and placed it on his desk over the death of the Sorensens' dreams. "Then tell me if you still want Marek Okerlund working for you."

Sanchez turned in the driver's seat of his parked pickup. Fear had an odor, the union representative thought, bitter and acrid, tinged with sweat, but bereft of tears.

He spoke softly to the man in the passenger seat. "If you tell me who, I might be able to help."

No sé. No sé. No sé.

"Don't tell me you don't know. You have to know. Or you won't live long." Sanchez leaned closer. "Listen to me, your family will suffer, if you don't tell me."

The man shivered in the too-large coat and, after a moment, gave him a name in a hoarse whisper.

As if someone could hear, out in the middle of nowhere.

Yes, fear had a smell, Sanchez thought again, and it smelled smoky.

Avoiding the sheriff's office, Marek walked up the stairs and into the commissioner's office, his spiel at the ready. He'd spent the night thinking on it. A pudgy hand rose before he could open his mouth.

"No, no, don't tell me. Let me guess." Harold Dahl settled into the indulgent curve of his chair like an oyster nestled in the half-shell. "You'd be Marek Okerlund and you're going to quit before Karen fires you."

So Karen had beat him to it, Marek thought.

"Guess what, she can't."

Marek dug his hands into his pockets. "She's the sheriff."

"Lucky enough, she's also your family. That's why you're under my thumb, not hers. Prevents what people in high places like to call a conflict of interest."

The Okerlunds might have a lock on the law in Eda County but the Dahls were found, and ticked off, on every ballot. But he kept his mouth shut.

"Now, I've a few things to say to you, Detective, before we get to your concerns. First, I told you straight off that Karen doesn't have much law enforcement experience."

Marek stared down at the commissioner. "You didn't tell me she was an Okerlund."

"That was the quaint belief that family knows family," he said with an inflection that told Marek he'd played this tune before, with Karen.

"You're a blind spot for her," Harold conceded. "I knew it when I hired you; I didn't realize quite how much until now. Always thought it was just Arne that couldn't stand the sight of you—and for reasons I'd wager have nothing to do with you personally."

Only that I'm a person at all, Marek thought.

"But Karen's not your boss, I am." Dahl held up a hand, even though Marek had made no move to speak. "Now, I don't want you reporting to me or anything like that. You take your orders from her, just not your marching orders."

The commissioner rubbed at his round face. "Hell, you got one of the finest families in the county itching to shoot each other—and they're the law. I know the both of you've had some hard knocks, but I'd like to knock your heads together all the same."

Hard knocks? Karen Okerlund? Talk about the original golden girl.

Harold swiveled to the floor, rose on his stubby legs, and walked over to the window. "You know, we all thought Karen would do great things." He looked down, presumably to where the sheriff's Suburban sat in its slot. "If she'd been born later, she'd have been in the WNBA."

Marek didn't disagree. He'd seen her play.

"After that, a sports commentator, reporter or anchor, even politics; she's a leader. But after all that mess in the Army, she made a life for herself in Sioux Falls, got a lot of awards as a dispatcher. She saved lives. Guess it doesn't get any greater than that."

What mess, Marek wondered. Had she been dishonorably discharged?

The commissioner went on, "I had a hell of a time prying her away from her job, even had the chief of police there telling me to get the fuck away from her." He cleared his throat and turned back. "That's a quote, you understand."

Marek rewound his mental tape recorder then had to suppress a smile. Cops spoke profanity as a second language: first, for some.

As if tired by the foray to the window, Harold nestled back in his chair with a gusty sigh. "After Karen told her father I'd hired you, Arne came in here and blasted me for being a viper in the breast—at least I think that's what he meant, but he actually said a leper in the vest—and that was the least of it." He looked more amazed than insulted. "Now, he might have *thought* that before the stroke, but he'd never have said it. But you know something? Karen's a good sheriff. I have confidence in her abilities and judgment, except when it comes to you. Just wanted to make that plain."

Marek nodded.

"But I've heard some disturbing things, Detective. For one, I've heard you won't arrest anyone for being illegal. It doesn't hurt to check people's papers if you pull them over."

He wasn't sure he'd heard right. "Even for traffic violations?"

"Yes. Everything. You're the law, Marek." The genial tone had disappeared. "Do you understand me?"

Let Karen deal with the consequences—or lack thereof. "Yes, sir."

"Just check their birth certificate or passport or green card or whatever it is they've got to establish legal residence."

Marek wanted to ask, do you have yours, but he wasn't suicidal. He couldn't afford to be with a daughter to raise.

"Now, I've got one more thing I want to cover," Harold said, "but first I want to hear what brought you here today."

Not long ago, Marek would have been appalled at what came out of his mouth. "I'm supposed to be part-time."

Harold misunderstood his complaint, saying, "You'll be paid. It'll be a strain on the budget but we can handle the overtime for a while yet thanks to PBI."

Marek felt his eyebrows rise. "Heard they got tax amnesty."

"Okay, so their workers generate revenue." Then Harold let out a breath. "I'm not saying it's a place I'd want to work, but it's keeping the population stable and revenues high enough to support the sheriff's department, the jail, the courthouse, the clinic...all the services we need if we are ever going to attract something better. Think of it as a stepping stone."

Those stones were people being stepped on, Marek thought.

"Okerlunds," Harold said after a long silence. "Good thing Karen's got the Halvorsen genes or I'd be talking to myself most of the time. All I'm saying is, if you're worried about getting paid, you needn't, so long as PBI is here."

Marek tried again. "It isn't the money I'm after."

"Then what is it?"

"Time."

"If you can't explain this to my satisfaction," the commissioner said, rifling through his desk then pushing forward a picture, "you can have all the time you want—because you'll be out of a job."

Marek stared down at a bound and terrified Blanca Jaramillo.

"Jaramillo hasn't said a word," Tammy told Karen at the dispatcher desk outside the jail. "He doesn't eat either. It's like he's decided it's the end. Believe me, I've gotten plenty of people to talk, some pretty tough characters too, because it's boredom city down here without it, but it's like I'm not there." The rolls of khaki shook. "And I'm not easy to miss."

Karen nodded toward the jail and their lone prisoner. "Emilio Jaramillo doesn't like women."

"Well, that explains it then. But at least he isn't violent."

In answer, Karen pulled out the picture she'd shown to Walrus and Kurt that morning. The same picture she'd made a copy of for Dahl.

"Okay, now I'm pissed," Tammy said, looking down at it. "I don't *want* to talk to anybody who can do that to a woman."

Why was it only women, Karen wondered, who understood that? Why had Harold Dahl told her, Listen to Marek. Why had Marek told her, Listen to Jaramillo. Why had both Kurt and Walrus said, What did Marek say?

Some things didn't need an all-points bulletin.

Stuffing the picture back in her pocket, Karen climbed the stairs back up to the office, where her gaze rested on the empty desk. She may be privately relieved, in some part of herself, that Marek wasn't fired. Yet. But she still needed him to do his job. "Did the principal send our favorite Polack to the dunce corner, or what?"

Kurt put a finger to his lips and Walrus jerked his thumb toward the windows.

Marek stood there, so silent, so unmoving, she'd overlooked him.

"I'm sorry, Marek." Basic management 101, she told herself. Never demean a subordinate to other subordinates. She knew better. Their complicated history, his threat to her job, and her shock at his stand on domestic violence, all mixed into a disorienting brew that had thrown her off balance. Big time. "Truly. I apologize."

First the eyelids trembled, then as if that small ripple moved outward, muscle to muscle, he took a breath, turned his head. "What?"

Relieved he hadn't heard her comment, she walked over to the window he'd been looking out so intently. She saw nothing but the stone bandshell in the park across the street, its curves rounded with snow. "What do you see?"

"Adobe."

If his mind had turned back to Albuquerque, maybe she wouldn't have to force him out if she didn't like what he had to say. But first, she'd listen, hard as it may be to hear. "Tell me why I should let an abuser like Emilio Jaramillo go."

Before Marek could speak, Darcie Ringold flew into the office like an agitated grackle, deep purple coat flapping around her black turtleneck and jeans.

The high breathy voice and the low rumble came out in stereo. "It's meth."

CHAPTER 23

KAREN BLINKED AT HER FORMER murder suspect. "It's *what?*"

"Methamphetamine." Darcie slipped her hands into her jean pockets—a tight fit. "Don't tell me you haven't heard of it."

Karen noted that the office had gone silent. "Of course I know what meth is, but what's that to you?" She glanced at Marek. "Or to you?"

Ignoring her question, Marek walked over to Darcie, dwarfing her. "You were with the Jaramillos at the clinic that night, weren't you?"

Marek's brain must be as tired as he looked, Karen thought. Different investigations.

But the thin shoulders hunched. "I think it's confidential. You know, doctor-patient stuff. The thing is, you've got to let Mr. Jaramillo go."

That didn't sit well at all. Not again. "Because?"

When Darcie remained silent, Marek explained. "Because he was trying to wean Blanca off meth in the only way he knew how—to tie her up, keep her away from it."

Karen felt like someone had snatched the ball from her in midair, just as she went up for a game-winning layup. Lost again. She sank against a pillar. If this new spin on the case played out...it made her dizzy to think of the ramifications, not only on the case but on her ability to do the job. What had she missed, that Marek hadn't?

Darcie turned on Marek. "Mr. Jaramillo told you?"

"No, I suspected as soon as I saw Blanca's face."

That puzzled Karen. "I thought it was *his* face you were going on about, Marek."

"I suspected meth when I saw her face: the decayed teeth, the pocked face, the brittle hair. But I knew it when I saw his face. When she told you to lock him up, Jaramillo looked devastated—and betrayed."

Darcie's hands came out of her pockets as if she needed to steady herself. "*Blanca* told you to lock him up?"

Marek glanced at the doctor wannabe. "She let us believe that her father abused her."

Kind of him to say *us*, Karen thought, then frowned. "What a minute. Blanca is his *daughter*?" She remembered the photo on the wall that had transfixed Marek: the little girl with an ear of corn in her hands. "That's not possible, Marek."

"Meth can age a person," Marek said. "How old is she, Darcie?"

"A bit younger than me."

In the peanut gallery, Walrus muttered, "Geez, you'd think a girl'd drop a drug that did that to her."

"That's why it's illegal," Kurt said. "Beats me why people do it in the first place."

Karen pushed off the pillar, pointed at the kicked-back Walrus, then thumbed him to the door. "Go pick up Blanca Jaramillo. If she won't come willingly, tell her we're going to charge her with obstruction of justice."

Walrus shot a disgruntled look at the standing and ready Kurt then swung down his hunting boots.

After Walrus tromped out, Darcie said, "I didn't want to get Blanca in trouble."

Karen leaned back against the pillar, one of several that kept two floors of governance from crashing down on their heads. "When did you get to know the Jaramillos, Darcie?"

"The teachers had us help the kids from trailer city that didn't know English." She raked a hand through her dark hair to the nape of her neck and left it there, like a gaudy barrette. "I tutored Blanca. She picked up English as fast as I could teach her. She worked nights at PBI and was always afraid that she'd have to quit school and work at the plant full-time."

Karen's own mother had had to fight to continue her schooling past the eighth grade and ultimately left family and faith to do so. "Blanca's father didn't want her to learn?"

"Oh, he did, since he doesn't have any education himself. No, it wasn't him but...finances, I guess. I went to her trailer once and she was so embarrassed that I never went again. I mean, it wasn't so bad, but she thought it was. Money was really tight. He'd saved up, Mr. Jaramillo said, to take her to the clinic. He was scared to go, but he was more scared of what was happening to her. He didn't know it was meth. I kind of, uh, stuck around for a while to talk to David Echols, after they left, until Dale called me."

From behind her, Kurt said, "We've gotten more drug traffic since PBI came to town. Couple overdoses, an accident or two, some petty crime."

The deputy's tone seemed to set Darcie on edge. "Listen, Blanca didn't...it wasn't like she wanted to get hooked. She just wanted to keep up."

Kids. In her day, it'd been alcohol. "With the *in* crowd?"

Marek stirred himself back into their dimension. "I imagine she means at the plant."

Darcie looked impressed; she wasn't the only one.

"It helped her, you know, keep her count," the girl said. "That's what they call it. I went to the plant once. Dale took me. He was proud of it, said it was all efficient, the latest, but it gave me the creeps. All that gleaming metal and blood."

Karen let out a short laugh. "Maybe you should rethink your career goals, Darcie."

After this boondoggle, Karen thought she might need to do the same.

"That's healing not killing."

Marek sat on his desk, which put him about on the level with the girl. "Where'd she get the meth, Darcie?"

Her hands dipped back into her pockets. "How would I know? All I cared about was getting her off it. Mr. Jaramillo said, after he found out about the meth, that Blanca won't ever have to work at the plant again. But she said she had to work, or they'd be—uh, they needed the money, that's all."

They'd be deported, Karen filled in, saw it in the face of her detective.

Karen dug the heels of her hands into her eyes, hoping it would correct her blurred vision, make her see what she hadn't. She waited, with the rest of them, for Walrus to return. When the door finally opened, she frowned. "Where's Blanca?"

"Beats me." Walrus batted his cap against his thigh and water spotted the rug. The snow must still be melting and dripping off the overhang. "The place was deserted. Jaramillo's car, though, is gone. Want me to contact the patrol, ask them to watch out for it?"

Darcie eyed her with dread. Marek disappeared back into whatever unfathomable dimension he'd been in when she'd first come into the room.

"No, not yet," Karen decided. "We've got a murder to solve. That takes priority."

"So you're going to let Mr. Jaramillo go?" Darcie asked.

"We need to check his immigration status. If it comes up legal, he's free to go."

"Oh, but…"

"Darcie, you've done your good deed for the day," Karen said. "Unless you like hanging out here."

The girl hastened out the door that Walrus held for her.

Karen said to Marek, "Harold wants us to check status, so it's not even my call. I can't let Jaramillo go until it's done."

His gaze fell back to his battered boots. She took it as assent to the legality and dissent with the humanity. "We don't make the law, Marek, we enforce it."

That lifted a quizzical brow. "Cops pick and choose what to enforce."

Kurt responded, "The law is the law. Period."

"If we went after everyone for everything still on the books," Walrus said equably, "there'd be precious few citizens in Eda County without a sheet."

Karen resisted the urge to jump into the argument, knowing it merely delayed what needed to really be said—in front of the others. "I should have listened to you yesterday, Marek." She swiped a foreclosure notice from her desk, whirled it into a hat, and put it on her head. "I was the dunce."

He just shook his head.

She whirled the paper back into the death of someone's dreams and laid it flat back on her desk. "You see Harold?"

"I did."

"Does he know?" At the blank look, she decided he must not have gotten much sleep the night before. Neither of them had. "Don't be dense, Marek."

"Oh. Yeah. I told him about the meth."

So she'd not only royally messed up in front of her men but her boss. What a wonderful way to win elections.

"If I'm not fired," Marek said finally, "do I get a gun?"

She'd assumed he'd been using one of his own. "Didn't you bring one, or is it coming in the van?"

"Turned it in with my badge."

Walter crashed down on all fours of his chair. "You don't *own* a gun?"

"It's a job requirement not a personal one."

Karen headed to a cabinet against the wall. "What did you have before?"

"Glock 17."

"Good gun if you need to conceal your weapon," Walrus said. Then he patted his holster. "Smith & Wesson .40 is what I carry."

So did she, but Kurt said, "All you need out here is a good revolver."

Like his broad-brimmed deputy's hat, Kurt Bechtold preferred the tried and true. A Colt, of course: a .32 Colt Police Positive Special, last produced in the 1970s.

Karen hunted through her keys, opened the cabinet, and peered in. "We've got plenty of revolvers, a couple 9mm semis, and a nice .45 automatic that our last night deputy used." She picked up the last, a Glock 21, and handed it to him, saw it fit easily into his big hand. "You'll want a duty rifle as well."

"I don't need—"

She reached back in. "You need."

"One gun is enough in a house with a kid," he protested.

"It's the kids you got to train," Walrus piped up, "not the guns, Okerlund."

Holding out the rifle, Karen said, "Lock it in your pickup if you don't want it in the house. You may be a detective but you'll still get the odd call about a feral pig or a loose bull or the like. Take it."

"Better an animal than a man," he said and reluctantly took the rifle.

"You do know how to use that, don't you?" she asked him.

"More or less."

Before she could press him, his cell phone rang. The Lone Ranger rode again. He took it, said, "Fine," then shut it down. "Moving van's here."

She didn't need to be a detective to figure out that was a question. "You can go." When Walrus got to his feet with a hopeful expression, she sighed. "You too, but you're on call." She noted the surprise on Marek's face. Did he think he was going to unload what she took to be a couple decades of accumulation by himself?

"I, um—Thanks. Appreciate it."

"We're here to protect and serve," Walrus said, going to the door. "Besides, I can see whether you've got a bigger TV, so I can crash at your place if my wife wants to watch *Dancing with the Stars* instead of football."

From Marek's face, she didn't think Walrus was going to get lucky, though whether it was the size of the TV or the football that didn't meet specifications, she didn't know.

"What about me?" Kurt asked.

"I want you here while I go talk to Jaramillo," Karen told him.

Marek hesitated at the door. "I can help translate."

She could translate too: he didn't trust her to conduct the interview on her own. And why should he? She'd screwed up big time with Jaramillo. Still, she was sheriff and this was her case now. "If I get stuck, I'll snag you later."

He hesitated for a moment longer then went out in Walrus's wake.

When the phone rang on her desk, Karen took the call. Emilio Jaramillo wasn't legal, she was told. Big surprise. She went down to the jail and told Tammy to take a break.

Sitting on the Spartan bed, Emilio Jaramillo looked like what he was, what Marek had seen, what she hadn't...a broken man. The tears glistened in his bloodshot eyes but, Karen thought, fell back into the hole in his heart, rather than onto his lined face.

She'd told him, in as plain English as she could, that the charges against him were dropped, but they were holding him because of his immigration status. Though she wasn't sure for how long. When she'd asked the Feds when they'd pick up her prisoner, the caller had laughed and hung up.

"Blanca," Jaramillo said. "Where?"

"She's not at your trailer. Your car is gone." She saw hope for the first time. "When did you find out your daughter was doing drugs?"

Hands fisted on his thighs. "I tell her bad. She say no."

No, that the drugs weren't bad? Or that, no, she wouldn't take them? Whichever, it didn't really matter. "She said yes."

"All for her. Lost. Drugs." He rocked back against the cell bars. "I pay all to come to America. Start over. Be free." His tautened face held a fury deeper than mere words could convey. "Not free. Lies. I feel murder. I work. Blanca all I have." Then the passion burned out. "Diablo say, work good job, need white."

Needed to be white to get the good jobs? Not true, as many of his legal coworkers proved, but it didn't hurt, unless he meant the management jobs. Which from Marek's verbal report, she knew were all whites. But who was Diablo? One of Jaramillo's coworkers, perhaps? "Your daughter took the drugs to work at the plant?"

"I want she go to school but Diablo, he say we owe. Always. More. Blanca not child, he say."

So maybe this Diablo owned the trailer. Rent wasn't headed south, even in South Dakota.

"Blanca sick. I take to doctor. He tell me not sick." He folded himself up on the bunk. "Wife, she is killed, but to Blanca, drug do worst." He made a hooking gesture from out of his chest. Heart or soul, she thought. "Gone."

A tear slipped its red-rimmed mooring.

So, the wife was dead. If Emilio Jaramillo had better English, she'd ask him how, but the man looked like he'd expended his language skills.

Or perhaps she'd expended hers.

Marek watched the sheriff's Suburban pull up behind Walrus's squad car at 21 Okerlund Road. What now, he wondered, but when Karen came over and peeked into the bowels of the moving van, she said, "I didn't get much out of Jaramillo. I'll let you talk to him tomorrow."

"Okay." When she remained standing there, a bit awkwardly, he got it. "You want to help?"

She grabbed a box labeled *Becca* that teetered on top of a chest of drawers. "Jaramillo's pretty broken up. If I could, I'd let him go. He's still not eating and that worries me." She snagged the other box on the chest. "I didn't get into this job to ruin people's lives."

He hefted one of the Paradigm floor speakers onto his shoulder. "Side effect sometimes."

When they got into the house, they found Becca sitting on the bottom of the upstairs steps with an open box of toys in front of her, a stuffed dog in her arms. She'd bought it with her allowance nearly a year ago now. It'd been meant for a gift but it hadn't made a transfer of ownership—and never would now.

"Hey, Becca." Karen sank down beside his daughter and swiped fingers through the plush fur of the floppy-eared spaniel. "I had one of these for real once."

Marek put the speaker down in one corner. "Don't encourage her." The last thing he needed was another mouth to feed. He turned at the huffs coming through the open door. Walrus had the twin mattress set in his grasp. Barely.

"Where do you want it?" Walrus asked.

Good question, he thought. "Pick your room, Becca."

His daughter held out her stuffed dog like a dowsing wand, ducked into the rooms on the first floor, then shot up the stairs where he found her, with Karen, a few minutes later, staring out of the bedroom window.

Karen pointed out across the street. "You can see my room from here when my blinds are open."

But they'd rarely been open when he'd been a kid and never at night. Maybe she'd been afraid he was a voyeuristic little prick. Or maybe her father had. Apparently they'd been open, though, that awful afternoon his mother had lost her temper with what she'd seen as intransigence in the schoolroom.

"You don't want this room," Marek said, putting down one of his own boxes beside the one of Becca's that Karen must have brought up. "You can have the big one in the—"

Becca stomped her foot.

They all stared at it.

His daughter's eyes rose slowly up to his face and he let out a breath. So much for reclaiming his boyhood room. "Okay, it's yours, but we'll have to switch out what's in here." He looked down at the queen-size box springs for the mattress he'd dragged downstairs their first night. "That bed won't fit Baby Bear."

Far too big for her. And, in fact, it needed to be hauled out to the dump. Wondering if anything more up here needed to be trashed, he went over to the attic door and found it padlocked. He pulled out the keys Alice Winke had dropped off for him and found one that fit.

Half expecting the space to be empty, he had to blink at the crammed contents. So that's where everything had gone. Just inside the door, he saw the pair of bookcases he'd made for his mother when he'd been a teenager, the one gift he knew had been truly appreciated. Last time he'd seen them, they'd been in the

Valeska house.

He stifled the urge to put it all back: the bookcases downstairs on either side of the hearth, the Oscar Howe print called *Blizzard Bath* in the master bedroom, and the Stickley library table in the combination spare room and den where his mother had graded papers and drilled him under the light of a Tiffany stained-glass lamp.

Instead, he shut the door.

"You done picking rooms yet?" Walrus bellowed from below.

Marek walked over to the stairway. "Becca's up here."

"Then we'll put you in the master," the deputy yelled back and floorboards began to creak. Remembering the draft in that room, he wanted to protest, but the spare room had looked in worse shape. The movers must have brought in his bed—a new one. He hadn't been able to face the idea of sleeping in the same one where Val's absence lay beside him.

Walrus huffed up the stairs with the twin mattress set and deposited it on top of the old queen. "Here you go, Bambi girl. Sweet dreams." He patted Becca on the head and trundled back down. Becca rubbed her head and gave Marek a look that said: Is he for real?

Or possibly, what did he do to my hair?

"Here Becca," Karen said, picking up the box she'd laid down on the floor. "This one's yours. Let me open it up for you."

Before Marek could stop her, she'd pulled out a Swiss Army knife and cut neatly through the tape. With an almost reverent silence, Karen pulled out the painted wooden icons, one at a time, and placed them on the bed.

"Are they angels?" she asked.

Marek glanced at the collage of haloed saints beaming up from the box springs. "*Retablos*. It's a Hispanic thing." When Becca pointed to her wall, he said, "I'll hang them up later."

When he glanced back down, he saw that Karen had opened the other box and pulled out two framed certificates: a commendation for apprehension of two armed suspects and another for the resuscitation of a child.

"The brass hand out awards like candy," he told her, wanting to snatch the box from her and stuff it in the storage room with his past life. "Makes them feel good and doesn't cost them as much as a raise."

Forestalling further revelations, Marek headed downstairs,

telling himself he'd better supervise the move or he'd have to redo everything himself later.

When he got back to the ground floor, he was stunned at the number of people who streamed in with arms full of his possessions. He cleared his throat and the assembly paused. "I'll send out for pizza."

"Oh, really, from where?" Walrus asked. "Sioux Falls?"

"Don't you worry your head about food." Alice Winke hustled in with a brushed-steel floor lamp. "Potluck's coming as soon as we get your table set up. The Bolvins are bringing the table in right now: solid oak, isn't it?"

She set the lamp down by the recliner her husband had put near the fireplace then stepped back to beam up at Marek. She must be over the moon, he thought, not to have to find another renter for the place now that he'd taken possession.

"Welcome home, Marek."

It was, he realized, the first time he'd heard it said.

In the darkness of the countryside, Blanca Jaramillo drove one way, then another, the beam of her one headlight skimming over the dingy white banks.

So quiet: except for the wind.

The gravel road shone with dark glints of dull ice—thawed and refrozen so many times, it looked like lava flow. Each day it flowed a bit more, thinned a bit more, until it was gone.

Like her, she thought.

Each turn, left, right, right, she expected to skid off the road. She'd never been out this far. Her world had been the school, the plant, the trailer.

A world so different than what she'd dreamed of, when her father had promised they'd make a new life in America, a life that her children would one day take pride in.

Tears flowed again. Then froze.

Finally, the one-eyed headlight picked out the building she'd been told to look for. The shadows rounded the square bell tower into something more familiar from home, *la iglesia*, a sanctuary, a beacon of hope.

The old Buick lurched then spun as she braked. When it stopped, she found herself pointed the other way, toward the pinpricks of light from Reunion. Blanca pried her fingers off the steering wheel. With difficulty, she got the door open. Nothing worked here. Except the people. Her people. For so little.

What was she doing out here, even in the shadow of that hope? Wasn't it an illusion, as America had been?

She wanted to go home to her Petén village.

But she knew that she didn't dare; it meant death. Even her mother's funeral had been conducted many miles away, by a priest neither she nor her father had known, on a moonless night, as if to bury a shameful secret instead of the body of a generous and well-loved woman.

No, Blanca couldn't go home.

Home was where her mother had been raped and shot. Home was where her father had been beaten unconscious and left for dead. Home was where she'd returned to, after preparations for *Semana Santa*—a weeklong celebration of the rebirth of Christ or, to Mayans, the rebirth of corn and the promise of a fruitful harvest—only to find her life gone.

They'd been legal in Guatemala. But the law hadn't helped them. No one had dared to even raise a voice in protest. The drug runners had wanted the Jaramillo's land as an airstrip and her father had refused to take the tainted money. That should make her proud, the priest had said, but over the grave of her mother, she'd thought: he'd killed her mother with his goodness.

Out of the shadow of hope, a voice spoke. "Do you need help?"

Her heart pounded. Salvation was at hand. "Yes, please."

"You need a tow? Where were you going?"

She tried to pick out the form of her savior but he was dwarfed by the structure behind him. "Please, I have no money. Only the car. If you help me, you can have it. I heard you can help...people like me."

The shadow moved then. Enveloped her. For a moment, she thought she had it all wrong, that she would die right here and be buried in the snow.

So white.

She would never get used to it, these pale people, with pale eyes, on pale land. She herself had been vibrant once, she knew. People told her so. At first. Before the plant.

The hand fell on her shoulder. Blanca shook. Please God, she thought, please.

He said, "You're cold. I've got blankets." The hand squeezed. "Come on in and we'll get you settled."

CHAPTER 24

T HE CELL PHONE WOKE MAREK from a post-move nap after he'd gotten Becca to bed. He checked his watch and found it wasn't quite midnight.

The voice said, "Mr. Okerlund, I call because you I trust."

It wasn't the idiosyncratic wording but the accent that gave Marek the identity of his caller. That and the caller ID. "Yes, Dr. Ahmed?"

"Please, I worry for Mr. Sanchez."

"The union rep?" That got his attention. "How so?"

"Men, they come to his trailer. I hear...awful noise. I learn to not see, to not hear, but this is America. It is to be different here."

America wasn't without its own kind of massacres. "Not that different."

The voice went on, almost inaudible, "You will not tell?"

The engineer turned meatpacker had yet to learn the art of anonymous phone tips. "That you called? Not unless I have to, Dr. Ahmed. Stay in your trailer and don't come out, not unless we come to your door."

After retrieving his Glock from the lock box, Marek flipped on the porch light then hesitated on the step. Did he dare leave his daughter alone in the house? Should he just call the night deputy to check on Sanchez? Or did he call the sheriff?

All these years, he'd never thought twice about leaving the house, even in the big bad city. But he hadn't needed to, with Val and her father there.

As he hesitated, the porch light across the street snapped on and the tall, shadowed figure of the sheriff emerged.

He met her in the street and told her about the call.

"Anonymous? I don't know, Marek, especially after the threat to Becca."

"I think it's the real deal."

After studying him in the light of the street lamp, she nodded and went back into her house. Moments later she came out with her father trailing her.

He carried a rifle.

Without a word, Arne Okerlund walked across the street and disappeared into the house he'd sworn he would never enter again.

"He's been itching to do something ever since the threat came in," Karen said, beckoning Marek over to the Suburban. "He cares about Becca."

"Why should he?" Marek slid into the Suburban and buckled the seatbelt. "She's mine."

"Marek, I've never understood why my dad had it in for you. I really don't. But you threaten a kid in this county and he'll shoot first and ask questions later." Karen shoved the key into the ignition. "You know what I think? He's had time to mellow and doesn't know how to bridge the gap between you. Family becomes more important as you get older."

The Suburban gasped, snorted, then gunned, saving Marek from a response.

Only when they'd parked in the plant lot, lights doused, did he ask, "Who's the deputy on duty tonight?"

"Bork is, but he's got a domestic in Dutch Corners. Rick's on call but I don't want to pull him in unless I have to. He's been putting in a lot of hours on the evening shift what with Two Fingers getting deployed again. Plus, we're still short two deputies on the graveyard shift. No one wants to work those hours for the pay Dahl is offering. Not for long, anyway."

When they got out of the Suburban, she pulled her gun. "You know which is Sanchez's trailer?"

Marek nodded, pulled his own gun out, and led the way between the shadowed hulks. The mud-stained paths had frozen over as the temperature had fallen and their feet crashed through the crust.

Some lights snapped off as they passed and some snapped on.

When they came to the last two trailers, Marek slowed to a laconic crunch. The first trailer, he knew, belonged to Dr. Ahmed. It was dark. The second was lit, if curtained, and quiet.

"I'm calling in Rick," Karen said on a breath behind him.

He turned his head and mouthed, "Why?"

"Your place."

A trap, she must be thinking, to lure them away from Becca. And why couldn't it be? Just because he liked Dr. Ahmed, that didn't mean the man couldn't be involved in Dale Hansen's death.

Marek nodded. And wished he were back in Albuquerque, where the highly trained apprehension unit could deal with what awaited them in the trailer—and he could get back to his daughter.

Karen moved away and made the call. Then she slipped around him and crackled her way right up to the door of Sanchez's trailer. Marek moved to the side to cover her. But as she knocked, she jumped back, and he saw that the door had swung inward.

Karen pointed a finger at him then down.

Stay.

He waited, gun trained on the crack of the door, as she plastered herself against the side of the trailer. "Sheriff's Department! Police! Throw out any weapons and come out with your hands in the air!"

But the only thing that came out was silence.

"Cover me," she said.

A minute later they both stood over the mangled body of Sanchez.

Arne Okerlund rocked in his father's old hickory rocker, rifle on his legs, his eyes darting from memory to reality.

The remains of a fire in the hearth spat out some heat in the cool room. Not cold, not as it must have been the night of the blizzard, but cooler than he kept his own place. No wonder Karen had insisted on bringing Marek and Becca home with her.

Didn't mean he had to like it. It was still his house, and he should have some say in who lived under its roof.

Then he relaxed his fierce one-handed grip on the rifle. Who was he kidding? He'd take anyone, even Marek Okerlund, under that roof as long as it kept his daughter there. Addressing a space in memory where his father had once sat, he said, "She's the sheriff here now, not your son. Bet you never thought that would happen, did you, old man."

Rundown old place, Arne thought, with satisfaction. He recognized little of it. Not surprising since the last time he'd seen it had been, what, going on forty years ago?

The place had been built sometime in the early 1900s, after Artur "Bear" Okerlund had left the old homestead to be the county's first sheriff. Artur's in-laws had built across the street at the same time, adjoining land they owned down the bluff into the flood plain. When they'd passed on, Leif Okerlund had moved there to start his own family, and it was where Arne had grown up, thinking he would one day own this place in his turn.

A cycle of generations, orderly, natural, *right*.

But then his mother, Kari Halvorsen Okerlund, had died in a freakish fall, harvesting apples from the small orchard she'd painstakingly nurtured. His father, not he, had moved to this house. That's when the trouble began. Janina Marek made her move on Leif Okerlund and produced her halfwit of a son.

Well, the joke had been on her.

The slam of a car door outside had him starting up from the rocker, his face heating, to be caught so unaware. Was that Marek or Karen? Not just his daughter, but his mother and his wife, would have berated him for his thoughts, if they knew. Maybe they did—like Becca's angels, looking down from heaven.

That didn't change that he could not, would not, ever care for Marek Okerlund. Karen didn't need more trouble in her life. A life that hadn't gone as she, or he, had planned. She'd had bigger plans than he'd at first allowed, ones that would take her, not only from Reunion, but from South Dakota, even from the country altogether.

But pride had let her go in the end.

Now she was back again, here, to many minds, nowhere. Guilt ate at him for that, wishing, as he often had since he'd woken in intensive care, that he'd been struck down dead, in one fatal stroke, a clean cut.

Instead, he'd become a burden.

But he'd supported Karen's decision to take his place as sheriff. At first, he'd told himself it was only until he could retake the reins himself. Even Harold Dahl had said as much, but the man hadn't met his eyes.

Then he'd known.

Arne raised his rifle and waited for the door to open. Might as well show Marek the ex-sheriff could still handle himself.

His finger jerked when the sharp knock startled him. Not quite enough, however, to trigger a shot.

What the hell was the halfwit doing, knocking at his own door?

Then Arne realized he couldn't see the man's head in the

transom lights over the door. Marek Okerlund was bigger even than Lenny Marek. He should be able to see him, what with the porch light on.

Maybe he didn't care for Marek Okerlund, but that little girl up there, that was different. If he had to kill to protect her, he would. If he was killed, he wouldn't mind, so long as he could return the favor.

Being useless sucked, plain and simple, and he had a great need to be useful. He wedged the index finger of his good hand more carefully into the trigger.

When the door handle jiggled, Arne steadied himself. One shot. That's all it took.

In trailer city, Karen noticed no one came out to look, despite all the commotion, the sirens, the strobe lights. So she banged on the door of the trailer closest to Sanchez's. "Police! Open up!"

The lights flicked on and the door edged open. A man stared at her through the crack, a pair of old eyeglasses perched askew on his lean face.

"I am Sheriff Mehaffey." She showed him her badge. "I want to ask you some questions."

"I have papers. You wish to see?"

"Papers? Oh, I see. No, I mean, I don't need to see—"

But he'd already disappeared back into the trailer. When he returned, the man thrust the papers at her. She shone her flashlight on them. "Dr. Ahmed Sabonovic." She snapped off the light. "You're from Bosnia?"

He blinked at her, as if surprised she hadn't stumbled over his name. "I am legal."

She handed the papers back. "I was in Bosnia with the peacekeepers."

He looked baffled. "You are peacekeeper?"

"That's one of my job descriptions," she said. "I am the sheriff. Head of police. Keeper of the peace. You talked to one of my men."

The lean face slackened. "Detective Okerlund, he tells you? But he promises."

Confused, she stared at him. Then it sunk in. If she hadn't sent Marek with the ambulance, she'd let him know she didn't appreciate being kept in the dark about their so-called anonymous tipster.

"We are talking to all the people near Mr. Sanchez's trailer," she told him. "You must have heard something. No way you couldn't have with what happened in that trailer."

The face blanked again. "I do not know language."

"English? You seem to get by well enough."

"English, it was not."

So much for union busters. "Spanish?"

"I do not know Spanish," he said. "I do not understand what is said."

Only what wasn't said: the language of pain was universal. Keeping her voice low, she said, "No one should suffer what Sanchez did. I am the law here. Nothing will be overlooked or swept under the table."

She saw the brief glint of hope; it died.

Marek watched the gurney disappear into the operating room through swinging double doors. Sanchez had regained consciousness only once on the trip to Sioux Falls, but when Marek asked who had done this to him, all that had come out was a wail in the smashed face.

"Don't look so glum," the EMT said from behind him. "Looks bad but most of its external now we've got the bleeding stopped. Your suspect will live to stand trial. What did he do, by the way?"

"Suspect?" Slowly Marek turned. "Victim."

"Oh, really? I just thought—you insisted on coming with us, so I thought he was a prisoner." The young man held up his hands. "It was just kind of freaky, everybody hiding behind the curtains, like they were afraid for their lives. Why'd someone do that to him?"

"It could be because he's a union man."

"Oh, hey. I'm union myself."

"Does he have insurance?" a new voice asked.

That brought Marek's head around to see a woman with a clipboard, her mouth pursed, her expectation: nil.

"If he worked for PBI," Marek said, "I'd say no, or little to nothing of it."

The face, if possible, showed even more disapproval. "Unemployed, then."

"He works for a union." Marek pulled out the evidence bag he'd stuffed into his pocket. "You got any latex gloves?"

She gave him a slighting glance. "This is a hospital."

The EMT laughed then turned it into a cough as the woman handed Marek a pair of gloves.

"They're the biggest we've got," she said, when he had difficulty getting them on. "People of healing don't generally have hands like yours, Detective."

He opened the bag and pulled out Sanchez's wallet. The money, the credit cards, nothing looked touched. "I like to think the hands of justice can heal."

That earned him a sniff but he snatched up a card. "Blue Cross-Blue Shield."

While the nurse filled in the information on the clipboard, Marek sorted through the rest of the meager documentation. No wonder he'd never heard anyone call Sanchez by his first name: it must have caused him grief as a kid.

Angel.

Sanchez had his social security card and, no doubt the result of being caught in raids, his birth certificate. He noted not only had Sanchez been born in Oregon but his parents had both been born in California.

Marek pulled out the three pictures in the wallet. The first showed a round-faced Hispanic woman with warmth in her dancing eyes. His wife, he thought. How could he stand to keep it, always having that face haunting him?

But Sanchez had lost his wife to the impersonal hand of fate. Cancer.

Marek turned to the next picture, a young man with much better looks than Sanchez and more height. Then a young woman, this one in the latest fashion, with Sanchez's thin face and her mother's dancing eyes. He turned that over and saw some writing on the back.

"Consuela Sanchez," the EMT read to his side.

"His daughter, I'd guess."

"Looks like he's got her phone number there too," the EMT said. "Want me to call her?"

"Go ahead. I'll talk to her after you do."

That way Marek wouldn't have to make a fool of himself. More often than not, when he was this tired, he switched the numerals in the phone number.

After the EMT talked to the young woman, Marek took the phone and identified himself. "Ms. Sanchez, does your father have any enemies?"

"He's union and Hispanic. What do you think?" Then something hit the phone, perhaps her hand coming up to dash at her face. "How is he, really? I'll drive up right away from Vermillion but—"

"No, don't drive up—" he began.

"Of course I'm going to drive up. He's my father. They won't even tell me how bad it is."

"He's in surgery now," Marek said. "It could be hours. You can't do him any good this late and you're upset."

"I'm coming."

"Then have someone else drive. Please. I've seen it too many times. DWD."

"What are you talking about? I'm not drunk."

She'd just proved his point. "Driving While Distracted."

CHAPTER 25

INSIDE MAREK'S BUNGALOW, KAREN TRIED to remain detached as she lightly fingered the bullet hole. "Clean," she said. "Through and through."

Her father was gone. And the evidence he'd left behind told her that he hadn't made it—to full recovery, that is. He wouldn't have made this mistake, pre-stroke.

"Thank God it went through door jamb instead of me," Rick Gullick said with a crooked smile. "Your dad thought I was the bad guy. Actually, he said he shot at me because I wasn't big enough to be Marek. Guess the guy's pretty big?"

"Marek's half a foot taller than me. And no lightweight."

"Like Walrus?"

"Think hulk not bulk."

He whistled. "Sounds like the legends I've heard about Old Man Marek."

A man she'd known as a girl was now a legend to her youngest deputy. She dropped her hand from the jamb. "Didn't you knock?"

"Of course I knocked." Seeing her dismay, he shrugged. "Hey, he missed. Said he missed on purpose as a warning shot, but I think he's pretty embarrassed."

Which may be why he'd left the scene.

"He's not the only one," Rick said. "I nearly shot him back. He, uh, didn't lock the door, so I walked right in with gun in hand, not sure what I'd be facing. Good thing he picked up the rifle instead of the shotgun he meant to or I'd be full of buckshot."

One mistake to be grateful for, then.

"Anyway, I went upstairs to check on the girl, to give your dad time to recover."

The doctors had told her, the brain had ways around damage, but it would never be quite the same. "Everything's okay here, then?"

"Yep, your dad went home and the girl's asleep." His gaze strayed toward the stairs. "Dad told me she's Mexican but she's a pretty little thing, isn't she."

New Mexican, she almost corrected, then gave it up. "Doesn't matter what she is—or who she is."

"Didn't say otherwise. I'm no bigot. I even went to the Cinco de Mayo festival in Sioux Falls last year. Had a great time." Rick jiggled the zipper on his coat. "Where's her dad?"

"Sioux Falls. I expect to—" Her cell phone launched into the dispatch line of *Adam 12*. "That should be him." She turned away. "Marek? How's Sanchez?"

His voice rumbled out into her ear. "Still in surgery. He won't be talking even when he comes out of it. They're wiring his jaw shut, his daughter tells me, and, no, she doesn't know who did it. Other than union-busting flunkies, that is. I have a feeling she thinks I looked the other way when it happened. You get anything from your end?"

"The only mystery I solved," she told him, "was the identity of your anonymous caller. Dr. Sabanovic thought you ratted on him. I'm not happy with you."

With resignation in his voice, he said, "So what's new."

"Marek...never mind." She felt like laughing, strangely. Punchy. "I'm at your place. Becca is asleep. Everything's fine." She crossed her fingers behind her back. "Just get back here."

A long pause came. "And how am I supposed to do that?"

"What do you mean?"

"You told me to go with the ambulance, remember? Doubt I can get a cab back."

She closed her eyes.

In the hospital parking lot, Marek eased down into the squad car's passenger seat. "Gullick?"

"Rick." The deputy's blonde hair stood up from his scalp like dried short-grass in August. "Sheriff was right. You're one big son of a gun."

"A big pain in the ass in her opinion, I'm sure." Marek had to slam the door of the squad twice to get it to shut; it must have been replaced and didn't quite fit. The boxy shape of the car told him it was vintage. "Thanks for coming."

"I don't mind." Gullick's fingers danced on the steering wheel as he pulled away. "I'm still wired from getting shot at by your—I guess he's your brother, isn't he. Half anyway. Weird, you being Karen's uncle when everyone says you're younger than she is." The sidelong glance told Marek the deputy doubted it. "Karen told me about the guy who got beat up. I bet the Mexican mafia did it. You must have run into them down in Albuquerque all the time."

Marek managed to keep his face straight as the deputy rambled on. He wasn't sure if it was nerves or normal twenty-something skitter-brain that had the deputy jumping all over the map.

"Why did Arne Okerlund shoot at you?" Marek finally broke in.

"Because I wasn't you."

Marek fiddled with the seat adjuster, almost gave up when it stuck, then pushed back with relief. "He'd be happy to shoot me, Deputy Gullick. Try again."

"Oh, I don't think you're supposed to know about it because the sheriff, I mean, both sheriffs—well, they're embarrassed and it's only a bullet hole so—"

"I take it the hole isn't in you."

"I dropped to the floor. I think I can still hear my heart pounding. Kind of a high, really."

Adrenaline junkie, Marek thought. Rick Gullick might be better suited to a city force than a rural one. Maybe he should send him to Manny to break in. "Who's with Becca?"

"Sheriff. Karen, I mean. Your daughter woke up when the gun went off but she didn't make a peep. I went upstairs and checked on her and—I..."

They raced around a slow-going Buick, almost clipping its bumper, and Marek tested his seatbelt. It held and so did he. "You what?"

"I should ticket that Buick for going below the speed limit," the deputy muttered. "What? Oh, I couldn't understand it—how she got those cool eyes." His own darted over to Marek's. "Guess she got them from you. But she didn't say anything, not even when I asked her about those saint thingies over her bed. Kinda creepy. Made me feel like I was being watched."

"They're called *retablos*. They're art." Okay, not quite the truth,

Marek thought, but some of Manny's *retablos* sold in his wife's art gallery, so it wasn't a lie.

Rick accelerated around a truck then darted around a snowplow, waving his hand at the operator. Marek closed his eyes. Maybe he'd have been better off walking home. "I don't usually see driving like this unless I'm in a car chase. Or in the back of an ambulance."

"Oh. Sorry. Thought you city cops drove like this all the time." The deputy eased back on the accelerator and set the cruise. "Better?"

"Much." Marek was surprised the cruise control actually worked—and that the squad had it at all. "You knew Hansen, right?"

"Oh, yeah." The deputy's fingers stopped dancing on the steering wheel. "I hope I'm not stepping over the line for saying it but—well, the guy was an asshole."

That brought Marek's head around from the enveloping darkness that told him they were now in the countryside. "Thought you two got on."

"For a while, yeah, because I thought he was a decent enough guy, just doing his job." Some of the youth leached out of his face. "I even helped patrol trailer city at night for him when I was on duty."

"What changed your mind?"

"I think he was trafficking."

Marek considered that. "Drugs?"

"No, I mean *human* trafficking. We had a special class on it in Pierre. I think—listen, I'm not sure, but I think Dale ripped off some of those people who worked there. He'd go with them to the bank and take most of their pay. Said they owed it."

"Hmm."

"Hey, don't go all Bork on me. Just thought I'd mention it. You want to stop at the Alford truck stop?" Rick's fingers danced again on the steering wheel. "I need caffeine."

Not hardly, Marek thought.

Back in her own home, Karen sank down into the easy chair opposite her father's recliner.

The closed eyes didn't fool her.

"At least Marek didn't notice the bullet hole," she said. "Maybe he'll think it was from a previous tenant. God knows, the place is a wreck."

Without opening his eyes, her father said, "Was just an accident. Damn fingers."

Karen knew a little about trajectories; it had been her father's good hand on the trigger. Oh, it had been an accident, but it had been the brain, not the fingers, at fault.

Sitting outside intensive care after his stroke, she'd prayed, pleaded, demanded. Let her have this one life. God had granted it to her. With a twist: she'd ended up in her father's shoes. While he'd struggled to speak again, to walk again, she knew that he'd have rather died than be a burden to her, to himself, to his job.

But her need for him had kept him there.

To keep tears from falling, over what they'd both lost, she told herself to be grateful how far he'd come, so very far.

"We didn't get anything, not one word, out of anybody near Sanchez's trailer," she said, as much to herself as her father. "Thing is, who would these people be afraid to speak of, and who would want to teach Sanchez a lesson, except for someone who wanted to squash the union? Which at the moment, appears to be a union of one."

She dropped her head into her hands. "I went and talked to Thompson. He was having a drink at The Shaft with Dale's replacement. Bartender vouched for them both."

When she looked up, she found her father had fallen asleep. With a sigh, she went to the closet, pulled out a blanket, and covered him. Then she leaned down and kissed his cheek.

"I love you, Dad," she whispered. "Happy trigger finger and all."

When she arrived at the office the next morning, Karen spun a 360. "Where's Marek?"

"You got kids," Walrus said with a shrug, "sometimes you're late."

Kurt hooked thumbs into his gun belt. "He didn't call."

"Well, we had a little excitement last night," she said and explained.

The door opened then and an old man came in, his step tentative, his face as white as the hair that stuck out beneath the seed cap. She knew him by sight. Iver Andersen. Behind him, her missing detective loomed in the doorway; he too looked shaken.

"What happened?" she demanded. "Is Becca all right?"

"She's at school."

Karen smoothed out the adrenaline rush. "So what's the problem, Mr. Andersen?"

"I was born in Sweden," he said with fear in his face. "Never tried to hide it."

She wondered if he was starting to lose it mentally. "Why should you? The Okerlunds came from there as well." Then it hit. "Oh, you've got to be kidding. Marek, he—"

"Pulled out right in front of me on Main. So I did what Dahl told me and checked his status." Marek kicked out a chair. "Sit down, Mr. Andersen."

The gentleness in Marek's voice kept the order more in the line of respectful attention. The old man sank into the chair with relief.

"I'll call his daughter," Kurt said. "She'll be home."

"Nah, the granddaughter, she took a spill on the playground," Iver said. "Gretchen went to take her to the clinic. That's why I drove. Needed more feed cake. Kids don't like me driving." His fierce look turned abashed. "Maybe they got reason."

Karen didn't see any obvious injuries on either Iver or her detective. She wondered who Becca's guardian was, if something happened to Marek. Undoubtedly someone back in New Mexico, but she had to bite her lip to keep from asking him.

"Any damage?" she asked Iver.

"Think we had, what, maybe an inch between us when we got stopped?" The old man glanced up at Marek, who nodded stiffly, as if his neck muscles were too tight. "But I got my front wheels stuck in the snowbank on the curb. Gotsch is going to pull it out and look it over. Anyway, Detective Okerlund said I'd have to pay a fine then asked me about my immigration status. Didn't understand that one 'til he asked where I'd been born and did I have a birth certificate."

Was Marek so shaken he didn't realize the difference between birth country and citizenship? "You're naturalized, that's all, Mr. Andersen. You don't have to have been born here..." But Iver was shaking his head. "Never did anything official."

After a few more minutes of discussion, she pointed at her men. "Kurt, you try to raise one of the Andersens. Walrus, get him some coffee. Marek, come with me."

Then she marched herself and Marek into Harold Dahl's office.

"Iver? What do you mean, he's illegal." The commissioner actually came out of his chair, with a plop, his ball-belly jiggling in protest. "For God's sake, his kids were years ahead of me and his grandkids are mostly grown. He's got greats now."

"Mr. Andersen was born in Sweden," she answered, forcing herself to be factual, to be the representative of the law she'd sworn to uphold. "He came to Canada with his folks when he was still in diapers; they moved to South Dakota a couple years later. They had some cousins down here and land was cheap. He didn't even know he wasn't born here until his daughter-in-law started doing the family history a while back. So far as he knows, no one in his family ever got naturalized; he doesn't have any papers. He isn't sure if he's got Canadian citizenship either."

"Hell, things were different then." Harold glared up at Marek. "I meant being illegal *now.*"

"How many years does it take?" Marek asked.

"Is it like common law marriages," Karen put in, "you stay here long enough, it's too late to send you back?"

When Harold didn't answer, Marek said, "We've got two men in custody for being here illegally. Mr. Andersen and Mr. Jaramillo."

For once, she and Marek were on the same team. "Same offense, same consequence, or it isn't justice."

"Though I don't know when the next deportation flight to Sweden is," Marek said.

"It isn't Iver's fault," Harold protested. "It's his parents who didn't get it taken care of." As they stared at him, the commissioner sank back down into the comforting curve of his chair and muttered to himself. "I'll be lynched if I put Mr. Andersen in jail or have him deported. Where would he go anyway? I'll bet he doesn't even know anybody in Sweden and how can you expect an old man to relocate away from his family at his age? It'll kill him. And the Andersens will kill me."

Glad it wasn't her call, Karen commented, "You'll get lynched if you let Jaramillo go."

"Will I? Who knows he's down there? Nails hasn't said a word. All he can talk about this morning is how nothing is happening on the Hansen murder. You avoiding him, Sheriff?"

"I dodged a call from him last night," Karen admitted. "This morning too. I didn't have anything to tell him."

Apparently Nails hadn't caught word yet about Sanchez getting beaten up, she thought, not that she had anything to tell him about that either.

"Telling the media you've got nothing seems to make them happy," Marek told her. "But if you actually tell them nothing, you just make them mad."

"Tell me about it," Harold grumbled then turned back to their illegals. "So you heard back from the Feds on Jaramillo, Karen?"

"Yes, finally," she said. "But when I asked when they'd pick him up, the guy laughed at me. Said if we had thirty illegals, maybe they'd come, otherwise we were free to keep Jaramillo on our own dime." She saw the twitch on Marek's face. "You *knew*."

"No one would listen to me."

That shut her up.

But it cleared Harold's face. "Well then, we can lay it on the Feds." A popular pastime in the Dakotas, she thought. "We can't be footing their bill," he went on. "Let both of them go. If anyone asks, point them to me."

Downstairs a few minutes later, Karen smiled at the man worrying his fingers around his cap like a rosary bead. "You're free to go, Mr. Andersen."

He looked at her uncertainly, opened his mouth, then wisely shut it. He plunked his cap back on his head and with their help, made it down the stairs and into the pickup that pulled up to take him home. One of the younger grandsons, she thought, who gave the old man a teasing grin. The affection in his eyes, though, told her that he'd likely not rat on his grandpa.

Marek watched them go. "What about Jaramillo?"

"Our jail's got to be better than that drafty trailer of his," she said as she went back into the office with Marek. "I'll let him go after our meeting this morning." She beckoned over her men. "Let's see if we can come up with something to tell Nails."

Walrus fluttered his moustache with disgust. "Geez, the man is all over us, wanting to know what we're doing—scratching our butts or planting our faces up them." He trundled toward the break room. "I'll get the drinks."

"I'll get the eats," Kurt said and disappeared after him.

Then the door jerked open and a man came barreling in.

"You've ignored me long enough." He headed straight for Karen. "And it's going to cost you."

CHAPTER 26

MAREK MOVED WITHIN GRAPPLING DISTANCE, his left hand going to his gun, but the man ignored him—his attention centered on the sheriff.

Was this, Marek wondered, the missing husband?

About the same age as Karen, with dishwater blonde hair, he had a battered look. The nose swerved out of alignment and an old scar creased down one cheek.

Karen took a head to toe inventory of their visitor. "Dirk Larson, I presume?"

"It's not Livingston," the man said, his lead-colored eyes widening as Karen looked him straight on.

Marek eased back, his hand falling from his gun. Larson. The agent who'd requested the autopsy report. So, it was true. Karen intended to hand off the case to the state boys.

Why that should hurt, he didn't know, given their history. Although at the moment, Karen looked less than thrilled with the cavalry.

Larson said to her, "You've got a hell of a nerve, lady, lying to a DCI agent."

She took the one step that divided the two. "Nerve is something desirable in a sheriff. And I didn't lie to you, Larson."

The agent didn't blink. "Crying uncle again? If you think you can take on a complex homicide like this one, just because your daddy was sheriff, then you've got another thing coming."

"What I've got," she said, "is a detec—"

"Squat," the man finished.

Marek didn't like being called squat but he was getting

used to it.

To his surprise, Karen's face hardened. "Don't take potshots at my men."

"What men?" Larson asked. "I'm talking about you. I don't care if you're a woman or a freaking alien but without experience, you're nothing in this game."

So Marek wasn't squat after all. Karen was. Interesting.

Larson continued, "Talk to me in a few years or, better yet, decades—not that you'll get the chance after your constituents see how badly you screwed up this investigation. Still, I've tried to keep things moving with the lab."

Karen cocked her head at Marek, eyes cool. "Did you?"

No, he hadn't brought Larson in. "I thought you did."

Marek saw a hint of hurt. Maybe it was time he cleared something up. "Agent Larson?"

"Butt out, Deputy. I'm not finished."

"I'm not a deputy."

"Then pardon me for plain speaking, whoever you are, but civilians don't have anything to say about this screwup until election day."

Walrus walked in with his mug of hot water and the coffee carafe. "Hey, didn't know you were coming, Larson. Just in time for our morning confab. Coffee?"

He got a snarl.

Relaxed now, Karen went to her desk. "Pull up a chair, everybody."

Larson didn't move, arms crossed, face mulish.

With a grin, Walrus sat, poured, and handed mugs around. Then he yelled back into the break room, "You pulled those flesh-whatevers out of the microwave yet, Bechtold?"

Whatever it was, Marek thought, it didn't sound appetizing.

Kurt came out with a tray, put it on the sheriff's desk, and rolled his chair over. He looked inquiringly over at DCI Agent Larson then shrugged when he got nothing but glare.

Karen plopped one of the fried turnovers onto a napkin. "Ah, isn't this nice. Good food, good company—or at least company—and, eventually, we get to talk." She dunked the turnover in ketchup and took a big bite. The aroma of hamburger and onion spilled out into the room. "Though I for one won't mind if we speed that part up. Got to multi-task these days, I hear, just like these big city folks."

After one bite, Marek didn't want to bother with condiments. He didn't care what it was called; it tasted like a Midwestern version of the breakfast burrito.

"Best *fleischkuchle* outside Schmeckfest," Karen said, noting his enjoyment.

As if Larson realized he'd lost ground by being the last man standing, he grabbed a chair and rammed it across from Karen's, sat down, re-crossed his arms. He didn't pick up one of the turnovers. "A tea party is about what I'd expect from a sheriff of your description."

Karen patted down a juicy line on her chin with a napkin. "Here I thought I was hiding it so well, Agent Larson. I confess: I'm an alien."

"You were born right here in Eda County," Kurt protested.

Walrus spewed pastry.

Larson flicked off crumbs. "What the bloody hell do you think you're—"

The blast of cool air stifled further hot words. A spindly teenager with a red, moon-round face came in, looking like a corn dog in the knee-length beige coat.

He held a small package in his hand. "Special delivery, Sheriff." His slow speech clued Marek in, if the face hadn't, that the kid had Downs. "Mom said you wanted this ASAP."

"Yes, thanks, Teddy," Karen said, taking it. "I know you guys had to halt production to get a one-off done. I appreciate it."

The young man gave her a salute, got one in return, and left with a broad grin.

Karen held the package out to Marek, a gleam in her eyes. "This would be for you."

Marek ripped it open then reached down to recover the cap that fell out. He fingered the silky embroidery. The word stitched over the patch didn't take any effort on his part to read, even though it blurred under his eyes. Had he ever wanted this? He hadn't thought so, so why the emotion?

"Lemme see," Walrus said.

A chair scraped back over the marble. "No way I'm sitting through a fashion show," Larson said. "Expect a call from Pierre, Sheriff, about DCI and crime scene protocol."

She glanced at Marek. "Stand up and let the man out."

Marek rose to his feet, adjusted the strap to its loosest setting, and set the cap on his head.

"Eda County *Detective*?" Larson whirled back to Karen. "Rural counties like yours don't have detectives. Besides, what kind of idiot would take a job out here in bumfuck?"

"Meet Detective Marek Okerlund." She gave Marek a smile—a real one. "My uncle."

Karen never thought she'd take such pleasure in making that introduction—and it appeared to have shocked both men. Marek recovered first.

"The proper term for me around here," he told the DCI agent, "is halfwit, not idiot."

Larson got his jaw hinged. "Alright, so the joke's on me. But I still don't know squat about you, Okerlund, except you don't look much like Arne, much less old enough to be his brother. No one in Sioux Falls ever heard he had one."

Marek said, "Different mothers."

Larson waved a hand. Would that the rest of them could dismiss that so easily, Karen thought.

"What experience do you have," Larson asked Marek, "and where'd you get it?"

"Agent Larson, we're not holding interviews here," Karen said. "All you need to know is that he's qualified."

"What, did he get his creds from a cereal box?"

"That's right," Marek said. "Life."

Walrus spewed again and Kurt handed him a stack of napkins.

Karen wanted to get back to their meeting. "Now that we've established that we do indeed have a detective here, Larson, feel free to go. We have a case to solve."

"Handily enough, that's why I'm here. I've got a theory that your killer is—"

"Agent Larson, we don't need you—"

"Here," Marek interrupted. "But you could do us a favor in Sioux Falls."

The last thing she wanted was for Agent I'm-in-Charge Larson to butt into their case. That he'd done so, without her knowledge much less permission, made her furious. "If you want to bring DCI in, Marek, you deal with them."

"Fine," Larson said, turning his back on her. "What can I do for you, Detective?"

"Talk to Sanchez for us."

What was Marek up to? Sanchez wasn't going to be talking any time soon, not with his jaw wired shut. She cleared her throat. "Yes, seeing as you're right there..."

Larson glanced back at her. "Who's Sanchez and what's the catch?"

After the DCI agent left, she wrapped up the short meeting then beckoned Marek downstairs.

"Get Jaramillo's things, will you, Tammy," she said, once they'd reached the dispatch desk. "He's the second course of our get-out-of-jail special today."

"I heard about Iver." The woman got up from her seat with a creak of relief. "Let me tell you, if Dahl hadn't sprung him, I would've done it myself. None of us would be left alive after the Andersen clan came after us."

Tammy went into the evidence room and came back with Jaramillo's clothes and a small clear bag. She flung it on the dispatch desk and it spilled out the pitiful few items: belt, wallet, and pocketknife.

Karen replaced them in the bag then saw the brown flakes, brittle on her fingers. "What is this stuff?"

Tammy glanced over. "Did it come from the wallet?"

Marek stepped up from behind her. "No, it's black leather. The belt too. Must be from the pocketknife." He looked down at her fingers. "Blood."

"What?"

"It's blood. Dried blood."

She lifted her hand to the flickering fluorescent lights. Through the kaleidoscope of light, she saw red.

CHAPTER 27

KAREN TIPPED THE FLAKES INTO an evidence bag. She sealed it—and, she hoped, the case.

"Karen...Sheriff, it's just blood," Marek said. "Could've come from working at the plant."

But she'd pulled on a thread Marek didn't know about. "He told me...he felt murder."

"I've felt it a time or two myself," he said mildly. "What's Emilio Jaramillo got against Dale Hansen?"

That stopped her. Then excitement rushed back. "He said something about whites getting the good jobs. It's racial, Marek. Whites out. Just like Nails said."

Tammy held up the keys. "Guess I'm putting these back?"

Marek said, "We've got nothing to hold him on."

"Not on murder yet," Karen conceded, taking the keys from Tammy. "But he's still illegal. We can hold him."

Tammy took herself back to the dispatch desk.

"I'll send Kurt with the blood flakes and the knife to the crime lab right away," Karen said, relieved to finally have something concrete to work with. "If that's human blood, Jaramillo's our prime suspect. DNA will take longer, of course."

Marek still didn't look convinced. "Go ahead, but even if he is our carver, that doesn't make him our killer."

Okay, she'd play his game. "If he didn't kill Dale, he still might know who did—I don't know if I mentioned it, but he's Guatemalan like the others who disappeared."

But when they went to see Jaramillo, all he wanted to talk about was his daughter. When told she hadn't been found, he looked more relieved than betrayed. After that, he wouldn't talk, not even to Marek, except to say one word: *No.*

Which, curiously enough, meant the same thing in English and Spanish.

But inside, she was saying, *Yes.* She'd got her man.

When they returned to the office, Rick Gullick awaited them.

"Hey, Sheriff, Detective, look what I found in the field at the old Hansen farm."

The eager young deputy held a coat aloft like a scalp. Then he brought it down and dug into the pockets. "Look, there's stuff in here, like Dale's cell and some kind of weird tag and..."

Karen let out a hiss of breath and grabbed evidence bags from her drawer. Rick turned the shade of the coat, a dull, unattractive red. "Oh, hell, I didn't think..."

"For God's sake, Rick," she said.

"Sorry, I'm just...not much sleep." The deputy dropped the items into the evidence bags like he was getting rid of live grenades. "I was just coming off the interstate and I saw the flash of red in the field, and I guess I was so excited to find it that I just...didn't think."

Marek asked, "Where?"

"Maybe fifty yards from the fence, still had some snow on it, so it's been there awhile—since the blizzard, I guess. Dale must have, you know, shed it off, like they say people who freeze to death do, thinking they're hot. I don't get that. How can you be so cold that you're hot?"

He jumped from foot to foot like a Mexican jumping bean. "Am I in big trouble?"

"We'll just take your prints," Marek said, "and send them to the lab for elimination."

Karen shoved the sleep-happy deputy toward the downstairs door. "Go get Tammy to take your prints. When you're done, go home and crash."

When the door shut behind him, she said to Marek, "Thanks for pulling him out of the fire. Rick's young. He's only a reserve, but he works hard and if he hadn't been so tired, he'd have known better."

"We all make mistakes. I've made my share." Marek picked up the cell phone, protected now by the plastic. "Dead. It'll need to be charged if we want to get anything off of it."

She'd wanted to learn, she told herself, so learn. "Like what?"

"See what phone numbers he stored, for one." He put the cell phone aside and pondered the dirty red coat. "Talk about mistakes. I've just made a doozy."

Karen tried to think what that might be—but came up with nothing. "What's that?"

"I've been assuming Dale Hansen was taken to that spot by the interstate and chained." He looked up from the coat. "Dale must have ditched it when he was wandering about in the field. So he wasn't on the interstate to start with, though he may have been headed there."

"So where was he?" Then she made the connection. "At the old Hansen farm."

Marek nodded. "We never checked. It didn't seem related, what with Dale on the interstate side of the fence and the farm a couple miles away." He picked up the last piece of evidence. "And this lockout tag points to the worker who lost his hand in the grinder. Chacón. Or someone who wanted Hansen to pay for what he did to Chacón. Or...it could be completely unrelated."

She got the message: don't assume. Still, she asked, "Sanchez?"

"But then who beat up Sanchez?"

"Stop messing with my head, Marek." She chafed her temples until the next step came clear. "Let's go out to the farm."

Twenty minutes later, they tromped toward the farmstead from the gravel road where she'd parked the Suburban.

"What's with the weather?" Marek asked, looking down at his mud-covered boots. "It's early January. It's supposed to be subzero."

She skirted a shallow lake of water. "It doesn't get as cold as it used to, or at least doesn't stay as cold, several brown Christmases, not much snow."

Karen walked through a thin white line of snow on the shade-side of the barn to wipe the mud off her boots. Then she went up to the farmhouse. Once white, it peeled now to gray, sunk under the heavy mercury of plummeting fortunes. The countryside was peppered with such abandoned farmsteads, what with consolidation and the farm crisis of years past.

"It's locked." She peered in through an uncurtained window. "It doesn't look like anyone's been in there. Neat as a pin."

"Let's check the barn."

She followed in his tracks.

The barn door sagged and groaned in the wind. When Marek pulled it all the way open, she walked in, her gun leading. "Police!

Anyone here?"

But the only sound was Marek's footsteps behind her. They kicked up dust that scattered in the dim light. "My God, that's lethal," she said then stifled a sneeze.

Marek held up a warning hand and she heard a faint, metallic clink.

She gripped her gun with both hands. Marek pointed. At first, she saw only the small stack of hay on the floor. Hay didn't clink, she thought.

Had someone moved in the shadows?

When Marek's finger rose, she followed its trajectory with her gun.

The object of his attention swung lazily in a draft of air. Glinting dully in the dust-filled light, a long, broken chain hung from a weathered cross beam.

CHAPTER 28

MAREK DROPPED THE COILED EVIDENCE onto Karen's desk. The chain looked never-ending, he thought, unless you looked close, to see the ends. But he couldn't see the end of the case.

Walrus wandered over then went *en pointe.* "Hot dog. It's *the* chain, isn't it. From the plant."

Marek had learned caution early in his career, when he'd nearly gotten an innocent man convicted for capital murder. He didn't let himself forget. "The lab's got the rest of the chain, so we can't be sure until they match it. Even if they do, the last person who had that hider chain, according to Chacón anyway, was Dale himself. At the plant."

"Where'd you find it?"

"Someone used it to chain Dale from a beam in the old Hansen barn," Marek explained, while Karen filled out an evidence tag.

The deputy stroked his moustache. "So how'd he get loose?"

"Probably used his feet to pile up some hay as a cushion, then swung on the chain." Marek scraped his heel against the turf-green rug. Flakes of dark earth sloughed off. "With the weak links, it didn't take much weight to snap, just as it did at the plant."

Karen attached the evidence tag. "The big problem is, we don't have a clue whether we've got just one suspect—or two."

She'd said just that on the way back, disrupting his thinking—of the same thing. He had to hand it to her, she learned quickly, even if she jumped too hard, too fast. But she'd also proven she could own up to her mistakes, in front of witnesses no less, a rare thing.

Walrus pulled on his moustache. "What do you mean, two?"

Hands free, Karen ticked her fingers. "First, somebody to chain Dale to the cross beam in the old barn—and then leave him there. Second, somebody to chain him to the fence out by the interstate after he got free."

"Tracked him down, that's all," Walrus said. "It's got to be the same person—or persons."

"Could be," Marek said. "But how'd they find him in the blizzard?"

Karen asked, "And if they meant to kill Dale in the barn, why didn't they just do it?"

Marek scraped the other heel over the rug. "Why do you think they didn't mean to?"

She looked at him in surprise. "With the heavy coat and vest Dale had on, plus the shelter of the barn, he would have survived the blizzard."

The flakes from his boots, Marek noticed, had turned the green rug to brown. "Not if he wasn't found."

"Oh." Karen stared down at the chain. "Sick."

"Geez, it could take weeks to die that way." Walrus shuddered, stared up at the ceiling, and studied the mottled plaster. "Wait a minute. We've got one padlock, right? Same kind as the plant."

Marek wondered what the deputy had seen in the plaster. "So?"

Walrus wrapped his fingers around his own wrist then jerked down. "When Dale breaks the chain, there's that bit around his wrist with the padlock still on."

The man had a brain under that gleaming pate, Marek thought. "Yet when we find Dale, the padlock's not only locking down that bit of chain but also the tow chain."

"Which was added later." Karen patted Walrus's shoulder. "One padlock. One key. One suspect."

"Or suspects working in tandem." Marek nodded toward the beaming man. "Good catch, Deputy. But why didn't Dale use his cell phone, once he got free?"

"Could be a dead zone," Walrus said.

"I bet Dale tried," Karen said, beginning to pace. "From what Uncle Sig said, land lines were working better than cells that night."

Just watching her stalk from pillar to pillar made Marek tired. She'd had the same energy on the basketball court—and on endless summer days, shooting hoops in her dad's driveway. The bounces, the boings, the swishes, they'd been the backboard of his childhood.

"Dale ditched the cell with the coat," Marek said. "That doesn't make sense."

"What's sense got to do with it," Walrus asked, "when it's 20 below and Dale starts stripping like he's on a beach in Waikiki?"

"Point taken."

An hour later, Karen forced herself to finish the foreclosure notices she'd been putting off. A dark shadow engulfed them just as she completed the last, for the little card shop on Norbeck.

She looked up and sighed. "Do you have a police fetish, Darcie?"

Then she recognized the lean, tanned man who ranged himself behind the girl.

His features had only honed with time like the scalpel he wielded with such skill. A plastic surgeon, she recalled. She wondered if he'd ever considered rearranging his daughter's face. Maybe he hadn't thought it worth the effort once he found out she wasn't his.

Karen nodded to him. "Troy."

After a baffled second, his grim face relaxed. "Darcie didn't tell me that the intimidating Sheriff Mehaffey was Karen Okerlund. I thought you were headed for bigger and better things than this burg."

His smile faltered at her silence.

"Dad, I mean, Troy—"

The man put a hand on the much shorter girl's shoulder. "Dad will do."

With that gesture, Karen reminded herself that Troy had been kind to her when she'd first started high school—an older boy who'd danced with the gangling girl she'd been.

"If you came all the way up from Arizona to rescue your daughter, Troy, you're behind on the news. She's clear. Not entirely innocent, but clear."

The girl bit her lip. "Dad came to make sure I was okay and we...well, we talked." She glanced back at him then stuffed her hands into her pockets. "I have to tell you something."

Karen didn't want to hear it, but given Troy might not know the score, she said, "Listen, if this is about Jaramillo, he's illegal. He told me as much, and we've confirmed it." She wasn't going to broadcast her theory that he was also a killer. "That's just the way it is, like it or not."

And she was finding more and more not to like about this job. Maybe she should just hand over the badge to the last Okerlund standing—which at the moment would be Marek, looking out the window again.

"But it was Blanca who got him in jail," Darcie protested. Then her father squeezed her shoulder and she redirected. "It's not about the Jaramillos. Exactly. It's about Dale."

Were they, Karen wondered, going to get yet another confession? "Third time's the charm, Ms. Ringold?"

That brought Marek around. "I think we should take this into interview."

Dr. Ringold stared up at the detective. "Marek Okerlund, I take it. I don't believe we ever met. Officially, anyway."

But his tone indicated he'd heard of him or, it not him directly, the Marek name.

With a touch of irony, Marek said, "You were well ahead of me in school."

The man's flush told Karen he'd heard of Marek's less than stellar academic performance.

Darcie asked Marek, "I won't get in trouble, will I, for not telling you everything before? I mean, I didn't lie, more omitted."

"I'm not making any promises," Karen said, yanking the chain of command back to herself. "Tell us straight this time. Troy, you'll have to wait out here, since Darcie's not a minor."

Darcie waited until she got a nod from Marek.

If this continued, Karen thought, Marek was going to win her job on a landslide in the next election—as a write-in candidate. She'd be hard pressed not to vote for him herself.

In the interview room, Marek surprised Karen once again with his first question.

"Would you like to revise your earlier statement, Darcie," he asked, "as to why you kicked your stepfather out of the Hummer?"

Darcie stared at him, then at the recorder, and sighed. "Okay, yeah, I would. That night, I did argue with Dale, but it wasn't about illegal immigrants. At least, not directly, but about meth. Blanca said she got hooked on it working at the plant."

"At the plant itself?" Karen propped one arm on the top of a bulging file cabinet. "Someone was distributing from there?"

Darcie put her hands over her face but nodded.

Marek studied her. "You can't hurt Dale now."

Karen finally got it—and got back on track. She now had another motive for Emilio Jaramillo wanting Dale Hansen dead. "Say it, Darcie."

"Dale gave meth to the workers and docked their pay for it." Darcie dropped her hands wearily. "He said it was just to help them keep their count, you know, to keep up with the chain speed. The company's always pushing: faster, faster, faster. Like people are Intel chips."

Marek ran a fingernail down a crack in the table's varnish. "Are you telling us all the workers at the plant took meth?"

"No, but the immigrants, they didn't know what it was, only that it would help them work faster. And some who did know, didn't care. Mr. Jaramillo, he figured it out real fast and told Blanca to stop." Outrage brought animation to the angled face. "Blanca lost her mother to drugs."

"Like mother, like daughter?" Karen asked drily.

Voice taut, Darcie told her about the drug runners in Guatemala. "Blanca was at her church when it happened or she'd have been killed too. She said they can't go back. Those people run the villages there."

Into the chastened silence, Marek asked, "Where was Dale getting the meth, Darcie?"

"I don't know. Maybe that guy I saw him with? You know, the Hispanic guy in the fancy mountain gear. Aren't the Mexicans supposed to be cornering the market these days?"

Though his hand fisted on the table, Marek's voice remained gentle. "So why did Blanca keep taking meth?"

Darcie looked at him as if stumped by having to divulge the obvious. "Because she couldn't keep up without it."

"Then why didn't she quit working at PBI?" Karen asked and had both Marek and Darcie staring at her. "What?"

"That night, at the clinic, Blanca told me why she was always afraid she'd have to quit school, why she *had* to work, why they had so little money. They paid to come here, took all the money they still had left, and were told that they'd have papers and become citizens. But once they got here, they found out otherwise— and they couldn't tell anyone or they'd be deported."

"That's illegal," Karen said.

The scowl didn't improve the girl's looks. "I'd expect you to take Dale's side about illegals."

At that, Karen planted her hands on the table. "I meant, human trafficking, it's illegal. I'm not the bad guy here, Darcie Ringold, and if you'd told us this before, we might have made more progress on this investigation."

Marek shifted in his chair. "I take it, Ms. Ringold, that you didn't go for a pregnancy test."

Karen watched that dark face redden high at the cheekbones.

"David Echols called me, from the clinic, asked me to come. He was kind of out of his comfort zone, and since it involved Dale...well, I went."

Now Marek's eyes lidded. "How long did you stay?"

"Until Dale called me. The Jaramillos, they left earlier, and I stayed and talked to David. About illegals, about how to treat addiction, about lots of things. But mostly I just had to let off steam...because it was Dale who got her hooked."

Tears welled into the dark eyes. "I hadn't seen Blanca since she got so bad. I didn't even recognize her; she's nothing like she was, all eager to learn, eager to be here, despite everything. She used to be so bright and now..." She dashed the tears with the heels of her hands. "Then Dale called. You know the rest."

Marek asked, "Why *didn't* you tell us right at the start?"

"I felt so stupid." She flung her hands out with her voice. "Here I was, feeling sorry for Dale, for having to take a shitty job like he did, for losing his farm and everything that mattered to him. And he was out there wrecking the lives of people who had it even worse." Now her hands drew back in. "Besides, if it came out, I knew my mother was going to catch flak."

Now this, at least, Karen could understand. Family loyalty.

"Truth?" Darcie said.

"That'd be nice," Karen muttered.

"I felt sorry for Dale. I can't say I liked him; he didn't know how to be liked. But he treated my mom well enough, gave her money and trotted her around. Which she enjoyed, so don't look like that, Sheriff. I won't need a man to keep me like she does. I've got no looks but I've got brains."

And she'd pawn them to the highest bidder, Karen thought, and be called a success: but not here. If the reunion with Troy was anything to go by, Darcie would be finishing her schooling in Arizona not South Dakota.

"That's the message," Marek said into the exhausted silence.

"What?" Darcie eyed him warily. "Brains?"

Karen didn't know if her detective lacked brains at the

moment—or if she herself did. "Marek, I can't take cryptic right now."

"Remember those packets Thompson offered you?" he asked her. "One of the workers said what Thompson thought was lite, snatched right away from underneath our eyes. But I'll bet it was *white*." He waited a beat. "Which is one of the street names for meth."

Karen sucked in a breath. "Jaramillo, he said Diablo—whoever he is, I forgot to ask you—said they needed white to work. I thought Jaramillo meant he needed to *be* white to work, to get the better jobs." She could kick herself. "I should've taped that interview."

"Was Diablo the man I saw," Darcie asked. "The one in that dark truck?"

The mouth beneath the scraggily beard curved. "Diablo? I don't think so."

Karen pounced. "You know him? Who is he?"

"I don't believe the devil drives."

"Dammit, Marek. Be serious."

"I can't be, not when we're talking pointy tails and pitchforks."

It finally sunk in. "Diablo means *devil?*" At his nod, she leaned back against the wall. "Great. That could mean anybody."

"You're missing the point," Marek told her, sadness dragging at his Byzantine face. "Who wanted meth out? White out?"

Darcie dropped her head into her hands. "Oh, God. Mr. Jaramillo."

She'd got her man after all.

CHAPTER 29

KAREN ITCHED TO CALL NAILS.

But after Darcie left the interview room, Marek recommended holding off on going public about their breakthrough.

"Did you take a good look at that jacket Rick Gullick brought in?" he asked her. "The right arm was coated inside with blood."

Karen labeled the tape of the interview they'd just completed. Do the details, her instructor had said, and they'll do the time. "So?"

"When I talked to Dr. White, he—"

"How'd you like our nattily dressed pathologist?" she interrupted.

"Well enough," Marek said, his tired eyes crinkling at the corners, telling her he'd gotten the joke of the pathologist's name. "He said the message had been carved well before death. When Darcie picked Dale up from the plant, she said he cradled his arm. So if Jaramillo did it, it doesn't make him a killer, only a creative carver..."

He trailed off, frowned.

That deflated her again. But she wasn't ready to let go. "Maybe he came across Dale again after Darcie kicked him out on the road."

Marek shook himself out of his frown. "And took him all the way out to the barn in his old clunker? Why?" He followed her out of the interview room. "And how would he even know it was Hansen's old homestead?"

"Maybe he did, or maybe he just knew it was abandoned. He could chain Dale up and no one would look for him there." When

Marek's silence dragged, she said, "Look, I know you like Jaramillo, he seems like a good man. But maybe Sig's right, under certain circumstances, anyone can kill."

Marek sank down at his desk. It held not one piece of paper, she noted.

The phone on Marek's desk rang; he answered it, grimaced, and mouthed *Larson.*

Then she heard Marek say, "*El Gigante,* you mean? That's me."

After a moment, he put down the phone.

Not slammed, she noted. Either he had better control than she did or Larson hadn't tried to steamroll him. "What's going on?"

"Seems Sanchez can write, if he can't talk. When Larson pressed him on what happened last night, he wrote that he'd only talk to *El Gigante.*"

She'd forgotten about Sanchez. "How is he?"

"Awake. Scared."

"Looks like you're going to Sioux Falls then." At his mulish look, she said, "I'm sorry, but that's the job. You want free time, solve the case, and you've got it. In the meantime, Dad will protect Becca." If nothing else, her father had proven he could still shoot. "You can check on Chacón while you're there. See if you can get anything out of him about Jaramillo. I want it on record about the hider chain from the plant. You told me we have to build a case. Well, go build."

Marek stood at the foot of the hospital bed.

The wild colors of insult—yellow, purple, black, and blue—stood out along with puffy red on the swarthy face. Only a slit of Sanchez's unbandaged eye was visible.

"About time you got here."

Marek looked up at Larson, who stood near the head of the bed. "Had to get my daughter from school and take her to the babysitter." Marek wondered how Arne Okerlund would react to that term.

Larson looked baffled. "Why couldn't your wife do it?"

Sanchez grabbed the pen by his side and wrote on the small notepad.

Marek didn't move so Larson glanced down. "Sanchez, you've got the worst handwriting I've ever seen. Looks like familia. Familiar?"

"No, *familia,*" Marek said. "Family."

Larson stared down at the battered man. "You saying family did this to you?"

Marek watched the slit turn from dark to white. Not a faint but an eye roll. "No, he's saying..." How did it translate into a hyper-individualistic Anglo culture. It didn't. Not the same way. "Just family. A family matter."

On cue, a young Hispanic woman hustled through the door. Marek identified her as Consuela Sanchez. "Who are you people and what are you doing here?" she demanded.

Her father's hand rose off the bed, dropped the pen, trembled for a moment before his fingers clasped hers, lightly, but with a tenderness that had Marek clearing his throat.

Larson spoke first, introduced himself, then said, "Thought your dad would want to talk to someone without any Eda County connections. Instead, he sent for the detective here."

When Marek gave Consuela his name, her fierce look softened. "You were the one who told me not to drive while distracted."

"And did you?"

"No, I got a ride up. I'm not leaving until my dad does."

"And I'm not leaving," Larson broke in, "until your father tells us who did this to him and why."

Sanchez picked up the pen and scribbled. Larson leaned over. "Dammit, quit doing that. He wrote *familia* again."

"It's not who did it, Larson, but who he's protecting." Marek looked into that puffy face, that insult, and that stubbornness. How did you combat it? "My daughter was threatened too, if I didn't stop the investigation into Dale Hansen's death."

The dark slit widened, looked puzzled, then just weary.

Consuela dropped down to her father's level. "Dad, you can't let them do this to you. They win. You have to tell them."

But Sanchez's hand dropped the pen to grab his daughter's hand again.

"Who's they?" demanded Larson of the daughter.

"Go look at PBI," she told him. "They're the ones who don't want a union. Do you know how hard it was, for unions to make headway, to finally make businesses treat workers halfway decent? How they fought for things we now think are standard?"

Sanchez had passed on his passion to his daughter, it seemed.

"But it's all going backward now. And when people like my dad try to even the scales, they get threatened and beaten. It's not the first time it's happened to him, but it's the worst. Usually they don't

like to break anything, in case the cops actually care enough to—"
She broke off as her father squeezed her hand and shook his head.

It just didn't make sense, Marek thought. Sanchez had been more than willing to get in Thompson's face over labor violations. And Thompson had ignored him, because the union never got off the ground. What did either have to fear now?

Larson scowled at Consuela. "If we didn't care, we wouldn't be here. If it's somebody at PBI, if the local cops won't enforce it, I will. Your father would have died if somebody hadn't called it in."

Now Sanchez did pick up his pen. Larson leaned over. "He says to thank...I can't read it. Oh, doctor."

Marek met the slit of eye, knew that would be Dr. Ahmed, and nodded. "I don't think this is coming out of PBI," he told Larson. "Not directly. Not union-busting."

Sanchez closed his eye but not before the shot had hit home. Larson must have seen it too, because he leaned over. "Tell us, Sanchez. You could still be in danger and so could your daughter."

Marek didn't need more than a few ticks of silence to guess the outcome. "We're not going to get anything out of him."

The agent grunted his agreement. "Sorry I dragged you up here for nothing."

But Marek didn't consider it nothing. After wishing Sanchez the best, he headed down the hallway toward the one-handed worker's room. But before he'd gone more than a few steps, Larson stopped him.

"You gonna tell me what Sanchez has to do with your dead body down there? And what you picked up from him that you're not telling me?"

Marek decided that, for all his blustery manner, the man was good. "I haven't worked it all out yet...but our homicide might've already been solved by a reserve deputy with far more hair on his head than years."

Apparently Larson took this as a criticism, because he said, "Sorry if I came on like a bull in a china shop, or tea shop, down in Reunion, but I hate incompetence. Even Arne, with all his experience, let me in on the crime scene most times for felonies. So when I have to hear on the news that you had a homicide in Eda County and no one even gave me a call, I got a little hot."

A change from his own style; when he got angry, he went cold— or disappeared.

"So, what made you leave Albuquerque?" Larson asked.

Marek reminded himself that the man was, after all, a detective. Probably knew his entire service history by now. As for why...he thought back to Sanchez. "Family, I suppose." Or escape from what had once been a family. "What made you leave Chicago?"

They reached a stairwell exit. Larson put his hand on the door. "Same reason."

Hearing undertones, he asked Larson, "You divorced?"

"Hell, yes, years ago. Wife took the house, the car, the kids—and more than a few of my colleagues to bed with her. Left me with all the debts. You?"

"Widowed."

Larson pushed the door open. "Better than bitter."

"Your opinion."

After Larson left, Marek strode down the hallway to see Chacón but found the room occupied by an old lady with her knee in traction. She gave him an affronted look and whipped the sheets over her sagging hospital gown.

He found a nurse and asked her if Chacón had been discharged.

"Oh, the Feds came and took him. He was illegal."

Marek fought to keep his anger from the messenger. "He was a person of interest in my case."

The woman glanced up at his hat then shrugged. "They're Feds. They've got jurisdiction over state. You're just county."

For the first time, he realized how far down the food chain he'd come. Justice shouldn't depend on a jurisdictional pecking order. The Feds couldn't stir themselves to pick up an illegal out in the boondocks but went out of their way to get this one; why, who had clout?

After a few questions, he found out; the nurse he'd heard saying she'd look into the matter turned out to be a shirttail relation of the US Congressman.

Disgusted, he walked back down the floor.

"Marek?"

He stopped, baffled.

A man in the waiting room off the main corridor sat, book in hand, staring up at him over half-moon reading glasses.

"I realize you chose not to keep in touch," the man said, rising to his feet. "I suppose that's my fault too, but I'd hoped now you were back—well, I tell my students, they shouldn't assume. Still, I thought I merited more than a brushoff, especially since I drove Consuela up here at your suggestion."

Students. Books. Consuela. Vermillion. "Dr. Kubicek?"

He got a nod. Blaise Kubicek. His mother's cousin, executor of her estate, and the man who'd changed the dynamics of Marek's relationship with her.

"You've certainly changed," the professor said. "I wouldn't have known you but for the cap and the resemblance to..." He caught himself. "But have *I* changed that much?"

Marek still hadn't fully processed the connections. "You know Consuela Sanchez?"

"Consuela is one of my grad students. She called to leave a message last night that she couldn't proctor an exam for me because of what happened. I was awake and picked up. Once the whole thing tumbled out and she mentioned your name...well, I insisted that I drive her up to Sioux Falls. I stayed the night with a colleague at Augustana and I'm here now to take her back if she's ready." He scanned Marek's face. "She didn't tell you."

"No, I had no idea." He found himself bumbling into babble. "Look, I know I owe you a lot and I meant to contact you once things got settled down but I just..." A professor probably heard a lot of lame excuses.

One hand swept off the reading glasses. "I heard about the homicide."

"Happened just as I pulled into town." Marek tugged on his cap. "Haven't had time to think of anything else except getting my daughter enrolled in kindergarten."

Why, Marek mused, did everyone seem so surprised that he had a child?

"I hope she has a better shot at a good education than you did. I just wish I had pushed Janina harder to have you tested for dyslexia when you were younger, but she wouldn't admit anything could be wrong except your...willpower."

"She saw her father in me."

Marek didn't have to ask; Blaise Kubicek had seen it too. Bumbling body, bumbling mind, bumbling hands. In Christmas stories, Bumbles bounced. Lenny Marek hadn't bounced. Not at the end.

Marek said, "Thank you for keeping everything for me at the house. I wouldn't have blamed you if you'd sold everything to cover my mother's medical bills. I thought you had."

"It was little enough to do." The professor fiddled with the glasses, put them back on, and in half-sight, said, "Jim Marek told me where you were. What you were. He'd contacted me first, thinking I would know."

Marek shifted his guilt. "Why didn't you get in touch then?"

"Time...it goes faster, the older you get. You should have had your inheritance a long time ago. I've kept all the records filed with the court. It's not much. The rent on your dad's place was better in the early years but lately it's been eaten up in property taxes. I think Alice Winke's about to land me with the management of it—she says it's not in good shape."

"I'm living there now."

"Surely you'll want something better."

"I can fix it up when I get a little time."

"That's right. You picked up some carpentry skills, didn't you, before you left for a better life."

The dismissive tone grated but given what Blaise Kubicek had had to fight to get into the ivory tower, he deserved some free potshots at the working class he'd come from.

"How long will your wife wait for these repairs to happen?"

"She's dead."

Had he said that before? Died, yes, but...dead. Marek didn't know if he liked that his brain, if not his heart, had made the blunt transition.

The professor raised a flustered hand. "I'm so sorry. I didn't realize."

Consuela Sanchez flew down the hall. "Oh, Dr. Kubicek, you found him. Thank God. I forgot to tell the detective you were waiting and you've been so nice, driving me up here and...my dad is finally asleep. I know you need to get back to Vermillion tonight but I've decided to stay." Her gaze challenged Marek but her lips trembled. "Until I know whether my dad will be safe going back to Reunion."

Marek reached out to touch her on the shoulder. "For what it's worth, I think both of you are safe for now. If I'm right, the message has already been delivered."

"Okay. Thanks. I'll be with my father." But she lingered, her gaze on Marek. "Family...it's everything, to him, to me, especially with my mother gone. I know he's trying to protect me, but I wish he'd protect himself and get out of the union." Then she deflated. "But he saw things when he was a kid, following his parents and grandparents on the migrant circuit, that never left him. He feels he owes them."

As the young woman departed, Dr. Kubicek said ruefully, "It's taken me a long time to see the value in families: for so long, I saw only their destructiveness. Like a psychiatrist, I suppose, who sees parents only as the harbingers of pathology. I have no wife, no children, no family to speak of, or who will speak to me, just my students and a handful of friends."

He paused then said, "I hope once this investigation of yours is done, I can meet your daughter and get to know the man I just saw comfort a very worried young woman."

"She's stronger than she looks," Marek said. "Women often are."

But the professor shook his head. "It's a gift your father had."

And so Marek went back to Reunion with the gift of his father's reflection and not his grandfather's in Blaise Kubicek's eyes.

When Kurt Bechtold came back from his trip to the crime lab, Karen was waiting for him. "Well, did they tell you anything?"

He placed his hat on the antlers of the jackalope before he turned back to her. "First off, they did initial testing on the blood on the kill floor—it was human. The blood on that pocketknife was also human."

After Marek's cautions, she simply nodded. "Good."

Then Kurt smiled, splitting that narrow face. "Hansen's bloodtype on both. It's rare. AB negative. You'll need DNA but it looks like a match."

She pumped her fist, twirled, and ignoring Kurt's raised eyebrows, mimicked a shot. "All net."

A carver, Jaramillo definitely was—a killer, they'd see.

When Marek pulled up at 21 Okerlund Road, he knew he'd been seen.

Becca would soon be on her way over.

Getting out to wait for her, he frowned at the package hung on the rusted metal flag of the mailbox. He didn't remember ordering anything; he hadn't had time. Not touching it, he walked slowly around it until he could see the addressee: Miss Rebeca Okerlund.

His heart started to pound and, without thinking, he drew his weapon.

"You gonna shoot it?"

Marek whirled at the derisive voice, gun rising then dropping. "It's addressed to Becca."

That wiped off the sneer—or half sneer that wobbled with effort.

"We don't have any bomb squad here," Arne Okerlund said. "Have to call CID."

Marek frowned. "DCI, you mean?"

"That's what I said," his half-brother snapped, his face flush in the cold air.

Instead of making the man eat his words, Marek looked away, back to the package. He'd taken enough ribbing about his own scrambled brain to take any pleasure in rubbing it in another's face. Finally he took in the sender.

Then he yanked the package off the flag.

CHAPTER 30

A
RNE OKERLUND STUMBLED BACK WITH a muttered oath. "What the hell do you think you're doing, yanking that package around like that."

"It isn't a bomb." Marek turned the package around so it faced the ex-sheriff. "It's from my partner, Manuel Trujillo."

"Forgot one *c* in her name," the ex-sheriff said doubtfully.

"It's the Hispanic spelling of Rebecca." He'd wanted to spell it that way, to acknowledge her heritage, but Val had insisted on the English way—no one would mispronounce it and say BEEKA instead of BEHKA. Besides, their daughter's heritage stood proudly in her middle name of De Baca. "I recognize the handwriting now. Just wasn't expecting anything."

Arne nodded over at the face plastered against his front window. "If you really want to protect that girl, go back where you came from."

Marek waited until Arne had gone into the house. "I did, old man. Only this time, you're not running me off." When Becca came out, he showed her the package. "Look, Uncle Manny sent you something."

His daughter snatched the package and ran up the steps.

After Marek got his gun secured, he found his daughter at the kitchen table. She held a butcher's knife, trying to get through the tape, her little fingers millimeters away from being sliced. He stifled the shout. "Becca, put that knife down, please."

She didn't put down the knife. But she did stop. He covered the distance in three steps, took the knife, and let out a breath. "Don't use the knives, sweatpea."

He slid the knife back into the butcher's block and dug out his pocketknife. He thought briefly of Jaramillo then shoved the investigation aside and attacked the tape. When he got the package open, his daughter dived into the wadded-up newspapers.

He'd thought nothing in the package was dangerous; he'd been wrong.

From under her desk, Karen spied the pointy cowboy boots first. Rhine-stone studded. Definitely not the swing shift deputy, Bork, she thought. She grabbed the pen that had rolled away from her and got hurriedly to her feet.

Under the flickering fluorescent light stood a tanned, silver-haired whippet of a woman in a pink-fringed leather jacket and slinky jeans.

It wasn't for show, Karen knew, or—actually, it was. Rodeo shows. A champion barrel racer, Josephine Lindstrom had a boatload of belt buckles to prove it.

"Mrs. Lindstrom, welcome home." Karen pasted on a smile for the former secretary, dispatcher, and all-around dogsbody. "You look...refreshed, rejuvenated, and relaxed."

To Karen's dismay. She'd hoped—well, so much for that fantasy. "So, how was the Caribbean cruise?"

"Nothing on the rodeo circuit," Josephine said with a snort. "The men don't know how to move with a body. Never stir off their butts except to eat."

Karen didn't like to think of the long-time widow and mother of three grown men doing the tango. "You miss the snow?"

Correctly interpreting Karen's question, the woman sighed regretfully. "Melted off just as I hit the US of A. It figures I'd miss the biggest storm since '75. But that's not the worst that blew in, from what I've heard. Bad business, the plant. I said so when it went up and haven't changed my mind."

Then she smiled, her white teeth glinting against the tan, showing a hint of the cowgirl from West River who'd lassoed a staid Lutheran Lindstrom, only to lose him in the Vietnam War. "You look right sitting there, Karen. I didn't know if you would, but you do."

"It feels right." Karen settled back in the chair that had cradled her father and grandfather. "But it's not mine to keep if the voters don't agree."

"You're on the hot seat on this one, all right, and Marek's been slow out of the chute—could get you disqualified if he don't start racking up some points." Now Josephine looked all business. "Harold told me about his dyslexia."

"That's a factor, but he's..." Then Karen stopped. "You talked to Harold?"

"Rumor is, you could use some help."

Now Karen swallowed. Hard. "Harold said we didn't have any money."

"Has a Dahl ever said anything else?" Unbuttoning her jacket, the woman revealed a western shirt in wild paisleys. She flicked a mangled paperclip off her old desk, caressed the computer monitor that still sat there, ran her fingers over the keyboard. "You're short-staffed by two full-time deputies."

"Three," Karen told her. "Deputy Two Fingers is shipping out tomorrow. He's been on leave for the last two weeks to say goodbye to his family in Flandreau."

"So there's money in the kitty, even with Marek's overtime. And while I've enjoyed kicking it up in retirement, I miss my place here." She leaned against her desk and crossed her arms, fringes mingling over the paisleys. "If you like, I could come back, say, part-time? Mornings, I think, would be best, with more time off during rodeo season."

What was this thing with part-time schedules, Karen wondered. "Our work doesn't fit in neat time slots."

The woman merely smiled. "Take it or leave it."

Because Marek couldn't hold his daughter's shocked gaze, he fastened on the *retablo* he'd thrown against the wall.

Sacrilege, he thought. That's what he saw.

And what, he understood, she saw. In him. "I'm sorry, Becca. I just...it hurts."

He knelt down and picked up the *retablo*. He cradled it, told himself the cracked corner could be repaired, even as he knew it never could be. Not where it mattered. His daughter tugged on his arm, made mewling sounds.

Sounds.

He froze: and the *retablo* was taken from his hands.

How did you explain to a five year old that it had been a betrayal, to use those faces on the angelic wings of saints.

Manny Trujillo didn't often speak of, or show, what he was: a *santero*. A painter of saints. Marek himself had only accidentally discovered it, at a time when the swaggering young cop had wanted nothing to do with his family's tradition. A cop drew a Smith & Wesson, not angel's wings. Manny's *retablos* had an edge to them that the serene traditional ones did not; it was what made his, not just primitive religious art, but Art.

Small fingers pushed the crack closed. But it sprang open again.

As penance, Marek got out his tools. When the wood glue had set, he removed the *retablo* from the clamps, and without looking at it, asked his hovering daughter, "Where do you want it?"

She ran upstairs to her room and he reluctantly followed. He figured she'd want the new *retablo* with the smaller ones he'd already hung over the head of her bed. Manny had given them to her over the years—saints for all occasions.

Val had allowed the *retablos* only because of their religious nature. Just as she'd allowed crafts into her home, like her father's Navajo rugs and her cousin's pottery, but never Art.

Becca pointed, not at the head of her bed, but at the foot, where she'd see the *retablo* morning and night. He wanted to refuse. Instead, he set a nail against the chosen wall and hammered it into place. Then he held out his hand.

Becca hesitated, *retablo* in hand, one finger tracing the face of the angel grasping the hem of the Madonna's mantle. He knew she hadn't seen that face; she'd been spared that. Or maybe, in the end, denied it.

Then she held the *retablo* out, he took it, and hooked it on the nail.

Might as well, he thought, put the nail through his heart.

Cell phone to his ear, Marek flicked on the light and stared at the clock. It was just after two in the morning. His brain couldn't track. "Say that again?"

"It's Bork. I'm at Mex-Mix and I think you'd better get over here."

"Mex what?"

"The Mexican restaurant on Clay."

Two streets off of Main. "There's a Mexican restaurant

in Reunion?"

"Mmm. Surprised no one's told you. I like the *huevos rancheros* myself. Been going for, what, three or four years, I guess, about a year after the plant opened. Anyway, we've got an incident down here. Vandalism. I'm trying to talk to the owner but she's not making much sense. I called the sheriff and, since you know Spanish and everything, she thought you might could help."

Marek had swung his legs off the bed before his brain clicked on. "I can't leave Becca alone."

"Karen says to take her over to her place. She'll take care of her."

So Karen wasn't going to be at the scene. She either trusted him or she didn't want to crawl out of her warm bed.

Part-time, my ass, he thought. Cold ass.

Ten minutes later, he stepped down off the street curb and his daughter went rigid in his arms. He'd hoped she'd stay asleep. "It's okay, Becca, I'm just taking you over to Karen's. I've got to go out on a call. I'll be back. I promise."

Her head lolled back against his arm.

Karen met him at the door. "I'll put her down with me so if she wakes, I'll be able to reassure her." His daughter didn't protest at the transfer; one arm snuck out of the blanket and encircled the sheriff's neck. "You okay with this, Marek? I wouldn't have told Bork to call you except that with everything going on, I think he should have backup and Mrs. Reyes wasn't very coherent."

"You know her?"

"Mex-Mix is the only place in town that still delivers. Walrus has been lobbying for taco pizza as a menu option."

"Good to know there's something besides the bakery and the café." Even if he doubted the fare could compare to what he'd had in Albuquerque.

"I don't like this any more than you do," Karen said. "People are stirred up and not thinking straight. Fear will do that—target anything different. Watch your back."

He watched her shift the slumbering head into her warmth. "Watch my daughter."

Bork met Marek outside the damaged restaurant. The large picture window was shattered, the remaining storefront covered with silvery spray-painted obscenities.

The deputy pointed over at a woman who sat huddled on a packing crate on the sidewalk. "Mrs. Reyes keeps saying something over and over. Sounds like, I don't know, moss durrow."

"*Mas duro*. Too hard."

Marek went over to her and sat on his haunches. She wore a coat, unbuttoned, over pajamas and worn slippers. "Mrs. Reyes, I'm Detective Okerlund."

She backhanded her tears. "You don't look like your father."

That threw him. "You knew my father?"

Bork cleared his throat behind him. "I think she's meaning Arne."

"He's my half-brother. Mrs. Reyes, can you tell me what happened?"

She looked over his shoulder, into the gaping hole of her livelihood, and clasped her hands. "I am American." The lights from the squad car gave her face hollows. "I don't understand."

He waited until she met his eyes. "Don't understand it. Defeat it. Tell me what happened."

Mrs. Reyes took a deep breath, looked down, appeared to realize her state of dress, or lack thereof, and pulled her coat closer. "I live over the restaurant. I was asleep. Then I hear this big crash. I think, it is just..." Her hands went out to encompass the dingy snow hiding out in the shadow of the curb, the dark starless night, the air. "The wind, it howls, I think it will drive me mad, sometimes. So strong. I think, so strong it breaks the window. Maybe I will go back to Texas now."

He kept his voice light. "I hope you don't. I'd kill for *huevos rancheros* and someone to ask me, red or green? And if you have *sopapillas* and a honey jar, I'll kiss you."

"You are not from here...but, you are."

"I lived the last twenty years, most of it, in Albuquerque."

"Oh. I see. I am from El Paso but my husband was from Columbus, New Mexico." A border crossing town, Marek knew. "The restaurant, I cannot afford to repair, but I will make you something."

She started to rise and he reached out to stop her. "It's not as bad as it looks. He didn't do any damage inside."

Of course there was damage inside, he told himself. Inside the woman.

"So what did you do," he asked her, "when you heard the crash?"

"I went downstairs, turned on the light, and I see all the glass. I was going to go back and get shoes, but then, I hear, like the night talking to me. The ugliness, the things he yelled, it was..." This time her hand gestured toward the obscenities—the kindest being Mex-Ho Go Home—glowing in the night. "Like that."

"You're sure it was a he?"

"Yes, a young man. Across the street."

"Only one?"

She nodded. "I finally see a bit of glittering on him. From paint, I think." Her hand rose to grip her shoulder. "I see it when he throws another rock at me."

He hadn't realized she'd been hurt. "We should get you to the clinic."

"No, it is just a bruise."

She didn't appear to be in pain: of a physical kind. "Why did you come here, Mrs. Reyes? To Reunion."

"My husband...I can tell you now...he wasn't legal. I didn't even know until after we were married. He was afraid to tell me. Then afraid to try to be legal, afraid we will be separated. It's harder to find jobs now. He heard about PBI from his cousin, that they'd make sure he could work, no problem. I told Miguel, the restaurant I had down in Texas, it will keep us, but he is a man, no? He wants to bring home the bacon. The beef."

Now she looked straight at him. "They say, he brought drugs here, that this is what Mexicans do, but many come here to escape them, you know? It is very bad in Mexico now because of drugs. Miguel always said that hard work, it was the best drug. He was a good man. He worked hard. He fell asleep at the wheel. But your brother, the sheriff, he told me, after the accident, Miguel had drugs in him when he died, and I did not believe him." The bottomless eyes flashed red then blue in the cop lights. "Is your brother a good man?"

He was saved from having to answer when an old town car pulled up. What looked like an entire village spilled out and enveloped the woman. From snatches he heard, he figured that most of them worked for, or had worked for, the woman.

Marek crunched over broken glass to Bork. "Anything on scene?"

"Mmm. Found the rock that went through the window. Doubt it'll hold prints."

"Spray can?"

"No such luck." Bork glanced over at the hatred that spanned ethnicities; there was even a swastika. "We've never had anything like this before."

Now that, Marek didn't believe. "No vandalism?"

"Oh, sure, mostly at the school, rivalry stuff or just profanity, but this...it's a level up."

"Down," Marek said. The gaping hole in the storefront needed to be closed to the elements, natural or human. "I think I might have something that will cover this."

He'd just shaken out the tarp from the back of his pickup when he heard Bork behind him.

"Uh, Detective. It's Nails."

"That'd be useful. I've got an extra hammer. Need it?"

"No, I mean, Nails Nelson. You know, from YRUN? He's on the phone. He wants to talk to whoever's in charge."

Marek bumped against the truck's utility rack, rubbed the back of his head, then rummaged in the toolbox until he found some nails himself. "Tell him I'm busy."

"Mmm, Karen, she always said, we should keep him in the loop. He's got a lot of pull in Reunion."

Marek took the deputy's phone. "Okerlund here."

"That's one word more than your big brother ever used."

"I'm a little busy, Mr. Nelson, and—"

"You'd like to send me to hell six ways to Sunday. First off, Detective, I want to apologize for placing you in Mexico. I should know better. The guy who dragged me off the rice paddies in 'Nam was from a little place called Pojoaque in *New* Mexico. I apologized, didn't I?"

Did he? YRUN wasn't on Marek's dial.

"As for the opinions of Arne Okerlund, they aren't mine, so you'll just have to prove our ex-sheriff wrong. Now that we've got that out of the way, I got the gist of what happened at Mex-Mix from the scanner, but I could use a sound bite. By the way, what's your cell number?"

As if, Marek thought. "Until the sheriff okays media contact, Mr. Nelson, I can't—"

"Media contact? Hell, Detective, you *have* been in the city too long. We don't even have a paper in this county any more. Now it's just me and I do it for free on my disability pension. Doubt the *Argus* or the networks will come down for this, though you never know, outrage always plays, especially with the race card. Hate in the Heartland."

That wouldn't make Karen happy. Or Dahl.

"Course, lots of people don't even know the Dakotas are in the heartland. You see that time, a couple presidential elections back, when they put North Dakota on top of Nebraska on the electoral map? What kind of idiot doesn't clue in that there's got to be a south in there. Probably a foreigner."

"More likely a New Yorker."

That earned him a laugh. "But if the *Argus* does come down, they'll more likely want an update on Dale Hansen. Speaking of which, anything new?"

"You'll have to talk to the sheriff."

"You're no fun, Detective."

Marek stared at the glowing obscenities; is this what he'd come home for, to have that kind of thing flung, not in his face perhaps, but his daughter's? Had things changed so much, even here, that this kind of thing didn't merit a blip on the *Argus*'s radar?

"Hate is never fun, Mr. Nelson."

A slight pause told Marek that Nelson had just collected his soundbite. When Marek hung up and handed the phone back to its owner, the deputy merely said, "Mmm."

Bork, bork, bork. "Let's cook up a cover for that window."

Between the two of them, they got the tarp up over the broken window and nailed it down.

Turning, Marek looked out across the street. A small huddle of people stood beneath the street lamp, turning shades of red, blue...and silver. Just a glint. On an arm? Even as he limned a figure out of the darkness, it moved, took a step back, and ran.

CHAPTER 31

"**C**UT HIM OFF WITH THE squad!" Marek shouted to Bork and launched himself after the sound of pounding feet.

The silver-glinted figure dove down a side street. Marek heard the clang of metal and a roll: the spray can. Despite his longer legs, Marek fell behind, stumbling in partially frozen potholes in the weak light of a stray streetlamp.

He'd gained a bit when the paint-glittered arm flung up, simultaneously with a startled cry, and the figure sprawled to the ground. Then the squad car rounded the corner and blinded Marek.

When he regained sight, he caught the silhouette of a man in the headlights—obviously not Bork—pinning the now struggling and cursing figure.

"Well, if it isn't Wayne Gotsch," the silhouette said. "Surprise, surprise."

Marek came up to them, breathing heavily, and leaned hands on thighs. He didn't recognize the voice nor, after his eyes recovered from the afterburn of the headlights, the man.

Not that he could tell much with the face turned out of the light, whereas he himself must be all too visible.

"You're Okerlund, aren't you."

"That's right. And you are..."

Handcuffs clicked over Wayne's wrists. "Two Fingers."

All he could think of to say was, "Why two?"

"Better than one."

Wayne Gotsch gave two one-finger salutes. But since he now lay face down into the grit of asphalt and ice, it looked like rabbit ears coming off his skinny butt.

Two Fingers turned into the headlights. Marek saw the sleek black hair, cropped close, and the high cheekbones.

"You okay, Detective?" Bork asked, emerging from the squad.

Not trusting his facial fungus to cover the heat in his cheeks, Marek looked down as he tested his foot. "Yeah, bad ankle, that's all."

He'd injured it his rookie year jumping over a fence and falling into the concrete *arroyo* to drag a gangbanger from the raging water of the monsoons.

He'd missed. By inches.

No one had blamed him except his own clumsy self. The occasional twinges reminded him that life could be lost by inches.

Wayne Gotsch snorted into a pothole. "I'd've outrun you if it weren't for Chief Two Fucks."

Marek didn't bother to respond. He was still getting his breath back.

Two Fingers yanked his prisoner to his feet. "Let me tell you, Wayne, you won't be running out of a nine-by-nine cell."

"You can't put me in jail. I'm a minor."

So one thing hadn't changed since he'd left: no room in the inn for a minor. He himself hadn't been a minor. Barely into his majority, he'd spent a terrifying night in the jail, unable to sleep, all his supports in life kicked out from under him, even the law.

"What you are is a major pain in the ass." Two Fingers nudged Wayne Gotsch into the back seat of Bork's squad. "And we can hold you for 48 hours before we have to transfer you to a juvenile facility."

He slammed the door on the profane response.

Marek took one last deep breath. He bet the trim, slightly aloof figure wouldn't be breathing hard after a couple blocks. Maybe not even after several miles; he looked like a marathoner, all lean muscle. "You're headed for Afghanistan, I hear."

"Thought I'd take one last cruise through town before I picked up my gear." He waved toward a barely visible black SUV. "Heard about Mex-Mix on the scanner and Wayne Gotsch ran right into my arms. I just stuck out a leg and he went sprawling." He glanced back at the squad. "You'll want to keep an eye on that one." Then he asked Bork, "Bad?"

The two, Marek remembered, worked together on the same shift.

"Rock through the window," Bork said. "Spray paint."

Marek said, "You're both welcome in on the interview, if

247

you like."

Bork socked Two Fingers on the arm. "Guess we'll have to go roust Myron Gotsch. That should get you ready for active duty again."

In the interview room, the elder Gotsch's fist thudded on the old table, rocking it on its uneven feet. "You've no cause to go hauling my son down here like a bunch of goddamn stormtroopers, three of you on one skinny slick of a kid."

Marek had heard variations of this theme since they'd rousted Gotsch from his bed. His wife, a flutter of a woman in a muumuu, had been brushed quickly aside by her husband and told to stop worrying and go back to bed. Now the man, his son, Two Fingers, and Marek sat crowded into the interview room with the tape whirring.

Bork had gone back on patrol.

Patience usually came naturally to Marek but he found himself short. "We weren't the ones painting swastikas, Mr. Gotsch. We found the spray can in the bushes in the side street where Wayne ran. We're going to get his prints. He's got matching spraypaint on the arm of his jacket. He fled the scene, refused to stop when ordered to, and took great pleasure in flipping off the arresting officer."

Gotsch let out a breath of exasperation at that. "Wayne—"

"It wasn't detective halfwit here, it was—" Once again he demonstrated his two-finger salute. Marek noticed that Gotsch not only got the reference but let it drop.

"Who's to say I didn't just brush against the paint," Wayne said, slouching into the chair. "Just came looking to see what the fuss was about then went for a stroll?"

"That was no stroll."

"You couldn't keep up with an old lady on a tricycle."

Marek hadn't expected to feel the prick of temper. He'd had killers in his face with far more venom. "You caused a great deal of property damage. Mrs. Reyes is—"

"Illegal."

Marek let out the steam before it hissed on his tongue. "It doesn't matter if she's a citizen or not."

"Then it doesn't matter if I did it or not. Law's the law," he mimicked, and Marek heard the echoes of Kurt Bechtold.

Gotsch creaked back in his chair. "If you won't arrest the Mexicans for being illegal, you've got no business arresting Wayne for trying to do your job."

"As it happens, Mrs. Reyes is a citizen."

"So she's got papers, but I'll bet you they're forged," Gotsch countered. "You got Mexicans here, there've got to be illegals."

"Who else would come to this town," Wayne muttered.

"Mrs. Reyes was born in Texas. She came here with her husband." Who had been illegal, Marek knew, but you didn't catch it by association. "He died in a single car accident when he fell asleep at the wheel after pulling three successive shifts at the plant. A hardworking man, by all accounts. The widow decided to stay and make a go of her restaurant."

"Heard the husband was a drug addict," Gotsch put in. "No one died of hard work."

Marek figured plenty of illegals, and legals, had died of hard work, but he figured it was pointless to argue.

"Get a whiff of the gold and you all cross the border," Two Fingers said into the silence. "Give us back the Black Hills, then we'll talk about illegals."

Wayne blew out air. "Ancient history. Get over it. You lost."

"The US Supreme Court sided with us, not you, and still, you want to give us money, not land. Whites don't respect the law unless it's in their favor."

Marek didn't know if he was included in the indictment, though he might be the only one in the room that it bothered. In the silence, the whir of the impartial observer broke into his consciousness. "Let's get back to what happened at Mex-Mix."

Wayne sneered at him. "Heard you got a little Mex-mix of your own."

It took a few seconds for that to translate but by then Gotsch was scowling at his son.

"Did *you* make that call?" he demanded.

"What call? Oh, *that* call." Wayne slammed back in the chair. "Give me a break. I don't threaten little girls."

"Just women," Marek said. "A widow barely treading water."

"Oh, stop the sob story, Detective," Wayne said. "We did fine in this town before the Mexicans got here. Now look at it. It's a dump. No work, no business, *nada*. Only losers come here." Wayne smirked at Marek. "You must be one really washed up cop."

Marek kept his cool with difficulty. Was this what grief did to you? "You planning to leave, then?"

"Sure, once I get me some money, I'm outta here. I'll go down to sun and fun; only I won't be coming back like you, because I'm smarter."

Two Fingers stirred again. "So smart you quit school at fourteen?"

"Didn't need any more."

Marek asked, "So, did you apply at PBI?"

"You kidding? Even the Indians won't work there; then, they never work anyway."

Two Fingers simply said, "I've got a job and you don't."

"Wayne's working for me," Gotsch countered, "until he can sign up with the Marines."

From Wayne's face, Marek thought that ambition was his father's, not his own.

If Marek couldn't get anything else out of the Gotsches, he might as well ask something else. "You still have Dale Hansen's pickup, Mr. Gotsch?"

The man stared at him, as if trying to figure out the trap, then relaxed. "Yeah, it's still there. Haven't figured out what's wrong with it. I told Dale when he got it, the more bells and whistles, the more to go wrong. Give me a rusted out old Ford or Chevy with a stick and windup windows any day. I can make it run. But all these computer chips and newfangled stuff, it's hell to find what's wrong. Wayne works on computers some."

"Not very hard, it seems," Marek observed.

"He's still kicking it up; he'll come around. People used to understand boys gotta get it out of their system. Now just one little fight and they're kicked out of school like they was a terrorist or something."

So maybe it wasn't just a matter of quitting school.

Gotsch fisted one hand and tapped his own chin. "In my day, fights were how you proved you weren't a sissy."

Marek said, not half in jest, "You want to take this behind the courthouse?"

"I'm just saying that Wayne'll be in the Marines and outta your hair in a couple years."

"I'm gonna be a SEAL, not a Marine."

The man rapped his son on the back of the head. "Yeah, like you know water from wheat. Be a man. Be a Marine."

In the end, Wayne went off in the recognizance of his father.

"They still send juveniles to Plankinton?" Marek asked Two Fingers as they watched the taillights disappear into the night.

"Some, yeah, but I'm not holding my breath."

Marek looked sideways at the deputy's profile. "You're Sioux? Lakota?"

The deputy turned his head. "Dakota and Nakota. Santee and Yankton. My mom's enrolled at Flandreau but I don't meet the blood quantum."

Marek said, "You look it."

"I'm the sum of many enemies, some Native, some not." The light didn't penetrate the black eyes. "The name Two Fingers comes from my grandfather. Mandan and Arikara. Original enemies out here. After traders gave them smallpox, what was left got kicked out by the Sioux; then the Sioux got kicked out by the US of A and their immigrant settlers. Someone's always kicking ass out here on the plains."

Two Fingers turned away from the darkened street. "Lots of so-called Mexicans who come here for a better life are Natives. Borders mean little if there's prejudice without justice. But you don't strike me as part of the gold rush."

Marek's left hand fisted, without gold, nor any rush for it. Not while the white lingered, a scar, a brand, an indictment. Too many dead. "You're an endangered species, Two Fingers. Come back from Afghanistan."

"I'm smarter than the Gotsches *and* the Okerlunds." The smile slashed white. "I'm Air Force. I'm safer there than here."

CHAPTER 32

KAREN CLOSED HER EYES TO the dawn leaking through her window.

Becca burrowed into her, the dark head resting in the valley between her breasts, little hands dug into her pjs. An interesting hair shirt, Karen thought, with the momentary embarrassment of a woman who'd spent much of her life sleeping alone. Having another's heartbeat, heat, and drool...well, it wasn't something she was used to.

She heard her father banging cabinets downstairs.

As a child, she'd often fallen asleep to, or woken to, impromptu meetings of her father with his underlings. The murmur of strategy, of tragedy, had risen through the vents.

She'd known, instinctively, as if in her genes, that what she heard in the circle of law stayed there. If nothing else, if she told, she'd never hear again. Her father should have known; this had been his room as a child. But she doubted he remembered his childhood much. He never spoke of it.

"You gonna lie in bed all day?"

Her father's voice came up through the vents. Okay, maybe he knew. Or remembered. He'd said once to her that the stroke stoked old memories.

Becca stirred, looked up with blurred eyes, and froze. Hope shot the eyes wide; then they fell. Along with tears. Awkwardly, Karen cradled the girl close, let her hand sift through the dark strands, so very different than her own.

Trying to think of something, anything, to comfort the girl—or at least distract her, her gaze fell on the kaleidoscope she kept on the night table.

She snatched it up then handed it to Becca. "Here, take a look at this."

The girl sniffed, eyed it blankly, and Karen had to demonstrate. When Becca raised it to the light and started to rotate the barrel, Karen said, "My grandfather gave that to me on my fifth birthday. Yes, the same age you are now. He tried to explain, how things changed, what with his new wife and son—that would be your dad. But the old pieces—like me and my dad—would always be part of his life. Even my grandmother who died, a piece of her would always be with us."

Whether Becca got the parallel, Karen didn't know, but she appeared fascinated with the kaleidoscope. Finally, Karen took it and put it back on the nightstand. "We've got to get you home and dressed for school."

When Becca didn't move, Karen laughed. "I know, school's the devil, but hey, it's only the next thirteen years—after that, it's up to you."

Karen got dressed and let Becca stay in the bed, watching her with those Okerlund eyes, with an almost adult guardedness. As if there were things going on in that head that had to be hid; but what did a five year old have to hide?

Shaking off the odd feeling, she scooped Becca up, blankets and all, and hauled her downstairs over her shoulder. Her father blinked at them, then after a second of what looked like disorientation, he said, "You're gonna be late."

Karen thought she knew what had thrown him: that she had a child. Well, she did, but he didn't know—would never know. The time had passed, the decision made, two decades ago, the same year Marek had disappeared. Nothing good could come of the revelation now.

Her daughter would be college age now. Was she in college? Where?

Ruthlessly, Karen shut down the speculation. If she didn't stop, she'd be blurting out her secret in no time, forever ruining her relationship with her father. Not necessarily because she'd gotten in trouble, though that had been a big fear at the time, but because she'd denied him the right to be a grandfather.

Maybe Marek's daughter could give him what she hadn't, a tie to immortality, to see those Okerlund eyes grow up here. "I'll go deliver Becca to Marek and then go on in to work and hope Kurt brought some of Eva's goodies for breakfast."

But her father's eyes hadn't lifted from the child. "She sick?"

That brought Becca up, nodding vigorously, but Karen ignored it. "No, she's not sick."

"Says she is."

"She's sick of school." Karen swung the girl down to her feet. "Sorry, kiddo, but I'm the sheriff of Eda County and I can spot a lie at a thousand paces. You can try it on your dad but I bet he's even better at it, being a detective and all."

A few minutes later, with Becca's enthusiastic help, Karen knocked on the door of the other bungalow. She wondered if Marek had noticed the bullet hole yet. He hadn't mentioned it.

The door jerked open.

A rumple-clothed Marek took his daughter from Karen. Then he put her down, oriented her to the inside, and pushed. "Go on, get dressed. I've got to take a shower."

After Becca disappeared reluctantly up the stairs, Karen said, "She cried. When she woke up. She thought I was her mother. I think it's good she can cry." Deciding that just about pushed the limit of the personal, she stepped back. "We'll hold the morning's meeting for you."

One hand rifled through the dark-corn-syrup hair. "Don't bother. I'll be in late. I have a window to replace."

Alarm had her wanting to run after Becca. "Someone broke out a window here last night?"

"Not here, at Mex-Mix."

"Oh. That's not your responsibility."

"Mrs. Reyes can't afford to repair the damage; she's talking about moving back to Texas."

That stopped her lecture on priorities. "Well, then, you're excused."

Marek walked quietly up behind the gang of scarfed figures attacking the restaurant. He heard a voice say, "Some things just don't fit. This here is one of them."

Another said, "I think it might...if we had a good carpenter."

Marek cleared his throat. "How about me?"

Heads swiveled in alarm then one of the rounder figures turned toward him. "Well, don't just stand there." The bifocals dipped to his tool belt. "If you don't use it, you'll lose it."

Titters sounded from the flanks and Marek felt warmth blossom in his face. "Mayor Dahl?"

The roly-poly woman grinned up at him. "And people think you're not too bright, Marek Okerlund. Got it in one."

"What are you doing?" he asked her.

"Heard on YRUN this morning what happened here." The mayor pushed her glasses farther up toward a dandelion fluff of hair. "Disgraceful, simply disgraceful, and I'm not letting Mrs. Reyes think that's the kind of people we are here in Reunion. We're painting those awful things over. Connelly's Supply donated some kind of special paint; it'll take down to 35 degrees and think we just hit that. Mel Olson down at the hardware store donated the window but it doesn't seem to fit."

So few things did in this town anymore. He said, "I know something about misfits."

An hour later, with some additional donations from the supply store, Marek had framed the new rough opening for the window. Not long after, with the help of several men who'd wandered over to see what was going on and got recruited by the mayor, the new pane was put in place.

He could only hope Mrs. Reyes hadn't left town yet.

"That's a nice tight job there," a voice said from behind him. "You hiring out? I've got some work I need done."

In the new pane, Marek saw the reflection of a man. No one he knew. Wore a Stetson.

"So do we," another voice chimed in.

Marek turned from reflection to reality. Next to the first, two more men stood, sporting faded red and blue ball caps, the logos long since burned off by the sun.

Stetson said, "Most of us know a bit of carpentry. Have to. But work like this, not everybody can do."

Marek shifted on his feet, not sure what to say, and settled on, "Once Dale Hansen's murder case is closed, I might have some time on my hands. Just as long as it's in the morning when my daughter's in school."

The men's faces tightened. So, Marek thought, they might not like blatant obscenities but that didn't mean they liked Mex-mixes like his daughter.

"I think I speak for us all," Stetson said, tipping his hat up with an arthritis-bent finger. "You need any help keeping that little girl of yours safe, we'll be there. Anytime, anywhere."

"Uh...thank you." Now he felt like the bigot. "I doubt she's in real danger, not with Nails on his case over it, but I appreciate it."

Red cap looked at the new exterior—or through it. "This was bad, all around bad, but just sticks and stones." He chewed on his lip. "Some things can't be repaired. Knew Dale Hansen. Dead long before it happened."

Hat dipping down again, Stetson said, "Saw Dale at the auction after he lost his farm. Wished I'd had the guts to do what my grandfather told me they did in the Depression. Penny auctions, they called them. Kept any serious bidders out by gunpoint and forced the auctioneer to settle for a penny. Then sold the farm back to the owner."

Blue cap rubbed at his jut of jaw. "Leastways Dale ended up back where he belonged, on the farm he loved."

He'd been in the ditch, Marek thought, not on the farm—but he'd come close.

Outside the school, Marek watched Karen stride toward him. Caught. He'd just stopped for a few minutes before heading back to the sheriff's office. Couldn't he ever catch a break?

"Got a call," she said.

"What now?"

"We got a report of a strange, dangerous looking man hanging around the playground, looking at the little girls."

For an instant, he felt his gut tighten then relax. "Me."

"You really need to trim that roughage you call a beard," she said, breaking somber with a grin. "Stop by the barbershop on the way back. You're going to start scaring off the citizenry we're here to protect."

She beckoned toward a group of teachers huddled next to the school building.

A red-headed woman detached and walked across the playground. She bopped one of the boys up the side of the head as he snatched the ball away from a smaller boy. "Tad Nelson, you give that back or I'm confiscating it." Then those flashing green eyes turned on Marek before landing on his companion. "Karen."

The sheriff gestured toward Marek. "Is this the man you've pegged as a blight on the innocence of Reunion Elementary?"

"Yes, it is."

Strange, Marek thought, you wouldn't think anyone with that many freckles could look so intimidating. She was almost as tall as Karen. Despite himself, he felt a stirring of interest.

"Laura Russell, meet Detective Marek Okerlund."

That froze the snapping eyes on him. "You're Becca's father?"

The doubt didn't recede until a small, bundled figure hurtled toward him from the playground. He scooped Becca up into his arms: as proof and a shield. "Tell me, Ms. Russell, if I was five-foot-two and a woman, would you have sicced the sheriff on me?"

Since her hands were gloved, he couldn't tell if she wore a ring.

"No, I'd've called my husband," she said, "but I wasn't sure he could handle you."

So, she was married. Just as well. And far, far too soon. If ever.

Karen lifted fair brows at the red-head. "I don't know that your husband would appreciate the slight, Laura."

"Walter's never shot anyone before," the teacher said. "I'd rather you do it than him."

Boy, he was slow this morning. Russell. "You're Walrus's, I mean Walter's, wife?"

"Me and his mother are the only ones allowed to call him Walter." Karen winced and Laura Russell laughed. "Well, Karen is allowed when he's being particularly dense." The smile left her face. "He told me about Becca. I passed the word."

Walter Russell was one very lucky man, Marek decided. "Whoever threatened her may not be a stranger, Mrs. Russell."

"You're the only man I've seen hanging around." She pondered him for a moment. "You know, try as I might, even taking out the beard, I can't see the kid who used to collect our aluminum cans by yelling at the back door, Bring out your dead!"

Really, really slow. "Laura O'Connor." He glanced at both women. "The twin towers. Good to see you're still hooked up. You two made a hell of a backcourt."

But Laura hadn't pursued college ball, he recalled. Perhaps that explained the stiffness he sensed between the two at his comment. Karen turned to Becca. "Hey there, kiddo. Making friends?"

None of the kids who'd gathered around looked willing to claim her. In fact, several looked away, guiltily wiping palms.

No wonder Becca didn't want to come back to school. Did nothing change, he wondered, just the names and faces?

You got Dale germs.

The sweaty palms had smeared from kid to kid on the hard asphalt of childhood recess. The squeals of the girls, the mocking hoots of the boys, and Dale Hansen...at the center of the cruelty and on the periphery of all else.

Were those childhood memories ever forgotten?

But now the queen of all she surveyed, elevated by the attention of adults, Becca eyed the other kids with a regal aloofness.

"Friends are good," he told her.

A guarded look passed between the two women that he couldn't interpret then a pint-sized girl stepped up. She wore a Carhartt jacket, jeans, and tiny workboots with more than a little mud on them. Her face tilted up with an *aw shucks* grin.

Not shy but he recognized it. "You'd be a Bolvin."

"How'd you know?"

He stared down from his great height. "Because I'm a detective. Is your father Nate or Nick?" He'd learned Nate was a bookkeeper in town.

"Uncle Nate's only got boys. So does Uncle Noel." Her hands went into her back pockets. "Grandma says one girl's worth ten boys. My dad says I'm worth ten hired men. He says the farm would stop dead without me."

Laura laid a hand on the girl's shoulder. "This would be Nick's youngest. Emily Bolvin."

"Em," the girl said.

No, not shy, to correct a teacher, especially this one. The bell rang and Marek let his reluctant daughter down. Em Bolvin looked at Becca: an oldcomer to newcomer kind of look, even if she had to look up at the taller girl. "The teacher says you don't talk. But that's okay. Dad says I talk enough for all the Bolvins."

And she proceeded to do just that, hauling Becca along with her to lead the peloton of kindergartners toward the school. The teacher came out to get them. One sight of Marek and her anxious eyes darted to her class, then fell on Becca with relief.

Marek thought that she was more afraid of him than of whoever threatened Becca. Or maybe, he thought, she was afraid of Emily Bolvin.

Laura Russell gave him a parent-to-parent look. "I warn you, if you want a girly girl, you won't get one if she teams up with Emily Bolvin. Pardon me, Em. Penny says it's an anagram for Me." Amusement sparkled in the green eyes. "She may scorn boys but only because she thinks she can outboy them. When she grows up she wants to be a wrestler like her Uncle Noel. That is, when she's not going to be the best Bolvin farmer there ever was."

Laura Russell clapped her hands together and strode forward into a swarm of older kids. "All right, class, recess is over. March. Hut, two, three..."

The ragged line took shape and marched back inside.

"Scary," Marek muttered.

"You don't know the half of it," Karen said. "Now, I expect you shorn and back at work in..." She glanced at her watch. "An hour tops. The barbershop's walk-in and shouldn't be too long a wait. Call me if it is."

Marek decided that Karen Okerlund Mehaffey was the other half of it.

"And find your hat," she said. "It's the only uniform you've got but it may prevent more callouts like this one."

CHAPTER 33

WHEN MAREK CAME THROUGH THE door, Karen noticed the beard had been reduced back to the Byzantine goatee. And he'd managed to find his hat.

"I must say, Marek Okerlund," a droll voice said from behind them, "you look a heck of a lot more intimidating in the flesh than on that New Mexico driver's license I pulled up."

He started and turned. "Mrs. L?"

"That's Josephine, Detective. Goes for you too, Sheriff. Since I'm going to be working with you, no need for the long form."

Karen wasn't surprised when Marek remained mute.

"Mrs. Lindstrom—uh, Josephine—will be transcribing your oral reports."

To Karen's astonishment, Marek sank to a knee before the woman. With a laugh, Josephine shooed him back to his feet. "Oh, go on. I'm just a secretary, not the queen." Then she hugged him, barely able to get her arms around him. "My, oh my, but you turned out a big one." She released him. "I'm so glad you're back home where you belong. I can't wait to meet that little girl of yours. Is she like—"

"You can talk later." Karen knew this could go on for some time. She'd watched it happen with Walrus and Kurt already. "Josephine is getting our records back in shape. And us. So, if you've got more tapes, hand them over to her. Right now, I want to interview Jaramillo again. He's had time to sit and think."

Josephine said in a *faux* whisper. "The Army did that to her. She used to talk and talk and talk. You never did, though."

"Somebody's got to listen," Marek said solemnly.

"That's what I love about Okerlunds," she returned with a grin.

Karen rose to her feet. "I'm one."

"No, you're a Halvorsen," Josephine said. "Through and through. Speaking of which, Sig called while you were out keeping the munchkins safe for another day of fingerpainting. He wants you to stop by when you've got some time."

That made her pause. "He say why?"

"Not to me, he didn't." Josephine turned as the phone rang. "Do I hold calls until you're done with Mr. Jaramillo?"

"Unless it's murder, yes, hold them." Karen snagged the tape recorder. "Unless it's Agent Larson. You can hang up on him or hang him, your choice."

The laughter followed them down to the jail.

Emilio Jaramillo lay on his bunk, staring up at the ceiling.

"He's like...I don't know, comatose or in a trance or something," Tammy said, letting Marek into the jail cell after the sheriff. "Except to whiz. Won't even eat. Had to chow down on his lunch myself to save the waste. The café makes a mean meatloaf."

Marek hadn't had meatloaf in years and wasn't sure he wanted to reacquaint himself with it. "I'm going to patronize Mex-Mix for a while."

If it was still in existence.

Tammy patted her ample frame. "You have the gratitude of me and mine."

The jailer went back to her dispatch desk before Marek processed that. "What? Why?"

"You've got to keep your dial on YRUN, Marek." Karen flipped the tape in the recorder. "Nails not only got your soundbite last night but snagged an interview with Mrs. Reyes. She said you convinced her to stay. You've got free *huevos rancheros* and sope—well, something—any time, she says."

"*Sopapillas.*"

That came from their prisoner. Not so comatose. Marek sank down on the cell's other bunk. "You know Mrs. Reyes?"

"Good *posole.*"

Dried corn soaked in lye-water and made into a hearty soup. "You don't like meatloaf?"

The man slowly swung his feet down off the bunk, ignoring or unaware of Karen, who'd switched on the tape recorder. "*No.*"

Given what he'd spent the last several years doing, Marek didn't blame the man, though *posole* also had meat, likely pork instead of beef, with other garnishes like cabbage, chile, and garbanzo beans. "I'll tell Tammy to get you something vegetarian. You need to eat."

But he just shook his head. "Over."

What's over, he wanted to ask, but saw it on the man's face. Life. "*La vida es difícil.*"

That didn't connect as it had with Sanchez. Perhaps because this man had known nothing else but a difficult life: why acknowledge the obvious? And yet, for a camera shot's moment, he'd known a good life.

Marek read the man his rights in Spanish then said, "Mr. Jaramillo, your pocketknife. It has Dale Hansen's blood on it."

A stretch of the truth, perhaps, until the DNA results came in. The dark eyes didn't so much as blink, as if it hadn't even registered. Black holes absorbed light, Marek recalled. Just when he thought he'd lost any hope of an answer, Emilio Jaramillo spoke. "*Sí.* Yes."

Karen bobbled the tape recorder. "Did you kill Dale Hansen, Mr. Jaramillo?"

Jaramillo didn't look at her. "He kill."

Marek didn't take that as a confession but an indictment. "Who is *he*?"

"White."

"Dale Hansen?"

"*Diablo.*"

Marek began to think that Guatemalans had nothing on Dakotans for monosyllabic riddles. "Dale Hansen, who is a devil, killed? Because of white? Of meth?"

"*Sí.*"

"Who did he kill?"

Emilio Jaramillo's hand went to his heart.

Karen said, "Your daughter isn't dead, Mr. Jaramillo."

Finally, the man glanced at the sheriff. "I dead to her."

What could you say to that? If his own daughter had been older, Marek may have gotten the same treatment. As it was, she didn't understand enough yet to hate him.

Karen sank down now beside Marek on the bunk to look straight at Emilio Jaramillo. "Did you carve the words *White Out* into Dale Hansen's arm?"

Again, the answer came slowly. "*Sí.* Yes."

Marek frowned at the man, thought about challenging him, then left it. "Mr. Jaramillo, what happened that night after you left the clinic?"

The dark eyes shifted, inward, not outward. "Tell Blanca stay in trailer. Go see *Diablo.* Think dead."

"At the plant?"

The man nodded. "Not dead." Marek felt Karen tense beside him. "Want dead. Cut. Go."

But Dale Hansen hadn't been stabbed to death; he'd been alive and more-or-less intact, other than the head wound and bloody arm, when Darcie had kicked him out of the Hummer. "And after? What then?"

"Blanca cry. Try to leave. Tie down."

To try to save her from herself. "After you tied down Blanca, did you kill Dale Hansen?"

"*No.*"

Back in the office minutes later, Karen ejected the tape and clutched it. Finally, something to hold on to, something she could pass on to Nails. ASAP. "We've got enough to hold Jaramillo on—what, assault? That's solid. But I still say he killed Dale."

"Saying so doesn't make it so," Marek replied, sinking into his chair. "I'd like to know where Dale got the meth."

Did the man always go off on these tangents? "I want you focused on the homicide."

Marek nudged the reports on his desk. "How did that happen so quick?"

"Mrs. L—Josephine—has the fastest fingers in the West." The fax hummed to life beside her and Karen snatched out the cover page. "Crime lab. Says, 'Rush per Larson.' What kind of pull does that man have?"

"It's getting results," Marek said. "Don't knock it."

She pulled out the next sheet. "Phone records. They must be from Dale's cell." She handed that to Marek as the next came online. "This one's the fingerprint report." She scanned to the conclusion. "Excluding the victim and incidental prints we submitted, no others identified. Well, that's no help."

Watching Marek concentrate on the phone numbers, she huffed

out a breath. "Give me that. I'll read them out."

"I can read."

"I can read *and* talk." He handed it over and she skimmed. "Okay, they've got the names he input for the numbers. We've got the expected: Krissy, Darcie, Thompson. Mex-Mix is on here."

Marek pulled out his cell phone. "I need that. What's the number?"

She read it off then went on to the next. "Aunt Mary. Uncle Dave. That would be Vanderwil, I believe. Bunch of Hansens. Bullard. Oh, that's right. His cousin Mindy married Cal Bullard. Yarnik. Do I know that one?"

"New operations manager at the plant."

"The cheery guy in the sunny yellow hat." She thought about him. "He was second in command to Dale, so that's not too surprising. Ringold. That must be Troy. I wouldn't think that one got used very often. It must be to do with Darcie. Hmm. He's got Gotsch in here."

"Dale's new pickup was in repair," Marek said. "Wayne Gotsch is supposed to be working on the electronics but he doesn't seem to be in any hurry."

She'd gotten the update on Wayne. Unfortunately, the Eda County state's attorney hadn't been inclined to throw the book at the boy despite community outrage. Not in small part, she thought, because the attorney's wife's cousin happened to be related to Gotsch. But if everyone stepped away from a conflict of interest in this county, there'd be no one to run it.

"Feedlots come next," she said, looking back down at the fax. "Iowa and Nebraska numbers mostly. Now this last one's just listed as MM. That's interesting. It's a New Mexico number." She put down the fax and picked up the phone. "I wouldn't think they'd be hauling stock in from that far."

But when she dialed the number, it was dead.

With its bell, the abandoned building reminded Blanca Jaramillo of her village church, where she'd been as the drug runners had destroyed her family. It had been the last place where she'd still been untouched by violence, still innocent in the ways of men.

That, she could no longer claim. Pulling the blankets closer, she laid her chin on her arms, rubbed at her irritated eyes.

The man had told her not to leave, that she'd be safe if she stayed here. He'd brought her what she'd needed, including food and more blankets. And she'd given him what little she could: what else did she have?

She turned on the battery-operated radio and listened to country western. Stories of sad loves and sad lives. Then it stopped, mid-twang, and a voice came on, wavering a bit over the distance.

"Good afternoon, folks, this is Nails Nelson. We've got a special report that I wanted to get out to you ASAP. There's been a big break in the Dale Hansen murder."

On the brink of turning the dial, Blanca sank back. Yes, who *had* killed him? She wouldn't be hiding out, her father wouldn't be in jail, if Dale Hansen was still alive.

"We're looking at a foreigner, an illegal to boot, so rack one up for the home team. The sheriff said she got a confession, not to murder, but to the carving of the words *White Out* on Dale Hansen's arm. But it wasn't a racial slur. So I got that wrong. Turns out it's about drugs. Hold on to your hats, folks, because it's going to take a while to explain."

Blanca rocked back on the hard planks, shaking her head back and forth, the scream of denial inarticulate in her chest, as she heard the names.

Her name. Her father's name.

Flinging off blankets, she rocketed to her feet, then stopped as a man stood silhouetted in the doorway, light cascading from the bell tower behind him, throwing his features into shade.

From out of that darkness, a long slender shadow reached out: the barrel of a shotgun.

Marek initialed the last report. He hated paperwork; every cop he'd ever known hated it. But he knew he'd caught a huge break with Mrs. Lindstrom.

The front door opened and shut. Marek rose to his feet, recognizing the sheepskin-clad farmer. "Mr. Gullick. I'm sorry I haven't gotten back to you on the fertilizer, but I do have the signed report here." Just barely. "I can make a copy for you, if you like, for the insurance people, but I'm afraid I haven't had time to pursue the matter further."

To his surprise, the man looked—what, chastened? Maybe Rick

had had a word with him.

"No, no, I understand. You've got a murderer to catch. I just wanted to tell you, I remembered something. You asked about anybody out of place around the farm. Before the blizzard hit so hard that day, I was on my way to town to get some supplies." He swept off his hat and scratched at his head. "Passed one of those, what do they call them, sport cars? Like what that Hansen gal—or Ringold I guess she still calls herself—drives, only not so queer looking."

"Sport utility vehicles. SUVs."

"Yeah, one of those. Some dark color. Right there on the section road. The guy driving, I didn't get hardly more than a glimpse but looked Mexican to me."

Marek thought of the black SUV that Darcie had seen. But what would it have been doing out there?

"Odd thing was, the plate. Bright colored, yellow or gold maybe. Not from anywhere around here." He twirled the hat then stuffed it back on his head. "Anyway, don't know if it means anything, but that's all that I could think of." The man craned his head around the room. "Where's the sheriff?"

"She went to talk to Sig Halvorsen."

A grunt emitted at that. "Who knows how long *that* will take. Won't wait for her then."

After Marek made him a copy of the incident report, Vern Gullick went on his way, apparently satisfied. But Marek wasn't. Instead of heading for Mex-Mix, he got on the radio, made his way through layers of command until he found his target.

"Southbound?" The radio transmission crackled. "Yeah, we had a couple stragglers come south that night. Better that than north."

"You get any plates?"

"Yeah, one guy, he had a light out on his souped up SUV, so we stopped him. Land Rover. Midnight blue. Beauty of a ride. Said he didn't know why anyone would want to live out here. Anyway, thought it was weird, two yellow New Mexico plates in one evening, but at least this guy was going the right direction, unlike the other idiot. You ever find that guy or did he end up in the drifts?"

"You're talking to him."

"Oh. Uh...great. Good. What'd you need?"

Marek took down the plate information, double then triple checked it. The Land Rover was registered to one Lawrence H. Montero. He started to pursue the lead then glanced at the clock. If he didn't get to Mex-Mix soon, Becca was going to go without supper.

CHAPTER 34

KAREN CHEWED ON JERKY WHILE she waited for Sig Halvorsen to usher out his last customer. Once he was done, he beckoned her back to his office.

When he sank into his chair, he looked...old, she thought, and her heart contracted. "What is it, Uncle Sig? What's happened?"

He stared up at the pressed-tin ceiling. Horns of plenty ran riot there. "I've been debating the last couple days whether I should even talk to you."

About to hook her feet into the stool, she let them fall back to the ground. She needed the earth under her. "Why?"

His gaze fell to hers. "Goodness, child, I'm not a killer."

She hooked her feet back on air. "I didn't think you were."

"No, but I think you're finding out if you treat people like animals, they'll turn into them." He glanced back up at the harvest that spilled out over his head. "You know, Dale Hansen used to win awards with his livestock. Those animals responded to him, some would say because he had a lot of the animal in him, but if so, it had no meanness to it. But what he did to those poor people...that was human. Ate of the tree, we did, and there's no going back, not once we learned the ways of evil."

Karen shifted on the stool. "You've heard the news about Emilio Jaramillo, then?"

"It's all my customers can talk about. Five to one, they think Mr. Jaramillo killed Dale, but three to one, they think they'd have done the same. A few, they're saying any illegal gets what he deserves, but it's muted. I wonder how many others Dale got hooked, how many of the missing workers...but maybe I should leave it alone."

Her boots thudded back to the floor. "You know where the missing workers are?"

He continued to ponder the tiles. "I heard rumors they're being protected by a church."

"Sanctuary? In Reunion?" That boggled her mind. "What do you want me to do, start hauling in pastors and grilling them?"

"Of course not." He ran his palms back over his temples then clasped his hands behind his head. "I just thought you should know."

She'd rather not. But it was just hearsay, after all, and if it was a crime, one for the Feds.

"And that's not all," Sig went on. "They're saying this guy who took over for Dale, Yarnik, he's trying to get parolees to work at the plant for really low wages."

Although that made her stomach clench, she wore her uniform, which meant she had no opinion but the official. "It's not against the law."

"No, it's not, Sheriff. But I think it would concern you."

"Concern, yes, but we've already got some ex-cons working at PBI," she told him. "The few I've pulled over weren't violent offenders. I think Dad had one up on burglary charges a couple years ago but he's long gone."

Sig shrugged. "Word is that Thompson and Yarnik are at odds over the plan. And a lot else. After your little news blast on meth, Thompson shut down the plant and called an all-staff meeting. He wants mandatory drug testing."

"Sounds reasonable."

"Yarnik, he thinks it's a waste of money, that people will do what they do, and you deal with them one at a time. I don't know that he's wrong. But apparently he stood up and said this business about Dale distributing drugs was bogus—just a cover for Jaramillo's hate crime and a smear on the workers at PBI. He got shouted down. It got ugly, I guess. People are desperately looking for another job. I wish I could give them one."

Karen rubbed at her own temples. "It shouldn't be like this, that you get run out of business for doing right by your workers."

"You'd think we were in Sanchez's boat," Sig said, with a wry smile. "How is he, by the way?"

"Last I heard, he'll be released tomorrow morning. I wouldn't blame him if he never sets foot back in Eda County. He would have died, Uncle Sig, if we hadn't gotten to him. We still don't know who did it. It doesn't make sense it was PBI. Marek doesn't think it was. But he's not been real open with his thoughts."

Her Halvorsen relation grinned. "You should be used to that."

"Maybe, but it's frustrating. He's still a mystery to me."

"Not like you haven't had a few other mysteries to deal with this past week."

"Is that all it's been? A week?"

"Coming tomorrow, it will be." The fjord eyes, mirrors of her own, welled with concern. "Take care of yourself, Karen. I don't like the feeling I'm getting, that this case of yours isn't so shut as some people think."

"I'll go with the odds," she said. "But whether we can actually prove Jaramillo killed Dale, that's something else, and what I'll have to live with, and get voted on, come election time." She hooked her feet back into the stool and leaned forward, propping her elbows on her upshot knees. "Now tell me about your wife and the twins."

With the burden off his shoulders, Sig Halvorsen's eyes twinkled, and he launched into his favorite topic.

Marek ditched the takeout containers from Mex-Mix into the overstuffed trash bag. He needed to get on the garbage pickup list. One more thing to do. To get back to normal.

What was it they told survivors? Get used to a new normal. He didn't want any part of it, but Becca needed it. So he had to figure out how to make it happen.

Marek eased down into the rocker and watched the flames flicker. The crackle of burning sap—juniper or red cedar, he thought, not the more plentiful riverside cottonwood—punctured the utter quiet. Other than the wind, the creaking and settling of the old house, not a sound. No honking horns, droning planes, wailing sirens, or booming rap music from cruising lowriders.

When the cell phone burbled, he dug it reluctantly out of his pocket. He wanted one night, just one, without having to haul his daughter off to Karen's or having Arne coming over and shooting up his house. He might hit something more vital than a doorjamb next time.

Marek looked at the caller ID.

Slowly, with deliberate premeditation, he flipped the cell

phone closed.

In the abandoned building, the man shook Blanca Jaramillo hard. "Where have you been? I told you, you were safe, if you stayed here, but you left. Where did you go?"

She couldn't see; the moon didn't penetrate and the light of the small fire didn't reach them. "Just outside."

"Liar, your car was gone," the man said. "Tell me where you went, who you talked to, or you'll put all of us at risk. Do you understand? All of us. *Tell me.*"

When her bones began to knock together, she told him.

And when she fell to the floor, he stalked to the fire.

CHAPTER 35

WELL AWAY FROM THE BUILDINGS turning deep night into daylight, Karen watched history disappear. Her immigrant ancestor, Alvar Åkerlund, had worshipped in that church; his bones lay in its churchyard, presumably free from the lick of warmth. His son Artur, the first sheriff, had attended the nearby school.

Beside her, about two dozen people, faces ash-dusky, huddled in blankets; their history had never touched this land. Until now. How many more, she wondered, hadn't gotten out in time?

Fatalities.

That dread word had come on the heels of Jordan Fike's call. She saw him now, pulling back, walking toward her.

He flicked up the shield on his volunteer fireman's helmet. "Looks like we've got three dead. Less than we'd feared but one's a child." He raised an arm, brushed against his forehead, and smeared ash. "The car out back, we've identified. It's Emilio Jaramillo's."

Karen sucked in a breath and looked again at the eerily silent crowd. She'd seen the flames flicker in those stoic faces, then watched the fire die with their hopes. Other than the various emergency crews and a few farmers from the area, the crowd consisted of the Guatemalans, the missing workers.

And none wore the face of Blanca Jaramillo.

Sig had been right; they'd taken sanctuary in a church. But not a living one: a dead one. Didn't the Mexicans have a special holiday, the day of the dead? Marek would know. Something about dressing up as skeletons, dancing in the streets with the bones laid bare.

"Both buildings are a total loss," Jordan said.

She could see that. "Cause?"

"From what I've heard, they were burning the flooring in the old wood stove to keep warm at night. Probably got out of control. Someone nodded off. But that'll be for the fire marshal." He pitched his helmet into the truck. "I'll go back and relieve Tammy."

Karen let her night jailer go. What else could be done here? She'd called her pastor and he'd woken others; cots and food awaited the survivors at the Lutheran church in town.

Sanctuary after all.

Technically, the lot of them were trespassing and likely illegal, but she didn't move to arrest any of them. For one thing, she didn't have the manpower to arrest them *en masse*—or the jail space to house them.

And, not to put too fine a point on it, it just wasn't right.

She hadn't called in the rest of her crew. If she had to go down for this, she'd do it alone.

"Karen."

She turned to find Vern Gullick beside her, hunched into his sheepskin jacket, hat tilted down almost to his nose. "Stopped to talk to your detective today—yesterday I guess, now—forgot to tell him about this place, about what I saw, and if I had..."

"You can't play those games," she told him, even though she'd been doing it herself. "What did you see?"

"Tracks in the snow, mostly. Not that unusual. Lots of people who've left, left their dead here; they stop by sometimes and check the graves. Saw an old white pickup parked out front here several days ago. Pretty rusted up."

Sanchez drove a pickup like that. But, then, plenty of people had white pickups. "No one could have predicted this, Mr. Gullick."

Rick Gullick pulled up then and Vern went over. Father and son didn't speak to each other, just stood in front of the squad car and stared at the smolders. In the alternating light of the silent strobe lights, Åkerlund and Gullick gravemarkers shone in shadowed letters.

There'd be more markers in the community of the dead after tonight.

When the last of the Guatemalans had been shuttled away and the fire crew called it a night, Karen got back in the Suburban and headed home. Her cell phone rang when she hit the outskirts of town.

Tammy Nylander's voice came through with less buoyancy than usual. Not unexpected given that she'd been rousted out of bed to cover for Jordan Fike. "We need you at the jail."

So much for her own bed. Karen turned on to Main. "Why are you using my cell instead of the radio?"

"It's Jaramillo."

Oh, hell. He'd have questions. "I'm only two blocks away."

Minutes later, she found Tammy sitting in a miserable mound at the dispatch desk. Jordan hovered behind her, hand on her shoulder.

"When I got in, I didn't want to wake him," Tammy told Karen. "I just waited out here in case more calls came through, then when Jordan got back, we talked about what happened...you know, how Blanca Jaramillo's got to be one of the dead and..." She rose, gestured into the jail. "I didn't even know he was awake."

Karen walked into the jail. And stopped. Dead. The body hung so still, so silent, with bulging, accusing eyes—so dark and wide she could fall into them and never find her way out.

Finally, she said, "I'll call Tish." Karen hated what had to be done. "And DCI."

"What? Why not Marek?" Tammy asked. "He's the detective. Not that you need one."

"Because it's a death under our watch." Or lack thereof.

She made the calls right there in the jail. Somehow none of them could break away from death.

Jordan turned his back to the bars. "I can't believe it. I just saw her. Now she's dead."

Karen shifted. "Him, you mean."

But her night jailer, his face still smeared with ashes, shook his head. "No, I mean Blanca Jaramillo. She came in to see her father tonight. In a real state, she was, so I...um, I let her. Guess that's one thing I don't feel bad about, that they got to see each other before—"

"Jordan," Karen interrupted, "why didn't you hold her, or at least call me?"

He looked confused. "Why should I? Is she illegal? Listen, I didn't ask. I didn't know."

She pressed her eyes closed. Was this, too, her fault? "It's been all over YRUN and around town."

But, she reminded herself, too late, that he slept days, worked nights. So she told him about Blanca Jaramillo's false charge of abuse against her father.

"That explains it, then," Jordan said. "The two shouted a bit. Oh, not so's I had to break it up, but lots of tears on her part. He just seemed to shut down after a while, like she was asking for something he couldn't or wouldn't give her, and he got tired of saying it. Then at the end, he reached through the bars, cupped her face, and said something to her. She left after that. He laid down and I thought he went to sleep."

After another long silence, Karen asked, "What did they say, Jordan? As near as you can remember."

"How would I know?" At her stare, he said, "I don't know Spanish."

"Did you pick up *anything*?"

"*Policía*. That's police, right? And Hansen."

Tammy hefted herself out of her funk. "I guess that shuts the door on the homicide. All parties dead."

CHAPTER 36

THE NEXT MORNING, KAREN TRUDGED up the walk—dingy gray with the melt and freeze of days, not unlike her brain—to the broken down bungalow.

She found Marek at breakfast and Becca still, thankfully, asleep.

"You want something to eat?" he asked her, uncertainly. "You look like..."

"Crap." She sank down into one of the sleek hardwood chairs at the table. It was surprisingly comfortable—or maybe she was just so tired it felt like it. "I haven't been to bed. I need to take a shower. Then I've got the media. That's why I'm here."

He looked at her with caution—and reluctance. "You want me to talk to Nails?"

The laugh came from somewhere, she didn't know where, and she felt light-headed. "No, I'm doing the talking, some of it anyway. But I want you there to back me." She rubbed hands down her face. "Larson is doing the rest."

He'd just set down the cereal in front of her. Now he paused with milk in hand. He must have had time to stop at Casey's for the basics. "Larson? Why?"

She explained what had happened, at the fire, at the jail, and watched him retreat, bit by bit. Not physically. He hadn't moved. But he'd gone away, into that mixed up brain of his.

And, she realized, he looked like crap too, despite having cleaned up. "Marek, has something happened since yesterday? Dad told me about that package for Becca but he said it was just some harmless—"

She broke off when he threw the plastic carton against the

kitchen wall. Milk flew against the faded wallpaper, splatted back, into his face, onto his shirt.

She felt the shock, not only of the act, but of his face. "Marek..."

"You don't understand."

Slowly, Karen rose, went to the sink, wetted the dishrag. "Then make me understand."

"That package...it reminded me of what I've been trying to run away from." Marek wiped at milk that threatened a whiteout in his sky-eyes. "If I'd been home instead of working on a lead that could've waited until the next day, if I'd gotten the damn milk, the accident wouldn't have happened."

So she wasn't the only one playing *what ifs*. If anyone, he should know the futility of it. Logic, not emotion, was what he needed now. And she didn't dare say what had been her first thought on learning of the accident: that Val shouldn't have gone out at midnight just for milk. "If it wasn't your wife who was killed, it might have been you."

"It should have been." A tear rivered down, tinged with white. "Then my daughter would still chatter like a magpie and my son would have lived to be born instead of being cut out of his mother's body—too late..."

He lurched to his feet and charged up the stairs.

Oh, God. His wife had been pregnant. Not his father-in-law, but his son, that had been Becca's second angel.

Karen stood there, rag in hand, wishing she could wipe it all away. She wondered if he was being sick. With the smell of souring milk unsettling her own stomach, she decided she should leave, then she heard the feet clomp back down the stairs.

Marek held one those wooden icons in his hands—she'd forgotten the Spanish word—only larger, darker, more compelling than the ones she'd seen in Becca's room.

He tapped the face of the Madonna. Or at least, that's what Karen thought it represented.

"That's Val. Her face, anyway." Duskier than her daughter and, at least by the face, more petite. "She was eight months pregnant."

His pale blue eyes rose with devastation large: holes in his world. How long had her own eyes held that look, she wondered, after what happened to Patrick. Did they still?

Marek's blunt finger trailed down to the winged angel who held to the bottom of the Madonna's mantle.

"I held him. He was so small. Manny insisted he be baptized."

His finger nearly obliterated the delicate face. "Joseph Leif Manuel Okerlund."

She got Leif. Manuel must be for his ex-partner, Sergeant Manny Trujillo, who she'd done a Google search on after Harold Dahl mentioned him. "Joseph?"

"Val's father. Joseph De Baca. I finished my carpenter's apprenticeship under him." He brushed milk and tears from his face. "We gave my son the names of all the men who made me who I am. But I pursued death and lost his life."

His hand trembled and she gently tugged the *retablo* away.

She looked at the duskily pale face, with its long lashes, curly black hair, etched face. Unearthly, she thought. "He's beautiful."

"He was perfect," Marek said so softly, so lowly, she could barely hear him. "And I had to bury him because I wasn't."

"That drunk you told me about is the one who's to blame." She turned, set the icon down on the counter, then fingered her ring. "But you aren't the only one with regrets for choices made, or not made."

His gaze fastened on her ring. She stared down at the plain circle of it, all they'd been able to afford, though Patrick had promised her better. But she'd said it was all she wanted: plain, solid, simple. The basis for the life they'd planned, including a large family, to replace what they'd both lost—or never had. Patrick had been in foster care most of his young life.

"Is your husband in the service?"

How carefully they danced around what strangers knew. "Actually, he might be. Truth is, I don't know."

"You don't know where he is?"

"He's in Sioux Falls. In an institution."

She could almost see the thought process. The state mental hospital was in Yankton. Sioux Falls had chosen a different institution to host.

"He's in the state pen?"

"Wouldn't that be a good campaign slogan: vote for the sheriff whose husband is serving a life sentence." She dashed away her prick of pain; it was nothing on his, she knew now. "Actually, Patrick is serving time behind bars—bed bars—at the VA hospital. He's been in a coma ever since a bomb blew shrapnel into his brain. I should have let him go. But I believed in miracles."

A rapid rush of creaks on the stairs had them both looking over. Becca ran to them, her face filled with panic, and she looked at her father like...well, like she'd been betrayed.

Until he held up his hands. "I didn't do anything to your *retablo*, Becca. Uncle Manny made it for you."

Karen wrapped her tongue around that word. *Retablo*. "Here you go, Becca. Your dad wanted me to see your mom and your brother. Your Uncle Manny is a very good artist."

To her surprise, Becca darted a fearful look at her father, then with exaggerated steps, bore off the *retablo* like it was the ark of the covenant.

"I, uh, didn't react well when it came," Marek said. "Manny's never done real people before. Just saints. You saw the ones up in her room."

She nodded. "I figured out that's where Becca got so obsessed with the idea of angels." Only the girl's drawings had been simpler, with wings like the snow angels, but still colorful, striking, and well beyond her years. "You must be inundated with them."

She looked over at his refrigerator. He had a Mex-Mix menu tacked up with a Curry Seed magnet but that's all. "You don't have any up yet? Dad's got our fridge papered with them. I've got one tacked up on my old corkboard in my room. My God, Marek, she's only five. What'll she be in ten, twenty years?"

The pale eyes chilled. "Not an artist."

"Why not? Is it the angels? I take it you're not religious but—"

He got up then. "I need to take a shower. And so, Sheriff, do you."

So the line had been reached, she thought.

Half an hour later, Karen threaded her ponytail through her cap. She'd given thought to hacking it all off, as it was more practical for her current position, but she hadn't been able to bring herself to do it.

Maybe after the election. If she still had the job.

Which wasn't looking good after the night's developments. And she wasn't sure Sioux Falls would take her back, even at entry level, after she'd ignored their warnings. Maybe she'd end up working at PBI. Wouldn't that be a kicker. When she went downstairs, her father stood in the foyer, fully dressed, ready and waiting.

Blinking back tears at his silent support, she holstered her gun. "Here we go, then."

When the sheriff had told him there'd be media that morning, Marek hadn't worried; South Dakota wasn't a magnet.

Then he saw all the vans and satellites. True, most were local. Because of the anomaly of similarly named and similarly populated cities, Sioux Falls in South Dakota and Sioux City in Iowa, the area had two of almost every network. He squinted against the sunlight. Twin Cities had come too, it looked like, even...yes, that was a Denver station. Was that CNN?

If it was, the world must have stopped; no one stopped for Reunion, South Dakota.

In Albuquerque, he'd gotten caught up in a few national media storms but he'd shoved Manny to the fore, a position his partner had relished.

Resisting the urge to pull off his cap, to remain anonymous, Marek made his way through the crowd to where Karen stood with Dahl. Even Arne Okerlund had come, looking uncomfortable in a dark suit.

"Good thing you got a haircut," Karen muttered when Marek came up to her. "I need you behind me on this, okay?"

Literally or figuratively? Likely both. He nodded. Then nodded again at Larson, who eyed the crowd with the bitter resignation of a scarred veteran.

However, the murmurs of reporters in their camera-eye bubbles were sedate. As Karen went to the microphone, all swung to face the small podium.

"Good morning. I'm Sheriff Karen Mehaffey. Please hold your questions until both myself and DCI Agent Dirk Larson have made our statements."

Karen didn't draw on her maiden name this time, Marek noted. She gave a succinct description of the night's happenings. He'd expected nerves; he neither saw nor heard them. She rocked a bit on her feet but, then, she never stayed still.

"The dead have now been identified as a family of three: Javier Ramirez, his wife Inez, and their infant son, José. They had been sleeping in the loft of the old church and died, the coroner believes, of smoke inhalation."

That was all news to Marek; their identities must have only just been confirmed. But what of Blanca Jaramillo, he wondered. Had there been a fourth body?

"The source of the fire remains under investigation this morning and I won't speculate ahead of the facts." Now she paused to take a deep breath—the first sign of nerves. "Many of you are aware that we have been investigating another death, that of Dale Hansen, the operations manager at Plains Beef, Inc."

Karen took them through the background, their investigation, and the confession of Emilio Jaramillo to carving the letters in Dale Hansen's arm.

She glanced over at her father then looked out at the cameras. "I am sorry to have to report that Mr. Jaramillo was found dead in his jail cell last night after the fire."

That's what had brought Karen to his door that morning.

At the murmurs of the crowd, Karen held up a hand. "Per procedure, we called in DCI. Agent Larson will tell you about his investigation. First, however, I want to say that, for what happened, I take full responsibility. I can only apologize to Mr. Jaramillo's daughter Blanca, wherever she might be, and to my constituents, for allowing this tragedy to happen."

Larson took the podium; he raked his bullet eyes over the crowd of reporters. "I know what you're thinking, that Sheriff Mehaffey neglected to put a suicide watch on Jaramillo. You're right. But it wouldn't have made any difference."

Marek admitted he'd thought the man would gloat; instead, he appeared to be defending the sheriff he'd turned his back on.

"Why not?" Larson's scowl pulled at the scar on his cheek. "Because someone strangled Emilio Jaramillo then strung him up to make it look like suicide."

Marek knew that, Karen had told him, but he was still pondering it, even if it wasn't his case. The agent answered the flurry of questions in rapid-fire bursts.

"The sheriff is not a suspect," he told them. "She was at the fire."

A reporter asked, "Who was the officer on watch?"

"The night jailer, a volunteer firefighter," Larson said. "He responded to the call immediately. Left the jail unmanned. Lives were at risk. It took his backup twenty-three minutes to get to the jail. During that time, someone came to the jail, took the keys from the dispatch desk, strangled Mr. Jaramillo, and got away clean. We've no suspects at this time."

He backed away from the microphone.

Karen took it back over. "Questions?"

She pointed at the grizzled Channel 11 reporter who asked, "How does a woman who took South Dakota one shot away from a

Division II national championship come to be sheriff?"

Larson looked even more startled than Karen did, Marek thought, but she answered without hesitation. "I stepped up when asked; if I falter at the buzzer like I did then, I'm sure the voters will let me know."

"That was a foul," another reporter yelled. "You'd have made that shot otherwise."

Marek agreed. He'd been there.

"Well, in this case, foul play is loss of life, not just loss of a trophy," she returned. "Now, do you have questions on any of these cases?"

The CNN reporter asked, "What will happen to the survivors of the fire?"

Marek stirred. "I'll answer that."

The sheriff blinked back at him but, after a moment's hesitation, yielded the microphone.

"The survivors are being cared for at a local church," he told the crowd. "They were brought to the US under false pretenses, scraping up their life savings to pay for what they thought were green cards. As such, they may be exempt from deportation per Title 18 of the US Code and subsequent acts."

That showed blank faces.

"Human trafficking," he said. "Go look it up. It's illegal."

"You mean, they are!" a voice shouted. "Fire is too good for them!"

Marek fastened on the man at the edge of the crowd. Yarnik. "The Ramirezes didn't deserve to die. And their child was an American citizen, born on US soil, and he had a name: José. I won't forget it." It came out before he could stop it. "Any more than the name of the son I lost six months ago to another kind of illegal, a drunk driver."

He stepped back rather than answer the questions that popped up; he'd just given them his private life on a platter. But if he had to guess, Karen would be well ahead of him in local interest.

Karen gave him a long look, not accusing, not approving, just a look. Then she took the podium again and finished off the last of the questions. Most of them had to do with the meth connection. That Dale Hansen had used it as a productivity booster seemed of more interest than the death of a Guatemalan-American infant.

Hopefully they'd go harass Jack Thompson or whatever corporate honchos spoke for PBI. The plant had thrived in anonymity. He'd have hoped, early in his career, that scrutiny changed things for the better, but he'd learned otherwise.

Once the heat died down, the weeds of human nature grew again in the cracks of the concrete of civilization.

Weedwhackers, that's what we are, Manny used to say.

Not weedkillers.

CHAPTER 37

KAREN FOLLOWED THE FIRE MARSHAL to where he pointed.
"Here," he said. The smoldering remains of the schoolhouse still smoked in lazy tendrils in the morning air. "It started here."

Behind her, she heard Marek, his voice masked to a rasp, ask, "Arson?"

"Or accident. Hard to say for certain," the fire marshal said, indicating melded metal, a sculpture of dysfunction. "We've detected chemicals and the remains of some apparatus here that make me suspect a meth lab. That's why I insisted on the masks."

She looked over the blackened earth toward the church. The scorched trees that stood taller than the rubble looked like they might disintegrate on touch. But when she'd brushed against one, it had been hard, like a shell of life.

"We thought it started in the church," she said. Instead, it started in the schoolhouse, a place where bells had rung to bring young minds to a world beyond their own. The Guatemalans must have made meth here, and when things got hot, they'd taken sanctuary in the nearby church. The meth lab changed the picture, once again, a twist of the kaleidoscope.

They left the fire marshal to finish his tests and went to interview the Guatemalans.

But after two hours of it, Karen and Marek got only indignation. Dale Hansen, the workers insisted, had handed out the *white* at the plant and docked their pay for it, even those who refused to take it. And while they all knew Jaramillo, none admitted to having been there when he carved the message into Dale Hansen's arm. Two, however, had seen Dale fall to the concrete floor when the chain snapped.

Yes, they'd seen lights at the schoolhouse, as well as Jaramillo's car, but they hadn't gone out to investigate, for fear of being discovered. No one had come out to investigate the church either. Except, one admitted, the union rep.

"Sanchez?" she'd asked.

The workers clammed up at the name, as if just speaking it put them all at risk. Maybe it did. But what did Sanchez have to do with the Guatemalans? Was he in on the drug trade? And who beat him up? Had they? Who were the workers afraid of, now Dale Hansen was dead?

Marek listened but, to her, seemed turned inward. Knowing what she did now about what and how he'd lost, she didn't let his disappearance bother her.

He'd be back.

When they returned to the office, she fielded a call from Jack Thompson, who demanded to know what she was doing, trying to get his plant shut down? Oh, and what had they done with Yarnik?

"Who?"

"My manager," he yelled through the line. "He went to your media shindig this morning and never came back."

"Cutting his losses, I'd say," she said to Marek after she hung up. "Yarnik looked like a survivor to me."

Unlike herself after this week, she thought morosely. For months, it had been summonses, minor assaults, drunk and disorderlies, domestics, accidents, and traffic violations. Since Marek had returned home, the town had burst into one major felony after another.

He was staring out the window again at the bandshell in the park, and she wished she could see into his mind. Was it adobe again, of what he'd left behind? Or was it his past in Reunion? Did he see any future here? And if he did, what of hers?

His cell phone burbled out its *Lone Ranger* fanfare. He started, took the call, then when he was done, asked her, "Can your dad pick up Becca?"

In answer, she dug out her own phone. After a bit of obligatory grumbling, her father agreed. "Where are we headed?" she asked Marek.

"Trailer city to see Dr. Ahmed."

That made her pause. "Who? Oh, Dr. Sabanovic. The Bosniak. Is this about Sanchez?"

"No, Jaramillo."

Ten minutes later, they watched the agitated man twitch his glasses as he explained what happened the night of the blizzard.

"Emilio, he come to me very upset. He wants to talk to Mr. Hansen. I have better English. We go to plant but Mr. Hansen, he is on floor. I find..."

He hesitated then put his own fingertips over his neck.

"Pulse."

"Yes, pulse. Emilio take out knife in pocket. I think, he will kill Hansen, but then, he drop knife on floor. Emilio, he is religious, no? No kill, he say."

The Bosniak's world-killed eyes told a different story of religious scruples.

"But Emilio say, this *white*, it must go, you understand? Ruin everything. He sit on the floor and cry. What you say, last straw? So...left message."

Marek shook his head. "That's not possible. Emilio Jaramillo wasn't literate, he couldn't wri—"

He shut his mouth. Karen opened hers, looked at Marek then at Dr. Ahmed, at the deep wells of resignation that lidded into fatality. If Jaramillo hadn't written the message, then this man had. If he got in trouble with the law, he'd be deported.

Marek had been right, Karen thought, cops made choices. She made hers. "What happened after the message was left on Dale Hansen's arm?"

Marek's mother had had little use for the passive voice, Karen remembered, but it might save this man's life.

"I help tie Blanca to bed," he said, eyes darting between Marek and Karen. "Only way."

"When did you leave the Jaramillos?"

"It is late. We sit, talk, drink coffee. Snow...it is everywhere. I almost get lost."

So, the whiteout had been in full force.

Emilio Jaramillo now had an alibi for the murder, an alibi he hadn't tried to give before, because of his daughter. If he'd only spoken up, if Dr. Sabanovic had, maybe none of this would have happened. *Ifs*, again. "Why didn't you tell us this all before—and why now?"

The workworn hands rose, palms up. "Emilio a good man. He try to, what you say, play by the rules. Pay all to come. Think he is legal, like I am. People trick him. In Guatemala. Here. You put him in jail. He die there. You kill him."

"We didn't..." she began then had to stop. They'd left the jail open for whoever killed him. "If you had told us..." He still would have been in jail, she reminded herself. But why did anyone kill him? What did he know? "I don't know what happened to him, Dr. Sabanovic. We will find out. Do you know where Blanca Jaramillo is?"

Now the blame bent inward. "I am upset at her. She run. If you find, I will take her." He pulled off his glasses and rubbed at his eyes. "Emilio and I, we should hate, but we like brothers. All brothers dead now."

Literally? "Do you have family in Bosnia, Dr. Ahmed?"

The unsteady glasses went back on. "Wife, she die, years ago, in birth of child."

She felt, rather than saw, Marek stiffen beside her.

"Two sons killed." He looked away, said a word, and it made her skin crawl. Srebrenica. "One daughter. She...the soldiers...I thought she is dead. She take another name. Pretend married, to protect herself. I come to America because I have education. Then I hear daughter is in refugee camp. Have baby."

Karen read what wasn't said; his daughter had been raped.

"She think I hate her because I do not bring to America. I write I love her, all of me left in world, she and Saban, but she not believe." He pulled out his wallet and showed them a young woman with her father's haunted eyes. The baby was now as tall as her. "All the time, she write, why? Why not bring. I try but government says nothing. I call, all the time, nothing. I think, almost, then 9/11. Everything stop. Tell me to stop calling. Can you help?"

Marek answered for her. "We are little people, Dr. Ahmed."

He looked up at Marek in bafflement.

"No power, he means. No one listens to us." Karen sighed. "Not in Washington DC."

Marek shifted on his feet. Was he eager to get gone? Well, so was she.

On the way back to the office, Marek asked her, "Why should they hate each other? Mr. Jaramillo and Dr. Ahmed?"

"Jaramillo would've been Catholic. Dr. Ahmed is Bosniak. Bosnian Muslim. The Serbs who killed his family, Christian. Ethnically. Not ethically. The Serbs massacred thousands of Muslims in Srebrenica."

"You were there?"

"No, the Dutch."

Marek looked straight ahead, not at her. "Why did you go into the Army?"

"I guess I was flattered to be recruited as leadership material. And I wanted to see the world. Make my mark." Karen turned into the parking spot, turned off the ignition, and thought of what she'd seen, heard, felt. "Instead, the world made its mark on me."

Walrus and Kurt awaited them in the office. She ignored Larson, who'd parked himself at Marek's desk and had a phone attached to his ear like a cochlear implant.

She'd called the others in for an incident meeting. Given what had happened to Jaramillo, it might be her last. Dahl would let her know soon enough; he wasn't one to drag things out. But for as long as she had the job, she'd do it.

"All right, have a seat." They did; she didn't. Marek went to her desk. Taking her spot already? But, no, he sat on the desk, not in the sheriff's chair. "Bork's on personal leave and Two Fingers flew out this morning, so it's just you three."

"The three musketeers," Walrus said with a paw pat on his partner's arm.

Ignoring that, Kurt asked her, "Why weren't we brought in last night, Sheriff?"

She heard censure in his voice. "Because what was done, was done, and if I could go back and do it again, I'd have gone to the jail myself to cover for Jordan. Rousing you or Walrus from bed wouldn't have changed the outcome; it still would've taken you too long to get here."

Marek asked, "Who called in the fire?"

Larson swung the phone away from his mouth. "Farmer. Forget his name. Lives close."

"That'd be Vern Gullick," Karen said. "He or his wife must have seen the fire."

The door to the downstairs flung open. Tammy came in, wide-eyed. "Got a call from the Feebs."

Larson raised a hand. "That'd be for me."

"Uh, no, sorry."

"For me, then," Karen said, reaching for the phone.

"Actually, it's for Marek. You really lit a fire under somebody important, Detective, when you asked the Feebs down in New Mexico for info on Lawrence 'Mince' Montero."

"Who the hell is that?" Larson demanded.

"Our mystery man," Marek said. "The one in the dark Land Rover that Darcie Ringold saw with Dale Hansen that night."

Karen absorbed that. He'd gone around her to get that information. Straight to the Feebs. Without so much as talking to her about it.

"The FBI wants you to back off," Tammy said, backing herself off from the heat in Karen's eyes. "Either that, or they want in, I'm not sure which, but they've got the gist of the trafficking."

"Which, drug or human?" Marek asked.

"Both, it seems. They're sending a team down. Sommervold and Wintersgill."

"The Seasons are the top guns at the resident agency in Sioux Falls," Larson said. "If anything out here can be called top."

Karen didn't think he meant the topography. Before Marek could move, she stabbed the button for the speakerphone. "This is Sheriff Karen Mehaffey. I hear you want to talk to my detective."

A pause came over the line. "That's correct, Sheriff. He's been stepping on toes."

Karen wondered which Feeb she was talking to: Sommervold or Wintersgill. Whichever, it was a woman. "Let me step on his toes, if needed. That's my job." And stepping on his shoes wouldn't hurt him much. "Anything else?"

"The Special Agent in Charge of the Minneapolis office wishes me to relay his personal displeasure that your detective tipped off Montero. The agency has been tracking him, building a case for years, and—"

"You *knew* about the people down here?" Karen interrupted. "The human trafficking?"

The voice cooled. "I, personally, or we, as an agency?"

"I think you just answered that, Agent—"

"Sommervold." The voice warmed unexpectedly. "And you're pissed. Good. The bigwigs didn't bother to give us a heads-up; they want Mince Montero for drug running not human trafficking, though now it's out there, they want that too. We'd like to depose the Guatemalans before immigration gets to them."

Marek leaned toward the phone. "Is immigration going to get them?"

Sommervold hesitated. "I think I can keep them out of lockup if they'll turn witness against Montero."

Like Sanchez had tried to do? Marek was right; it wasn't PBI.

The union rep had been asking questions about Montero. Had Montero's goons also been the ones to threaten Becca? If so, she'd be at more risk down in New Mexico than here in Reunion.

"Good luck getting the Guatemalans to talk," Karen said.

"They've got incentive; it means citizenship."

Marek spoke up again. "It might also mean death given Montero's connections."

"Let us worry about that."

"Happy to," Karen said. "But why don't you think drugs were involved?"

Another voice came on. "What makes you think they were?"

Wintersgill, she presumed. Had he been on the line the whole time? If so, he didn't breathe. "Meth was involved."

"In your homicide, apparently, but you've got the culprit—or you did."

Karen wasn't about to tell the agent that her prime suspect, her dead suspect, now had an alibi. "The investigation is still ongoing. As Jaramillo was himself killed, we're not assuming anything."

Marek's eyebrows rose at that. Well, she could learn, couldn't she?

"Larson's been assigned to that homicide from DCI, hasn't he?" Wintersgill said. "Is he still there?"

"Parked out here, yes," she said. Larson had finally disconnected himself from the phone and, like Walrus and Kurt, appeared to be entertained by the conversation.

Sommervold cut back in. "Then we'll see you all soon."

After she hung up, Karen said, "Marek, why did you contact the FBI without letting me know first?"

"It wasn't an official call," he said, gazing down at his boots as if wondering how hard she was going to stomp on them. "I just asked someone I know down in the Albuquerque office what they could tell me about Lawrence Montero of the dark Land Rover." He looked back up. "I was going to fill you in but the call came first."

She didn't see anything but tiredness in his eyes. "Okay, I won't mangle your toes."

The side door opened then. She blinked at the pudgy figure framed in the arched doorway like a croquet ball under a hoop.

"What have you stirred up down here, Sheriff?" Harold Dahl asked her. "My cousin in DC just called me. You know, the one with the FBI."

Karen frowned at the commissioner. "He's upset?"

"Officially, I suppose, but—" Harold's gaze fell on Larson.

"Don't mind me," Larson said. "I'm officially deaf."

Taking him at his word, which Karen thought naïve, the commissioner said, "It looks like we're going to be getting some big press soon; the FBI just picked up this Mince Montero character at the Albuquerque airport along with three others."

Harold almost burst out of his buttons. "They were set to fly off in a personal jet to Guatemala City. Had more than enough dope on board to hold the three of them without bail while the FBI scrambles to pull in their associates from cell phones they confiscated. It'll be a big haul but hurried."

The commissioner looked over at Marek. "The FBI didn't like it that a lone county detective in a backwater town upset their apple cart—or drug cartel—before they'd decided it was ripe for the picking."

Shaking his head at Walrus's thumbs up, Marek said, "Don't tell me my little soundbite about human trafficking went national."

Harold's hands inched around his paunch and tap danced. "Seems someone up here tipped off Montero—you know, about the Guatemalan workers."

Marek grimaced. "I've got a guess on the tipster."

Karen had one too. "Yarnik?"

Her detective nodded. "I don't think he was directly involved; he let Dale do that. But he's the sort who'd have nosed it out and kept it under wraps until he saw reason to sell it to the highest bidder. But I should've kept my mouth shut. Montero's still got connections and he's going to think Sanchez rolled on him. He'll be at risk."

Larson propped his elbows on Marek's now-papered desk. All belonging, she'd bet, to the DCI agent. "The Feds could protect Sanchez."

"It's not himself he's concerned with," Marek said. "But his family."

"Where are they?"

"Spread out. He's one of twelve."

"I thought you meant *his* family. Doesn't he have any, then?"

Her detective's face tightened. "He has a son and a daughter."

Marek had had a son, Karen thought, and was left with a daughter. If anything happened to Becca, well, she didn't think he'd live—even if he lived.

"Montero's connections to Guatemala may have a familial link," Marek continued, "but it's more likely a different kind of family: a gang. Instant conduit for drugs and dupes."

Harold scratched his head. "Dupes?"

"The duped," Larson said drily.

"Workers for the sex trade, most often," Marek explained. "But sweatshops too."

"How did Dale Hansen contact Montero in the first place?" Kurt asked, finally entering the conversation.

"Yeah," Walrus echoed. "I mean, Dale? Come on."

"According to what I heard from my Albuquerque connections," Marek said, "Mince Montero saw one of the little flyers Dale Hansen had people tack up in Tijuana, before things got so anti-immigrant here. All about beautiful downtown Reunion, South Dakota. Montero thought it was so amusing, he had some of his people track Dale down. Told him he could get him workers."

Larson grunted. "For a big finder's fee."

"A big chunk of the cleaning contract at PBI, I'm guessing," Marek said. "And, of course, Montero took whatever he could get from the workers before they left Guatemala—double dipping. Apparently, Dale Hansen put in an order with Montero for more workers."

Karen pondered. "Do you think Montero's people killed Dale? But why, unless he double-crossed them somehow?"

"It's possible," he said, "but why mess up a good racket if you can just send some goons to rough him up, like they did with Sanchez?"

"Wait a minute," Larson said. "Are we sure that's what happened to Sanchez?"

"It won't go in any report," Marek said. "Not one I'll ever sign off on."

Larson looked disgusted. "How can we get Montero for trafficking, then?"

Karen broke in, "That's for Sommervold and Wintersgill."

"And that's it for me," the commissioner declared, turning in the doorway to contemplate the stairs up to his office. "Good work, Sheriff, Detective. Keep me updated." And with a look reminiscent of mountain climbers on the last leg of Mt. Everest, he braced himself and began the ascent.

When he'd gone, Karen turned to Larson. "Your case and ours are linked. We need to find out who killed Jaramillo to find out who killed Dale Hansen."

"Jaramillo killed Dale," Walrus said.

"No, Jaramillo had an alibi." As she saw the surprise on her deputies' faces, she said, "We've just come from trailer city."

After she explained, she opened up the floor. "Who had reason to kill Mr. Jaramillo?"

"Depends on the motive," Kurt said. "I don't know that I agree that whoever killed Dale, killed Jaramillo. Could be a hate crime."

Walrus looked over at Marek. "Didn't you have the Gotsch kid in for that kind of thing?"

"Wayne?" Karen shook her head. "From what I hear, he's too chicken-hearted, not to mention chicken-armed, to strangle a man like Jaramillo."

"I wouldn't put it past him," Marek countered. "But he couldn't have known the jail would be left open. And I doubt he'd be hanging around here after the other night."

Larson put his oar in. "Someone had to know that the jail would be unattended. Don't see it as luck. Not in the middle of the night. Who's got a police scanner around here?"

"Nails has one," Walrus said.

"Who?"

"Local radio personality," Karen said.

Irritated, Kurt got to his feet. "He's out: wheelchair."

"What about you, Okerlund?" Larson asked.

That brought her detective awake. "I was asleep."

"His truck was in the drive when I got the call." Karen didn't think Marek even noticed that she'd alibied him. He'd sunk back into himself. "And when I got back, it was still there and the house was dark. He wouldn't have left his daughter."

"I'll need to check on the rest of your deputies—" Larson began.

"No."

The DCI agent glared over at Marek. "What did you say?"

"You won't need to check because I know who did it."

Karen wondered if he'd wandered too far into loss—and lost the thread of the investigation. "Who did what? Killed Dale Hansen?"

"No, I know who set the fire," Marek said, "who cooked the meth, and who killed Jaramillo."

"What do you mean, set?" That leap didn't have a solid springboard, she thought. "The fire marshal hasn't determined the cause yet."

Larson kicked back in his chair. "You're telling me you know my perp, Okerlund?"

Karen took a stab. "Was it Yarnik?" When Marek turned bleak

eyes on her, she breathed out, "One of *us*?"

That brought Walrus to his feet. Kurt, already on his, stiffened to military attention. Karen slowly walked over to them, turned, and faced Marek.

Her detective registered the wall he faced. And for a moment, it looked like he wouldn't say anything, wouldn't break it down, but then his eyes shifted to Larson.

"Rick Gullick."

CHAPTER 38

WALRUS BROKE FIRST; HE LAUGHED. "Good one, Okerlund."
But Marek noticed Kurt didn't laugh.
Nor did Karen. "You're serious," she said.

"Oh, come on, guys," Walrus said, catching his breath. "Can't you take a joke?"

Larson stirred. "I'd say, no joke. Who is he?"

"My night reserve deputy." Karen crossed her arms and stood hipshot. "Just where did you jump off into lala land with this, Detective?"

No one connected the dots, Sig Halvorsen had said. What he hadn't said was, when you did, people got mad. "It started with fertilizer."

"Bunch of manure, that's for sure," Walrus muttered.

"Anhydrous ammonia," Marek said. "It can be used to make meth."

Karen dropped her arms back to her sides. "The Gullicks reported the fertilizer missing. That's hardly something they'd do if they were using it to cook meth."

"Vern Gullick called up your dad as soon as he found the tank empty," he told her. "Didn't think it was right to have his son report the theft. I went directly out there with your dad." When he got the stone wall of silence, he plugged on. "Tell me, Sheriff, did you see Rick at the fire, when you first got there?"

"No, not until later, but—"

"Vern Gullick told me he'd seen Montero out near his place just before the blizzard started." That pricked interest, he saw. "But Montero was with Dale Hansen when the storm started to kick up—

Darcie Ringold saw him—and he left and was identified by the highway patrol at the Iowa border. I checked the times. He didn't linger. Besides, Montero'd hardly be stealing fertilizer; he doesn't make the meth and has plenty of his own supplies."

"Maybe he went to put the fear of God in the Guatemalans." As if remembering where they'd sheltered, in the abandoned church, Kurt said, "So to speak."

"No, the Guatemalans didn't move into the church until *after* the blizzard. The only tracks in the snow out there were in front of the schoolhouse, not the church." And if he'd checked it out, things might have happened differently. "So tell me, why would Vern Gullick lie, try to redirect my investigation, with information he could only have gotten from his son?"

The wall slid back into place.

"All along, there's been a leak." He built his case. "Jaramillo gets arrested, threatening the entire enterprise. Rick must have figured the man would talk about the meth being distributed at the plant— why wouldn't he?" He kept his gaze on Karen now. "Next thing you know, you get a call that threatens my daughter if I don't back off."

"It wasn't Rick's voice," Karen countered. "I would have recognized it."

"Maybe, maybe not, but he would have changed it, muffled it. But even way back, there was a leak: think the raid by the Feds. All the Guatemalans disappear, as well as a few illegal Mexicans like Chacón. Rick could have been the leak. He'd been friends with Dale, or at least friendly, until just recently. And Rick's the one who pointed me to the human trafficking."

"And haven't you just proven him right?" Karen asked.

"Yes, but Rick also wanted me to tug them for the meth. All neat and tidy."

"And so it should be," Kurt said, his thumbs hooked into his gun belt.

"Geez, Okerlund, get a grip," Walrus said. "We've just heard from the Feebs that Montero had his fingers in both. All you could want in one handy package: slave labor and the drugs to keep them going. Sort of like the cattle, now I think of it: crowd them in and shoot them up."

"It may have been headed there," Marek acceded. "In fact, I think that's what was behind Dale Hansen's death."

Larson kicked back in Marek's chair, absently tracing the scar on his face. "I thought you said it was Jaramillo's killer you'd pegged."

"And maybe Dale's as well," Marek said. "I'm not so sure about that. We had two different things going: drug trafficking and human trafficking. I think the drugs were coming through Rick to Dale."

"So you say," Walrus muttered.

He hadn't managed to break down the wall, Marek thought, but at least they hadn't strung him up yet. "Dale had a separate account for the cleaning crew, a lump sum, since they were supposed to be independent contractors; he had free rein to make them work, take their money. I think as time went on and he didn't get caught at it, he started skimming more and more. Not from Rick, I don't think, but from the workers—and it spread out to bogus equipment charges and the like. And I don't think Rick liked that."

"If Sanchez got beat up for poking into the human trafficking," Karen asked, "why not Rick?"

"Rick was a cop and a risky bet. But Sanchez, he had no clout, no backup, and when he started to ask around about Montero, he got the crap beaten out of him and his family threatened. Sanchez won't ever talk."

No one contradicted him. "But I think Montero was here to make another pitch besides more workers; he wanted to cut in on the meth trade. Not just at the plant, too small a market, but as a stepping stone to the northern states and even into Canada. My guess is, Rick got wind of the deal, maybe he was even the one who picked up Dale on the road that night. Remember, Darcie Ringold saw a squad car out that night."

"That was me," Kurt insisted, "on my way to rescue *you*."

His tone made it clear he wished he hadn't bothered. "It might have been. Or it might have been Rick. Either way, no one's going to pay any attention to a squad car. You expect them to be out on a night like that, tooling along Main, to and from the interstate."

Larson leaned back in Marek's chair. "So you're saying Dale Hansen was going to cut off his buddy Rick's profits on cooking meth by getting it cheaper from Montero?"

"That's what I think. Vern Gullick said something about his son doing really well with the county; how it had helped save the farm. He's a reserve. On-call work."

That quieted them all.

Larson whistled through his teeth. "So this night deputy of

yours, he took Dale out to that barn by the highway and had a private little Buy American rally."

"But the chain, the lock, they came from the plant," Karen protested.

"And so did Dale. I'll bet he had those on him, in his jacket pockets, most likely, because he wanted to get rid of them, away from the plant, to prevent OSHA shutting them down." Marek continued to build his case, relentlessly battering against the wall of loyalty. "Remember, Rick had his prints on the tag and the cell phone. We had the crime lab eliminate them—but I no longer buy he forgot he shouldn't touch the evidence."

Did he see a gap in that wall, finally?

"Why would Rick do it?" Walrus's moustache fluttered. "He's a bit impulsive but he's a good kid."

Kurt nodded stiffly. "He's from good people."

Marek caught the tone underneath: *he* wasn't. The Marek name trumped Okerlund once again. "When I met Rick Gullick, he was pumped up, his eyes red, but he didn't have a cold. You said he got a little aggressive, knocked in Sanchez's door on that union-busting incident. I'd guess he took meth himself and it escalated from there to distribution."

Karen hissed out a breath. "Meth addict, my ass."

Marek sighed, rubbed at his own tired eyes. "Rick probably got hooked for the same reason many outside the normal drug scene do: to keep up, to stay awake, to bolster a shaky ego, to be more productive."

Walrus stomped over to his desk. "You're off. Way off."

"One way to find out." Larson got to his feet. "Where's this Rick Gullick now?"

Karen glared at the agent. "He should be at the farm."

"Let's go, then." He paused when no one moved. "Of course, I can do this alone."

That got them moving.

"I'll lead the way," Karen said as she put her hand on the door. "Marek, you're coming with me."

Keep your friends close and your enemies closer, he decided. And if he'd ever had a chance to become the former, he'd just lost it to the latter.

"Walter and Kurt, go together," she continued, "but stay behind, back on the road, and don't enter the farm unless you're called in. Got that?"

At the Gullick farm, Karen got out of the Suburban and slammed the door shut. She'd like to slam it on Marek Okerlund and wipe him off the face of her earth.

But some part of her, deep down in the gut, had knotted. She stalked up the steps and glared back at Marek. "Keep your mouth shut."

She turned back, braced herself, and knocked.

Clara Gullick opened the door. A petite woman, broad only at the cheekbone, she smiled at Karen with delight. "Why, Karen, it's so good to see you. You haven't been out to the farm in a good long while, have you." Her eyes fell on Marek. "And your...nephew?"

"My uncle," Karen reminded her.

"Oh, yes, sorry, it's the ages that always throw me. Goodness, the same thing happens with Rick. Being so much younger, he's of age with the kids of his cousins. Come in, come in, is this about those poor souls in the church? Or is it about the missing fertilizer? Vern's about the farm somewhere but..."

She trailed off as she finally gauged the look on Karen's face.

"What is it?" She reached out to grip Karen's arm. "Rick? Vern?"

"So far as I know, Mrs. Gullick, they're both fine."

The hand slipped off her arm and went to her heart, where her men lived and were loved. "Whatever's got you looking so grim then, Karen?"

"It may not be anything, Mrs. Gullick." She couldn't do it, shoot out friendly fire into that familiar face. "We're looking for Rick."

"If you couldn't reach him on his radio, did you try his cell phone?"

Karen let her silence be taken as assent. "Do you know where he is?"

"He made up some sandwiches a while ago, said he was going to eat on the run, and I haven't seen him since. He must've let the battery die on his cell phone. He'll be mad at himself for it, I'm sure, as he takes pride in his work."

And she in him. The knot twisted harder. "And your husband?"

"Oh, last I saw him, he was headed for the barn; the old barn, come to think of it. We're still cleaning up after the blizzard."

Karen nodded, exchanged a bit more chitchat, then beckoned Marek. But Clara Gullick stopped him. "Detective, I never got to meet you properly."

She held out her hand and Marek took it gently. "Pleased to meet you."

Karen started to see past her own anger and to his face. Even he couldn't hide the misery. He didn't *want* it to be Rick.

And, she thought, maybe it wasn't. Maybe they'd all go home happy. Well, except Larson. When they went back outside, the DCI agent awaited them, leaning against his car. "Well?"

"Rick isn't home."

He stared over their shoulder to the front windows. "Right."

Karen didn't have to look to know Mrs. Gullick stood watching them, no doubt puzzled to see the agent, though not unduly worried. Why should she be?

"He made lunch and left in his squad," she told the agent. "Vern Gullick's in the old barn."

Larson took out his gun.

"Put that thing away."

"I don't go after a killer with polite nothings, Sheriff."

"We don't know that Rick's a killer, much less his father."

Karen headed toward the barn. Vern Gullick walked out and met them halfway.

"You all look mighty official," her father's best friend said. Was it her imagination, or did the tone sound forced? "Come to tell me what happened to my fertilizer?"

"Your fertilizer got spread over something more profitable than dirt," Larson said. "Black as dirt, isn't that how the saying goes? Only it's honest dirt. Your son, Mr. Gullick, turned a profit on what his buddy Dale called *white.*"

Karen saw it, just the flicker before the farmer's eyes lidded. Hadn't she told herself that she'd have to question, arrest, people she knew? "Mr. Gullick, don't lie to us." Not again, she thought. "Where is Rick?"

The outraged stance held for a moment then sagged. "I don't know."

"You mind if we look in that barn?" Marek asked.

"You got a warrant?"

"I can call up Judge Rudibaugh and get one," Karen said evenly. "Is that how you want to play it, Mr. Gullick? Is Rick in there?"

Vern closed his eyes. "She's there."

"Blanca Jaramillo? She's alive?"

The man opened his eyes to glance at the house. "Wife doesn't know. I don't want her knowing. Not until....unless Rick is...it was just..."

She almost choked on her own regurgitated naiveté. "You're telling me you've been holding a scared young woman against her will in a drafty old barn?"

"Hiding her, not holding her," he growled. "Old barn's better built. She's got warm blankets, plenty of food, and we're looking for a job for her. Rick was watching after those Guatemalans, you know, at the old church. I didn't know, not then, what was going on. After what Dale Hansen did to those people, he deserved to die."

Larson hadn't put away his gun, though he held it at his hip, away from Gullick's gaze. "Did your son kill him?"

That lifted the grizzled brows high. "You're outta your mind."

An engine gunned in the silence. Rick's squad car barreled out from behind the old barn and onto the road.

Larson cursed and ran to his car.

Yelling at Marek to drive, Karen ran to the Suburban and grabbed the radio. She hailed Kurt and Walrus, even knowing Rick would be able to hear. "Rick Gullick is headed your way. Stop him if you can." Marek fishtailed around to the section line road to follow Larson. "Rick, I know you can hear me. I don't know why you ran but there's no reason for it. Stop the car and we'll talk. Hiding Blanca isn't going to get you in big trouble. I promise."

He wouldn't know, couldn't, that they'd tagged him for bigger trouble.

"You know I'm on your side, Rick. I'll do whatever I can for you." She waited for a few seconds. "Rick, talk to me."

She grabbed at the dash as Marek braked and slung the Suburban across the road. He'd seen what Walrus now reported at the top of his disbelieving voice. "He's turned back. Headed your way. He rammed Larson!"

Remarkably, Larson did a one-eighty in his dented car and followed Rick's squad. Marek jerked open the Suburban's driver's side door and pulled out his gun. "Come out this way," he told Karen, "or you'll get rammed."

She slid out. "You point a gun at Rick and he's not going to give up, Marek."

Once out, she looked over the hood at the approaching squad. "Dammit, Marek, he's not going to ram us."

But she had to take that back, and a step back, when Rick didn't slow.

"Don't you dare shoot," she said.

Too late. The shot rang out over her order.

But it didn't hit the windshield.

Some part of her had to admire the control Rick exerted over the squad car after its front right tire blew, even as she whirled in frustration to watch the taillights disappear down the section line. The Suburban covered the road but it hadn't covered the ditch.

"Get in," Marek yelled. "He's headed for the interstate."

It took precious seconds to get the Suburban headed in the right direction, with Larson and the other squad bottlenecked behind them. She contacted the highway patrol and hoped they'd have some backup in the area to cut Rick off.

Marek followed the distant taillights with singular intensity; she knew she was a good driver, but he drove the Suburban like it was a Ferrari.

Larson had fallen back at the last turn. Kurt and Walrus were farther yet behind.

She grabbed the radio again. "Rick, the interstate will have plenty of commuter traffic. It isn't worth your life or theirs. Stop. Please. You're sworn to protect lives, not take them."

But all she got was static then the hail of a highway patrolman passing Alford. Too far north, she thought with frustration. She watched Rick turn to take the highway ramp at high speed, two wheels off the snow-scuffed concrete. Fortunately he'd hit the siren, the lights, and those in his path moved out of his way, thinking he was after one of them.

Not imagining, she knew, that he was the trouble.

She closed her eyes as Marek performed the same maneuver in the Suburban. Braced for a rollover, she wondered if time had stopped.

"You can open your eyes now."

She did. And found they'd traveled a full mile. Now she heard another hail. From the south. Rick would hear that too. He'd have only one exit: the Reunion exit.

He took it. But when he turned onto the county road, it wasn't toward Reunion. She held her hand up against the glare of the plunging sun.

"The old Hansen place," Marek said as he followed. When they braked hard behind the abandoned squad, Karen saw its door had been left open.

From behind the protection of the squad, Marek reached in and turned off the ignition and pocketed the keys. He held his gun in the other. Pointed toward the open barn.

That panicked her but she kept her voice low and controlled. "Let me talk to him. I can get through to him."

Protest flamed on his face as the setting sun hit it. "Karen..."

"That's an order, Detective." She ignored the pileup of squads behind her. "Rick!" she shouted. "It's Karen. I'm coming in. We can talk."

"Get the hell down," Larson shouted behind her. "You want to get killed?"

She kept on walking and Rick came to the barn door.

His gun rose toward her. That shocked her into stopping. "Rick, put it down." She made a slow sweeping-down gesture. "You don't want it to end like this. No matter what you've done or not done; it's not the end."

"You're wrong," he said, his eyes wild with...what? Paranoia? Betrayal? "You came for me like I was one of the ten most wanted with that jerk-off agent." His eyes darted over her, behind her, and his voice went thin. "If you'd let me alone, I'd have ended it myself, but you brought *him* here."

She wasn't sure who it was he meant: Marek or Larson.

But she didn't have time to find out.

The pain as she hit the ground took her breath, even as her ears registered the echo of the shot—or shots—and heard the thud of a body.

CHAPTER 39

"GET OFF ME," KAREN SAID, striking out at the mound that was Marek. He rolled off with a wheeze that told her she'd struck windpipe. "Call for an ambulance!"

She clawed into the ground, propelled herself toward Rick, then knelt by her fallen deputy even as Marek kicked the gun away. She jerked off her coat and balled it up. Pressed it against the red.

Rick lay awkwardly on his back, one leg trapped underneath him. Kurt moved the leg, gently, while Walter corralled a nearby crate to use for elevation. Keep the blood in the torso, she thought dimly. Larson and the highway patrolmen stayed back. Had it been one of their guns that had done this?

If Marek hadn't knock her out of the way, she thought, they wouldn't have had the angle. As it was, only one shot had hit the bullseye. Or close enough.

"Why, Rick?" she asked.

"Meth?" Rick flicked at blood-flecked lips with his tongue. "Helped me...stay up nights. Thought harmless, like coffee, you know. Nobody can outwork a Dakotan." His boyish smile twisted. "'Cept maybe those Guatemalans."

He coughed blood and Karen pressed harder. "Hold on, Rick."

"Dale thought...it could help at the plant. Speed things up. But got greedy. Hurt people. Brought in that Mexican. Montero. Didn't mean for it to go bad. Helped the Guatemalans. Didn't think the fire'd go from the old school to the church. Just wanted to...start over."

He coughed up more blood: dark, the river of life, flooding out of its banks into the shallow plain of a wasted life.

"Did you kill Dale?" she asked.

"Chained him in the barn. Got loose..." He coughed again. "Blizzard killed."

With a little help from a tow chain, she thought. Had it come from his squad?

"What about Jaramillo?"

Rick tracked toward Marek's gentle voice, identified the speaker. His lips trembled and a tear made inroads into the blood. "Went to get him out, tell him...Blanca was safe, get both away, but he said...people the same. All over. Bad. Told him it was done, no more drugs, but he just kept saying... *White* out, must stop, that he'd tell you, trusted you to stop it. I just lost it."

He clutched Karen's arm. "Just wanted him to shut up. Didn't mean...knew it was over then. Should've done it myself. Tell Mom and Dad...sorry. So...stupid."

Karen pushed harder on the welling spring of red, even knowing the ambulance wouldn't get there in time: the rural death penalty. She tried to keep him with her as the last of the sun set in his eyes. "Who supplied you before you got into the business, Rick? Those Guatemalans?"

His answer was a convulsive and bloody no.

"Who, then?"

"Always said...wife's coffee sucked. Caught him one night. Said did it for a couple years, on and off. Just trying to do...the job and keep the farm." His eyes unfocused. "Tired, so tired, isn't right."

"Who?" she demanded, wanting someone, anyone, to blame, to arrest, to answer for the waste beneath her hands.

"Ca—"

A consonant drowned in his mouth and the light went from behind his eyes.

"No, geez, no." Walrus sank down to his knees beside the young man, buried his face in his hands, and wept. Kurt put a hand on his shoulder. Karen couldn't move, hands still pressed hard against the unmoving chest.

"Cal Bullard," Marek said quietly. "We need to get him before he hears and takes off."

Karen's mind shifted to a thermos, a wired man, and a name on Dale Hansen's contact list. The plow operator who'd called in Dale Hansen's body on the interstate and who'd married Dale's cousin. Was there no end to the family's pain? "Dammit, Marek, Rick could have meant anything. Can't, for instance, instead of Cal."

Face as remote as one of those *retablo* saints, Marek knelt and pulled her bloodied hands away from the spring that had gone dry. "We can't let it lie. That's what Rick did and it led to this..." He turned up her palms and she barely kept from throwing up. Kurt brought a wetted towel and Marek cleaned her hands like a child's.

The Gullicks pulled up then: ran to their son. Karen watched, in the headlights, the life go out of their faces. Blanca Jaramillo had come with them, huddled in a blanket, and she cried too, not yet knowing it was for the man who'd killed her father.

"If you're not going after Bullard," Marek told Karen as they moved out of the way, "I am."

Karen wanted to tell him to go to hell. But she could see he was already there: and she felt the kinship of it. It was, after all, their family business.

That lasted until, in the Suburban, Marek began to hum. If she hadn't had her hands on the wheel, she'd have strangled him. No wonder he was a murder cop. Hands bloody one minute and humming a tune the next.

Then she caught herself. She'd jumped on Marek before, seeing his actions in the worst light, only to regret it later. Was she more like her father than she'd thought?

So instead of spewing, she asked, "What's that?"

He broke off. "What?"

"You're humming."

He reddened then cleared his throat, and...sang. Awkwardly, quietly, but the lament laced with then strangled her anger.

Come sit down beside me and hear my sad story
I was shot in the chest and I know I must die

Had she known Marek could sing, and like that? No, no more than she'd known that he'd been dyslexic. Her mother's letters hadn't mentioned much about Marek once he'd moved to Valeska. Not until Janina Marek Okerlund had died and her son had left town right after the funeral with tornado sirens on his tail.

"I didn't know you could sing," she said into the lingering echoes of lament.

He hunched in the seat. "I don't except in the shower. Not since high school. I didn't even know I was humming. Nick Bolvin put it in my head, and it fit, but I didn't want you thinking..."

She rubbed her thumb against the steering wheel, flaking off the last of the blood. "It was nice. Strange, but nice."

If she were in charge of Rick's funeral, she'd ask him to sing it again, but she doubted the Gullicks would want him there, probably not her either. Maybe her father could talk to Vern and...God, her father. She'd have to tell him, unless he already knew, from the scanner he kept on in the kitchen.

As if to confirm it, her phone burbled its dispatch tune. "Dad? It's not a good time to talk. I'm headed for—"

"It's Cal Bullard."

"How'd you know?" she asked, surprised. Had he, too, seen what she hadn't? "We're on the way to his farm right now."

"He's here. He's got Becca." She braked so hard that her seatbelt engaged and dug into her heart. "He wants you and Marek to come. Alone. Honey, don't—"

But the phone must have been snatched from him. All she got was a dial tone. She swerved into a dirt turnoff, headed the Suburban back around, then stopped dead in the road.

Karen tamped down the panic enough to speak over it, to tell Marek what happened. "Do we call for backup, for snipers? I can use an encrypted channel, but..."

She read the answer in his face; it mirrored her own. No way, no how, would they risk all they had left of their family on the competence of strangers.

Useless.

Stupid and useless.

Arne Okerlund sat in his recliner, trapped by Bullard's gun. When the door had flung open moments before, he'd thought Karen had come in, to tell him what he'd already heard on the scanner— that Rick Gullick was dead.

Becca had rushed down from upstairs when the door opened, probably thinking it was her father—and fell right into Cal Bullard's arms. Now she sat, mute, tied to a kitchen chair.

Arne dug hands helplessly into the slits of the recliner. His gun was where it was supposed to be with a kid in the house—locked up. All he felt was the damned remote. Too bad he couldn't use it to turn Bullard off. "You're not thinking straight, Cal."

The man paced the kitchen floor. "I'm not the one who had the stroke, old man."

He wasn't all that old. "You want an ostrich—I mean, hostage—take me."

"Nah, you're not worth much, stuck in that damn chair all day. Sheriff'd be happy to have you off her hands, what with one dead weight in the family already." Bullard nudged Becca's head with his revolver. "This one, they'll negotiate to hell and back for."

"Why didn't you just take off?" Arne demanded, wanting the gun away, far away, from that dark head. What had Cal done—had he killed Rick? The scanner hadn't given the how, the why. "Why come *here*?"

"Rick called me, from his squad, said the game was up—that the sheriff knew. But I told him, it's nothing that can't be worked out." Under the seed cap, Bullard's eyes striated red with irrational reason. "We'll get Rick to come, once the sheriff and that idiot detective gets here, and we'll work it out."

"That's right," the ex-sheriff said on a long breath, realizing Bullard didn't know that Rick Gullick was dead. The scanner in the kitchen, set on the Eda County channel, had fallen silent. What, exactly, had Rick kept quiet about? And what did it have to do with that young man's death? "Just ease off, will you. She's just a kid."

And kids could die on you, Arne thought, thinking of Vern and Rick, himself and Karen, Marek and Becca. Kids would die, if he couldn't do the job, this one last time. And he was going to have to do it with his mouth, not his gun.

But outside, the Suburban—silent lights wheeling red, white, and blue over the paired bungalows—screeched to a halt.

Karen grabbed Marek's arm before he could launch himself out of the truck. "Wait, don't rush in." She felt the muscles under the coat quiver. "That's what I did at the old Hansen place and look what happened." She'd have done better, she thought, to reach Rick from behind a dispatch desk. "Think a minute."

He shook off her hand and put his own in his pocket. Did he have a gun there? No, he pulled his hand back out again, empty. "We don't have a minute."

"Cal Bullard's not a killer. We need to—"

"Get in there."

"And talk, not fight. Cal's got to be scared to death to pull something like this." She doused the overhead lights and waited for her eyes to adjust to the dimmer light of the street lamp. "Okay, let's get out. Slowly. Don't draw and don't talk."

"I'm not the one talking."

No, that would be her responsibility. She'd need to draw on all her experience as a dispatcher and tactical responder. Not that she'd had much actual experience with the latter, though before her father's stroke, she'd been in talks with the chief of police in Sioux Falls about turning negotiator on his tab.

Karen led Marek up the walk. Stay calm, she told herself.

But it was hard, Karen decided a moment later, to do so when a shaking Cal Bullard trained the gun on the back of Becca Okerlund's head.

"Throw your weapons out the door. Now."

The size of Marek Okerlund, Karen thought, must intimidate the slight-built farmer and plow operator. "Cal, we're just going to talk. There's no need for—"

"Now!"

She unholstered her gun, threw it behind her, and heard it hit. The safety held. Marek's heavier gun clanked, slid, then skidded into snow—maybe into the remains of one of Becca's angels.

Karen would call on all the saints her Lutheran forebears had disavowed, if it would get them all safely out of this situation.

"Shut the door and get in here."

In the dim light, Karen met her father's eyes then saw them shut in frustration. What did he think, that she'd send in her deputies, when she wore the star?

Marek closed the door behind him. "Mr. Bullard, let me take my daughter's place."

The man laughed. Nerves, Karen thought, not humor.

"Bunch of heroes. Just like Rick." Then he frowned. "He must've turned off his damn phone. I can't reach him." He gestured at the chairs at the table before him. "Nothing's gonna happen to the girl, so long as you do as I say. Sit down."

So, he didn't know Rick was dead. A plus for their side.

Karen scraped the chair over whatever Marek might have said. He didn't move, apparently frozen by his daughter's fright. Karen had to pull on his arm so he'd sit beside her, across from Becca.

"Sure, Cal, we'll sit and talk," Karen said, even as she recognized now what she hadn't in Rick. Cal Bullard had sampled the product before showing up here—and that made him much more dangerous than the panicked family man she'd expected to deal with. Always call for backup, her instructor had said; better to get ribbed for it than riddled with bullets.

But her only backup was her mouth.

Marek reached out toward his daughter, to link their hands, but Cal said, "Hands off until the deal's done." But when Marek jerked back his hands into his lap, Cal became agitated. "Keep those hands where I can see them!"

The big hands, the left highlighted with the white band of his loss, splayed out.

"Yours too, Sheriff."

Karen complied and hoped he wouldn't see the sweat dribble off her palms.

They said, as you got older, time sped up. But right now, it slowed, and the familiar room came into unbearable focus. Harvey Dunn's *The Prairie is My Garden* hung on the wall, her mother's cheerful red-and-white-checkered kitchen mitts dangled off a peg, and the yellow cookie jar she'd kept full for all comers sat empty on the counter.

Maybe it'd all be captured in a photo in DCI's evidence files. Would Larson investigate? Damned if he would. She focused on the people: all that remained of the Okerlund family sat in this room. Divided we fall, she thought, then forced her attention back to Bullard. "What do you want, Cal?"

He wiped his upper lip with the back of his free hand. "Same deal as I had with Rick."

That stumped her. "You want to give us meth?"

He snorted out a laugh. "Just keep quiet, that's all. It's just you two that know, right? I came here just after I got the call from Rick."

"The meth's not such a big deal," she said. "We can handle that."

Cal nodded at her, as if he'd expected no less. "No skin off yours. What with the old school gone up in smoke, we're not gonna be making any more meth anyway."

That put a different spin on matters than a bit of family barter.

"You're a damn drug dealer." Her father echoed her thoughts.

Aloud. He wouldn't have done that, before the stroke. Or, actually, maybe he would. She hadn't ever worked with him before, so she didn't know. But it wasn't smart.

"I'm no drug dealer." Cal appeared sincerely shocked. "You want one of those, go after Montero. I'm just trying to make a living."

Rick must have told him about Montero. Karen shot her father a warning glance and pulled Bullard's attention back to herself. Establish rapport, she reminded herself.

"Farming's never been an easy living," she said, wanting to get up and pace, feeling trapped with her hands drowning in sweat.

Cal scratched at his pocked face. "Mindy, she'd burn my ass if I lost the farm like Dale did. All I want is what everybody wants, right? A decent life."

His gun hand tilted up and away from Becca as he put both palms up. In her peripheral vision, she saw Marek tense, as if to spring. No, she thought desperately, don't. You'll be dead—and right in front of your daughter. Wasn't it bad enough, that Becca had already witnessed one parent's death?

"That's all Marek wants," Karen said hurriedly, drawing Cal's attention to her detective. Marek didn't untense—but he didn't spring either. She imagined if she could read his mind, it would scorch her. "It isn't easy for anybody right now," she went on.

Cal's attention jittered back to her.

"Farming's all I ever wanted to do," he said with a nod. "It's what my dad did, but he didn't have to work so many other jobs just to keep afloat. I can't keep up anymore. We got debts from paying for that big combine last fall." He rubbed at one redshot eye. "They say, keep up with the latest or you're sunk. I kept up, more acreage, bigger yields...but it's those backward Germans down by Fink who're living off their oxen and plows, not me. Bet they sleep better at night, too. That's why I take the stuff, not to get high, to keep up."

Now he gestured toward the still-frozen Marek. "Just look at him. He could use a jolt, just like Rick did."

Once again, Karen pulled his attention back to her, needing for Cal to stay on target—and off the realization that he wasn't making much real-world sense. "So, what you want is a deal for our silence then you'll leave us alone." She glanced over at her father. "All of us."

"That's right," Cal said, voice dropping as he relaxed. "I mean, what really happened? Somebody froze to death in a blizzard, happens all the time. It isn't like I meant for Dale to die."

The chain she'd been weaving of his faulty reasoning broke. Not Rick's tow chain. Cal's. And her mind swerved. Bruce Wilson, the convict whose prints had been on the chain. She'd bet anything that the seasonal DOT worker had operated Cal's plow.

She'd been wrong. Dead wrong. Cal Bullard was a killer. But she had to pretend, to believe even, that he wasn't, since she saw her father's face go cold. He'd spout off again and antagonize Bullard if she didn't keep talking.

"Of course you didn't mean for him to die," she agreed. "I mean, you saved that guy caught out in that RV, right? So, what happened the night of the blizzard?"

She ignored Becca, afraid if she really looked at the child, she'd lose her mind—and she needed it.

"Dale left a message for me. Said he wouldn't be needing the *white* anymore. The meth. He was going to get it cheaper elsewhere." Bullard shook his head in disbelief. "I called Rick. He was cruising the roads and found Dale walking back to the plant. Handcuffed him and called me. We decided to take him out to the old Hansen farm. Talk to him, that's all."

"Right. Just a cozy little chat," Arne muttered from his recliner.

Karen held her breath but Cal either didn't hear or didn't care, intent on telling his side of the story. "Dale laughed at us. Talk about dim. We had a gun on him, he was chained up to the rafters, and he thought he had leverage. We left him there. Rick took his cell, but Dale had the coat. That old barn was built well enough; he'd have survived, though he might've got some frostbite. We weren't real concerned with fingers and toes after the way he double-crossed us."

Karen badly wanted to wipe her hands. "What happened after you left Dale?"

"Went back to work, of course. 'Bout an hour later, the idiot tried to flag down my plow after he stumbled across the highway. Fate, that's what I'd call it."

Karen frowned at a rivulet of red coming off her right hand. Had she hurt herself? Then she snapped her attention back—she couldn't lose focus. "So you chained Dale to the fence."

"I didn't mean to leave him there all night," Cal said, letting the gun lower a bit farther. "I left the construction cone so I could find him again. Then I went to get gassed up before I took him back to the barn. But when I was fueling up, they decided to pull everybody off the road. Wouldn't even let me go home. By that time, Rick couldn't get out there either."

The gun dipped again. "Dale's my wife's cousin, but I figured it's kind of rough justice, isn't it. Family's supposed to mean something, right?"

When Karen spared a glance toward Marek, she was surprised

to encounter one of his own. But she didn't know if it meant, we're family, or if it meant, get ready.

Cal's chin fell to his chest. "I didn't mean to...hell, Dale would've seen the light by morning and none of this would've happened. I panicked once Rick told me you'd taken Jaramillo in. I don't know what went wrong with that daughter of his, what was her name...Blanca, that's it. I've been on and off meth for years. It's not addictive. Just gets you revved up to do what you gotta do."

You keep telling yourself that, she thought.

Marek's chair creaked and Cal's head snapped up. "Don't move." He swung an agitated hand in the air, tugged at his hat, then dug into his pocket. "I need to call Rick again. He knows you people better than I do, whether your word's any good."

Karen could feel the frustration rising in Marek's tensed form.

Cal opened his phone with one hand, punched a button with a calloused thumb, and held the cell phone to his ear. No one would answer, Karen knew, and wondered if she could get him back on track.

"Who's this? Where's Rick?"

Now it was Karen's head that snapped up at Cal's voice. What the hell?

"Dead! What do you mean, dead." He listened for a moment, his face hardening. "No, doesn't matter. He won't need the message."

He flicked the phone shut. "That was the coroner. Said I about gave him a heart attack, the phone ringing like that, when he was loading the deceased, as he called him, and..." He trailed off. "This isn't news to you guys. Dammit, you knew and didn't tell me."

Danger zone, she thought. Big, fat, screaming danger. "We didn't want to upset you."

"Yeah, right," he said, waving the gun wildly. "You shot him, didn't you. Shot him for a little meth. He was a good kid and you—"

"Suicide," Karen interrupted. "That's honest truth, Cal."

"God, he...how?"

"By cop," she told him.

Her father almost came out of his chair, hot eyes on Marek, and Karen realized if she brought the highway patrol and her two deputies into the picture, it would all be over.

"I did it," she told him.

Arne sank back, stunned.

Cal looked at Karen with something like respect. "Didn't think you had it in you."

If you have to tell a lie, her instructor had said, do it as close to the truth as you can. "He held a gun on me."

"Rick did? Boy, he must've really lost it." He laughed, a twisted horror of sound in the room, laced with hysteria. "Guess he did me a final favor, though. Anything comes out now, it all goes on him, you hear?"

"I hear," she said calmly. "You want to walk out of here with our silence. But I want something from you in exchange." Another little tidbit from her training: don't let it be too easy. "You'll quit the meth, right? Dealing and taking."

"Sure," he said. "I don't need it. I'll just dump Mindy's coffee for the stuff at Casey's." Cal nudged the back of Becca's bowed head. "Tell your dad to deal."

Even as Karen realized Cal must have been the one who'd phoned in the threat to Becca, the girl raised her head, her mouth working silently. Not "deal" but "daddy."

From behind her, Cal made a sound of disgust. "Come on, kid, cat got your tongue? Tell him to deal."

"Deal."

That decisive word—short, low, almost a growl—hadn't come from Becca. Marek. The first thing he'd said since he'd sat down. Even though Karen agreed with the strategy, employed it herself, she felt he meant it. And why shouldn't he? Hadn't he already lost his wife to the job? With his agonized eyes on his daughter's, what choice did he have?

Not that it mattered. That it hadn't yet occurred to Cal that, once freed, they'd go back on their word, could only be the meth talking. Once he came down, he'd either give up—or kill them all.

"Okay," Cal said. "It's a deal."

He started to lower his gun—when a disembodied voice floated through the kitchen.

"Sheriff Mehaffey, please respond."

CHAPTER 40

CAL BULLARD SWUNG TOWARD THE kitchen counter—his body, but not his gun, to Karen's despair. "What the hell's that?" he demanded.

"It's a police scanner." Her dispatching skills had gotten her so close to talking her out of this, only to be foiled by her own dispatcher. "I've got to take that," she told Cal. "It's set to the county channel. It'll be something routine—but I've got to respond."

He seemed torn. "Where's your radio?"

"It's in my vehicle," she said. "I didn't think you'd want it in here."

"Sheriff Mehaffey?" Tammy's voice dropped the professional tone. "Please copy." Silence beat into the room. "Detective Okerlund, respond."

"Next will be a call for backup," Karen said.

"Go ahead then," Cal snapped, gun still trained on the back of Becca's head. "Answer the damn thing."

But as she rose, Kurt Bechtold came on the radio. "Sheriff Mehaffey and Detective Okerlund went to pick up Cal Bullard for drug trafficking. Call for backup, Tammy. Now. I'm on my way."

Within two heartbeats, Tammy's voice, after a quick intake of breath, said, "Possible officers down at Bullard farm." Tammy rattled off the address.

Cal wouldn't be there, neither would she or Marek, but they'd figure it out. Eventually.

Seeing Cal's horrified face, she knew the damage had been done.

"You lied!" Cal put both hands on the gun and pointed it at her. "They know about me and the meth!"

"Don't make it worse, Cal," she said, even as other hails came over the radio.

"Worse? What's worse than losing my farm? My kids? My freedom? There's nothing left." His hands tightened on the revolver. "But I'm not going out alone. If I lose, you all lose."

She caught a movement from behind Cal and gathered herself for a last leap—better go out hitting the boards than sitting back on your heels—then she yelped as a loud whoosh roared into the room.

Cal twirled.

Simultaneously, Marek leapt up and hauled Becca and her chair right over the table and into his arms. A fraction of a second later, Karen leapfrogged over the table, dragged out her cuffs, and restrained the man lying stunned on the kitchen floor.

Adrenaline. What a rush. She looked up to see her dad shake his good hand from the blow he'd given Cal. The other hand dropped its lifesaving instrument onto the floor.

The TV remote.

The static of a dropped signal on the TV still roared into the room. A blessed sound. A saving sound. "Turn it off, Dad. It's going to destroy Becca's ears."

He reached down, switched the TV off, and ignored Cal, who moaned into the linoleum.

Like her, Marek must have seen her father's cue—he'd reacted too fast otherwise, all done in Okerlund fashion, without a word spoken.

"Were you telling the truth?" her father asked her. "Did you kill Rick because he held a gun on you?"

"Wait a sec." She went to the scanner. "Sheriff Mehaffey here. Suspect apprehended at 22 Okerlund Road. Both officers on scene are code four."

"Code four?" Tammy echoed, practically in operatic ranges.

The standard codes had been dropped in favor of plain English in most places—if they'd ever been adopted at all.

"A-Okay," Karen radioed.

"Oh, good...great, I thought it was lights out for—" began a relieved Tammy.

"Redirect Deputy Bechtold to pick up the suspect at this address," Karen cut in, in full professional mode. Who knew who listened in—perhaps a prospective employer.

Kurt came on. "Copy. On my way."

Opening a drawer, Karen pulled out a bread knife and went at the ropes on the kitchen chair. It wasn't easy, with Marek holding onto his daughter, but the ropes finally came free. Karen eased the chair back down to its place at the head of the table.

Then she stepped over Cal to stand in front of her father. "Rick did pull a gun on me, but I didn't shoot him." And now, with the latest crisis averted and nothing left to do but clean up, her grief melded with anger. "It didn't have to happen."

"Did *you* kill Rick Gullick?" the ex-sheriff demanded, shaking a finger at Marek, his fury finding a target. "Your badge won't be worth tuppence in this county if—"

Arne broke off when Karen lifted a tired hand. "He didn't kill Rick," she told him.

"You're hurt," he said, the anger draining from his face.

"No."

"There's blood on your hand."

Baffled, she looked down at it, remembered the blood mixed in with the sweat on the table. "It must be Rick's."

But Marek had washed off her hands. And only one hand, her right, had blood on it. What had she touched? She thought back then looked at Marek's left sleeve where she'd grabbed him in the Suburban. To find the ragged slash of leather—and flesh. She moved her hand horizontally from the graze to her own chest. And fisted her bloodied hand over her heart.

"It's Marek's blood, not mine." She opened her hand again to show the stain. "He saved me."

"From who?" her father blustered.

"From Rick." She looked into Marek's still-wild eyes. "I'm right, aren't I?"

He kissed the top of his daughter's head. "You were looking into Rick's face. I was looking at his finger. He pulled it just as I hit you and—" He broke off. "Did you hear that?"

Karen swung a look at Cal, saw him still dazed, secure on the floor. "Hear what?"

In answer, Marek tipped up his daughter's face. "Did you say something, sweatpea?"

Burrowing back, Becca shook her head—into his heart, Karen thought.

"I heard or felt—well, whatever. Must've imagined it."

"Heard what?" Karen repeated.

"Daddy, I thought." Marek covered Becca's exposed ear with his hand. "They figure that's what she was yelling that night, strapped in the minivan." The pools of regret in his eyes made her ache. "And that, by not speaking now, she's punishing me for not coming."

"My dad saved her this time," she said. "But you saved me."

Stiffly, the two men nodded to each other, Okerlund eyes lidded to half staff. Would that bury the old feud, she wondered. Or, the owing balanced on both sides, would it just continue?

Then she heard it, between the hiccups of tears, muffled into Marek's body.

Daddy. Daddy. Daddy.

She saw the tears leak down Marek's face before her own vision blurred. "I'll, uh...take you and Becca to the clinic before we head back to the office."

Because she didn't think he'd be letting go of his daughter anytime soon. She turned into her own father's arms. Hugged him. Then stepped away. "I thought that was it."

"Me, too." Then he smiled—a half-smile. "Not so useless after all."

"Not by a long shot." Even if he took out a doorjamb in the process. Then she wondered what he'd have said, if he'd been asked to deal for her life. She turned back to Marek. "Did you mean it, Marek? You'd have dealt?"

Marek took one hand away from his daughter, stuffed it in his pocket, and pulled out his little digital recorder. "Never go in without backup."

So that's why he'd put his hand in his pocket before they went in, to turn it on. But it wouldn't have saved them. It would, however, have given them justice.

"Karen," her father said again, his smile fallen. "What all was Rick up to?"

"He killed Jaramillo," Cal said into the linoleum. "You won't pin that one on me."

"That can't be true," her father said then saw it in her face.

She didn't have the emotional energy to tell him the whole— about Vern. Another father protecting his child. "Later, Dad."

A sharp knock on the door cut off his protest. Karen hurried over to let Kurt in. "Bullard's on the kitchen floor. Go ahead and take him to the jail. I'll send the doctor over to check him out."

Kurt didn't move. "Why didn't you call for backup?"

She didn't want to get into a tangle over procedure with her senior deputy.

"Had backup," the ex-sheriff said, rubbing his knuckles. "Got a problem with that, Kurt?"

The deputy said not another word as he entered the house and got Cal to his feet.

"Guess Mindy'll get control of the farm now, for all the good it will do her," the farmer mumbled into the accusing silence. "She'll lose it. Then maybe she'll understand what it does to a man to lose what he's inherited, worked all his life for, and wants to pass on to his kids. It isn't fair."

He wouldn't get any sympathy from Kurt Bechtold. But some small part of her understood, that he'd taken that first turn to preserve a way of life. In the Dakotas, small was beautiful—but dying hard. Sometimes harder than needed.

"Think he'll go down for murder?" she asked her expert after Kurt led Cal out.

"Voluntary manslaughter," Marek said, arms still tight around his daughter. "But he won't be getting out any time soon with what he tried to pull here. That's on record."

She picked up her hat from where it had fallen after her leap over the table. "At least he'll get three square meals a day and a bed. I'd really like one of those—a bed, I mean, though food would be welcome too. Why didn't you say something about your arm earlier?"

"Didn't feel it," Marek answered. "Do now."

When they returned to the office, Marek's arm patched up, two strangers awaited. The Seasons, Larson had called them, Karen remembered, and it fit. Spring in her eyes, winter in his, summer in her hair, autumn in his.

"The Guatemalans won't talk to us," Summer said, the female of the duo. "They're more afraid to implicate Montero than be deported. It's crazy. Montero is behind bars and, even without the human trafficking, he's facing major drug charges."

Karen wondered if the woman knew what they'd been through this evening and decided that she must but had her own agenda. Still, Karen could only think, who cared?

"His influence isn't limited by bars," Marek answered, over the head of his daughter. She wasn't sure when he'd let Becca go. Maybe when she reached high school.

"If no one talks, they all go back to Guatemala." Winter spoke in dryness. "Why die there if you can do it better here?"

"I will talk."

Startled, Karen looked back at the young woman still huddled in the blanket.

Agent Sommervold shifted weight to one hip to see around Karen. "Who's she?"

"I am Blanca Jaramillo." Despite the ravaged features, the tattered life, she spoke with dignity. "My father, he dies, because he wants for me to live without *white*."

As the eyes of the two whites narrowed, Marek said, "Meth."

"Because of me, he is killed. I will pay."

The Feds didn't seem to know quite what to do with a martyr-wannabe; but they recovered quickly and requested the interview room.

"Go ahead," Karen told them. "We can interview her tomorrow."

Agent Wintersgill held back. "You'll need to talk to the press tonight."

She just nodded and the agent turned into the interview room. With a limp. Maybe he'd been put to pasture out here—his elegant suit and New England accent didn't jive with his partner's flatter Midwestern accent.

Do the steps, Karen told herself. "You don't have to stay, Marek."

"Do you want me to?"

She rubbed her hand against her face and smelled blood. His blood. And death. "I'd appreciate it. I'm not sure what's going to come out of my mouth. If I'd listened to you, to Larson, maybe..."

"It wasn't your fault."

"What's fault?" she threw back at him then winced. "I'm sorry. I didn't mean..."

"I know what you meant," he said quietly. "Now you know what I meant."

CHAPTER 41

After the press conference, Karen knew she should go home. She'd told Marek not to check in until Monday. Let him have the weekend with Becca, holding her, rocking her, singing to her, for all she knew—all the tangible ways to assure himself he was still a father.

But Karen wasn't ready to face her own father. He still didn't know about Vern Gullick's coverup of Rick's meth dealings. Obstruction of justice, at the very least.

The phone rang then; she glanced at the readout. DCI Pierre. What did they want at this hour? She connected and identified herself.

"Hello, Sheriff Mehaffey, it's Gary Longwell."

Law enforcement instructor, her brain told her, after a momentary glitch.

"Sorry for the late call," he said into her silence, "but I figured you'd probably still be in the office. I just caught your press conference on the ten o'clock news. Wish all my students were as steady behind the microphone; maybe I should advocate for more former dispatchers in the job...or former basketball stars. I didn't realize you're still something of a legend in these parts."

"Yeah, I lost us a national championship," she said. "What can I do for you?"

"I'd like your permission to use this tape."

What tape, she almost asked, then groaned. The tape of Darcie Ringold's interview. "As what? Evidence?"

A laugh greeted her question. "In my class."

Marek would kill her. "Oh. Well, I don't know..."

"Of course, with the permission of Detective Okerlund," went on the affable instructor. "It's a masterful interview."

Karen may have, in hindsight, decided that Marek had gotten what was needed, but masterful?

"He's polite, he keeps from leading the witness, and he keeps her off balance. Most lies are thought out linearly. Most cops think linearly too, so I pretty much instruct it that way. But if somebody's making it up, they'll have made a story of it, from beginning to end. If you jump around, you'll interrupt the story, and you might get snatches of truth that will trip them up."

When she didn't say anything, he said, "You didn't do so bad as bad cop either."

"Seems that was pretty much my role for the whole investigation."

"He's got years of experience on you, Sheriff. Besides, it isn't just about investigating crime, not these days, and you put a good face on it. Not often do we get a case that jerks the chain of the FBI. Maybe your detective can come talk to our next class. Heard from Dirk Larson that he's got experience as a homicide detective in Albuquerque and a good rep down there. How'd you ever get him to Reunion?"

So Larson hadn't told him. Maybe he didn't find the topic of interest. "Family ties."

The kind, though, that bind: and cut off life if pulled too tight.

"Maybe we'll steal him from you."

She forced a gritty tone. "He's mine. Hands off."

But would Marek keep his fingers off her badge, come election time? And did she care if he did? After she hung up, she sat with her head in her hands in the quiet room. Jordan Fike, her night jailer, was downstairs with his new clientele, but she felt very alone right now.

The front door opened and Laura Russell strode in.

"Why didn't *you* kill him, *Sheriff.* Why did you make Walter do it?"

Karen focused on the furious face. "Kill who? What are you talking about, Laura?"

"Rick Gullick."

That brought Karen's arms down over the preliminary report on her desk. "Laura, no one knows who fired the fatal shot."

That stalled Laura's advance. "Walter took a shot, he said so."

"So did two highway patrolmen and DCI Agent Larson," Karen

replied truthfully, even though only Walrus had had the angle for the killing shot. But until ballistics came in, it wasn't fact. "My money is on Larson."

He could take the hit, even if undeserved. Then she recalled the DCI agent had defended her, at the press conference, and decided to stop shifting the blame. She rose and met her former friend full on. "But if you want to find fault, fine, I confronted Rick when he was still panicked…because I didn't think he'd kill me. I was wrong. DCI dug the bullet out of the side of the old house, said it was headed for my heart." She rubbed that part of her anatomy. "And he hit it. Is that what you want to know? Don't talk to me right now, Laura."

"That's a ripe one." Laura collapsed into Marek's chair. "We always talked. We got detention for it and had a grand old time, kept right on talking. That's what we do. In our different ways."

"Rick didn't want to talk."

"Walter won't either." Laura propped her arms on the desk. "Rick Gullick was in the first class I ever taught at Reunion, did you know that? I just can't stand to think of him dead."

At that, Laura sank her head into her arms and cried. Karen herself had never cried that easily. It still balled up in her. Like her jacket, which she'd pitched, knowing she could never wear it again, even if the dry cleaner could get the blood out of it.

"Rick didn't think the meth affected him," Karen said, trying to outtalk her grief. "It did. I believe that. More aggressive, more impulsive, more than a little paranoid. He just wanted to do the job, he said, a shot of something to stay awake."

She'd already chugged a liter of the legal option. Coffee. Sister's Blend.

Laura sniffed and palmed her tears. "I know Walter did what he had to do. But he won't *listen* to me and he won't *say* anything and he—"

"Probably can't get a word in edgewise. Go home, Laura."

"Only if you do." Seeing Karen wince, she said, "Your dad can't blame you for what happened."

"Vern Gullick is his best friend. Or was. I don't know if a friendship can last something like that."

As soon as the words were out, Karen wished she could take them back. She'd told her father there'd been no fight between her and Laura. True. But there'd been hurt and hidden lies. It was time to woman up—she'd sabotaged their friendship, not Laura. She'd lied, again and again, that last semester of their senior year, hiding her academic unraveling, her drinking, and finally her weight gain, under cover of the loss of a national championship.

The big unforgivable: she'd told Laura she couldn't be her maid of honor that summer, claiming she'd be at basic training and unable to get away. Instead, she'd been holed up, waiting to give birth, only two people in the know: her coach and her ROTC instructor.

And still, Karen couldn't tell Laura, only hope the past was past.

Laura rose, walked over to her, and laid her hand on Karen's shoulder. "When life settles down a bit, we need to talk, girlfriend."

Her shoulder slumped—in relief. "When's that, when the moon turns to cheese?"

"I'll throw the kids at Walter and run. That should keep his mind off Rick. How about next Saturday? We'll do the café or, heavens, run off to Sioux Falls. Your new detective can take your calls."

That's what she was afraid of. But she forced a wry smile. "It's a date."

"Why didn't you return my call?" Manny Trujillo demanded of Marek. "Why do I have to hear from the FBI that you got a big tie-in to one of our most wanted down here?"

Marek had been too disoriented from being woken from a deep sleep to take in the caller ID. Now he regretted the ingrained response to flick it open.

"I got all the scoop from them," Manny went on when Marek didn't answer. "I should've gotten it from you. Did Montero show up there, like they're saying? I can't see it. He's a homeboy or migrates south. It's only you Anglos can stand the cold."

Marek gave up his silence. "Yes, Montero was here, but he must've agreed with you, because he didn't come back. He did send a couple goons to rough up a union rep for asking too many questions."

"The Feds can use him to bolster their case."

"No, he won't talk. He'll face down management without a blink but not Montero and his ilk. He's got two kids in college here plus...*familia*. Besides, he's had enough grief."

"Marek, every homicide we worked meant somebody lost someone."

"I'm tired of losing."

"Then maybe you're in the wrong job." The jab hit. Then the heat died. "You didn't call me, Marek. You pissed at me?"

"It was sacrilege."

Manny didn't have to ask what: the *retablo*. "My priest would think so, to put real people in place of saints, but you're not exactly Catholic, even if Val was. Besides, it wasn't for you. Did you even give it to Becca?"

"It's tacked up on her bedroom wall." He got to his feet and wandered out of the master bedroom. "Dammit, Manny, they're gone. It's just prolonging her grief." He snapped on the stairwell light and headed up. "She's drawing angels in class instead of doing her homework."

Angels that showed that, while she might not have inherited his dyslexia, she'd inherited another undesirable trait. A talent for art. But not from his side of the family, not this time.

"What kind of homework does a five year old have except drawing?" Manny asked with better humor. "How can anyone tell they're angels anyway?"

He remembered the drawings the teacher had showed him. "They aren't what you'd expect from a kid that age," he said tightly. "Even twice her age."

A long pause greeted that. "Marek, being anti-art was Val's hangup, not yours."

Marek peered into the darkened room. "Val isn't here."

"So you have to inflict her prejudices on Becca for her, is that it? Bull. Listen, I liked Val, but you have to know, she could barely stand my *retablos* and thought my wife was a pimp for running an art gallery."

"I know. I'm sorry." He reassured himself that his daughter still slept—that nothing threatened her dreams. "But Val had reason."

"It wasn't art but the artist who hurt her."

"Adrienne Fiat claimed Art was to blame," he said, going back down the stairs. "She didn't even show for Val's funeral, Manny. Her own daughter."

"You let her know?"

"I sent a telegram to her agent in New York." Snapping on the living room light, he sat down in the rocker. "Figured she should know."

"Maybe she thought it'd be in bad taste to show up to the funeral of the daughter she abandoned over thirty years ago."

Marek heard the creak of wood: chair or desk. "Listen, I didn't mean to hurt anybody, you know that. I just felt compelled to paint that *retablo* and, when it was done, I thought of Becca. She's my goddaughter. I miss her. You gonna bring her home?"

Marek looked around in the half-light of the dimmed lamp; it softened the shabbiness of the wallpaper, the watermarks, even a hole in the dry wall he hadn't noticed before. Had someone put a fist through it? So much to repair. "I don't know."

"You still set on staying?"

Again, he said, "I don't know."

When he hung up, he checked out the other side of the socked-in wall. He flicked on the light in the spare room. The fist hadn't gone all the way through. Small blessings.

As he reached to flick the light off again, his eye caught color on the dresser against the far wall. He walked over to it.

One of the movers must have put it there: a picture of his family that no longer was. Turning quickly away, he left the room in darkness.

But it burned in his mind like a negative, all shades of black and white.

And he thought of two other family photographs: of Emilio Jaramillo and his daughter and of Dr. Ahmed's family. At least the latter still had a daughter, a grandson, though each year the connection would be more strained, he'd guess, without hope.

On that thought, he picked up the phone. It was late, he knew, but Senator Frank Elwell was a renowned night owl. He'd still be burning midnight oil in his capitol office.

Marek had told the senator, he didn't owe for the sins of the son, but the man had, after all, been the sponsor of the freely flowing liquor.

He was put through at once; maybe the senator's spin doctors were afraid he'd changed his mind, decided to go after him, smear and conquer.

"Detective Okerlund, what do you want?"

I want my wife and son, Marek thought. You want your son. Neither of us is going to get what we want. "I'd like your help reuniting a man with his daughter and grandson."

"If this is about illegal immigrants, it's not an easy time for any of us to get exemptions." He paused with that pregnant silence of public speakers. "No matter what you threaten."

"I'm not threatening you. I told you, that's done. This is legal—

and deadlocked."

This time, when Marek hung up, he powered off the cell phone.

He was going to get a good night's sleep if it killed him.

Karen let herself into her father's home, but she couldn't make herself do anything but drop into the nearest chair, in the dark.

One thing to be grateful for. Her father had gone to bed instead of sleeping in his recliner.

She felt sick, sick to the soul, betrayed, angered, all the words that encompassed what should not be, could not be, but was. One of her deputies, corrupt, one of her father's oldest friends, imprisoned—even if fleetingly.

Then she heard a shuffle on the hardwood floor, the light snapped on, and she dashed away the tear that had streaked down her cheek. So, she could cry.

"I heard," her father said. "Vern called me from the jail. He doesn't want a loo—I mean, a lawyer. Says he'll take whatever the judge hands out; losing his son, and the way of it, is already the worst he could have lived through."

Sadness pulled down the side of his face. "He didn't know about Jaramillo, Karen. Just about the meth, stumbled over the setup when he stopped to check on the old schoolhouse, what with all the footprints out there, and found Blanca Jaramillo. He made Rick promise to stop. That's why Rick burned it down. To end it."

Why was her father suddenly the one with all the words. Even though they weren't accusatory, for which she was grateful, she couldn't speak.

"He's sorry, honey."

That sparked her tongue. "And that makes it right?"

"No, that makes it wrong." His hand rested on her shoulder, squeezed, then slid off. "I wish..."

"That you were still sheriff?"

"Yes," he said, not giving her the lie, but it was with regret, not resentment, and a father's care to keep a child from hurt.

His mind must have gone the same route: or a similar one. "A man'll do what he wouldn't otherwise, Karen, to protect his child."

"Even something illegal?"

He didn't hesitate. "Even."

She'd been forced for the last year into a different relationship with her father, guardian and adult to thwarted child, but he was better now. Maybe it was time to put that relationship back, no, not back, but forward. He wasn't the same man he'd been, more approachable, perhaps, less hard edged.

"Dad, how do you keep going, when the people you work with, the people you thought you were serving, can't be trusted?"

He sank down across from her. She doubted he ever thought much about why or how; you just did.

Finally, he said, "You work, you serve, you trust, but you're no longer..." He searched for the word. "Surprised. You're not the first to have a deputy go bad and won't be the last. You think you know people—that's the trap."

"What would you have done with Rick?"

He sighed. "I'd have tried to talk to him. It's a hard lesson to learn."

"What am I going to do about Marek?"

That turned his tone testy. "What's he done now?"

"He solved it, Dad. He saw it when I couldn't."

"He had better to see it, being an outsider."

"Dad..."

That got a humph. "Don't ask me to go liking him. Not when he's in your way."

"In *my* way? It could be, Dad, that I'm in *his* way."

Then it all tumbled out: what had happened to Val Okerlund, to Becca Okerlund, and ultimately to Marek Okerlund.

"That girl needs family," he said when she finished.

"And does she have it here?" she asked.

"I've no problem looking after her." He shifted uncomfortably. "Should be yours."

She'd heard some of that after his stroke, the bow to mortality was easier if there were grandchildren to leave behind, but once he'd recovered, he'd stopped. How tempted she'd been, to tell him—and, indeed, in the ICU, she *had* told him, when he'd hovered between life and death. But he had no memory of it or she'd have heard about it.

"Dad, unless you want to do what grandpa did and marry someone half your age, there's not going to be a babe in arms in this family again."

His eyes held denial; she felt it reflect back. It was the first time she'd said it. The first time, perhaps, that she believed it, let herself believe it, because of Becca.

"You could discon—" Her breath caught. Then he frowned over the word. "No, not disconnect. Divorce. That's it. Divorce Patrick."

That her father had made even that stretch made her goggle at him. While they'd never directly talked of it, she knew one thing without a doubt. "You don't believe in divorce."

"Should've died right then and there; he'd have wanted it. You don't *have* a mirage—I mean, a marriage to break. So maybe, well, disconnect *is* the right word. He's gone, honey. Been gone a long time."

Maybe the stroke had changed his mind—in more ways than one. "Dad, even if I decided it was the right thing to do, I can't. Not now."

If it had happened when it should have, right after he'd been flown to Germany, no one would have blamed her. She'd have only been doing what the doctors had suggested, after they'd run tests. But she'd abandoned one difficult relationship already, that of mother, and wasn't ready to relinquish that of wife.

Her husband had been military police. In a not terribly flattering way, she knew some her constituents thought of her as her husband's stand-in, not unlike a politician's wife who took up the reins of power after her husband's death.

Later, after saying goodnight to her father, Karen made her way up the stairs, stared out the window. For a long moment, all she saw was darkness, then her eyes picked up the drift of fat flakes, white, soft, falling in the light of the streetlamp.

No wind. A rare thing.

Then why, she wondered, did she feel so cold; she'd had to get out more blankets, even though the temperature had risen. Her eyes ranged over the cozy room where she'd spent her young life...and might end her life. Not at all what she'd imagined.

Then she saw it: the hole. For God's sake, no wonder she'd been freezing. Her dad had taken out another house besides Marek's. Too tired to deal with the bullet hole, she slapped a large adhesive bandaid over it.

If only she could have done that with Rick.

When she crawled into bed, she couldn't sleep, her system tripped in the *on* position. She turned over and stared at the alarm clock. Midnight. Reaching out, she pressed down on the radio button. Might as well catch Nails Nelson's hourly playback of his last commentary. Maybe Nails would pull the plug for her.

And maybe, just maybe, she'd let Patrick go and still have the life she'd desired, though time was running out on having a child.

Another child, she amended.

In a few minutes, Nails came on live. "Well, folks, I can't settle tonight."

"Glad I'm not the only one," Karen muttered.

She heard papers shuffle in the pause. "One of my superiors told me once, Soldier, you got crow to eat, you swallow it whole, before you got time to taste it; it'll go down easier. So...I've got some apologies to make. First off, Emilio Jaramillo, may you rest in peace. You got shafted every which way but up in the land of dreams."

He'd be a citizen of American soil soon enough, she thought, naturalized in the way of all men in their time. Ashes to ashes. Earth to earth.

"And, incidentally, if you want to contribute to a headstone for him, as well as the Ramirez family, just let our new detective know. Speaking of Marek Okerlund, I officially declare him a genius."

Big newsflash there. Marek Okerlund for sheriff was sure to come next.

"Now to some fine folk went down the wrong road...won't be the first time. Can't say I never took a wrong turn in my life. Can't say I never tried to drown it in things that ain't precisely legal."

Karen was surprised, not at what he'd said, but what he hadn't.

"So I'm not figuring to be judge or jury here. Rick Gullick's dead, his father's going to do some community service, and Cal Bullard's looking at some serious jail time, leaving his wife and kids to mind a farm that will likely go belly up. Sometimes I think that's what we're set up for out here on the plains: set up for failure."

Was he going to get to her now?

"Sheriff Mehaffey told me Emilio Jaramillo was a farmer, lost his land, his wife, to drug runners. The Gullicks, well, what were they doing but trying to hold on to their land? Rick took that night deputy job to help out. Dale was a farmer too, come to think of it, lost his farm by taking more care for his animals than his books. My coach used to say, in football, there are takers and protectors, and you'll get the most applause for being a taker; in life, you should be a protector. Seems to me we've forgotten how to do that in this big country of ours; it's all take."

Karen let him ramble on about the rise and decline of American civilization as she finally drifted off.

CHAPTER 42

KAREN PULLED OFF THE ROAD in the inky darkness. Pulling her dad's coat closer around her, she rubbed at her eyes. Bork had called her out of her bed, told her she had to see this. Why, exactly, she wondered, had she given up predictable hours and a hefty paycheck for the Chinese water torture of callouts?

She inched farther off the road to let three semi-trucks pull away from the picked-over bones of PBI. Thompson stood out front, arms flapping. Whatever he was arguing, it wasn't flying with the man holding the clipboard.

After the last truck left, Thompson stood alone in front of the gutted building. Even the sign was gone. No press conferences, no glittering promises, just gone.

Karen got out of the Suburban and crunched over to Thompson.

"Consolidation, they say," he told her. "Bull. They just don't want to deal with the bad press. They'll change their name, go to some other town, make promises, break them, move on. What do you bet, after they spin this, the stock will go up and the rest of us..."

"Will go down," Karen finished. She looked over at the huddle of workers nearby, at the trailers lit up behind them, the hulks like submarine wrecks in the deep sea of pre-dawn. "What about these people?"

"They'll follow or look for jobs elsewhere. I don't see many sticking around here."

"What about you?" she asked. "You moving on with the trucks?"

"I'm fired." He sank down onto the curb as if it only now hit him. "Eleven years they've taken off me. Terminated. Said I must have known what Dale was up to." His head fell to his chest; he must be staring right at his paunch. "When I said I'd take a lie detector test to prove I didn't, they said, I should've known."

She sank down on the curb beside him. "So who's to blame for what happened here—not just the meth, but all of it? The CEO?"

"He's just trying to get his slice before he gets the axe himself. It's the crazy market; the stockholders want action. Cut prices, cut protections, cut ethics, cut people..." He trailed off.

She rested her chin on her arms. "Isn't the whole thing based on competition?"

He snorted. "Not all that long ago, people were laying down railroad tracks side by side, just to compete—forget common sense. Government had to step in. That's what it's for—set the ground rules and referee the game. Now all it does is step aside, like a drama queen lifting her skirts, afraid she'll wade into the shit that keeps her in baubles."

Karen couldn't help but smile. "You know, Mr. Thompson, you might have a future as a government meat inspector."

He gave her a dark look then, to her surprise, laughed. "Sure, I can look the other way as easily as anyone else."

Deciding Thompson wouldn't slit his own throat, she left him to explain to his former workers that their jobs had gone south. Or West or Far East.

On her way back home, watching dawn rise over the fluffy white stuff, she got another call. Harold Dahl, this time. She listened to his grim tone then replied, "Yes, I'll be there in a few minutes."

Karen headed for the courthouse, wondering what other cuts were now on the table.

Later that afternoon, Marek woke to a scrape, a crack, a thud, then a dead silence. He jolted to his feet from his half-doze in the rocker where he'd planted himself after plugging the bullet hole in the doorjamb. "Becca? Becca!"

He rushed up the stairs and found his daughter lying in the middle of the room, her eyes wide and staring. He felt the fear dry his own. Then he blinked it away as she swung her feet to the side and got off the broken sled.

She'd dragged it out of the attic storage. He should've locked the door again; kids loved to poke into hidden corners.

Becca tugged on his jeans, pointed at the sled.

"All right, all right, give your old man a bit of leeway, he's having issues." Marek looked down and decided that, as issues went, at least this one had some possibility of resolution. "Let's see if this thing can be fixed."

Karen pounded on the door of 21 Okerlund Road, finally giving up when she got no answer, even though the Silverado was parked out front. She noted the bullet hole had been repaired beside the door.

She started back down the walk, glanced to the west, then stopped. Marek stood out on the edge of the bluff, in the circle of the sun, an outline and an enigma. On either side of him, sun dogs—smears of rainbow, small suns of ice-light—gamboled.

She joined Marek on the bluff edge. "Where's Becca—" she started to ask, then she saw the bob of a dark head, lit into glittering obsidian by the sun. The girl careened down the bluff on an old sled, a mini-blizzard in her wake.

After a moment, Karen said, "If it weren't for the blizzard that night, you might have found Dale Hansen on the highway. He was right there: but invisible."

"Sort of like meth." Marek didn't turn. "But PBI won't pay—not like they should."

"Um, actually, PBI left town this morning." At his silence, she said, "I don't know if I'm glad or not...or if it's justice, that they'll get off, just by up and disappearing. There's been some grumbling about a lawsuit but no one's got the money for it. But, on the bright side, maybe Uncle Sig can start up his plant again."

"Think he'll risk it?"

"That's the Halvorsen motto. Take a risk." Only she wasn't, pussyfooting around the message she'd been told to deliver. "Harold Dahl wanted me to talk to you."

Marek didn't look away from his daughter.

Her mind stuttered. "He said you got some offers to do carpentry work in town. I could use some at my place. Funny thing, there's this bullet hole in my bedroom wall." Karen shifted on her feet when she got no response. "I'm sorry about the hole in your doorjamb, I'll pay for it, if you let me know..." He shook his head and she stared down the bluff. "There's something I've got to tell you."

"I'm fired."

"*What?*"

He finally turned his head. "Laid off. Whatever. I figure I'm the most expendable."

Marek was, she reminded herself, a detective, someone who made connections. The loss of PBI meant the loss of county revenue. "You're not laid off, but you'll need to take some time off. At least a month, barring any major felonies, while we juggle finances to keep your part-time detective position. The benefits, though, are ongoing."

She'd told Harold they wouldn't have a chance in hell to keep Marek without health insurance when he had a kid to look after. "We can't compete with what you had, what you can have elsewhere, but I—well, I didn't think we did too badly together...at the end."

He turned back into the sun; his profile didn't give her anything.

Finally, he said, "I'll take it."

Was that relief she felt? Yes, it was. But she still needed to know. "Are you going to run for sheriff, come election time?" She plunged on. "I mean, I can understand it; you've got the experience. You even look like a sheriff. Well, except the funny boots. And you don't have the bushy moustache but you can ditch the goatee for one."

She held her breath and, still, he didn't respond. "I'll dispatch, if I have to, but don't think I won't fight you for the sheriff's position. Give me a few years and I'll have a moustache too." She finally took a breath and knew now, as it seemed to slip from her grasp, what she wanted. "Because I want this job."

The girl trudged back up the hill, breathing out puffs of white cotton candy.

"I don't."

Karen let that sink in. "Why did you come back, then, if not to prove you could be the sheriff of Eda County?"

He nodded toward Becca.

"You thought it would be better for her, here?"

"Thought I'd have time for her, here."

"Oh."

A curve molded his mouth. "That, and she turned into a Scandinavian."

Karen frowned at him in concern. "Isn't she talking again?"

The curve turned down. "Not since yesterday. It'll take time, the doctors said."

Well, time she could give him. She offered another olive branch. "Um...my dad, he wants to keep looking after Becca when you can't. I think...well, he's felt pretty useless, what with the stroke and losing his job. He grumbles but it's just token."

Before he could reply, Becca made it to the top, pointed at the sled, at Karen, then at Marek. They looked at each other, down at the old sled, a Flexible Flyer that showed signs of recent repair, and Marek said, "Won't work."

"Sorry, Becca," Karen said, "but that would break the sled right in two."

"You and Karen could give it a spin, though," Marek told his daughter. "My work should hold."

For a flash of time, in his grief-gentled eyes, Karen saw her grandfather. He'd often taken her sledding on this same hill. "Okay, Becca, let's get this show on the road."

She cradled the girl in front of her, propped her boots on the steering bar, whooped her way down the hill, and sent them straight into a snow bank.

The soft, light tingle of laughter rose with the light white snow and disappeared into the spectrum of color.

ACKNOWLEDGMENTS

To the many friends, family, and teachers who have encouraged me throughout the years. And to Linda M. Hasselstrom and John Robert Marlow, who believed in me before I did. Also, to Jodie Renner and Anne Victory, who gave me the final nudge.
.

ABOUT THE AUTHOR

M.K. Coker grew up on a river bluff in southeastern South Dakota. Part of the Dakota diaspora, the author has lived in half a dozen states, including New Mexico, but returns to the prairie at every opportunity. Website: www.mkcoker.com

Made in the USA
Monee, IL
25 February 2024

53993424R00204